Remember me

MAUREEN LANG

Kregel
Publications

To my husband,
the man behind my heroes.

Remember Me: A Novel

© 2007 by Maureen Lang

Published by Kregel Publications, a division of Kregel, Inc., P.O. Box 2607, Grand Rapids, MI 49501.

Unless otherwise indicated, all Scripture quotations are from the King James Version of the Holy Bible.

Scripture quotations marked NIV are from the *Holy Bible, New International Version*®. Copyright © 1973, 1978, 1984 by International Bible Society. Used by permission of Zondervan. All rights reserved.

Library of Congress Cataloging-in-Publication Data
Lang, Maureen.
Remember me : a novel / by Maureen Lang.
    p. cm.
    I. Title.
PS3612.A554R46 2007
813'.6–dc22   2006103430

ISBN 10: 0-8254-3672-9
ISBN 13: 978-0-8254-3672-7

Printed in the United States of America

07 08 09 10 11 / 5 4 3 2 1

ACKNOWLEDGMENTS

THERE'S NOTHING more affirming to an author than having someone else "get" our writing. Special thanks to my editor, Paul Ingram, who gets it. I'm so grateful for his input and hard work on this project.

And once again, thanks to all of the Kregel staff for not only giving me a format to share the characters in my head, but making the process a pleasure.

Remember me, O Lord, when you
show favor to your people.

(Ps. 106:4a NIV)

CHAPTER *One*

WASHINGTON, D.C., 1917

JOSEF SWUNG his legs over the edge of the bed, jolts of pain stopping him abruptly. He couldn't guess why moving his feet should hurt his head. Carefully grabbing a nearby chair, he leaned on it and struggled to stand.

He'd make it to the bathroom today.

It must be fewer than a dozen steps across the single-room flat. He pulled in a breath as he pushed the chair, then hobbled behind it. It might take fifteen minutes and every ounce of his strength, but he'd make it.

"Hey, what's this? What are you doing?"

Annoyed rather than relieved to see prospective help, Josef eyed the man entering the room. Hank, lean and middle-aged, tossed aside the bundle he carried in his arms.

"I'm going to the bathroom."

Josef gave the chair another push, letting it take much of his weight.

"The bedpan—"

"—is over there." In a forgetful moment Josef pointed with his head. Ice and heat shot through his forehead. He took another step, and sweat poked from above his upper lip.

"All right, all right," said Hank. "Then let me help you."

"Just stay out of the way." Josef took another step, every inch like walking through a tunnel of needles.

The older man stayed put, vaguely surprising Josef. Hank had been hovering like an overpaid nanny since Josef woke up a day ago. He'd awakened in this room where everything was wood: ceiling, floors, walls, headboard, kitchen table and chairs. Each had a different finish, but Josef was in no mood to care about the decorating, or lack thereof. The pounding in his head alternated with lightning slicing his forehead. And through the pain, Josef had been concentrating on remembering—everything . . . anything . . . something.

Nothing came, absolutely nothing. Not even his name.

Between fits of vomiting and dizziness, Josef had questioned the man who cared for him well but gave no answers. He'd told Josef his name and given his own name as Hank. That was all he'd say, except that Josef shouldn't trouble himself with memories.

Not trouble himself? Didn't the man realize how troubling it was not knowing one's own name or a single day of the past? He looked back and saw nothing but emptiness to call upon. He wondered what kind of past he must have if this man thought it would trouble him to start remembering.

But those frustrations weren't long on his mind now. Hope touched him for the first time since he'd gained consciousness. He'd made it to the bathroom.

He cared for his needs, then turned to the chair he used as a crutch. Hank stood by, as if ready to act. Josef started the long return. Ten paces, nine, eight, all the way across the room.

For the first time, the pillow felt soft.

"Good. That was very good, Josef. You're on the mend now."

Josef looked at the man who was so obviously pleased. It was hard to know how to feel about him. He was a nice enough fellow, but a stranger so far as Josef knew.

"Yes," Josef said, "I'm on the mend. Maybe now you'll answer some of my questions."

Instead of showing an interest in doing so, the man stooped to pick up the package he'd cast aside. He opened the bundle, holding up a pair of denim pants and a blue work shirt. Plain, sturdy clothes like Hank's, for a working man.

"I thought you might be up and around soon," Hank said, "so I brought these for you. You can try them later for fit."

"You had to buy clothes for me? Where are mine?"

Hank folded the pants and placed them at the foot of the bed. "Gone. All gone."

"How could I lose all my clothes? In a fire?"

Hank shook his head. "No, nothing like that."

Josef swallowed a fit of frustration aimed directly at his tight-lipped caretaker.

"Will you sit?" Josef's voice sounded steadier than he expected, with his insides roiling.

Hank turned the chair Josef had used and sat facing the bed. He didn't look Josef in the eye.

"My name is Josef," he began, staring at the older man. "That's all you've told me. I've tried to remember, but I can't. You're going to have to fill me in. *Now.*"

The man slowly shook his head, but Josef didn't give up.

"Don't tell me again that you're waiting for me to get stronger. I'm strong enough. What's my full name? Who are you to me? What do I do for a living? How come nobody else comes to this place? I've been awake at least a full twenty-four hours, and the only face I've seen is yours. Don't I have any friends? Neighbors? It seems to me when somebody's sick, friends and family show up." He gently touched his bandaged forehead. "And if I can remember how to function—talk and eat and use the bathroom—how come I don't remember anything else?"

Hank ran an age-spotted hand through his light-colored hair. His hair seemed surprisingly thick for someone who was obviously past fifty. Apart from the gray, his hair was exactly the color Josef had seen when he looked into the bathroom mirror. The man sighed heavily. At last he leaned forward, meeting Josef's gaze. "I haven't meant to make it harder. I only wanted you to rest. Do you see that?"

Slowly, mindful now that any movement brought pain, Josef nodded. "But I can't rest while I have so many questions."

"Yes, I see that now. We will talk. Do you want something to drink? Milk? Tea?"

"Just answers."

"You know that your name is Josef; that much is familiar, isn't it?"

"I . . . don't know. Nothing's familiar."

Hank nodded. "All right. Then I will tell you what should be familiar, starting with your mother." Hank sat back, and a smile softened his face. As some wrinkles stretched out around his mouth and the lines around his eyes deepened, somehow he looked younger. He still showed a hint of the good looks that must have once been his. "Your mother was born in Baden-Württemberg. That's in Germany. You speak German, Josef. Do you recall that? Can you say anything to me in German?"

Josef searched for a word in anything but English. "No."

That didn't seem to ruffle the man. "You were born here in America, Josef, but your mother spoke German to you, even as she taught you English. I suppose your American friends helped you learn to speak. She always spoke with an accent, but you don't have one, even though you went to German schools. Do you remember your mother, Josef?"

Josef concentrated, waiting for an image to appear. None did.

Hank continued. "She was fair. Hair. Skin. Her eyes were blue, like yours. I always remember her smiling. She was happy, and everyone wanted to be around her." He sighed again. "She was happier still when you were born. *That* I wish you could remember, Josef. How she loved you."

"Do you have a photograph?"

"A picture? Yes . . . yes, I have pictures."

He crossed to the bureau in the corner. The cheap dresser was like the rest of the furniture, notched here and there as if weathered by more than a few moves. Without the rich patina of fine furniture, it reflected the simple wear and tear of life with someone who apparently didn't pay much attention to detail. From one of its drawers, Hank retrieved a small, black box and opened the lid.

"This is your mother, Josef. See for yourself how beautiful she was."

Josef stared at the picture. Light hair was obvious in the gray tones of the image, with eyes that indeed looked like they might have been blue. Cheeks and lips were of darker shading. Arched brows, high cheekbones, well-formed mouth, small nose—a beauty. But the girl pictured was a beautiful stranger to him, and far too young for this to be a recent picture. He handed it back, curious about what other photos might be in that box.

Hank handed Josef another picture. "This is you, not long after you were born." It was a full shot of the same woman with a child in her arms. She smiled merrily and wore a dark gown with puffed sleeves, tight at the waist, accentuating the curve of her slight figure. The gown flared at the floor, with something like sequins or jewels winking light at the camera. Her hair was loosely tied atop her pretty face, her light eyes joyous and youthful. She looked tenderly at the baby she held.

"And this is you when you were a year old."

A chubby infant laughed into the camera with two straight baby teeth and a hint of a dimple just above the left corner of his mouth.

"Here is my favorite. You were three."

A blond haired boy sat astride a pony, trying hard to resemble a fearless cowboy on a herd drive.

"Where is my mother now?"

"She's passed now, oh, some time ago. In heaven."

Josef wondered if he should feel grief. "How old was I when she died?"

No answer came right away. Just when Josef was about to repeat the question, Hank looked up from the picture. "You were eight."

"How did she die?"

"She got sick, and then she died."

"Can I see the rest of those?"

Hank hesitated but handed the box to Josef, who flipped through the items inside, hoping something would trigger a memory or give him at least a feeling of familiarity. Nothing did.

"This looks like you." Josef held up a picture of a cheerful trio in front of a cage at the zoo.

"By the lions. We could hear that lion roar clear across the park."

"You're with my mother and me. Who are you to me, Hank? Who were you to my mother?"

Hank looked at the picture but did not answer. His hand trembled as he took it from Josef to look at it closely, as if he wanted a better view of the memory.

Wondering if more pictures might hold the answers this man clearly did not wish to give, Josef glanced through the box again. He found nothing remotely recent. "There aren't any photographs in here from after my mother died, are there, Hank?"

He shook his head, taking back the box and placing the photograph from the zoo on top.

"Hank? Are you going to tell me?"

Perhaps in an effort to control—or conceal—his uneasiness, Hank slowly returned the box to the bureau. He pushed the drawer shut without turning back. "She was your mother, Josef. I hope you remember her someday. It would be a great loss to you if you didn't."

"And you, Hank? Who are you?"

"I am your father."

On a Farm Near Culpeper, Virginia

Lissa Parker stared at the solemn faces of her mother and father. The only sound was the chime of the old grandfather clock marking the hour in the front hall. One. Two. Three o'clock. The large farmhouse had been home to four generations of Parkers. The original house had survived the American Revolution but burned some years later. It had been replaced by a brick dwelling that had survived another war. Both Northern and Southern soldiers had billeted in all the homes nestled among the trees and hills of the Piedmont, depending on who controlled the section at the moment.

It was impossible to tell what her parents were thinking about the announcement she'd just made. She expected her father to be pleased. Her mother? Well, it was always hard to tell how she would react.

"Somebody should say something. Aunt Bobbie?" Lissa turned to her father's sister, who sat on the chair Lissa's father had made for his mother, back when he fancied himself a woodworking craftsman and made large pieces of furniture. Now he only created cedar chests and small toys. Aunt Bobbie was the only one who'd known about Lissa's plans, and she'd had a week to digest them. Now she tried to smile, but Lissa guessed it took effort.

"Well, Lissa," she began, with the slight lisp that gave her speech an added charm. "None of us could stop you, even if we wanted to. You're twenty-three years old."

"Yes, of course, but I was hoping for approval and support. What about you, Father? Aren't you pleased?"

Frank Parker rubbed his hands on his knees, as if emerging from a shock-induced coma. "Liss, we're all supposed to follow where we're led. Your mother and I are surprised that you think your leading is to a battle-field. With only daughters, we thought we would be spared that worry."

"Nearly every generation of Parkers has gone to war for America, Father. Don't you want me to carry on the tradition?"

Her mother's lips pursed. "Oh, Lissa, don't be ridiculous. This has nothing to do with Parker tradition."

Lissa turned back to her father, her best hope for approval. "But it does. It's true. I can't be a soldier like you were, Father, but at least I'll be support-ing the soldiers. And I won't be on a battlefield. I'll be behind the lines."

Aunt Bobbie stood to her full, albeit meager, height of five feet, then crossed the room to take a place beside Lissa. She patted Lissa's hand. "You must understand your parents' point of view, Liss. Since Chelsea, they have a right to be a little protective, haven't they?"

Lissa took a deep breath. This was an argument she'd prepared for. "No, I don't see it that way at all."

Her mother gasped.

Lissa met her mother's hurt surprise. "You've done all you can, you and Father, to raise your children. You've taught us our faith, our loyalties, our manners, our work ethic. As I see it, you've done your job. Now it's our turn to make decisions. Cassie chose, and now she's engaged to William. As for Chelsea, you did all you could."

Her mother stood, and Lissa followed on her heels. Adelia Parker was tall and thin, with dark hair always pulled back to a neat bun. Her face was narrow, and Lissa had grown to wonder if that was why she smiled so rarely. There just wasn't enough room.

"The fact that she died is nobody's fault, Mama. She's with the Lord. What more could any of us have done?"

Lissa's father stood, too, and put his hands on Lissa's shoulders. He was a big man, compared to his petite sister. Though Lissa was small-boned like her mother, she was tall like her father. "Stop houndin' your mother, Liss. You make it sound like we've grieved long enough. It was the Lord's doing, you say. Well, we believe that, too, but you don't stop missing your child, grieving that she won't get to do all the things we hoped for her, no matter how much time goes by. It's been less than a year."

Aunt Bobbie approached. "But this isn't really about Chelsea, is it? We were talking about Lissa and her decision to join the Red Cross and head overseas."

Lissa's mother turned and Lissa faced her as her father's hands dropped to his side. She squared her shoulders, prepared to meet her mother's objections.

"Do you have any idea what it will be like?" Her mother's voice was shrill, the way it sounded when she was tired or worried. "If you think it'll be some romantic, heroic jaunt, you'll be disappointed. The papers tell how they don't have proper supplies, proper care, proper food. That war has devastated Europe these past two years, Lissa. And you want to join in?"

Lissa had a ready retort about having seen the same newspapers. That was part of the reason she felt compelled to go, precisely because of the great need. But she choked back a hasty reply. Instead, she went the route she'd rehearsed. "Mama, why should I stay here, in the comfort of my own home, when our country has just declared war? Because I'm a girl? Why should this family be spared from the war because I have no brothers? Do you think Grandma wanted Father to go when we fought the Spanish? Do you think Grandpa's mother wanted to see her sons fight for the Union, against other Virginians, in the War Between the States? All the way back to the battle for Independence, nearly every one of the mothers in our family had to watch children go off to war for the good of this country—until now."

She paused, only because she was afraid her mother had stopped listening, but when her mother looked at her, Lissa started again. "I'm not going to the battlefield, Mama. I'm going to support the soldiers, to bandage their wounds and try to ease their suffering as best someone can." She turned back to her father. "Isn't that what the Parkers stand for?"

He put a hand on one of her shoulders, and the promise of a smile touched his face. "Lissa, you make me proud ever' day. Your words are Parker, through and through. And maybe I'm a selfish Parker, selfish to think we've lost enough, your mama and me, with Chelsea. Once somethin' bad happens, you know you're not immune. We don't want to lose you, too."

"Oh, Father, why should you lose me? I'm in the hands of God, you know."

Lissa welcomed his laugh. She watched her father find her mother's gaze and hold it steady. "Is this the way it should be, Addie? Our own Lissy Rose should remind us of our faith, the faith God gave her through us?"

Her father drew Lissa into his arms, and with his long reach pulled his wife into the embrace. Lissa saw her mother's face soften, even as her eyes swelled with tears.

"Well," her mother said unsteadily, "I could remind you of all the responsibilities you have here, like working with Dr. Sherman, and the children who need you at the school. How will they get along without the best nurse in the county? Besides that, how will Aunt Bobbie carry on all those meetings you hold with the Daughters?"

From beyond their huddle Lissa heard her Aunt Bobbie guffaw. "Oh look out; she's pulling out the big guns now, Liss! Not even a member, and she's worried about the Daughters of the American Revolution."

"I think Aunt Bobbie will manage to take care of the group," Lissa quipped, enjoying her parents' embrace. She knew they weren't exactly supporting her decision, but she could ease their worry or at least put it off. "I won't go until after Cassie's wedding. I'll still be home for the next few months."

Her mother pulled back and raised a brow. "What about Penny? Have you told her yet?"

Lissa smiled broadly. "She's coming with me."

CHAPTER *Two*

WASHINGTON, D.C.

To HIS eight-year-old eye, the ships, lined in rows at the New York dock, looked larger than anything he'd ever imagined. He didn't know which of them would carry his mother back to the fatherland. After the long ride to the pier, his father had spoken at last, telling the young Josef about his mother's voyage home. But he was so busy staring at the merchant carriers, freight ships, tug boats, and barges that he'd forgotten which was the huge passenger liner his father pointed out.

Papa talked to the captain, farther down the dock, but the boy knew they wouldn't go aboard. How many times had he heard his father tell him about the journey from the homeland, how hard it had been, how he'd felt so sick he'd wished for death. Even now Papa wouldn't so much as walk the long platform leading up to the ship's gangplank.

The boy wanted to go on board, to see where they would put his mother, but he was too afraid. He didn't want to be, and didn't tell his father of his fear. His father always said he shouldn't be afraid of anything.

Still, he wanted to see if they put her in a nice place. It must be a long way back to the homeland. It made him sad to think his mother would be alone. All alone in that box on that long journey. What if there was a storm?

What if the box slid about? He was old enough to know his mother was beyond hurting, but he didn't like to think of her tossing about.

At last his father returned and wordlessly took his hand. They walked away without pausing, although the boy looked back many times. They walked to their big, black motorcar nearby. The other vehicle, a shiny, black horse-drawn hearse that had delivered Mama, was already gone.

The boy opened his side of the motorcar and climbed aboard, sliding into the front seat. He wondered if he would be told to sit in the back, where he always sat when Mama was up front. But Papa seemed not to have noticed. With some effort, Josef pulled the big door closed with a bang and waited for his father to take his place behind the wheel.

His father closed his own door but it barely clicked shut. He did nothing after that. He didn't start the engine, and the crank he'd given the handle up front quickly unwound itself. If Papa wanted to go, he'd have to get out and do it again. But he didn't. He just sat there.

"She goes home now, Josef," his father said in German. Then he covered his face with his big hands and sobbed. The boy stared. He'd never seen his father cry.

At last Papa looked up, his face wet and shiny. "I should have taken her back when she was alive. Not like this. Not like this." Then he breathed deeply, and eyed the boy. "You will go there, Josef. When you are older. You are German, Josef. You and I, we belong to the fatherland."

The boy nodded. He already knew where he belonged. Papa had told him again and again how he was German and must honor his fatherland above all, even though Mama had given birth to him in the United States. Papa had come to the U.S. for business, and it was good to them—good enough that he could afford a fine home and a motorcar, and other grand luxuries. But it was only a place for business, not for loyalties. Only Deutschland, the fatherland, was for that.

His father got out to turn the crank again, then he started the engine, and they drove off. Josef stared out the window. He couldn't see the ships any more, but every once in a while, between the tall buildings, he caught a glimpse of the wide river port from which his mother would sail out to sea. It was the only road home.

Josef opened his eyes, and for a moment felt no pain. For the first time since he'd awakened two days ago, he felt nothing except the inescapable frustration born of confusion. But even as the pain registered with his first movement, optimism took a place beside his confusion. It had only been a dream, but it was so real that it must be more than that. He remembered being there, remembered those ships. It was the first memory of anything that had happened outside this room.

But was it a real memory? How could it have been? The man in the dream was his father; Josef was sure of that. But that man wasn't Hank.

Josef had studied Hank's pictures. He probed his mind for some memory of his mother, his father, his parents together, the house where they lived, a neighborhood. He looked at the pictures again and again, but they didn't help.

He was left with more questions than answers, not the least of them was why Hank had nothing recent of Josef's. There were no pictures of him when he was older than perhaps five years old. There were no keepsakes. Nothing.

Josef sat up, noticing Hank sitting under a light at the table, reading a newspaper.

"Mind if I have a look at that?" Josef asked.

"Take a look, but we don't have much time. We're going home this morning."

"Home?"

"I live in this flat when I come to the city to conduct business. I do occasional work as an inquiry agent here in Washington. But home is in the country. There I make my living: Virginia; Saddlebrook, near Culpeper."

Josef felt a prick of annoyance. "Is any of that supposed to sound familiar?" He was so accustomed to being given selective answers that he asked with low expectations.

"No, it won't," responded Hank. "You've never been there."

"You're my father, and I've never been to your home?"

"That's right."

Josef crossed his arms, ignoring a stab of pain. "Maybe you could explain that, or do you think it's too much for me to handle?" The sarcasm wasn't lost on Hank. He might be a man of few words and have a bent toward sadness, but he was not a whit short of brains.

"Your mother and I went separate ways long ago. I'm not proud of some of my past, Josef, which is why I'm reluctant to tell you. I wish you could know me better before I tell the worst of me, so the rest might bring some balance. But there is no way around it. You must know something. You didn't know the truth even when you had your memory."

"I didn't know you were my father?" Images of the other man, the father of his dream, replayed in his mind.

Hank folded the newspaper and stood before Josef. "That's right. You were raised by your mother and her husband until she died, and after that by her husband."

"My mother was married to someone else? Not you?"

"That's right."

"Were you married to my mother before that?"

Hank shook his head.

Josef looked away. "I guess that explains why she was dressed so nicely in the pictures. I didn't think she fit this place." He glanced at Hank, taking in his denim shirt and pants, somewhat faded at the knees—"Or you." He leaned back. "So, I'm illegitimate."

The word should have brought emotion. Josef wasn't sure what to feel. Shame? Humiliation? Like someone with a secret? At the moment, he felt nothing.

Hank interrupted his thoughts. "All you need to know for now is that you're my son, and I intend to take care of you until you can do it for yourself again." Hank must have noticed the scowl Josef felt forming on his face, because he went on, "I'm not a doctor, but I have common sense. You bumped your head, and it's bruised. If you bruised your brain, or however they describe what happened to you, it's best to let it heal on its own. It seems better to let the memories come back when it is time. I don't want to confuse you with a bunch of things that were never in your memory anyway. So, come. I'll help you get dressed, and we'll take a ride to the country."

Josef glanced out the window; it was dark. "What time is it?"

"Just past five."

"In the morning?"

"That's right."

Hank acted as if it were perfectly normal to be up and about before the sun, although to Josef, even without a memory, it seemed odd. Josef insisted on dressing himself, even though when he stood to pull up his pants the dizziness returned. But he made it to the bathroom without the chair, and that accomplishment eased some of his frustration. He may not know much about his history, but he was beginning to suspect something of his personality: he was an optimist. He'd get the facts figured out, with or without Hank's help.

When they left the apartment, the sun was barely a promise over the eastern horizon. Josef had little choice but to hang on to Hank's arm for support down the steps. It was impossible to navigate through the dizziness without him. By the time Josef sat in the front seat of Hank's motorcar, his vision was sufficiently cleared to see that the motorcar was a new, but dusty, model B55 Buick. It was open at the sides, and a canvas top stretched from bars at the four corners of the seats. A low glass windshield did little to keep out road dust. Yet, somehow, from within his mind came the thought that this model was the best that Buick had yet made.

Why did his bruised brain remember that but so little else?

Josef raised a hand to his throbbing head while Hank put a pillow behind him. They left the city and its almost empty paved roads for the deserted country lanes. Each bump jostled Josef's head, but the pillow eased the ride. Neither spoke for some time, and Josef wondered how long he would have to endure the jostling. Though he'd slept through the night, he couldn't shake the fatigue or nausea.

By afternoon the scenery became more rugged and the trees more plentiful. But Josef wasn't looking at the sights. He closed his eyes to ponder the man in his dream, the one who raised Josef.

"You are German," the man had said.

"You said I was born here, in the United States, Hank?" Josef asked. He had no idea how much longer their journey might be, how much time he'd have to ask questions, or if Hank was likely to answer any.

Hank nodded.

"I'm an American citizen?"

He nodded again, this time taking his eyes off the road to glance at Josef.

"I don't remember anything, German or American," Josef grumbled.

"What are you thinking, Josef?"

Unable to put the jumbled thoughts to words, he closed his eyes and leaned against the pillow. "Nothing."

"Your mother was German. I am German," Hank said. "The man who raised you as his son is German. We have in common that we all left Germany."

Josef opened his eyes again.

"Why? Why did you leave the land of your birth, to live in a country of mongrels?"

Where did that come from? Hank didn't speak right away, never taking his eyes off the road.

"The U.S. may be the land of mongrels, Josef, but my observation of dogs is that the mutt takes the best characteristics of the breeds in his heritage. America is a democratic republic. I don't know how much of history you remember, but I will tell you that Germany and the U.S. are as different politically as two countries can be. Germany is run by the Kaiser; the United States is governed by representatives elected by the people. Here, we have a vote, and it means something. Political leaders don't use the army to intimidate their own people."

"My mother and her husband left for political reasons?"

"Otto—your mother's husband—left Germany because he saw America as a business venture. He's a capitalist, despite his loyalties to the Kaiser. Your mother left because her husband wanted her to. Politics played no part, one way or another."

"So, my mother wasn't loyal to her husband or her country."

Hank's glance was harsh. "Don't be quick to cast judgment on your mother. You don't know the circumstances. We were young—rash, I suppose. We were raised to love people and our community, but did whatever felt right at the time. We were short-sighted, self-indulgent people with a foolish sense that the here and now was all there is."

"And that's my heritage?"

"No, it isn't. Some time before your mother became ill, she received a new life, and she passed on a new legacy to you."

"Through this other man she was married to?"

Hank laughed. "No, not through him. He never listened to your mother. I think that's part of the reason she never told him you were not his son."

"Then how did she find a new life?"

"God used you, Josef."

Josef felt the pierce of Hank's eyes and glanced away, wondering what the man wanted from him: A memory of something he'd done? Realization of the faith Hank spoke about? Skepticism? Surprise?

Josef didn't know how to react. He didn't know what he believed. But he was interested in finding out how he had helped his mother to find God.

"When you were four, you ate some poisonous wild mushrooms. Your mother was frantic. She couldn't call me to let me know what she was going through for obvious reasons. The man she was married to was by her side, worrying along with her. He loved you, too. They took you to the hospital, where your stomach was flushed out. You were given some kind of tea remedy and then they were told to wait through the night to see what would happen.

"A chaplain had just come from visiting another child in the ward when he noticed your mother crying. He asked if he could pray for your healing. Then he prayed that your mother would know how much her Creator loved her, no matter what happened. I think that's what took hold of her heart. She was hungry for someone to love her and want to be part of her life. It astonished her that God loved her so much He took on human life, then died for her. She didn't come to it all at once, mind you. She was still beside herself with worry over you. But it was the beginning. And then, that very same night, you started to get well. She never saw that chaplain again, and to the moment she died, I think part of her believed he might have been an angel, sent from God to tell her about His love.

"You came home from the hospital the next day, and after that, she began going to a new church and taking you along. It was no longer just a social ritual. She read the Bible every day. She started thinking about what she was doing, how her thoughts and actions might affect you."

"She didn't start her soap box with you, the father of her illegitimate child?"

Hank drew in a breath and let it out slowly. "You judge our old selves, not the forgiven ones. Once we looked at Christ, God changed both your mother and me. Our old selves thought whatever we wanted to do was right, so long as we didn't hurt anyone. Before, we thought if her husband never found out, what was the harm? He seemed to care more about his business anyway. We didn't know it was our souls at risk. We saw that shame brings a pain all its own. We're all given a conscience by a moral God.

"I didn't see your mother again until a month before she died, when she knew she wouldn't live. She let me say good-bye to her, and to you, for which I will always be grateful. You may have been conceived in sin, Josef, but if it wasn't for you, neither your mother nor I would have come to know the greatest joy in life. That joy is the knowledge that we were created for a reason, and that reason is nothing less than to serve our Creator, and to let others know He loves them and gives them a way to spend eternity with Him."

Hank took his eyes off the road again to give Josef a long glance. Josef wanted to feel something inside, but didn't.

"You were a young child when your mother took you to church, but she told me that you learned all of this and believed."

Josef closed his eyes. He didn't remember believing in anything. Nothing felt right to him: not this man at his side; not the memories of his mother; not a faith he might or might not have had. He didn't know who he was or what he believed. He wearily closed his eyes and brought up the next subject on his mind.

"Where is he now, the man who thinks he's my father?"

"In jail."

Josef opened his eyes and looked at Hank in surprise. "What for?"

"He helped a man who was committing criminal acts."

"He's a crook, then?"

Hank shrugged. "Not by profession. He's actually quite a successful businessman, as world standard goes."

"Soooo, then, when he got carted off, I came to find you? I must be, what?—twenty-five, twenty-six years old. What's wrong with me? Can't I live on my own?"

"You can, once you're back on your own two feet. For the time being, you're in need of a friend, Josef. When Otto was arrested, they seized everything in his house, including all of your possessions. You have nothing in Washington."

"How long is he in for?"

"I don't know. He was arrested only recently. As far as I know, there hasn't been a trial."

"Maybe I should see him," Josef mused.

"Why?"

Josef wondered if he heard a hint of panic in Hank's question. "Maybe he can help me to remember. And maybe he needs a friend."

"To get your memory back, you must rest and regain your strength. Beside that, I doubt Otto wants you to see him in jail."

Josef didn't reply. He had no recollection of the man beyond a vague dream. Perhaps he was a proud man.

"In any case," Hank continued, "what you need now is fresh air and rest, and Saddlebrook is the place for that. We'll let the memory problem work itself out. Why don't you try to get some sleep?"

Sleep. At least he wouldn't have to talk. He had plenty more questions, but given what he'd just learned, he was hesitant to ask much more. He had enough to sort out.

Despite the bumpy ride he did doze, for how long he didn't know. The sound of gravel beneath the rubber tires woke him. The motorcar rocked gently, quite a change from the deep ruts of country public roads.

"What part of Virginia is this?"

"We're on Saddlebrook land now, son. Everywhere you look is ours."

Rolling green hills led in the distance to a ridge of blue-tinged mountains along the western horizon. Ivy climbed out of thick underbrush on lush trees. Now and then the trees parted to reveal a white fence, stark and clean against the emerald background of pasture. Stretching before them, a mottled gray road of crushed gravel curved toward a house. Three-story white pillars supported an overhang. The façade boasted long, narrow windows on each floor and a massive pair of white doors centered above a half dozen steps. The porch itself was wide and inviting, with lacquered wooden chairs that beckoned a guest to watch the sun rise in the east or set over the hills in the west from its expansive southern exposure.

Josef was more curious than ever about Hank. If he was a working man, he was a successful one.

"How, exactly, does an inquiry agent afford all of this?"

"Oh, a combination of blessings, you might say. A long time ago, a wealthy banker needed someone to help him collect evidence on a man he suspected of stealing money from his business. He needed someone new to Culpeper because the suspect was known by everybody in town. The banker hired me, and we told everyone I was a friend of the family in need of a job. So I worked at the bank while I watched the man until we had enough to prosecute him. But while pretending to be a friend of the family, I got to know the banker's daughter. We had a similar dream about a farm with horses to breed and sell, and that was the beginning. Jaylene and I were married a year later. Her father leased us the land and bought us the first two horses we needed—good stock, mind you; what any business needs to succeed. We did the rest ourselves to build up Saddlebrook."

"You're married."

Hank nodded as he directed the motorcar down the circular drive toward the wide white porch.

"How long ago?"

"Twenty-one years."

The numbers clicked through his brain. "If I'm twenty-six, you married before my mother died."

"That's right."

"You said you loved her."

Hank seemed startled by Josef's accusing tone. "I did."

"So you married somebody else?"

Hank had reached the house and now turned off the engine. "You were not quite four when your mother and I decided to stop seeing each other. I loved her; I love her memory still. But there was no hope that we could marry. She couldn't leave her husband, and it wouldn't have been right for me to ask her to. I met Jaylene soon after your mother and I parted. She is a godly woman who loved me despite my past. She knows about you. She consented that I see you before your mother died."

Josef's gaze went to the house.

As if guessing Josef's thoughts, Hank spoke up. "She's not here. She's off with our daughter to New York for a shopping holiday."

"Your daughter?"

"Your half-sister. You also have a half-brother, at the university, thank God."

The last words were muttered as if Josef wasn't meant to hear as Hank slipped out from behind the wheel.

"What's the matter with him?" Josef called after Hank.

Hank leaned down to look at Josef. "Who?"

"Your son, that you thank God he got into the university."

Hank shook his head. "No, no. He's a bright boy. I'm thankful he's there and not—" He stopped short. He walked around to Josef's side of the car and helped him out. "You don't remember, do you? Our country has joined the war."

Josef leaned heavily between the car and Hank, once he'd heaved himself up. For a moment everything went black and his head spun, but then his vision restored itself, and he saw Hank in front of him, ready to help him up the stairs.

"War?"

"It's a long story. There's been a European war for a while now. In April, we joined in. Our boys are just getting ready to go over there."

"What are we fighting for?"

Hank raised a brow. "That, Josef, is a very good question. The president says it's for democracy."

Halfway up the porch, the door opened, and a woman stepped out, evidently a maid by her plain blue uniform and starched white collar. She stopped at the top of the stairs. Her skin was the shade of cinnamon, black hair pulled back tight into a single braid wrapped in a coil at the nape of her neck. Her light-golden-brown eyes gave Josef an appraising glance. He noticed that she was tall and thin, appearing even taller because she carried herself with regal grace as she swept down to help bring him up the stairs.

"Welcome home, Mr. Tanner," she said with a slight sing-song, foreign accent of precise English diction. "Whom have we here?"

"Well, Ulu, maybe you ought to be sitting. Meet my son Josef."

Long, tapered fingers rushed to halt the gasp that made it past her lips anyway. "You might have given me a chance to reach that chair, Mr. Tanner."

Looking at her, Josef noted that this woman didn't look or sound like a servant; more like the queen of some English colony. Despite her obvious surprise, she recovered quickly enough to hold the door open for the men.

"He's injured."

"He was in an accident and I brought him here to mend. I'm taking him to Caleb's room."

"Well, then, what can I get for him? Tea? A meal?"

Josef tried to shake himself free of Hank's grip but didn't have the strength. "He's able to speak for himself," Josef muttered.

"All right, then, are you hungry?" She flashed bright white teeth in a smile.

"No, just tired."

"Then maybe you'll let me help you up those stairs," his father said. "There's sixteen of them, boy, and you won't make half by yourself."

"Shall I call Dr. Sherman?" the servant asked.

"No, Ulu," Hank called over his shoulder, "he'll be all right. He says he's not hungry, but bring some tea and toast anyway. And see if you can find one of Jaylene's headache pills."

"I know just where they are."

She disappeared as Hank led Josef up the last of the stairs. "She speaks with an accent I can't place," Josef said, catching his breath. "Where is she from?"

"Ibo," Hank said. Josef looked no better enlightened. "That's in Nigeria."

"Nigeria," Josef repeated. "Africa?"

They were both breathing a bit heavier from the exertion as Hank led him along the upper hall. "Ulu's grandfather was one of the last slaves brought to the United States. He was a young man, and his wife and child were left behind. When he was freed, he earned enough money to bring his son and granddaughter."

He eyed Josef. "You knew Nigeria was in Africa. I'd like to know just what you do remember, how your mind is working."

"So would I," Josef said, half to himself. Then he added, "I don't know what I know. Africa is in that war you talked about, isn't it?"

"Yes, they're fighting in Africa. Maybe you are starting to remember." Hank's voice took on a new tone, as if he was not completely happy at the prospect.

Josef didn't mention the dream memory. From the look on Hank's face, he suddenly doubted that Hank wanted all of his memories to surface. Or maybe Hank was just tired from the long drive and nearly carrying Josef up the stairs. In a moment Hank opened a six-panel white door and led Josef into a large, square bedroom, decorated in browns and blues. A wide, four-poster bed occupied much of the space, a tall bureau was set off to one corner, and small tables were placed along each side of the bed with a lamp on each and sulfur matches for lighting the wicks. The furniture in this house looked nothing like the furniture they'd left behind in the city: this was rich, polished, pampered.

"Watch this, Josef." Hank paused just inside the door to press a button on the wall. An incandescent light affixed to the ceiling filled the room with brightness. "You've had electricity in the city for awhile, but not many places can get it this far out. Just so happened they were running a line across country. Some of us paid for the right to put in what was needed so we could run electricity."

Josef was barely listening. All he could hear was the pounding in his head. It grew louder and more painful by the second. He eyed the bed, hoping he'd make it that far without collapsing.

He didn't.

CHAPTER Three

"No, NOT pink!" Lissa said resolutely when her sister held up a swatch of frothy chiffon in the softest shade of the pastel. At her younger sister's sudden look of dismay, Lissa tried to smooth over her words. "It's just so, so— *pink.*"

"I like pink."

"You like liver and prunes, too, but you wouldn't serve them at the wedding."

"What's wrong with pink at a wedding?" asked their mother from the corner of the parlor. "It's a perfectly lovely shade, and you girls will look charming."

"Yes, well," said Lissa slowly, "I suppose if you want your wedding party to look like every other wedding party this year, it'll do."

Lissa looked through the other swatches for an alternative and held up a midnight blue. "What about this?"

"Oh, yes, I did like that shade." Cassie smiled then frowned when she looked in their mother's direction. She took the material from her sister's hand, replacing it on the table and lowering her voice. "But Mama said it's too dark for a morning wedding."

"With the brightness of the sun reflecting in your eyes, Cassie, nothing is too dark," Lissa said.

Her sister giggled then looked from Lissa to their mother, who just shrugged but offered no further objection.

"It's your wedding, Cassie," Lissa reminded her. "Pick what you want. Mama will come round to anything you choose."

Cassie looked doubtful. "Think so?"

"Tell her, Mama; tell her you want her to love each and every moment of her special day."

"She's right about that, Cassie. It's your weddin', not mine."

Cassie scanned the scraps in front of her and suddenly her eyes widened. "I choose this one, then." She held up the brightest shade of red Lissa had ever seen.

"Oh, now you've done it, Lissa," said Mama with more of a groan than a laugh. "You'll all stand for the nuptials looking like a flag."

Cassie frowned. "Don't you like it? It's fire engine red, and you know William is a volunteer fireman. And with Lissa going off to the Red Cross, I thought it would tie in everything that means so much these days, especially if William and the other men wear blue tuxes, and me with white. You know—red, white, and blue. Everything should be patriotic these days, don't you s'pose?"

Their mother set aside the knitting needles in her lap and stood. She never talked about the war, and especially about Lissa's upcoming adventure, even though she'd given her tacit consent. Whenever the subject came up, she either left the room or fell silent.

"I'm going to get the door," she said, and Lissa and Cassie exchanged glances.

"I didn't hear anything," Cassie said.

"I saw through the window. A motorcar is coming up the lane."

A moment later they heard the familiar voice of Ulu, their neighbor's African housekeeper. Every other servant or farmhand used the back door, not because the Parkers insisted, but because most white folks did. But Ulu was proud and had been born and raised without the history of racial class system in her own life. She'd learned which homes welcomed her like other visitors, and which didn't. The girls stood when they heard her melodious voice rise above its normal happy tone.

"And he passed out, just like that, at Mr. Tanner's feet. I came straight away; didn't wait to be asked. Mr. Tanner told me he didn't need Dr. Sherman, but I thought Miss Lissa wouldn't mind coming to have a look-see."

"Who is the gentleman, Ulu?" asked Lissa's mother as Lissa and Cassie came up behind her.

Ulu looked uncharacteristically tight-lipped. "Oh, I didn't even have a minute to catch his name, poor sick boy." Light brown eyes cast their gaze Lissa's way. "You'll come, won't you, Miss?"

"Of course. Let me get my kit, and I'll follow you back."

"I don't mind driving you back and forth," Ulu volunteered. Lissa had often tagged along with Ulu, ever since Mr. Tanner's first Buick when Lissa and Penny Tanner were girls.

"All right. It'll be quicker if I just come along. On the way, you can tell me more about what happened."

They hurried out the door, down the front porch, and across the lawn to the Tanner vehicle Ulu used, the motorcar she drove each Monday and Thursday to market. Mr. Tanner had taught all the women in his household to drive, insisting he needed someone he could trust to run errands between their farm and Culpeper and sometimes even Washington. Ulu was usually his messenger. Mr. Tanner was the first to have more than one motorcar for miles around. He had three Buicks because he was fascinated by every advance in the industry and couldn't wait to try out the new technology as soon as it was installed in a Buick.

This afternoon Ulu had the top on, though it made little difference without a windshield or sides, especially when it rained.

The drive from Lissa's farm to the Tanner's Saddlebrook was ten minutes, past wide fields and pastures between the trees and hills that lay before the bigger, bluer hills just west.

"He was talking sensibly when Mr. Tanner brought him home, Ulu? You said he passed out."

"Yes, that he was. He looked a bit pale, but it's hard to tell. He's a fair-skinned boy with light hair. I've never seen him before, so maybe he's pale all of the time."

"Did Mr. Tanner say what might be wrong with him?"

"Said he had an accident, that was all. He must have hit his head. It's bandaged at the forehead." She tapped the side of her head to show where, then returned both hands to the wheel. It was growing dark and the unpaved country road held dangers of its own even in dry weather.

"How old is the boy, Ulu?"

"Oh, fully grown, miss, but a boy to me, you see. Older than you would be my guess."

"I see." Not since her training at the hospital had she helped a fully grown patient, but while it might be cause for some hesitation she relished the prospect. In just a few months she'd be tending soldiers, so this was a wonderful opportunity to test her skills. "A head injury," she mulled. "That could be serious." She looked at Ulu. "Mr. Tanner said he didn't need Dr. Sherman?"

"That's what he said, Miss Lissa."

Saddlebrook sprawled before them in the dim glow of twilight. She'd always loved this farm, full of beautiful horses, inviting pastureland, and neatly planted cornfields. The same creek that babbled through her family's land widened along the back of Saddlebrook, and many were the days she and Penny Tanner had met on their horses for long rides through the countryside.

Ulu parked the sedan behind Mr. Tanner's newest and now favorite Buick, then quickly led the way up to the front door.

"He's in Mr. Caleb's room," said Ulu.

As many times as Lissa had been in the Tanner house, she hadn't been in Caleb Tanner's bedroom since she was seven years old, when she, Penny, and Caleb had engaged in games of hide-and-seek. Penny was two years younger than Lissa, and Caleb a year younger than that. Somewhere between the time Caleb was five and six, he'd discovered that girls had cooties. After that, he no longer played with his sister and her friend.

They passed Penny's room, Mr. and Mrs. Tanner's room, and finally came to Caleb's. Ulu quietly pushed open the door.

"Ah, there you are."

Lissa heard Mr. Tanner's calm, low voice. He was the kind of man anyone in town could depend upon for help. Most likely this young man had sought Mr. Tanner's aid.

"Yes, Mr. Tanner, and I brought Miss Lissa."

Mr. Tanner's eyes shot to the door as Lissa entered. It was the first time she could recall that he didn't send her an immediate smile of welcome.

"Lissa?"

"Hello, Mr. Tanner. Ulu says you have a patient here."

Lissa glanced at Mr. Tanner's face, which showed surprise or even alarm, then focused on the occupant of the large bed. Lying with his eyes closed was a blond haired man who appeared to be sleeping. She ignored Mr. Tanner's odd reaction to her and reached for the patient's right wrist. As she took his pulse she noticed the bandage, his skin tone, his steady breathing. His heart rate was stable. She wanted to look into his eyes to check for dilation, but hesitated before doing any more.

"Ulu said he passed out. Did he regain consciousness?"

The man himself opened his eyes, fixing a blue gaze directly on her. She made several observations in that moment, not the least of which was that her patient was a very handsome man. The nurse in her noticed that his pupils were a bit dilated, but that could be because his eyes had been closed for a time.

"He hit his head a couple of days ago." Mr. Tanner neared the opposite side of the bed. Even though she listened, Lissa didn't take her gaze from the patient. He was studying her so keenly she found herself unable to look away.

By sheer habit of initially talking to parents and teachers rather than to her own young patients, she asked Mr. Tanner, "Was there a great loss of blood?"

"No. Well, it happened in the water, so I couldn't say for sure. Mainly he's been tired and weak, and he's passed out twice. This time I think it was because of the trip here."

"How far did you come?"

Mr. Tanner's hesitation gave the patient himself a chance to break in, still eyeing Lissa. "Is there some reason you won't talk to me?"

She gave a laugh that sounded less confident than she wished. "Actually, there is. Our town has two nurses—one for adults, that's Henrietta, and one for kids, me. I usually depend on parents or teachers to tell me what I'm looking for in a screaming child."

"If I try not to scream, would you mind directing your questions toward me, then?"

"Of course." What kind of nurse was she that she couldn't see to the needs of a grown man? Could she be a nurse only to children, then? Fine time to find out, when she'd be tending wounded soldiers soon.

"Do you have much pain?" she asked.

"Hank gave me some kind of pill earlier. It eased my headache."

Lissa looked at Mr. Tanner. "An aspirin."

"Why do you think you fainted earlier, Mr. . . . ?"

This time it was the patient who exchanged glances with Mr. Tanner.

"Josef. No 'Mr.'; just Josef." He cleared his throat and tried to sit up, and Lissa moved automatically to take the unused pillow at his side, adding it to the one already beneath his head. She saw that he never took his gaze from her as she leaned close, but she refused to give in to nervousness. "I was tired," he said. "My head hurt and my knees gave out. That's all."

"Mr. Tanner said your accident happened a couple of days ago. Has there been any vomiting?"

"Some."

"How often?"

"Just the first day."

"Nothing today? No other feelings of nausea?"

"Some, I suppose."

"And have you experienced paralysis of any kind? Is it ever hard to use your limbs?"

"They're sluggish, not paralyzed."

"How is your vision? Fuzzy or clear?"

"Clear."

"I assume you've experienced dizziness. Ulu told me you couldn't walk up the stairs on your own."

The patient didn't deny it.

"I'm not a doctor, Mr.—Josef," she said awkwardly, "but I do know a little about accidents and the brain. It's nothing to shrug off. You should go to the University Hospital in D.C. for something called a radiograph. It's a picture of your brain, to see if there is a fracture in the skull or a swelling of any tissue."

"We just came from D.C. I'm not going back, at least not tonight."

Lissa looked at Mr. Tanner with surprise. "You brought him all the way out here, when you were in Washington?"

"That's right," said Mr. Tanner. "I thought all he needed was rest."

"I'm sure the trains are comfortable, Mr. Tanner, but still—"

"We drove."

Lissa barely felt her jaw drop open. Mr. Tanner had driven an injured man over those awful, bumpy roads from Washington? She could think of nothing to say, she was so shocked at Mr. Tanner's departure from his usual good sense.

"I'm just tired," said the patient.

Lissa looked between the two of them. "Neither of you seem to understand the risk you're taking by not seeing a specialist. The brain is a very complex structure. If you hit your head hard enough, hemorrhaging might have occurred. There isn't a lot of room in our heads for excess blood to float around. It could compress the brain and cause permanent damage—even death. I strongly recommend—"

"What's your name?"

The quiet question from the patient, so calm in such stark contrast to Lissa's whirling mind, stopped her cold.

"Did they call you Liesel?" Josef continued, almost whispering.

"No!" Hank's reaction brought both the patient and Lissa to turn his way.

Lissa recovered and turned back to the man in bed, shaking her head.

"My name is Larisa Rose, but everyone calls me Lissa—Lissa Parker. I live next door."

The man who'd introduced himself as "just Josef" gave her a lopsided smile. "Near as I could tell when we drove up, next door is a barn."

She couldn't help but smile, too. "I mean the next homestead over. At the edge of Saddlebrook. My family owns a farm, and I live there."

"Well, Larisa Rose," Josef said, saying the name slowly as if to let the sound linger on his lips, "do you want my own, untrained opinion of my condition?"

She nodded.

"I don't remember much about what happened, but Hank tells me I hit my head on a rock in a river. I agree it must have been a solid hit, because I still have one doozy of a headache. But the way I felt when I woke up felt, uh, familiar to me: like a sick bug. I think when I was a child I must have drunk some river water and got a sick stomach. That's what it felt like. I think that's a part of why I'm tired and weak and why I threw up. All I want to do is sleep. I think if I can do that I'll be feeling better in no time."

"You did fall in a river when you were six," Mr. Tanner said, "and you did get a belly ache. Swallowed too much of the river."

"There, I knew this felt familiar."

Lissa looked at Mr. Tanner. "Sounds like you've known him for quite some time."

Mr. Tanner nodded, offering nothing further.

"Nonetheless, you still are taking undue risk," Lissa said in as professional a voice as she could muster. "I think you should see a doctor."

Mr. Tanner backed away from the bedside, beckoning Lissa. "We appreciate your opinion, Lissa. Perhaps we'll go tomorrow, depending on how he does tonight. But you agree that he needs rest? Let's leave him alone so he can get some sleep."

Lissa followed with an unmistakable feeling of failure. How could she make them understand that head injuries were nothing to treat lightly?

"Larisa," said Josef in a voice that sounded more loud and clear in the quiet room.

Lissa turned back at the foot of the bed.

"You're a credit to your profession, a regular Florence Nightingale."

Lissa tilted her head to one side. "I'd hardly call myself that, Josef. I can't even convince my only adult patient to get the care you need."

"Can't blame yourself if your patients are mule headed, now can you, Larisa?"

Something about the way he said her name made her smile. She nodded, at the same time hoping she wouldn't regret being more insistent. Then she reluctantly followed Ulu and Mr. Tanner out of the room.

CHAPTER *Four*

LISSA LET herself in quietly through the kitchen door. She and Ulu had shared a cup of tea that turned into an entire pot before they were finished chatting. Lissa made her way silently through the dim evening light. No sense disturbing her mother, who heard every little noise. In their house it was early to bed, early to rise.

After a brief stop at the upstairs bathroom to wash her face and get ready for bed, she went to her room and was surprised to find an oil lamp lit. Cassie was curled on the foot of her bed like some giant feline dressed in white cotton.

"Well?"

Lissa untied her robe, throwing down the yellow, flowered coverlet at the head of the bed.

"Well, what?"

"What happened at the Tanner's? Who was hurt?"

Lissa felt a momentary flutter in the vicinity of her heart, recalling the face of the handsome young stranger. She had the odd temptation to giggle and give Cassie a vivid description of the deepest blue eyes she'd ever seen, how he'd called her only "Larisa" instead of "Lissa," and how it came out sounding like a caress.

What she did was climb into bed with a yawn, and turn down the wick until she could just barely see her sister clearly.

"He wasn't so badly hurt, but I argued that Mr. Tanner ought to take him to see a specialist, or at least ask Dr. Sherman to check him."

"But who was hurt? If Ulu didn't know him, he isn't from around here."

"That's right."

"Well, who is he?"

Another yawn. "I don't know. His name is Josef, but I didn't catch his last name."

"Where is he from?"

"I'm not sure. Perhaps Washington. Probably Mr. Tanner knows him from there."

"Oh, do you think so?" Cassie fairly beamed with interest. "Maybe he's somebody from one of his cases. Does he look like a criminal?"

Lissa laughed. "I'm sure Mr. Tanner isn't in the habit of bringing criminals home, Cassie."

"Well, what did he look like?"

Lissa looked away from what Cassie might see in her enthusiastic quest for details. "Oh, a bit older than me, I think, but only by a few years. Nice looking."

"Nice looking? How nice looking?"

Lissa lay back, fluffing the pillow to adjust it comfortably. She purposely avoided Cassie's stare, struggling to maintain the composure of an older, wiser sister.

"Just nice looking, that's all."

"Okay, let's have it," Cassie said firmly. "If you want to get rid of me and go to bed, you might as well tell me what I want to know straight out. What's the color of his eyes?"

"Blue," she answered without hesitation.

Cassie pointed a finger at Lissa as if she'd solved a mystery. "You must have thought him a modern-day David, or you wouldn't have noticed."

Unable to hold back a smile, she gave up her effort to look disinterested. "You would have noticed, too, Cass. In fact, I'd be willing to wager you would've forgotten about William, at least for a moment."

Cassie burst into laughter. "This is better than I thought. You've been struck, dear sister. Cupid's arrow has found you at last. Just when I was beginning to think you were settled into old-maid-hood at twenty-three."

"There's nothing wrong with a woman being independent, Cassie." Lissa had defended herself before against the romantic notions of Virginia society, and didn't hesitate to do so now. Most of her friends had married right out of high school and those who went to college were mainly interested in finding a good match. Lissa had entered one of the few education programs where women were readily accepted. She'd taken nurses' training a couple of years ago at the hospital in Washington, after a two-year college program. Her studies kept her too busy to get to know anyone special, but since being home, more than one young man had tried courting her. She just hadn't been interested in any of them, until maybe today.

"You can be independent and married, too," Cassie said. "That's my intention."

Lissa smiled. "Have you checked with William to see if that's okay with him?"

"Oh, posh, Liss. William wants me to be everything I want to be."

Liss couldn't help but frown. "In that case, why don't you wait until you're finished with college? You have two years left, Cass. That's not such a long time."

Cassie rolled her eyes and stood. "We've been through this before, Lissa. William graduates in two weeks, and he starts his job two weeks after that. I might live near enough to some university to take a class now and then, and you know I read a lot. But once I have kids, what's the point? Besides, William is ready to be married, and so am I. Maybe when you get to know this Josef what's-his-name, you'll know what I mean. You wouldn't want to wait two years, either."

"Oh, I see," Lissa said gently. "You haven't done anything that might get you into trouble, have you?"

Cassie's cheeks pinked nearly the shade of material she'd considered earlier in the evening. "You know we wouldn't do any such thing. But it is hard, you know. Well, you will know if you let yourself care for somebody again."

Lissa turned away, unwilling to take a turn in the conversation toward the high school sweetheart who'd jilted her after graduation.

"I'm sorry," Cassie whispered. "I shouldn't have said anything about that."

Lissa shrugged but didn't turn back. The hurt was still there, but somewhere along the line the memory had lost its power over her. She loved children, and she was good with them, but maybe it was best that she wasn't married with only her own to care for. God had something else in store for her, at least for the time being.

She extinguished the lamp wick. "Good-night, Cass."

She felt the bed shift as Cassie stood. "Pleasant dreams, sis . . . maybe with deep blue eyes in them."

"Mmm," said Frank Parker with a deep breath. "Smells good. Your mother's recipe?"

Lissa nodded. "Here, Father, taste it. I can't taste a thing, I've been breathing it in all morning."

She gave him a small bowl of the pungent chicken soup, watching him blow on the first spoonful.

"Ah, that's good! Nothing like a Saturday to get the best meals of the week."

"Sorry, Father," Lissa said, turning back to the pot, satisfied that it was acceptable. "I'm taking this over to the Tanners. Mama said she'd make you a sandwich."

"What? Why is it that every time somebody makes something special around here, I never get any of it? I have to move to a neighbor's house to enjoy my own family's best cooking."

"Oh, posh, Father. I just gave you a bowl, didn't I?"

"You gave me just enough to taste what I'm not getting."

Lissa laughed at her father's theatrics. "All right, Mr. Parker, fill your bowl and keep your complaints to yourself. I'm taking the rest next door, so you'd better get it while it's here."

Even while she prepared to take the soup, she wondered if her actions were wise. She'd never pursued a man before, and her motives now felt alarmingly akin to that very thing.

Lissa squelched the incriminating thoughts. Suppose the man Mr. Tanner had brought home was eighty? Wouldn't it still be the neighborly thing to bring him some chicken soup? So why shouldn't she do it for this virile young man with the unforgettable blue eyes? She was just being neighborly.

Lissa knew she was being more than neighborly and maybe more than a little transparent. For once, she didn't care. She was too eager to see Josef again, and she'd lain awake last night trying to think of a way to go back that wouldn't be untoward.

She had some justification in that she had a vested interest professionally in the man. If his condition had changed one little bit for the worse, it was no less than her duty to insist that he allow Dr. Sherman to see him.

She'd be denying her chosen profession if she didn't at least check on him, same as any patient on Dr. Sherman's rounds.

Lissa was alternately excited and apprehensive as she drove carefully around the ruts in the road to avoid spilling her cargo. She stopped before turning into the winding lane to the Tanner house, pulling a mirror from her purse to make a final check. She'd taken special care with her appearance that morning. Yesterday her honey colored hair had been pulled back in a bun, the way she always wore it to work. Today it hung free, curving out from her face in a gentle wave. Her eyes weren't nearly as fascinating as his, though more than one person had described her eyes as her best feature. She thought they were just plain light brown, but one male classmate in college had called them gold. That sounded far more exotic. Perhaps they were gold in some lighting.

Her high school sweetheart had said she was the most beautiful girl in town, and he'd made her feel that way. Around him, she could even accept the shape of her mouth, which she thought too wide. For a long time now she'd scoffed at the "vanity" of thinking about her beauty, or lack of it. Since the boy whose opinion she valued had rejected her, she'd drifted back into thinking of herself as average or even plain. Her eyes were just brown and her mouth too full. Her hair was less the color of spun sugar butter than the brown of old hay.

But today she'd tried to compensate. Though she wore no lipstick to draw attention to her mouth, she did tint her lashes and add a bit of color to her cheeks. That was all the makeup anyone in town wore, and that only recently, since the picture shows had opened up showing close-ups of the flicker stars. Even in the dull gray images projected on a large white-washed wall, girls could see all the makeup they wore. Even Mama and a few of the other older women in church had decided that cheek color wasn't just for loose women, so Lissa knew she wasn't creating a scandal. She was glad her hair had obeyed today, its fullness flowing past her shoulders in curls only at the bottom. And maybe the tan of her shirt tucked into her beige skirt did make her eyes look maybe just a little gold in contrast.

She only hoped Mr. Tanner didn't see through her ruse. He was the only one she could possibly fool. Ulu would know the moment she saw Lissa wearing a skirt on Saturday. There was nothing Lissa could do about that. She was just glad that Penny and her mother weren't home, imagining the ribbing she would take from them.

Lissa pulled up in front of the house and alighted from her father's Model T, carrying the hot soup pot with towels to protect her hands. She was relieved when the door opened for her, just as she reached the top of the steps.

"Well, what have we here, child? Don't you look pretty today."

"Why, thank you, Ulu," said Lissa in as casual a voice as she could mimic. "I brought some soup for Mr. Tanner's patient. If he won't take my advice about seeing a specialist, the least he can do is take my home remedy."

"Ah, your mother's recipe, then? The best in town. Such a treat."

Ulu followed Lissa to the kitchen, where Lissa made herself at home by settling the pot on their stove. Then, because Ulu seemed to have stopped at the doorway to merely watch, Lissa found a bowl in the wooden cupboard and a porcelain ladle in the drawer, and proceeded to prepare a bowl for the man in Caleb's room. The ride over had cooled the soup to just the right temperature.

Lissa couldn't avoid Ulu's eyes forever. Hoping her cheeks weren't pink, and wishing Ulu would think it was just from the steam of the soup, she glanced at her. "He hasn't eaten lunch already, has he? How is he today?"

"Oh, he's awake, I heard him shuffle about. And no, I haven't taken up his lunch. Even if I had, my plain broth wouldn't compare to the feast you have here."

"I was just doing what any neighbor would do. Will you bring it to him, or shall I?"

Ulu laughed in her typical loud fashion. "Oh, my little dear, I wouldn't dream of depriving you of what you came for."

Lissa wasn't quite ready to give up. She feigned confusion. "What do you mean?"

Ulu placed two strong, firm hands on Lissa's shoulders. She was even taller than Lissa, and looked down at her with a gaze that took in everything. "You are a lovely girl, Lissa Parker, inside and out. Just you remember, okay?"

Genuinely confused, Lissa cocked her head to one side. "Thank you, but, Ulu, why say that now?"

"Because there is a boy upstairs who isn't wearing a wedding ring, and I confess that last night I dreamed of the angels dancing at your nuptials. Now go. And you could have worn lipstick. You have a pretty mouth, especially when you smile."

Lissa did smile, relieved that Ulu saw through her pretense but didn't think her foolish. She turned back to the soup while Ulu gathered a tray, a glass of milk, and a napkin. Lunch complete, Lissa hoped she could calm her sudden trembling long enough to make it safely up the stairs without spilling a drop.

She paused at the kitchen door. "Is Mr. Tanner with him?"

"No, indeed not. He's out with the stock. That's why you should go up right away. You know he'll head there when he gets back."

Lissa nodded, suddenly feeling like they were co-conspirators.

She made her way up the stairs, glad her skirt was sufficiently above her ankles to be out of the way. The only good thing that had happened since the beginning of that awful war was higher hemlines.

That's it. She took a soothing breath. *Think of everyday life, and maybe you'll convince yourself you're not nervous.*

Setting the tray on the hall table, she knocked quietly at the door. If he'd fallen back asleep she wasn't sure she should wake him. The soup could wait, and rest was more important to his health, even if it did mean Ulu would have to bring lunch to him later. Lissa couldn't hang around long, or Mr.

Tanner would think her absolutely silly. She was never there when Penny wasn't home. She was relieved to hear Josef's voice a moment later.

"I'm awake. Come in."

"It's me, Mr.—It's Lissa Parker."

"Oh." He sounded surprised but not impatient. She waited for him to bid entrance before turning the knob, hearing movement from the other side of the door.

"I'm decent, Larisa. Come in."

After retrieving the tray from the table, she laughed lightly when she saw him. He must have had his shirt off. He was buttoning his blue pajamas askew, as if he'd donned them in a hurry. Her laugh sounded far more comfortable than she felt.

"I can help you with that if you like. I'm used to buttoning others' shirts."

He looked down at what he was doing. "Probably better at it than I am, but I think I'll manage."

He unbuttoned again and found the matching sequence. She couldn't help but notice his chest. His skin was pulled taut over a smooth and muscular, totally fit middle. Other than his head injury, she guessed he was in perfect health. She was glad he'd refused her help. Undoubtedly her hands would have trembled, or worse, she might not have been able to perform the task at all. Surely he would guess she seldom buttoned the shirt of anyone over the age of ten.

"I have soup for you." She brought the tray to his side. "Since you wouldn't take my medical advice last night, I thought I'd resort to the home remedy. Chicken soup is a guaranteed cure and preventive. Or so said my great-grandmother, and she lived until she was eighty-nine."

"Then I'd say she knew what she was talking about. Mmm, that's the first thing that's smelled good since I woke up a few days ago. Hank may be a good Samaritan, but he's a lousy cook."

"Didn't Ulu bring you breakfast? She's a wonderful cook."

"I'm not much for breakfast, at least today. But this is wonderful."

He took a spoonful and closed his eyes as if he'd tasted a bit of heaven. When he opened them again he looked directly at her.

"This was very kind of you," he said, nearly whispering. "I knew I wasn't exaggerating when I called you Florence Nightingale."

She felt herself blush and looked away. It was hard not to stare into those eyes.

"Sit, will you? I could use a visit. Hank's the only one I've talked to for days now, and he doesn't say much."

Lissa looked around for a chair but there was none. "Mr. Tanner doesn't say more than he thinks'll be heard, that's true."

"Sit here," he said, moving his feet beneath the light blanket even though there had been plenty of room before.

Lissa glanced back at the door. It was wide open, and no one would think anything improper was going on. Yet she hesitated.

"It's a big bed, Larisa," he said, looking at her in much the same way he'd looked last night. "Plenty of room for both of us."

She couldn't help but laugh again. His words were much bolder than any he'd said before. She felt foolish standing there but she shook her head. "No, Josef, I think it's best if I stay where I am."

He looked at her steadily, nodding. "Yes, maybe you're right."

At last he took a spoonful of the soup, and Lissa breathed a bit easier. Folding her arms, she paced near the foot of the bed once.

"How is your vision today, Josef? Any changes in how you feel?"

"Ah, so this is an official visit." He looked up at her again and frowned. "I was starting to think you came to see me because you liked me."

"I did. I do," she assured him, perhaps a bit too quickly. She smiled self-consciously. "Perhaps the visit can be partly social and partly professional."

"Hmm, I'd like to think it was more one than the other, but I'll answer your question anyway. My vision is perfect, my headache is easing, and I'm not as tired as I was yesterday. In fact, I was out of bed this morning, and if I could find what Hank did with my clothes, I'd be dressed."

"Just so you don't over do it," she cautioned. "Head injuries can have a lasting effect. I still think you ought to see Dr. Sherman. I'm sure he'd tell you to have a radiograph."

"I think your chicken soup is enough to get me back on my feet, though I'm wondering what kind of jaybird I am to admit that. If I'm perfectly healthy, you might not visit me any more. Then what would I do?"

She smiled down at him, folding an arm about one of the tall posts at the foot. He was so charming, she supposed she should guard herself. He might be this engaging with every woman he met.

Deciding knowledge was the best course toward judgment, she chose one of the many questions she had about him: "How long will you be visiting Saddlebrook?"

"I'm not sure."

"So where will you go when you leave?"

He finished the soup and raised his free hand in a momentary shrug. "At the moment, I'm not sure about that, either."

Perplexed, she wondered what kind of man could have such vague responsibilities. "Don't you have a job to get to? A home to return to?"

"I did have a job; I'm pretty sure about that." He set aside the tray and leaned forward. "But before we get to me, why don't you let me ask you a few questions first?"

She was still wondering at the uncertainty of his last answer. Now with the interrogation turned her way, she hoped her cheeks didn't turn beet red. Maybe the rouge camouflaged a blush under his scrutinizing attention.

"Like what?"

"How long have you been a nurse? You seem experienced, but you don't look old enough to have been in a career for very long."

"I've been nursing two years now, well, nearly three. Henrietta, that's Dr. Sherman's other nurse, is getting on in years, and she doesn't tolerate youngsters well. So that's become my job. It's not so difficult since I like children...."

That was definitely more than he needed to know. I'm babbling.

But even as she chided herself, a smile spread across his face, making him more handsome than ever. "I'm thinking that the young boys around here get sick often, just so they get to see you."

She shook her head, but smiled at the silvery compliment.

"Yesterday you said you lived on the farm next door. How far is it? I looked out the window, but I couldn't see anything except hills."

That he had looked to see where she lived pleased her. "Saddlebrook is pretty big. You can't see beyond its borders from here. I live about ten minutes by motor."

"You drive here then?"

She nodded.

"Am I wrong in my assumption that it's unusual for women to be driving?"

"I've been driving Model Ts around the farm for years. The back wheels slip off and adjust to the plow. We all help with the farming."

He looked surprised, and she wondered if he might be of the school that thought women should only work inside the home. "Do you think there's something wrong in that?"

"No," he responded absently, as if the idea had crossed his mind for the first time. He wasn't looking at her just then. "I guess I think that if a person is capable of working at something, they should just go ahead and do it."

"That kind of thinking still puts us in the minority. You know the war is leaving an awful gap in the work force, and women my age are racing to the factories. Not only are they getting hired, but they're doing a good job."

"That's fine, except who's taking care of the homes?"

"It's mainly single women going after the jobs, or married women whose husbands are gone and who don't have children at home. That's just it: there isn't anyone to take care of the family if the mother has to work."

He nodded slowly. "So you're a career woman, then? Crusading for the rights of women?"

She chuckled at the characterization. "Well, I do believe women should have the vote. Even though our brains are technically smaller than men's, it doesn't necessarily mean our capacity to learn is limited. I've met women who are much smarter than most men I know." She interrupted her own thought to see him still watching her with that intense scrutiny that seemed to be in his nature. She continued, slightly flustered, "But I guess I still think that if a woman chooses to marry, and if she is blessed by God with children, then she is better equipped than a man to stay home and care for them. God made most of us that way. If I were to get married and have children, I hope I'd be able to devote myself to my family, that my husband would provide the financial security necessary to do that."

"A man would be a rattlebrain not to try providing that for . . . someone like you."

For a moment Lissa let herself study his face. His nose, she decided, was perfectly straight. His brows were somewhat darker than his blond hair, and his mouth suited his face faultlessly. His jaw was solid and strong, jutting from the top of a neck that was neither too thick nor too thin, above shoulders that were square and strong. She wondered how tall he was. She hadn't yet seen him out of bed. With a glance to the length of his arms and size of his hands, she guessed he was somewhere around the height of her father, about six feet. Taller than her own five-eight, she was sure of that.

"I want to say something that might sound childish, inappropriate, and forward," he said softly. Even though the full length of the bed separated them, she had no trouble hearing him.

"What is that?"

"You are the most beautiful woman I've ever seen."

No amount of rouge could hide the blush she felt reach all the way to her hairline. She smiled even as she averted her gaze at last.

"I knew I shouldn't say that. I guess I believe people should say what they're thinking, if it's good. I'm sorry I embarrassed you. I'm not sorry I said it though."

Unsure of her voice but realizing she must speak, she cleared her throat. "I should say thank you, but I can't take credit for what I look like. That was between my parents and God."

"Your parents chose each other wisely, then."

"And God? What about His part? Do you believe in God, Josef?"

"What would you say if I told you I don't know what I believe?"

She felt her heart sink with sadness for him, knowing he was missing something she could not imagine life without.

He leaned back, and his gaze went to the window. "I guess I can say this much. I look at what's around us, the trees, the sky, us. It seems obvious that someone put it all together. Hank tells me that when I was a child I had faith in Jesus Christ." He glanced back at her, as if searching for a reaction. "But I seem to have forgotten even the simple things, like what I knew as a child."

"That's all Christ wants from us, a simple, childlike trust in Him. He said as much in the Bible."

She'd noticed Caleb's copy of the Scriptures on the bureau. It was a hefty volume, too unwieldy to take along to the university. "Here, I'll show you."

She flipped to one of her favorite passages and read, ending at a verse that she had made a needlework stitching of to hang in her bedroom:

"... And whoso shall receive one such little child in my name receiveth me." She looked up. "There are lots of verses about children in the Bible. Society may not value them much, but our Lord did."

"You do like children, don't you, to remember the verses about them."

She nodded.

"Mind if I take a look at that?"

She rounded the corner of the bed and handed the Bible to him, taking away the empty tray at the same time. She knew she should take it down to the kitchen. The sensible thing to do was to say good-bye and go home.

She set the tray on the bureau.

"I suppose you realize that the way you say things raises more questions than you answer about yourself," she said as she turned to him. He'd placed the Bible on his lap, open to the passage she'd read.

"That's because I don't have any answers. Here's the man with the answers."

His glance to the door alerted her of someone else's approach.

"Hello, Hank. Back so soon?" Josef asked.

"Hello, Lissa," said Mr. Tanner, with barely a glance her way. Apparently he was no happier to see her today than he had been yesterday. Why shouldn't he welcome her help in tending to someone who was hurt?

"What kind of answers?" Lissa asked.

"Oh, just about everything. Hank's quite the authority."

Lissa looked between the two men. There was tension between them, and Josef's words had an edge. Neither man seemed ready to reveal the answers to which Josef referred.

"There's the real authority, right on your lap, Josef," said Mr. Tanner, pointing to the Bible. "Maybe that will help you sort some things out."

None of this exchange made sense to Lissa. She did know, however, that she should leave to encourage Josef to give full attention to the Scriptures.

She turned back to the tray. "I should be going. I'm glad you're doing so well today, but if you notice any change in your vision, or the dizziness returns, call for me. Or better, ask Mr. Tanner to send for Dr. Sherman."

Josef nodded, but he was looking at her in that intent way of his, as if doctor visits were the last thing on his mind. "Thank you, Larisa Rose, or should I call you Florence?"

She glanced from him to Mr. Tanner, who seemed to be watching all too closely, then Lissa left the room.

CHAPTER Five

"I've learned a few things about myself," said Josef to Hank after Larisa left. "I'm fairly liberal in my political thinking, and I like women. At least, I like that woman."

Hank said nothing, but he seemed displeased by the disclosure.

"I wasn't . . . married or anything, was I?"

To Josef's immediate relief, Hank shook his head.

"Have a seat, Hank," Josef invited, feeling stronger by the moment. Larisa's chicken soup was having a remarkable effect. "I have been collecting a lot more questions, and you're not leaving until they're answered."

Hank smiled like an indulgent parent to a spoiled child who made threats but couldn't do anything about them. He sat on the end of the bed.

"I'm glad to hear your voice so strong, Josef," he said. "You sound better every day."

"Speaking of which, I'd like to know where my clothes are. I'd like to get dressed."

"I think you could spend one more day as the invalid," Hank suggested, and when Josef started to protest he went on. "I have a bargain for you, boy. You rest one more day and I'll answer your questions now."

"Done."

"What do you want to know?"

"My legal name. I didn't even know what name to give Larisa, except Josef. If my legal father is my mother's husband, then I must have his last name, not yours. So, what is it?"

Hank pursed his lips, and for the barest moment Josef wondered if he would get his answer. So much for the bargain.

"It's Warner. Josef Warner."

"You said you all came from Germany. Warner sounds English."

Hank shook his head. "My own baptismal name was Heinrick Tahnenheiser. Hank Tanner is easier to pronounce in English. I changed it when I came to America, and it's all I'm known by now."

"How did you and my mother meet?"

"On the boat from Germany. I met her husband first, at the beginning of the voyage while he was still coherent. He became so sick he never saw the light of day until we docked in New York." Hank gave a half smile that didn't look very happy. "I always thought it odd, but if it wasn't for Otto, I never would have spent time with your mother. He asked me to watch out for her. We were all traveling second class, and he was worried about her."

"He asked the wolf to guard the sheep?"

Hank frowned but didn't offer a defense.

"If my mother found God and banished you from our lives when I was four, how come you knew about me being sick from river water when I was six?"

His lips tightened again, as if Josef were trying to pry open one too many secrets. "Until she became sick, she sent me a letter at your birthday, giving the highlights in your year. That was our only contact."

"All right, enough history. Now about the recent past. I assume I held a job?"

"You sold glass and coking coal to markets along the East Coast. Your legal father started in the coal industry and eventually opened a glass factory in D.C. You sold both products, and very well, too, from what I saw."

"Just what *did* you see? Why were we together when I had my accident if I had no idea of your existence? Did we keep in touch somehow, after my mother died?"

Hank shook his head. "I didn't see you again until two months ago. Your mother's husband, Otto, remembered that I'd taken a job at a detective agency. He tracked me down, found I was still doing an odd investigative job from time to time, and asked me to help him out of trouble. I couldn't do anything to keep him from going to jail. The first time you saw me since your childhood was the night Otto was arrested. That night you ran off and slipped on a rock and ended up in the Potomac River."

"How did you find me?"

"I was following you. I knew I couldn't help Otto, but I could help you—and I did."

"What kind of trouble is Otto in?"

Hank leveled a stare at Josef. "It's a long story."

"From you, anything over ten words is a long story."

His old, blue eyes took on a thoughtful look as he considered his answer.

"There are a few things you must understand. These are hard times for Germans in this country, Josef. The war has been going on overseas for two years, and people over here have had to choose sides. Otto has always been loyal to Germany. Two years ago it didn't matter. But when Germany started sinking American ships sentiment swayed toward the Allies. Against Germany. President Wilson asked Congress for a declaration of war and that tipped anyone still on the fence to the Allied side. Sad as it is, this country has been as wild with war fever as Europe was two years ago. We haven't learned much from watching all the new graves being dug in Europe."

"And Otto never gave up German citizenship, you said. He thinks people born in Germany should side with Germany, I'll bet." Josef remembered his dream, and it all fit. "So why was he arrested? Don't we have freedoms about our opinions here?"

"Freedom to voice any opinion is a little harder to defend during a war. German soldiers with relatives who live here are shooting down our boys. Freedom of speech can turn into the crime of sedition. Giving money to German sympathizers who operate here during the war begins to look like treason. That's the kind of crime that Otto was arrested for committing."

"So he's not a typical criminal, just someone who believes in an unpopular cause and acts on those beliefs." Josef's gaze fell to the Bible at his side. "That seems much like what that book expects its readers to do."

"There is a difference," Hank said quietly. "That book contains the truth. Otto was so obsessed with Germany that he stopped caring about what is true."

But Josef's thoughts were elsewhere already.

"I don't get it. If Otto never gave up his German citizenship, why did he Americanize his name once he got here?"

The older man was staring at the floor. "He was a businessman, Josef. That's all I know."

"So an American business owner is more likely to be successful here than a foreign one."

Hank brushed his hands briskly on his denim pants. "So now you know it all, Josef—why you are here with me and why you cannot go back to Washington."

"I don't see why I shouldn't go back," Josef said. "He still has businesses to run, doesn't he? Maybe I could help. I must have known the industry if I worked for him."

Hank was shaking his head before Josef finished speaking. "You have no recollection of those skills now, so what good would you be? In any case, everything in Otto's name has been frozen until the government determines the extent of his criminal acts. They'll want to know if the business was a cover for German espionage."

"Was it?"

"I don't think so, but they will take time to prove it, one way or the other. At the moment, you shouldn't make any plans. You need to rest, regain your strength. When your memory returns you'll be able to decide for yourself what to do. I do warn you that Washington is teeming with so-called patriots who look for German spies in every shadow. By virtue of Otto's involvement, you would be a prime target if you went to him now. My advice is to wait until you know and are sure. The last thing he would want is for you to come to his side and be subject to ridicule and social ostracism."

"I don't care about that."

Hank looked at him. "Otto would for you. And so do I."

Hank stood and went to the door but hesitated, turning back. "I have one more bit of advice, Josef. Something you may not want to hear. Don't spend too much time with Lissa."

Surprised, Josef said, "Why not?"

"It's not fair to her, is it, letting her get to know you when you don't really know yourself?"

"Maybe we could find out together what I need to know."

"Josef, stay away from Lissa."

"If you're going to give that kind of fatherly advice, you'd better follow it up with a good reason, Hank. I don't think you've earned the kind of trust that I should blindly obey you."

"Why don't you spend some time reading that Book next to you instead? Penny told me Lissa reads it every day."

"Penny, my half sister? She and Larisa are friends, then?"

Hank nodded.

He was nearly out the door but turned once more. "Flip toward the back, Josef. Look for the Gospel of John. Start there."

Josef was already turning the pages.

———

Lissa felt the wheel firmly in her grip but she was floating, her heart pulling her up to the heavens.

He thinks I'm beautiful.

She hadn't felt so giddy since she was a teenager.

Oh, Lord, watch over me now. I thank you for the gift of emotion, but don't let me forget the Author of love. But I do think You did an especially fine job when You created him. Help me keep my mind fixed on You, even when it wants to wander earthbound. And Lord, help him to remember the faith of his childhood.

CHAPTER  Six

THE CHURCH was filled with sunshine and worshippers, and the hymns seemed to lift away nearly every frown from the faces of the congregation. Lissa was always amazed how the gift of praise could ease the deepest sorrow or enhance the greatest joy.

She prayed fervently in her worship. She prayed again that Josef would rediscover his childhood faith, not just because of her attraction to him but because she'd seen something in his face yesterday that seemed *he* wanted to remember. He already acknowledged God, so evidently he'd let some details get muddy when he became a man.

After the service, she looked for Mr. Tanner and his guest, though her training rejected the notion. She hoped Mr. Tanner wasn't foolish enough to take Josef down the long road into town.

Yet as she followed her parents outside, she scanned the heads of those nearby anyway.

"Miss Lissa, there you are."

Lissa turned to see Ulu behind her and smiled a welcome greeting. Ulu, dressed in brown cotton with stark white hat and gloves, greeted the Parkers then turned to Lissa. "I was hoping you'd come home with me in the Tanner motor today, Miss Lissa, to be the nurse just one more time for our visitor."

Lissa's heart skipped, partly from eagerness to see Josef and partly from sudden alarm. "Has his condition changed?"

Ulu started to answer but Lissa's mother spoke first. "I've been wondering since the other day how the young man is doing. Lissa said perhaps he should see a doctor. How is he?"

"Oh, he's so much better. Such a strong one, that boy. He wants a stamp of full recovery to get Mr. Tanner to stop hovering, which is why I'd like Lissa to come and break the tie. My vote doesn't seem to count."

"I doubt mine will, either," Lissa admitted.

Cassie, at Lissa's side and holding William's hand, nudged her from behind. "But that won't stop you from voicing your opinion, now will it, Lissa? It never does at home. You go with Ulu."

Lissa shot her a glance and a smile.

As Lissa followed Ulu to the motorcar, she heard her mother ask, "Lissa, will you be home for supper?"

"I don't know, Mama," she called back, her steps never hesitating.

Ulu closed the doors of the sedan. "Ah, that was easier than I thought."

"Thanks to Cassie," Lissa added.

"Yes, that girl is wise beyond her years."

"No, she's just a sneak. She enjoys being in on something my parents haven't a clue about. For someone planning her own wedding, Cassie thinks too much about my lack of one."

"Perhaps we will change that, yes?"

Lissa glanced at Ulu. "Now who's the sneak?"

"Go ahead; try to deny the obvious, young lady. But it won't do any good to disclaim with words something your eyes have already given away."

"All right, I admit that I find him charming and handsome," she laughed. "How is he today, Ulu? He must be better if he's arguing with Mr. Tanner."

"Ah, that he is. He's up and dressed and was sitting on the porch when I left. He even asked to ride one of the horses. Mr. Tanner nearly exploded, just hearing the question."

Lissa grinned at the good news.

"He also asked if he might visit you today," Ulu added, her voice suddenly little more than a whisper.

"He did?"

Ulu nodded. "Mr. Tanner refused, though. Now that, I do not understand. But I told the young man I'd bring you out after your services today, and that made him happy."

"Not Mr. Tanner, though?"

"Well, child, I don't know what's gotten into him since he brought Mr. Josef home. He's not quite himself. He even called me a meddler today. Me, who's taken care of his family all these years. A meddler?"

"If it's any consolation, I don't think he's been himself, either, Ulu. I was hoping to see him at services today. Did he think he had to stay with Josef?"

"Well, that was the best thing about the morning. Did you know that our patient found Mr. Caleb's Bible? I think he must have been up all night reading. Mr. Tanner was delighted and stayed behind to see if Josef had any questions."

Lissa could hardly believe the words. How quickly God answered some prayers.

The rest of the ride to Saddlebrook couldn't go quickly enough, but at last Ulu pulled onto the lane. When they reached the house, there sat Josef in blue denim clothes. He looked as if he'd never been injured, except for the wilting white bandage still affixed to his forehead. He seemed to belong there.

"Good afternoon," Lissa greeted.

Josef stood, and she saw that he was taller than her original estimate. His legs were long and lean in the loose denim, his shoulders wide, tapering down to a narrow waist. As she walked up the half dozen steps, she slowed to stand in front of him.

"You're looking especially fit today, Josef," she said.

"Out of bed and on my own two feet."

"That's the first thing I look for in my patients."

Just then Mr. Tanner came out the front door. He looked from Ulu to Lissa without a smile for either of them. In his hand was a tray of lemonade and two glasses.

"You went into my kitchen, Mr. Tanner?" charged Ulu as she stepped up to the porch. Evidently Mr. Tanner's frown didn't sway her boldness.

"Yes, Ulu, I found the glasses and the tray and the lemonade you made this morning. You'll find your kitchen is still intact."

Ulu winked at Lissa as she headed inside, no doubt to go and see for herself. Lissa watched Josef move to another chair, looking for any sign of weakness or dizziness. But all she saw was the natural ease of someone who moved with athletic grace.

Josef looked her way as he motioned to the chair he'd vacated. "You might as well know, I asked Ulu to bring you here, Larisa. And I suppose you're about to ask, 'Any changes in vision? Is the dizziness still gone?'"

"Well?"

"No to the vision question. Yes, the dizziness is still gone. Do I have a clean bill of health?"

"I'd love to say yes, but I can't." She was entirely serious, despite his coaxing smile. "Brain injuries are so unpredictable. I still think you should have a radiograph. I'd also like to change that bandage and have a look at the wound."

"Very well, Nurse Larisa Rose." He leaned toward the table and handed one of the full glasses to her. "That is, I agree to changing the bandage. The radiograph can wait."

"Some head injuries can have a slow effect on the brain. They need to be watched six months, at least. So why don't you just go to the doctor and see if anything unusual is happening up there?"

He shrugged. "I don't believe in wasting a physician's time. I'm fine, I promise you. In fact, I don't recall ever feeling better in my life."

Lissa saw Josef and Mr. Tanner exchange a glance. There was still something they weren't saying. She was uneasy about several veiled references she'd heard Josef make to his memory. But she didn't pursue it, with Mr. Tanner still showing such disapproval that she was even here.

"Well, Lissa," said Mr. Tanner, amicably enough despite his lack of welcome, "Ulu brought you here to tell us if you think Josef should be up and around so soon."

She wondered if she would be dismissed after voicing her opinion.

"I think he'll manage. Maybe you could spot him on the stairs from behind, just in case, for a few days, anyway."

"There's an idea we can both live with," he said. "Josef? Now how about a nap?"

"A nap? That's all I've done for the past four days."

"And it's done you good."

Josef looked at Lissa with what looked like an apology. "He's a mother hen."

"He only wants what's best for you. I do want to change that bandage, though. Mr. Tanner, do you have gauze and adhesive? I don't have my kit."

He nodded, then headed to the door, glancing back at Josef before going inside.

Josef turned to Lissa. He didn't merely turn his head, he stood for a moment and shifted his chair so his whole body faced her. She wanted to giggle like a schoolgirl, feeling his total attention.

"I'm glad to have a moment alone with you," he began. "There are a few things I'd like to say. The first is that I believe I really am remembering the faith I told you about, the faith I had as a child. When I read some of the Bible last night, I wasn't sure. Then, when I read about Jesus, the wisdom He had, the attitudes He presented in His words and actions, it made sense. More than that, I was awed by it. I don't know much about a lot of things, Larisa, but I think I do know something about people. This Jesus, He knew it all. He knew the worst in the hearts of men and loved them anyway, even so long ago."

Lissa nodded. "Yes, it's incredible to me, too. Who should know us better than our Creator? Yesterday, today, and tomorrow."

"Exactly." He seemed excited by the revelation. "A book like that couldn't have been written without God's help. It's full of more wisdom than any man can claim."

Could this be real? Could this man, so vital and handsome, so kind and considerate—not to mention so obviously interested in her—could he now even share her faith?

Lissa smiled. "I'm so glad for you, Josef. I couldn't imagine going through life not acknowledging God, or realizing how much He loves us."

But even as she acknowledged her inner joy, she saw a shadow cross his face. "This all ties in to another thing I have to tell you, Larisa."

He sounded so somber. Whatever this was, it couldn't be good.

"What is it?"

"It's about why I'd forgotten the faith I had as a child." He leaned back in his chair and looked out. She looked, too, at the view she'd seen many times before from this porch: the hill covered with trees, the finger of river, the green grassland, the blue sky that stretched down to the hills and mountains. Then Josef's gaze returned to her, and she looked at him again.

"My faith is not the only thing I've forgotten, I'm afraid."

She bit back her fears and approached him as a nurse.

"Let's see. You weren't certain you had a job, so you've forgotten that. Have you forgotten a family as well?"

She swallowed the lump in her throat. Had she really asked that?

He laughed, and she knew instant relief. "No, I haven't forgotten a family. That was the first thing I made sure of after I met you."

"You didn't know until you asked?"

He leaned nearer, and she thought for a moment he might take her hands in his. Then the door swung open and slammed shut. Mr. Tanner moved between them with a handful of medical supplies and a scowl directed at Lissa. The last time she'd seen that look on his face, she and Penny had, with all the confidence of youth, tried to ride a newly purchased stallion after Hank's specific warning to stay away from him. No one had been hurt, but it was the only time she'd heard Mr. Tanner raise his voice.

"You can change the bandage, then be on your way."

Lissa stood, receiving the items from Mr. Tanner and laying them on the nearby table. She didn't look at either of them as she sorted, giving herself a moment to calm herself after Mr. Tanner's unfriendly tone.

Carefully she peeled away the old bandage and cleaned the area with hydrogen peroxide and cotton. Looking at it, she was distracted from Mr. Tanner's words.

"Hmm. This wound, it doesn't look like a blow from a rock. It's more of a streak."

"Those rocks are sharp," Mr. Tanner interrupted roughly. "He has a knot above the ear, too."

She touched the area indicated gently. Whatever swelling had been there had gone down. That was probably good news. "This wound is deeper than it should be, and it's an odd shape for the kind of injury you've described. I still think you ought to see Dr. Sherman."

"Just cover it up and be done with it, Lissa."

She would have done so, but Josef gently reached up and stilled her hands, looking at Mr. Tanner. "Why are you being so rude, Hank? You're only like this when Lissa is around."

He said nothing.

Josef withdrew his hands from Lissa's, letting her finish the task. After she finished, rather than allowing her retreat, he indicated the chair. "Sit, will you, Larisa?"

"I'm sure her parents are expecting her home for dinner, Josef."

Lissa had wondered if Josef ever directed his intensity at anyone except her. Now she had her answer, though the potent look he directed Hank's way was of an entirely different sort.

"Hank, you've had your say about Lissa and me. I never agreed to follow your advice, did I? So either tell us why we shouldn't spend time together or leave us alone."

Instead of answering or leaving, Hank took a seat. He folded his arms and returned Josef's stare with an intensity that looked surprisingly similar. Lissa wished she could slip away from this looming confrontation. Part of her wanted to stay. She wanted to talk to Josef, to get to know him better. But not if it caused a rift between two friends.

"I should go," she suggested softly.

"No, you shouldn't," said Josef with such firmness she wasn't sure what to do.

"I don't want to be the source of tension." Then she looked at Mr. Tanner. "I don't understand why I've felt so unwelcome, Mr. Tanner. I've been like a member of your family ever since I can remember—until lately."

He didn't deny her words, didn't even look her way. He still glared at Josef.

But Josef wasn't looking at him; he looked at Lissa. "And I want you to stay. I want you to know everything about my injury." He glanced Mr.

Tanner's way a moment, then looked at her before speaking again. "I can't remember a thing before a few days ago."

In some corner of her mind she knew she shouldn't be shocked or even surprised. Hadn't she thought his memory seemed fuzzier than just the loss of how the accident happened? Yet his words still jolted her.

"My memory—it's gone."

Lissa gripped the arms of her chair. Fortunately it was solid compared to the sudden tremble in her fingers.

"All of it? You should have mentioned this earlier, Josef. Now I really must insist I fetch Dr. Sherman."

But Josef shook his head, somewhat gingerly. His gaze grew intense again, toward her, without the anger directed at Mr. Tanner, but still arresting.

"I don't need a doctor, but I want you to understand at least one reason why Hank's such a bear." His gaze gradually softened. "Apparently he thinks I should regain my faculties before I encourage anybody to want my company. I happen to disagree with him."

Lissa glanced at Mr. Tanner and back at Josef. "Do you remember anything—anything at all?"

"Hank's filled me in on some of it. And I had a dream—a memory, I guess, that came in my sleep. I was about eight. I was in a shipyard and they were taking my mother's body back to Germany to be buried." He looked at Mr. Tanner, who registered surprise. "At least if it was a dream, it fits with what Hank has told me since then."

"Memory loss can be temporary," Lissa said, trying to recall anything helpful from her training. Little had been taught on the subject. "Sometimes it only entails forgetting the accident and maybe what led up to it. But your whole life? I don't know."

Mr. Tanner stood, turned his back on them at the railing, and leaned on it to look at the Saddlebrook lawns.

"I don't think doctors know much about how that part of the brain works, Josef, but if anyone knows where to get help, it will be Dr. Sherman."

"No, Larisa," whispered Josef. "This is something I'll work out on my own."

"Why not see a doctor?"

Josef shrugged. "I don't want to be examined like I'm some kind of oddity. If it's all right with Hank, I'll stay here a few more days. Maybe by then I'll have everything sorted out. I think what I need most is a quiet place."

Lissa put two fingers to the bridge of her nose and closed her eyes as she shook her head. "I don't understand this at all."

She felt a hand on her wrist and looked up. "I didn't tell you this to upset you or make you feel you have to do something. I just need a friend I can be honest with about this. And I want you to understand why Hank is being so rude. He's only trying to protect you."

"Protect me from what? From you? I do want you to be honest with me, but I also want to help you. Let me just check to find out if someone in one of the big hospitals in Washington knows about memory loss."

Mr. Tanner turned to them. "No."

From that single, firm word, Lissa saw that she had pushed that option as far as she could. How could they be so reckless? She might have tried another angle if she didn't hear the sound of a motorcar on the gravel lane.

Mr. Tanner turned to the sound. "Oh, that's it. I'm done in." Though he'd muttered, his words were all too clear. He walked to the top of the steps and waited as Frank McPhearson's tin lizzie pulled to a stop. Waving from the seat just behind him were Jaylene and Penny Tanner.

The motor was barely disengaged when Penny flew from the side door. "Oh, Daddy, I hoped you'd be back! Just wait until you see what Mama and I bought in New York."

She stopped to take a breath and noticed Lissa standing nearby. Penny looked like she was about to jump from her father to embrace Lissa when her eye caught Josef.

"Oh, we have company."

She paused only long enough to bestow the intended hug on Lissa, then faced Josef, who was slowly rising from his chair.

"I'm Penny Tanner," she said, with an outstretched hand. "How do you do?"

Josef appraised Penny nearly as intently as he'd looked at Lissa that first time. But his assessment of Penny had a different demeanor, without a trace of a smile.

"I'm Joe Warner."

Penny shot a wink Lissa's way. "Are you a new friend of Lissa's?" She untied the ribbon at her chin, taking off her hat to reveal her curly, copper-colored hair. "I leave for a week and your whole life changes?"

"Actually, I'm a friend of your father's," said Josef.

"Oh. From Washington, I suppose?" She looked at her father for a better introduction and instead watched her mother walk slowly up the stairs to stand beside her husband. "What is it, Mama? You look like you've seen a ghost."

Lissa looked at Mrs. Tanner. Without a doubt, she did look pale. Her normally glowing cheeks were white, and her blue eyes held none of the merriment usually at home on her face. She ignored Frank McPhearson, who was unloading their baggage at her feet on the porch.

"How do, Hank," said Mr. McPhearson.

Mr. Tanner seemed not to have heard. He stared at his wife.

"Josef. Josef . . . Warner?" Mrs. Tanner whispered.

Josef nodded. He didn't move.

"Hank?"

"You're home early, Jaylene," Hank said to his wife. He looked as flushed as Mrs. Tanner looked drawn, closing in behind her as if he was ready to catch her if she fell.

Mr. McPhearson, ignored by all, headed quietly back to his motor. "Thanks for the ride from the station, Mr. McPhearson," Penny called after him, glancing at her mother to see why she'd lapsed from proper behavior.

He lifted his clerk's cap briefly. "Pleasure, Miss Tanner. Saddlebrook was on my way, anyway."

Penny smiled, turning back to Lissa. "He has to deliver a telegram to the Kranbeers, down the road. Oh, lemonade." She looked greedily at the last unused glass and, after taking off her travel gloves and tossing them along with her hat into a vacant chair, poured a drink for herself. "How I've missed Ulu's lemonade. Mama, here; you should have some. You look positively peaked."

She offered the glass, but her mother shook her head. Lissa watched Penny with affection. No situation, not even odd parental behavior, could sway Penny's bubbly optimism. She might be two years younger than Lissa, but she was years beyond Lissa in her gregarious nature.

"Your mother and I are going inside," said Mr. Tanner, holding open the door.

With her glass already half empty, Penny shoved aside her hat and gloves and plopped into the seat. She watched her parents quietly retreat, then eyed Josef with suspicious curiosity. "What are you doing at Saddlebrook, so far from Washington, Mr. Warner?"

"Your father was kind enough to offer me a place to recuperate."

She lifted her glass, as if in a toast toward the door through which her mother and father had disappeared. "That's Daddy. I noticed the bandage, of course, but I was being polite by not mentioning it. What happened?"

"I fell into a river and hit my head on a rock."

"Well, there's a concise answer. What were you doing in the river?"

"I don't remember," he said, still studying her with interested reserve.

Penny laughed as if it were a joke, but when neither Josef nor Lissa joined in, her laughter faded. "Oh, you really don't remember, do you?"

Josef shook his head.

"How much have you forgotten?"

"Everything."

"Everything?"

Penny turned in alarm to Lissa. "What does Dr. Sherman say about that?"

Lissa raised an eyebrow. "That's what I'd like to know."

"What does that mean?"

Josef spoke up. "It means Larisa is put out that I don't want to see a doctor."

"Who have you seen?"

"I've seen Larisa."

"Liss?" If Lissa didn't completely agree, she might have been offended at the shock in her friend's tone. "Lissa's a great nurse. She inspired me to want to follow in her steps. But Lissa's no doctor."

"I've tried to tell him," Lissa said. "He won't listen."

Penny leveled her eyes on Josef. "Why not?"

"As I told Larisa, I don't like wasting a physician's time. I feel fine, other than a lingering headache, and it is easing. Memory problems usually fix themselves, and there's nothing a doctor can do anyway. I'm pretty sure I wasn't a doctor before I lost my memory, but I don't think there's a treatment for this sort of thing."

"What if the memory problem is being caused by a blood hemorrhage, which can be relieved?"

Larisa turned to Josef. "You see, she agrees that a hemorrhage is a possibility, even now."

"Do you honestly think my head would be clearing so well physically if I had a brain hemorrhage?"

"The point is, I don't know," Lissa said, warming up yet again to the argument. "But a radiograph—"

"Larisa, don't you think you've plowed this ground enough times? Let's wait a few more days. If my memory isn't restored, we'll talk about it again. All right?"

Lissa looked into his eyes to secure the promise. "All right, and you know I'll hold you to your word, Josef."

"I believe I'm a man of my word," he said. With a grin, he added, "Well, I suppose I can be anything I want for the time being, can't I?"

Penny laughed. "Here you sit without a single clue to your identity, and you can make light of it. I doubt I could do the same."

"But if this happened to you, your family would be there to fill in the gaps, wouldn't they, Penny?" Josef asked.

She nodded, then frowned. "How sad it must be for you. Maybe you have family somewhere?"

Josef rose to his feet, not quickly but smoothly. He stood at the banister much as Mr. Tanner had when he'd wanted to avoid talking to them earlier.

"Your father seems to know Josef well, Penny. He's helped a bit, and Josef has had at least one memory come back. I think that's a good sign that the rest will come, eventually."

"I wonder how my father knows you. Did he say you worked together in the city?"

"No," Josef said, looking over his shoulder. "I think you'd better ask him for the details."

Penny finished her lemonade. "I guess I will."

"I'll go in and say good-bye to them," Lissa said. "I have to find Ulu for a ride home."

Lissa felt Josef's gaze and cast him a warm smile. She would have liked to stay longer with Josef and Penny, but thought she shouldn't, given the odd behavior of Mr. and Mrs. Tanner. It was obviously best if she went home, before Mr. Tanner could ask her to leave again.

Lissa went inside and peered into the large parlor. It was empty. So she walked past the stairway toward the kitchen in search of Ulu. As she passed the nearly closed door of the library, she heard the voice of Jaylene.

"I can't believe you brought him *here*, Hank, under the same roof as our daughter!" Mrs. Tanner's unsteady voice was louder than Lissa had heard it in years.

"What else was I to do? Leave him there to drown?"

"But did you have to bring him out of Washington?"

"I had to, Jaylene. I couldn't leave him to a lynch mob. And that's what they'll do if they find him. It wasn't his fault. Otto had him so engineered, he was like a puppet. I had to bring him here. I don't see that I had any choice."

Lissa stepped back, her heart pounding. She didn't want to remain where she was, listening like the worst kind of snoop, but she didn't seem capable of moving.

"But here. If anyone finds out who he is—it could come down on us all, Hank. Are you willing to risk that?"

"Now that he's getting better, maybe I can take him somewhere. We drove all the way from Washington. I was afraid to take him on the train in case someone might spot him. I'll drive him into the mountains, I suppose. I'll find a place."

She heard Mrs. Tanner sigh. She sounded like she was crying. "No, I don't think that's fair, either. I don't know what should be done."

"I only know one thing, Jaylene. God wanted me to bring him here. He prayed this morning. Josef prayed with me. He didn't know what he believed before, but now, after being away from Washington, away from Otto, he prayed."

"Oh, Hank . . ."

Lissa was sure Mrs. Tanner was crying now. Stepping away at last, Lissa hoped the floor wouldn't creak. She was ashamed of having listened, but the words left her shaken. Was Josef some kind of criminal, then? Who else would have a lynch mob after him? What had Josef done?

Lissa left the house without looking for Ulu. She would certainly spot that something was wrong, and wouldn't stop hounding until she pried out whatever had upset Lissa. She returned to the porch.

"Where's Ulu?" Penny asked.

"I couldn't find her."

"I'll give you a ride, then."

Lissa shook her head. "No, you've just traveled all the way from New York. If it's okay, I'll borrow the motor Ulu uses and return it later. My father won't mind bringing it back around this evening."

"You'll come too, won't you?" Josef asked, stepping closer to her.

She felt Penny's curious gaze on them, but Lissa was too confused to be either embarrassed or exhilarated by Josef's attention.

"I'll see."

She felt his fingertips land gently on her forearm. "Forget Hank," he whispered.

She looked up at him, drawn once more to the blue eyes that seemed to hold so much. But in those eyes she could not see who, or what, he was. How could she let herself care for someone who didn't even know himself? Maybe Hank was right to discourage them from spending time together.

She tore her gaze from Josef and hurried to the motorcar, gripping the wheel all the way home.

"Coward," she called herself now that she was alone. "What a coward you are. No wonder you're alone, Larisa Rose Parker. And little wonder you'll be alone the rest of your life. Coward!"

CHAPTER *Seven*

Hank opened the library door, stepping across the hall into the kitchen, where he found Ulu.

"Will you bring Penny and Josef into the library, Ulu?"

She set aside the bowl of peas she'd been shucking and, with a look of concern, walked silently past Hank to do his bidding.

Hank returned to the library to Jaylene. Her gloves and hat were where she left them, on the table next to the long leather couch. She stood at the window with her back to the room. The mountains were in the other direction, so this view offered nothing but trees. Hank knew she wasn't really seeing anything. She looked so alone, her arms closed around herself. He wanted to touch her, to take her in his arms and hold her, but he wasn't sure she'd welcome him. It was too soon on the heels of seeing Josef.

"Are you sure you want to do this now?" he asked. "We could wait until Caleb is back. He'll be here in a couple of weeks."

She turned to him after what seemed too long a silence.

"Putting it off will only make it more difficult."

He agreed, but wanted to make sure that's what she thought, too.

In a moment they heard Penny, talking, as usual, this time about Saddlebrook and the horses.

"What's this all about, Daddy?" asked Penny as she took a seat on the couch. "If you're going to properly introduce Josef, well, that's pretty much done."

"No, Penny, you've not been introduced. Not really."

She laughed. "His name is Joe Warner, and he's from Washington. And at the moment he's without his memory. What more do we need to know? I don't think he can fill us in on much more, but maybe you can." She raised a hand to one side of her mouth as if to hide her words from Josef. "He told me about the memory lapse."

"That's part of what we're going to discuss."

"Good. So, you're going to fill in the blanks? Just how do you know Josef so well, Daddy?"

Hank let his gaze linger on Penny. He wondered if she'd look at him with that love and admiration after hearing what he had to say. She'd always had an easy way of displaying her affection for him. Josef had judged him, and he didn't trust him as a father. How much harder would it be for Penny, having witnessed—and believed—all these years that he was a godly, upstanding man?

He looked from Penny to Jaylene. The tip of her nose was still red, but she had recovered herself otherwise. He had her support, he knew that. He could only guess what pain his past sin had caused her. Now it was Penny's turn.

"What's the matter, Daddy? Having a memory lapse of your own?"

"No," he said slowly, going to the plush leather seat that matched the couch on which she sat. Josef lingered nearer the door. Jaylene came to stand behind Hank, and it was perhaps her movement that gave him the courage to start. He sat on the edge of the seat, leaned forward, and took Penny's hands in his.

Penny glanced from Hank to her mother and dropped her frivolous smile. "Mama, you've been crying."

Jaylene said nothing.

Hank squeezed her hands gently. "Penny, there's something I must tell you. It won't be easy to hear."

"Oh, Daddy—something hasn't happened to Caleb?"

He quickly shook his head and patted one of her hands. "No, no, nothing like that. It's about our family. Well, it's about something that happened a long time ago that affects our family. From before you were born. Before I ever knew your mother."

"Oh, Daddy, what could be so serious if it's ancient history like that?"

He squeezed her hands again.

"A long time ago, I met a woman who became special to me. When we first knew each other we were very much alike, but both of us changed over time. We went separate ways. Not long after this woman and I parted, I met your mother, and you know how your mother and I fell in love and got married and had you and Caleb."

"So what's the part I don't know, and why should it matter now?"

"When I knew this other woman, an important relationship was missing in both of our lives. Neither of us knew the Lord. We lived for ourselves and acted foolishly, without thinking about consequences."

"What were you, Daddy, partners in crime? Did you rob a bank or blow up a building?"

He tried to smile and shook his head, noticing Josef showed no reaction to the mention of explosives.

"Okay, so I guess you and this other woman were married?" She glanced at Josef with a ruffled brow.

He took a deep breath, knowing he couldn't stall any longer. "No, Penny, but we did have a child."

The sparkle in her eye gradually faded.

She turned her head to look at Josef. "That's where you come into this, isn't it?"

Josef did nothing, but the lack of denial from all fronts confirmed the truth. Slowly, she pulled her hands from her father's. She stood, turning her back on everyone and taking the place her mother had occupied by the window.

"None of this is easy, Penny," said Hank gently, "for any of us."

"But I'll bet it was plenty easy for you twenty-five years ago, or thirty, or however old he is." She pointed at Josef and glared at her father. "You've done nothing but tell me to control every aspect of my life, from the words I say to the thoughts I think. But you didn't, did you?"

Her mother stepped nearer. "Penny . . ."

"So are you defending him, Mama, when he just brought his sin here to our home?"

"Your father is my husband, and we came to terms with this long ago." Anger touched her words. "He doesn't need to defend himself to you."

"Don't overlook the miracle in all of this, Penny," Hank said. "God was able to turn a sinner like me into someone very different."

"Penny," said Jaylene firmly, "while you're casting stones at your father, or even at Josef, who carries no blame in it, just remember what Jesus said about who gets to cast the first one."

Penny stood stiff, raised her chin, and, with the first tear tumbling down one cheek, pushed past her parents and ran from the room.

Hank watched as Jaylene turned to Josef. He met her eyes steadily, calmly, and when she held out her hand, he took it.

"I want to welcome you into our home, Josef," she said softly. "Hank told me he had a son, he didn't keep anything from me, and I married him anyway. I think I knew someday we'd meet. I will tell you a secret, though. If I ever felt a minute of jealousy about your mother, a thousand times more I thanked her."

Josef's brows lifted. "Why?"

"If it wasn't for her, Hank might not have come to know the Lord. God used her, and your birth, too, for that matter. For that I'll always be grateful."

Josef raised his other hand to enclose hers. "To tell you the truth, Mrs. Tanner, I don't remember her at all—what kind of woman she was, what love I may have felt for her. Thank you for saying that about her."

Hank came up and clasped his wife's shoulders. He'd never loved his wife more than he did at that moment.

"Is Penny Tanner back?" Lissa's father asked from the porch.

Lissa rose from her seat in the parlor to stand at the screen. "Yes," she said, watching with him as a Tanner Buick tore down the lane, leaving a cloud of dust in its wake.

"Goin' kind of fast, isn't she?"

Lissa nodded, coming out to the porch. The motorcar suddenly stopped, well beyond the usual spot, and Lissa waited, expecting her sunny friend to alight with a friendly wave the way she always did.

But nothing happened.

"Penny?" Lissa called. "Penny, are you coming in?"

Lissa exchanged a curious glance with her father. "Better go see what's up," he said. Even as he spoke, Lissa was heading down the porch steps.

Penny's face was splotched, her eyes puffy.

"Penny, what's the matter?"

"Oh, Liss, he—he's my brother."

"Josef?"

"Josef!"

Lissa leaned toward the open side of the motorcar, gripping the metal rail that held up the canvas top.

"My father, my own father. He made some woman pregnant. They weren't even married."

Lissa turned back to see if her father might have heard. His face showed only questioning concern, so she guessed he was beyond range.

"Move over, Pen. We're going for a ride, and I'm not letting you drive."

Penny obeyed, and Lissa sent her father a reassuring wave, then slipped behind the wheel. She engaged the clutch and pulled around the circle in front of the porch, then headed back to the main road. She didn't know where to go but turned in the opposite direction from Saddlebrook.

"Okay, tell me what happened after I left."

Penny wiped away fresh tears and took a deep breath. "My father called us into the study and then—boom—he said Josef is his son. Just like that. And my mother—my mother stood there as if it was all perfectly natural, nothing odd about it."

"Well, she didn't look so calm when she first saw Josef. She knew about him. Josef is a bit older than you. It probably happened before your father even knew your mother."

"That's what they said. But it's ... well, it's just so ... so shameful!"

Penny erupted into crying, so that most of her words became incoherent. From all that tumbled out, Lissa picked up garbled sentences about Penny playing the piano in front of the church and people gawking and pointing at the sister of Hank's illegitimate son. The whole family was forever stained.

Lissa pulled the car to a stop. The road was deserted, nothing but tall trees in every direction. She gave her friend a hug.

"Go ahead and cry. It's good for the soul."

She did, deep sobs that wracked her body. Lissa wished she could offer a hanky, but she'd left the house with nothing.

Hank's son. Illegitimate. Yes, that would gather some notice in the community. No wonder Hank was so out of sorts, and Mrs. Tanner beside herself. It even helped explain the anger that seemed to lie below the surface in Josef toward Hank. Lissa's heart ached for them all.

"Oh, Penny, I'm sorry you're going through this. I'm sorry for all of you."

Penny, her tears beginning to subside, gave a hard little laugh. "I hope you aren't feeling sorry for my father. Or him."

"Especially for the two of them. Don't you see the pain this causes them?"

"Them! This is all my father's fault, and this Josef, what'd he come here for? Why couldn't he have stayed in whatever hole he's been living in?"

"You don't know anything about him, Penny. How can you say such a thing? Maybe he had no one but your father to take care of him when he was hurt."

"How can that be?" Her eyes suddenly widened. "You don't think my father's been in contact with him all these years? That he's been living some sort of double life and has a whole family in Washington? He goes there often enough."

"Don't be ridiculous. Your father is one of the most respected men in the county, a church leader, and a fine Christian man."

She looked away. "I guess we know better than to believe that now."

"But he's still your father and always will be. He needs you to see things through his eyes. You said he knew Josef's mother before he ever met your mother. There was nothing hidden from your mother. He obviously told her about this woman and Josef. He told her the truth."

Penny said nothing.

"This must be very hard for your mother."

A new set of tears beset Penny. "It must be awful for her. People will say horrid things."

"What other people say will be a blessing or sin on them. It's their business, and we won't worry about that right now. I want you to think about your parents, Penny. Forget the others. And don't forget to think about Josef. Think how lost he must feel, with no memory and nowhere to get help that he doesn't feel like an outsider."

"He's an interloper, and if he thinks my family is just going to accept him, well, he's in for a surprise."

"Why?"

Penny looked shocked. "Why should we just accept him? Take him in, just like that? Oh, that would be fine, having him inherit Saddlebrook when he's never put in a day's work on the place or watched it change or loved it and lived there."

Lissa raised a brow. "So this is really about money? You're afraid Josef will try to claim Saddlebrook?"

Penny nodded, then shook her head. "That sounds selfish, doesn't it? It's just—he scares me. Who knows what he wants? He's a complete stranger."

"Yes, he is," Lissa said, "even to himself. I know him a little, and I don't think he wants to steal anything from you, Pen. Who knows what he left behind when he was injured? He only talks about getting well enough to leave. Maybe you'll never hear from him again."

"I couldn't hope for more."

Lissa frowned again. "Don't you think your father will want some contact with his son, though?"

"You're not much help, Liss."

Lissa took one of Penny's hands. "I know this seems like it'll change your life, Penny. I suppose it will. But yours isn't the only one. I can't help but think you need to be strong for your family right now. Try not to judge your father. He's always needed a Savior, just like the rest of us."

Penny looked away. "That's what my mother said, sort of. She told me to remember what Jesus said about casting stones." She took a deep, steadying breath and looked back at Lissa. "But it's hard, you know. I'm angry that my father messed up what I thought was a near perfect family. Josef is a living, breathing threat to everything."

Lissa couldn't help but laugh. "No family is perfect, Penny. If you lived with mine, you'd see the same."

Penny shook her head. "Oh, I doubt that. I've been around your family enough to know. They're every bit what I thought my family was."

Lissa shook her head. "No, Pen. No family is really that image you had. We're all needing the grace of God, especially in our own families." Lissa turned back to the steering wheel. "I have an idea. Why don't we go into town for a treat, then I'll take you home?"

Penny didn't object, and Lissa put the motorcar into gear.

They had a Coca-Cola and talked about anything except their families, concentrating on their upcoming adventure in the Red Cross. That was sufficient diversion to put them both in better spirits. Penny looked forward to getting away more than ever now.

As Lissa drove Penny back to Saddlebrook, she couldn't keep her mind from leaping ahead. She didn't deny she was still excited about seeing Josef again, but the conversation she'd overheard between the Tanners replayed in her mind. Some of it made sense now, the hesitation on Mrs. Tanner's part for everyone to know of Josef. But there was more. Lissa was sure she'd heard Mr. Tanner say something about a lynch mob. People didn't lynch a young man just because he was illegitimate.

It wasn't her business, except that she was attracted to Josef, and he seemed to like her. She wondered if what she'd heard would mean any more to Josef than it did to her. One thing was certain: all of the mystery and the truth that had now come out only strengthened her feelings. She wanted to know the whole truth about him. She wanted to help him.

Maybe she was becoming a little less of a coward.

Lissa and Penny stopped on their way to retrieve Ulu's Buick. Penny might be reluctant to go home, but she was calmer than when she'd left and fully capable of driving. So Lissa drove behind her in the borrowed vehicle after letting her parents know where she was headed. Now Penny drove so slowly down the Saddlebrook lane that Lissa nearly killed the engine to avoid rolling into her. At last they parked on the side of the lane and walked the rest of the way.

Penny had no trace of tears, but her trademark smile was conspicuously missing. Lissa put an arm about her shoulders. "It'll be all right after a while, Pen," she said.

Penny shook her head. "Don't say anything more, Liss, or I'll start crying again."

Lissa dropped her arm and gave her an encouraging smile anyway, and Penny sent a meager one in return. They found Penny's parents in the parlor. Josef was nowhere in sight.

After a long, awkward moment of silence, Penny spoke. "I . . . want to apologize for my selfish behavior earlier." Her parents stood and seemed ready to come near for an embrace, but she took a small step back and raised a palm.

"No . . . I'm not ready for that yet. I haven't adjusted to everything. Talking to Lissa helped, and I'm sure what she says is true, that things will be all right after a while. I need some time. Daddy, I need you to tell me one thing: Are you still committed to Mama and to our family?"

Hank looked ashamed that his daughter felt she needed to ask. "Of course I am. Don't ever doubt that, Pen."

Penny looked from her father to her mother. "And, Mama, I want you to know I'm sorry if I added to your pain earlier. This must be hard enough without me adding to it."

Lissa backed away, already feeling like her presence was becoming an intrusion. She went to the kitchen to look for Ulu. If Lissa happened to see Josef, maybe she could give him a reassuring word before asking Ulu to take her home.

She found both of them in the kitchen. They seemed completely at ease, sitting at the table enjoying iced tea. It was a pleasant contrast to the turmoil in Penny and her parents.

When Josef caught sight of her, he rose to his feet.

"Hello! I wasn't sure when I'd get to see you again."

"I came back with Penny."

Josef frowned. "How is she?"

"Better, I think."

Ulu went to the cupboard for another glass and filled it with tea. "She'll be fine, that one," said Ulu. "I always thought when the Lord made her, He forgot to give her the frown. Well, maybe she had one today, but it doesn't come natural to her."

"She's an optimist, then?" Josef asked, pulling out the chair next to him for Lissa. Ulu and Lissa gave a collective emphatic nod. "That's interesting. One of the first thoughts I had about myself and the kind of person I must be, is that I'm that way. Perhaps Penny and I have more in common than she'd like to think."

"Josef," Lissa said, leaning forward in her seat while he took his nearby, "I know I must be a bore."

He laughed and shook his head, showing just a little wince at the pain. "Why would I think that?"

"Because I'm about to say something for the hundredth time. You are at a disadvantage about your past, if nothing else, unless you can get help for this memory problem." She'd placed her hand on the table and he put one of his over hers, a contact she welcomed.

"It does bother me, what I don't know, but I'm also a realist. I'm in perfect health now. A doctor would only send me home." He squeezed her hand and added, "I still think your chicken soup was all the medicine I really needed."

She couldn't help but smile, and glanced from him to Ulu, who looked smugly pleased. "You know, I have a lot of work to do in this kitchen, and I work best on my own. Why don't the two of you go across the hall to the library? I'll send Penny for you if she comes looking, Miss Lissa."

Josef was already standing, and Lissa came slowly to her feet. Her heartbeat quickened at the thought of being alone with Josef. Even with all of the questions she had, she couldn't deny the truth. She wanted to be at his side when Josef discovered the past he was missing.

"I like this room," Josef said as they stepped into the library. He looked around at the oak shelves, which rose to the ceiling on three of the four walls. "It reminds me of somewhere."

"The Tanner library is famous around Culpeper."

"What kind of books do you like?"

"All kinds. I especially like history. United States history in particular. My aunt belongs to a women's group called the Daughters of the American Revolution. She persuaded me to join last year. I do admire their goal to preserve the past, and I've helped her sift through documents about our ancestors, and how this country came about."

"Sounds very patriotic," he said. "I like that. I can imagine I must have been loyal. . . ." His voice drifted away, as if he wasn't sure why he'd said such a thing.

"Mr. Tanner hasn't been in this country all his life, but I can tell you he's every bit American. He's told Penny and me a thousand times that his citizenship means so much because he chose it. He wasn't just born into it like the rest of us." She went to a section of books at the corner, one that displayed a little flag floating from a small holder attached to the woodwork. "This whole shelf is full of books about our country. Most of them were written by Americans, but there are some written by others about our democracy, and why it works so well, why it's unique."

She searched for her favorites and handed him two volumes. "This one is by Thomas Jefferson, and this one is by a Belgian who was so impressed by our system he wrote an entire volume about democracy."

Josef accepted both, putting one under his arm while he flipped the pages of the other. "I have a lot of learning to do," he said, so softly she wasn't sure she was meant to have heard. Then he looked up. "You know, I think I went to college. Maybe that's what this room reminds me of, a big school library for study." He shook his head, as if the memory was so clouded he needed to clear it away. "But I don't know that for sure."

"Not yet, anyway," she said gently.

He smiled. "You're quite the mentor. First you gave me the Bible to read, and now this." That smiled faded as he added, "Are you sure you want to associate with me, Larisa, given the circumstances of my birth?"

"That wasn't your fault."

"Some people won't see it that way. Penny doesn't."

"Penny will adjust."

"Maybe, but I doubt she'll ever accept me with open arms." His gaze settled intently on her again so that she couldn't look away. "What about your family, Larisa? I assume they hold the same beliefs you do, about the Bible?"

She nodded.

"What would they say if they knew you are helping an illegitimate man?"

"Of course they would want me to help you," she said confidently. "Why shouldn't they?"

He took a small step closer, close enough to create an intimacy of space and block out the rest of the room.

"If they knew I wanted to kiss you, and that you wanted me to, maybe they would object."

A smile touched her trembling lips. "I'm of an age to consider their opinions and any objections, then make my own judgment, so long as I heed the Word of God first."

He leaned closer, making the distance between them even narrower. "Hank read a passage about honoring thy father and mother."

"I do, but maybe we need to discuss how to honor your father."

Her words were enough to shatter the moment. Lissa wasn't sure she was relieved or disappointed that Josef stopped his slow advance.

"I'm sorry. I don't know why I said that."

He looked at her closely. "Are you sure?"

"What do you mean?"

"Maybe you aren't so sure you want to have someone like me kissing you after all."

She shook her head. "That's not it. I'm just bothered that Mr. Tanner so strongly disapproves of us together."

"I still think he's trying to protect you. I suppose he's right. I don't know anything about myself. How can I expect you to know me?"

"Can't we find out together?"

"That's what I thought. Maybe he thinks it's best if I have a whole life to share with you, instead of a few days."

She frowned. "What if you don't ever remember? You may simply have to create a new life, with nothing more than what you know of yourself right now."

He took the books from under his arm and turned to a nearby table. "That may be what I choose to do, whether I remember or not." He looked back at her with something like excitement lighting his face. "As I see it, I have more freedom at this moment than anyone in the world. I can do anything, without a past holding me back. And if I do remember, who's to say I have to go back to whatever I was doing before? I suppose if I liked it enough, I'll want to, but don't I have the freedom now to choose just about anything?"

"Apart from being a history teacher, I suppose that's true."

"I imagine I can do anything with the right training. I'm young, I'm healthy. All I have to do is choose."

"What do you want to do?"

If he seemed about to answer he suddenly stopped and emitted a brief laugh. "I have no idea, except . . ." He turned to a discarded Culpeper newspaper on the desk. "When I was reading this earlier, I wondered if there might be a reason God put all of us—you, me, everybody alive right now—at this time, right here. There's a war going on, Larisa Rose. They say in the paper it's the war to end all wars. Practically a global one, the last conflict for civilization. There must be a reason God has us alive during this time, right? Aren't we supposed to do something to make a difference?"

"I've always thought so." Her words suddenly slowed. "That's why I've signed up with the Red Cross to go overseas as a nurse."

His dark brows rose, so stark in comparison to his blond hair. "You're going to be a nurse in the war?"

She nodded, averting her gaze from the sweet concern and touch of admiration on his face. "My family has fought in every war since this country was formed. We believe in freedom. Now there's only my father, who's too old to go, and my sister and I. My sister is getting married in a couple of months, so that leaves me. Should I stop the Parker tradition of supporting our country, just because I'm a woman?"

"I can understand that." He smiled before a frown took the place of whatever approval he had a moment ago. "It troubles me that you'll be going to a war zone, but if that's what you're led to do, you should do it. I think that's what God intends."

"That's what I keep telling my family."

"They don't want you to go?"

"They're not forbidding it, but I think they'd rather I stay."

"It must be hard to let somebody you love go to a war, or even get close to the fighting." Then he went back to the newspaper at the desk. "Maybe you can help me with something, Larisa. I've not been able to quite understand why we are fighting against Germany."

Lissa followed him to the desk. She paused before answering. "I've asked myself that, Josef. I read the newspapers but it's hard to believe everything. Sometimes I think the papers are as full of propaganda as some of the leaflets that used to float around. Of course, the government calls everything sedition now that doesn't support the Allies."

She went to the couch and sat down, folding her arms in front of her and leaning forward. "There's a man in town who's kept every Culpeper newspaper for years now. He stores them in crates in one of his sheds and loves it when someone looks through them. I borrowed some boxes and spent weeks reading old articles about what people thought of Europe before everything went crazy. There were alliances, agreements, treaties, and family ties between the rulers, but nobody trusted anybody. So they started building up their armies to feel secure. But more arms just meant less security, with everybody doing the same thing. Then the Austrian archduke went to Bosnia. Probably he shouldn't have, because there's always been trouble in the Balkans. But he did, and he and his wife were shot. Russia mobilized to protect Serbia against Austria because it was a Serbian who shot the archduke. Russia was protecting the Serbs against bigger, stronger Germany, Austria's ally. And Germany decided to declare war before she was attacked."

Lissa shook her head. "It's all so ugly now. The Allies control the seas, at least around the ports that let things go in and out of Germany. They've set up a blockade, and I think the German people must be starving by now, it's been so long since this awful war began. Everybody thought it would be a quick fight, but somehow it turned into a stalemate. I think the best that could happen would be for a negotiated peace that wouldn't give a real victory to either side."

"I'm German. Well, German descent anyway," Josef said slowly. He looked at her squarely. "Do you have sympathy for the Germans, because of this blockade, even though our country is at war with them?"

"Of course, for the German people. And there are many Germans farming around here, including Mr. Tanner." She sighed deeply. "I read a new book, written by an anonymous German, about why he thought this war began. He writes that Germans invoke the name of God every day. God's name is even on soldiers' belt buckles. But he admits that this war is the opposite of what God would want. God taught us through His Son that He wants love and sacrifice. We're to look forward to the kingdom in heaven, not build up a kingdom on earth. The Kaiser said his people should let their hearts beat for God but their fists on the enemy. They want a place in the sun, but I don't see love or sacrifice in that goal."

"A place in the sun?" he repeated, as if the phrase were familiar.

"Like the British Empire, with colonies all around the world. Evidently some believe that Germany's power gives them the right to be the greatest kingdom on earth. But it's all wrong, that line of thinking. I'll lend you the book, if you like."

"Yes, I'd like to see it," he said slowly. "So this war was begun by Germany?"

She shook her head. "Germany officially declared war on Russia first, but Russia actually invaded Germany first. Most people believe Germany pushed the Russians too far with their ultimatums. What I saw in the news accounts was that Germany invaded Belgium after promising to honor her neutrality. Sympathy for Germany was forgotten after that. Belgium is all anyone remembers."

"Sounds like quite a mess. What's it all for, then?"

Lissa had no answer. "I don't know, but I think it was inevitable for us to be on the Allied side, even if Germany hadn't violated treaties and laws when they marched through Belgium to get to France. We have so much in common with Britain. That may be why all the newspapers from the beginning, at least around here, tended to side with the Allies. But I'm not ready to lay all the blame on Germany, the way some want to do."

"It doesn't sound like you think either side is totally right or wrong."

"I've tried to understand both sides," she admitted. "Germany *was* wrong to invade Belgium, even if Germany did think she had to strike on the western front because she was about to be struck. Russia had already invaded Germany, and France was Russia's ally. Technically, I suppose, that put them at war automatically.

"In any case, I'm not sure this war is right for us. Our founding fathers never intended for this country to participate in foreign wars. The President says we're fighting for democracy, a war to end all wars, as you read. I want to believe him. But the fact is, Germans aren't any more evil than we are; certainly not the German people, anyway. We're all just human beings, capable of great good or great mistakes. I'm afraid if one side or the other gets too damaged, it could lead to a frightening future—not an end to war but a beginning. All I can do is support our troops. Mostly I want it to end."

"That doesn't sound like what soldiers want to hear when they go off to battle."

She frowned. "I think some are actually afraid this'll be the last war. They want to see one while they can. Maybe it's enough to send off sons and brothers and husbands with the ideal that fighting is more than a duty. It's right and moral and unavoidable if we want to live in a better world. I suppose that would justify it better. I want to believe that."

"Larisa Rose, you're supporting the troops without supporting the war, aren't you?"

"Yes, but I don't think that makes me less a patriot. This world is stained by sin—personal and national. It's as you said, Josef, God put us here right now, during this war. We can hate war and still love the warriors, just like we can hate sin and still love the sinner. If God put us here to make a difference, then as I see it the best way to do that is with the golden rule. Supporting the troops is the best way to do that, don't you think?"

CHAPTER *Eight*

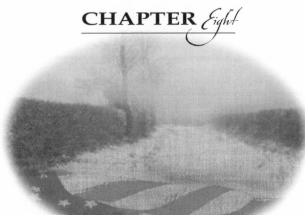

THOUGH THEY'D left the library door open, Mr. Tanner appeared none too pleased to find them seated on the couch, poring over one of the volumes Lissa had given to Josef.

"I'm ready to take you home, Lissa," he said, his mouth taut.

Lissa placed the book, which had partially rested on her lap, into Josef's hands. She stood, feeling like a schoolgirl who'd been caught in some infraction.

"Hank," Josef said, "why don't you let me go along? I'd like to do some driving. I'm pretty sure I haven't forgotten how."

"We'll see about that on our own." Hank did not look at Josef. He was still looking at Lissa, perhaps expecting her to follow more quickly. She hastened her step until Josef moved around her and stopped between her and his father.

"I know you've had a hard day, Hank, but I just don't understand you. Larisa gives me the Bible to read, a book you obviously believe in. Now she gives me a book off of your own shelf that upholds what you believe about democracy. Plus, she calmed Penny and brought her home. But you're still acting like Larisa is your enemy. It can't be that you don't like what she's trying to fill my empty head with. And I assume it can't be because you don't approve of her, since she seems to be all but a member of the family. If it isn't Larisa, it must be me. I'm your son, but you don't think I'm good enough for her. Why is that, Hank?"

Rather than answer, Hank turned away, characteristically stoic.

"I'm coming along," Josef said, more to Lissa than to Hank, who was already walking out of the room.

Lissa followed Mr. Tanner outside, but just as he was about to climb into his Buick he stopped. Lissa saw him look down the lane as she heard the crunch of gravel under the approach of another motorcar.

"Get in," Hank said quietly. Lissa moved to do so, but when Josef hesitated, she did, too.

A moment later Hank turned to Lissa.

"Lissa, take Josef to your house, will you?" His voice sounded strained, more strained than it had inside. "I'll follow in a bit."

"Who is it?" Josef asked Lissa.

Lissa had no idea, it wasn't a familiar Model T, and with the onset of twilight she couldn't make out the face behind the wheel.

"Go now," said Hank.

Lissa sat behind the Buick's wheel with Josef beside her. Pressing the electric start button with her foot, the engine chugged to life. She directed the vehicle around the circle in front of the porch, passing the man in the Model T with little more than a glance. He seemed to study them as she passed, but Lissa didn't slow under the scrutiny.

Josef looked behind as they drove off. "You've never seen that man before?"

"I couldn't get a good look at him, but no, I don't think so."

"I wonder if he has anything to do with me?"

"Wouldn't Mr. Tanner have asked you to stay, then?"

Josef shrugged. "I suppose. I can't figure out why Hank would've changed his mind so quickly about you and me being alone together. He sure shoved us off in a hurry."

Lissa stole a curious glance back. "Yes, he did."

"Why wouldn't he want me to see somebody from my past?"

The words *lynch mob* came to mind, but Lissa didn't speak. How could she say anything when she didn't know what was going on?

"Maybe it was someone from his business in Washington."

Josef settled into his seat. "Well, whatever the reason, we're left alone again. Maybe his objections don't run as deep as we thought."

Lissa glanced back once more even though the Tanner house was out of sight. Mr. Tanner's objections couldn't have changed that quickly. Perhaps concern about the visitor ran deeper than his objection to them.

––––––––––

Hank watched his Buick disappear down the lane as the man in a black suit emerged from the Model T. Only when the other motor was well away did Hank turn to the man, giving him his full attention.

"Help you?" he asked.

"My name is Agent Greg Donahue," said the man, stretching out his hand in greeting. Hank accepted the handshake. "I'm from the Bureau of Investigation."

"What can I do for you, Mr. Donahue?"

"I have a subpoena here for you to testify at the trial of Otto von Woerner. Recognize the name?"

Hank nodded. He'd wondered if they would drag him into it.

"Did you know he was arrested last week?"

"Read about it in the paper."

"Mind if I ask who that was just driving off?"

"My son and a neighbor girl," he said. "Well, sir, you've done your job as I see it. Any reason for you to linger?"

"None whatever, except to say your country's depending on you to help us keep this man locked up for a long time. He might have paid your bill, or maybe he didn't if he was arrested before he got to it, but your duty is to your country now, not to a former client."

"I don't need a lesson on my duty from somebody young enough to be my son," said Hank, maintaining his calm but directing a hard look toward the young man.

"I'm glad to hear that," said Agent Donahue, unruffled. "I thought maybe you forgot, considering who your client was. He's in jail for good reason, Mr. Tanner, and maybe, just maybe, if you'd remembered your duty earlier, we could have nabbed him sooner."

"Agent Donahue," said Hank, continuing to challenge the man with his eyes, "if you have a case against me, I suggest you bring it to the courts. But I've been involved in enough cases to know you won't get anywhere. All I did was locate the son of a client. Now if it's still true you've no reason to linger, I suggest you go."

The man tipped his hat, then turned back to his Model T. He took a long look around, drawing out his moment of departure. He couldn't see that the back of Hank's neck was prickling with perspiration or hear his pounding heart. He stood immobile until the man was out of sight.

"We should go on to my house," Lissa reminded Josef. They'd stopped at one of her favorite spots on Tanner property, the lake that fed the small brook along her family's property. It was, she thought, one of the most beautiful spots in the whole county. Gently rolling green hills, copse after copse of light barked birches, colorful wildflowers, and a sparkling lake right in the center. Who could deny the existence of a Creator after seeing this place?

That's why she'd pulled down the little offshoot before reaching the main road. Sharing a pink and purple sunset reflected on the water had been too beautiful to pass up. But now it was dark.

They sat on the edge of the pier, their legs dangling over the side but not reaching the water. So far, the summer had been dry, and the water level was low.

Josef tossed the long blade of straw he'd been chewing into the water, then leaned back on his hands, showing no interest in getting up. "I think I could stay here for a good long time."

She slapped a mosquito. "At least until the bugs start swarming."

He smiled and touched her arm where a welt was forming, as if his light touch would heal the bite. "All right, we'll go. But I want you to know I'd rather stay here with you. I like having your company all to myself."

Her heart twirled.

He leaned forward, sitting Indian-style in front of her, once again so focused on her that all she could do was stare back.

"I like the way you think, Larisa Rose. I like the way you make me think. I have questions about who I am, what I believe, and what I should do next.

But I can see that you have all that figured out for yourself. I admire that. I may not remember many people, but I doubt many people I have known are like you. Half the population probably doesn't think through what they really believe, or the reasons why they believe it." He smiled. "Do you know, Larisa Rose, I have decided that I want to be just like you?"

She laughed at his ridiculous statement. "I'm not sure that's ever been said by a man to a woman." Though her words had started out at a normal tone, they ended in a whisper, for he was descending upon her, and she had no inclination to move away.

His lips were warm and firm, gentle yet unwavering. He raised his hands to cup her face and she raised her hands to touch his, not to pull him away but rather as a tender affirmation. His kiss drew out, and she leaned into him, even as he did to her, as if that kiss alone could bind them into one.

When he lifted his mouth, he left his hands where they were and rested his forehead on hers.

"I've been wanting to do that since the first moment I woke up, when you were holding my hand."

She laughed. "I was taking your pulse."

He shook his head. "No, that was just your ruse to make it seem appropriate, since Hank was in the room." She didn't have to look up at the darkening sky to see the stars sparkling in his eyes.

Then in one smooth movement he was on his feet, pulling her along. He took her in his arms, holding her around the waist. "There's just one thing that I ask, Nurse Larisa Rose."

"And what's that?"

"When all the soldiers in France fall in love with you—and they will— be kind and compassionate without feeling too sorry for any of them. I'm the only patient I want you to get emotionally involved with. Selfish, I know, but there it is. Evidently I'm a possessive kind of fellow."

She pushed back his hair, which had blown across his bandaged forehead. Then, studying him a moment before speaking, she took in his face. In the dark his eyes were not quite so blue, but she was coming to think that, whatever he looked like, he was a perfect creation. He was gifted by God with a countenance with which no one could fault.

"I'm sure I'll be far too busy to get to know any one patient."

"That's good," he whispered, then kissed her again.

This time she gently pulled away. She wasn't at all sure she should be letting him kiss her like this so soon after they'd met.

"It's a good thing God made you the way you are," Josef whispered.

"And what does that mean?"

"I am a base man with all kinds of natural instincts, any number of which I'd like to give in to right now. But because I know you—actually better than I know myself—I know enough to control those instincts." He held her close, her head against his chest. "Hank may know something about me that I'm not worthy of your love. I don't know what kind of man I was, Larisa. I know what kind of man I want to be, a man of faith and honor and self-control that you can respect. I can't see God giving you anything less."

She looked up at him, feeling unworthy and yet believing he found her somehow deserving of such a man.

He pulled away, taking her hand as they headed up the pier. "God is a God of balance; do you know that, Larisa? Where God makes a man weak, he makes a woman strong, so she can help him aspire to something better. I guess there'd be chaos if men didn't have women to consider. We'd be a bunch of animals, fighting and killing each other."

"Like France is today, you mean?"

He paused, losing his smile. "Yes, I guess that's true."

They went to Mr. Tanner's Buick, and Josef slid behind the wheel. He shot her a smile. "If I didn't like motorcars before, I sure like them now. Trust me to drive?"

She took the passenger seat, and he drove off. He went a little faster than Lissa normally did, but not so fast that she felt unsafe. He hugged the road as if he'd been driving for years which, judging from his obvious ability, he had.

They came to Roland's hill, which was famous for its steep incline. Another way to her family's home was more direct, but Lissa was in no hurry. "I can never take this road when I'm driving my father's flivver," she said. "Too steep."

"For a Model T?"

She nodded.

"Try it in reverse," he suggested. "The fuel line is probably going dry—it won't do that if you turn it around."

"Oh?"

Glancing at her, he added, "And don't ask me how I know."

"But you are remembering, Josef. That's good. Perhaps more will come every day."

He shrugged. "I'm finding that I care less all the time." He reached over and squeezed her hand. "I don't know if that's good or bad."

They came to Lissa's home and both got out of the motorcar—and that was when she noticed another Tanner Buick. Lissa and Josef exchanged glances, guessing Mr. Tanner must be inside. Certainly he'd had enough time to beat them there if his visitor hadn't stayed very long. He'd come to retrieve Josef, still under the mistaken impression that he shouldn't be driving.

"I was wondering how I should introduce you," she whispered as they approached the porch. The front door was open, letting the cool evening air in through the screen—along with any spoken word they might utter loudly enough. "Now I guess I can let Mr. Tanner do that."

"He can always introduce me as your beau," Josef teased quietly in her ear.

"Oh, wouldn't he love that? And my parents? This is happening too fast for me. I can only imagine what they would think."

He pulled her into his arms. "I don't mean for this to go too fast."

She stroked his face from the temple to his hard jaw line. "I didn't mean either one of us is pushing things. It feels more like being swept away by something neither of us can control."

He smiled, and for a moment he looked as if he had all the answers, shaking his head so patiently. "We're in control. We left the lakeside, didn't we?"

She nodded.

"Then I suggest we just enjoy this feeling growing between us. God is a God of love; didn't He give us this capacity?"

"Josef, I think the faith that began in you as a child was never abandoned."

"Yes, I think you're right about that." Then he frowned. "As much as I want to declare myself your beau—right here and now—I think for your sake we should wait."

She cocked her head to one side. For her parents' sake, she could understand. But for hers?

He touched her cheek with a gentle caress. "I want you to be sure about me, Larisa Rose. Right now I'm a clean slate, eager to write on it everything you believe in. But I need to mesh all of what I want to be with what I was. Does that make sense?"

She nodded. "Yes. I know you must remember, Josef. I want you to. I want to know all of you."

"I hope you will. I hope I will." Then he tightened his hold even as he frowned. "There is another reason to wait, Larisa. I'm not sure any parents would welcome me into the fold right now. Not only is my past a mystery, the circumstances of my birth are, shall we say, less than honorable."

"The circumstances of your birth have nothing to do with you, Josef. If my parents are going to judge anyone, let them judge your parents. Even then, it's not their place to do so. Once my parents know you, everything will be easier."

"After they know me. After you know me. After I know me."

She welcomed his light tone of voice, that he could still find something to jest about despite the massive gap in his memory. They pulled away from each other, but he slipped his hand around one of hers as they walked up the steps. Only when they stepped inside the front door did his contact break.

Lissa found her parents in the parlor with Mr. and Mrs. Tanner. Her parents sat on the two big chairs her father had made so long ago, and the Tanners sat, holding hands, in the middle of the couch.

"Well, here they are," said her father, who looked unaccountably relieved to see them. Goodness, they couldn't have been gone more than an hour at most.

Everyone was standing then, and Lissa noticed her mother's face was tense and drawn. She came to stand beside Lissa, a look of reprimand just emerging from the uneasiness.

"Mr. Tanner was worried about both of you," she said. "What took so long?"

"We stopped by the lake to watch the sunset." Lissa tried to sound as if it were what anyone would have chosen to do, given the opportunity. "What's to worry about, Mama?"

Mr. Tanner spoke. "I told them about Josef's injury, Lissa."

"Well, I suppose you might worry about Josef, then," she conceded, "but let me introduce you to him. Mama, Father, this is Josef Warner. Josef, these are my parents, Frank and Addie Parker."

Josef extended a hand first to her mother, then to her father. Although he was greeted cordially enough, Lissa sensed an underlying wariness.

"Pleased to meet you," said Josef. "I'm grateful you have a daughter trained in medicine. I'm sure if it wasn't for her I'd still be in the sick bed."

Lissa laughed, wishing the sound would wash away the mood of both sets of parents. "But I didn't do anything."

"The chicken soup, remember? The best home remedy there is."

She saw her parents exchange a glance. "It's my mother's family recipe, actually, so I can't take all the credit."

Josef smiled Addie Parker's way. "Then I'll thank you, too."

"I'm sure my father believes all thanks should go to him," Lissa added. "He's always complaining that when we make anything special, we deliver it to someone else's house."

"Okay," said Josef, "thanks all around."

Lissa laughed again, and even to herself she sounded nervous. Why were her parents just standing there, not saying a word?

"It's time we were home, Josef," said Mr. Tanner.

Josef leaned closer to Lissa and said loud enough for all to hear, "Looks like we're being dismissed." Then, in a whisper, he added, "Am I the only one who feels like a school kid?"

Lissa nodded in commiseration. "I'll see you tomorrow, I hope." Then he left with the Tanners.

Lissa's father closed the door once the others drove off in the B55, leaving Ulu's car once again behind.

"Lissa, come into the parlor, will you?" asked her mother. Lissa had only heard that tone of voice on occasions she didn't live up to her mother's expectations. Her father followed. No one took a seat. Her mother stood in the center of the room, arms crossed, a slight frown touching her forehead. She watched Lissa approach.

"Your father and I don't want you to see that boy again."

Lissa let out a breath, something between a sad laugh and a quick sigh. "Mama, I don't . . ."

"Let's sit down a minute, shall we?" said her father, and he put a gentle hand to her elbow and directed her to the couch. Lissa's mother followed. "Mr. Tanner told us that Josef is his son."

Lissa stopped herself from springing to her feet, pressing her palms into the cushions beneath her. "You don't want me to see him because he's illegitimate?" Her voice trembled, there was no helping it.

"No, that's not it. I just want you to know that we were told."

Her face still serious, Lissa's mother leaned forward, elbow resting on the arms of the chair. "You know nothing about this young man, Lissa. His own father doesn't seem to know much, apart from the boy's childhood. And this man, this Josef, remembers nothing. How can we let you spend time with someone who has no recollection of what sort of person he is? He could be some kind of criminal for all we know."

Mr. Tanner shook his head, patting Lissa's hand as she stared at her mother.

"This boy has a lot to sort out, Liss. He needs to do that before he can offer anything to anyone else."

"Frank, it isn't just that. What if his memories come back at once, and he has some kind of—oh, I don't know—a seizure, a fit. Who knows how he'll react, depending on what he remembers? Maybe there's a reason he's forgotten everything. Some kind of shocking past that's too painful to recall." She shook her head as if the possibility was too awful to consider. "We don't want you anywhere near him, Lissa. Not alone, at any rate."

Lissa closed her eyes for the briefest moment, taking a deep breath. *Lord, guide my words.*

"I appreciate that you're both concerned." She looked at her mother then her father, and believed her own words. "I know that you always want to protect me. But, for heaven's sake, I'm twenty-three years old. How can you continue to filter who I spend time with?"

"We're not doing any such thing!" her mother insisted. "We'd be less than parents if we didn't speak our mind. And you cannot discount our opinions, Lissa. It's obvious you're interested in this boy. Perhaps you're not looking at it quite as logically as we are. I guess all I'm saying is that we don't want you to be alone with him until he has his memory back, and we can know a little something about him. We really cannot allow—"

Lissa leaned forward, grabbing both of her mother's hands in hers.

"In just a couple of months I'm going to be overseas, making every single decision on my own. I feel fully equipped to do this, thanks to you and Father giving me such a wonderful start in life. You'll have to let go then, Mama. Why don't you start now, by trusting my judgment about Josef?"

Her father stood, and if her mother had an argument, she kept it to herself while she looked up at her husband. "She's right," Frank said.

Lissa's insides did a little leap of independence at the words. Her mother obviously had other ideas. "You can't possibly mean . . ."

"Yes, Addie, I do." His gaze went from his wife to his daughter. "We left out one very important ingredient in our fear—trust. We need to trust our daughter. We don't know a thing about this young man, but she does, even if it is limited. Don't you think she'd steer clear of the boy if she thought he wasn't a worthwhile sort?"

"Not if she's so smitten by his good looks that she won't see other signals."

Lissa had her father's backing. That was all she needed.

"Well, thank you for that confirmation, Mama. I think he's pretty good looking, too. But honestly, do you think I'm so shallow I can't see beyond that? He can't remember much, but he does remember his faith. I doubt he could do anything to hurt someone, if that's what worries you."

Lissa and her mother stood at the same time, and Lissa watched her father put an arm around her mother's thin shoulders. "We're trusting your judgment, Lissa. And we don't need to say anything to anyone else about all the rest, either, about who his father is or that he can't remember things. You go on, now. Let me work this out with your mother, then."

Lissa hugged both her parents. Her mother still wore a sour expression, but she hugged her back tightly.

"It's just because I love you, you know," her mother whispered, voice trembling.

Instant tears sprang to Lissa's eyes. When was the last time her mother had said that?

"I love you, too, Mama."

CHAPTER *Nine*

ON HER last day of visiting patients around the countryside with Dr. Sherman, Lissa got out of his Model T with a wave and a smile when he dropped her off at her home. He wished her well, telling her he had a job waiting for her when she decided to return to the medical field on the home front.

His words reminded her that time was suddenly passing. In three weeks, after Cassie's wedding, she would begin her training in New York. After that she would ship off for France.

Three weeks.

Nothing had changed her commitment to the Red Cross cause, but in the month since Josef had so unexpectedly entered her life, she found herself less eager to leave.

They had spent at least a portion of every day together since they'd met, once Mr. Tanner finally believed Josef was up to activity. He seemed to have resigned himself to the inevitability of them spending time together. They walked or rode on Saddlebrook land, picnicked near the lake, and sometimes brought Mrs. Tanner's Victrola out to the porch and listened to the music. On Saturday afternoons they took excursions into town to visit the ice cream parlor or attend social events, everything from a spelling bee to listening to a military band concert in the park. They watched as preparations were made for the annual Culpeper horse fair, coming up in July, and one evening they dressed up and dined at the Waverly, then saw a show at the theater.

On rainy afternoons they sat on the porch at Saddlebrook, sharing pages of the Exponent, the local newspaper, or books from the Tanner library. Their tastes in reading were so similar Josef joked more than once that God must have mixed some of their souls together before releasing them to life.

Lissa watched as Josef made one discovery after another, amazing both of them with his math skills when she shared her chore at bookkeeping. His athletic grace surfaced as they rode horses or played tennis or catch on the baseball diamond. His memory of recent things surprised her. If he read something he could recall its content later, nearly word for word.

As for other talents, he could fix any machine on the Tanner or Parker farm, from an old rusty bicycle to the engine on her father's truck, the one he used to haul grain to town. Lissa's father was so impressed by Josef, she was convinced that he was ready to make Josef part of the family, whether or not Lissa had anything to do with it.

Even her mother had come around. She liked seeing evidence of Josef's manners and the way he talked seriously about what he'd been reading. It was impossible not to love him.

Yes, Lissa could say to herself, she did love Josef, even though those words had not been exchanged aloud between them.

She would go to the Tanner farm this very evening for dinner. It was her turn to go there, since Josef had come to her house the night before. Her anticipation to see Josef was as great as ever. Perhaps tonight they could celebrate the new phase in her life, ending one job while awaiting the start of the next.

The mood at the Tanner house was celebratory. Lissa could tell the moment she drove up and spotted Josef coming out to greet her. Light, laughter, and loud voices burst from open doors and windows.

"My long lost little brother has come home at last," Josef announced, leading her to a corner of the wide front porch. "It was nearly a month since the school year ended, but his trip to New York with a fraternity brother was too important to cut short."

They looked over the garden where Mrs. Tanner grew the best lilies in the county. As eager as Lissa was to welcome Caleb home, she couldn't help but want to linger outside with Josef. "What did he think of you, Josef? Was his reaction anything like Penny's?"

"He was the first one to take me as good news. He said he'd prayed for a brother when he was little but never knew God had answered him before he said his first prayer." Josef turned from the fragrant garden and folded his arms as he leaned on the porch banister. "He seems like a good kid."

"Why the frown, then?"

He glanced at her. "Was I frowning?"

She nodded.

"He came home with tales of boys being drafted from his university. They're older than Caleb, of course, but I couldn't help thinking he's not much younger than all those twenty-one-year-olds going off to shoot people." He sighed then and ran a hand over his forehead, where a scar remained from his accident. "And then it made me think of you going over there."

"Nobody's going to be shooting at me."

"Oh, you're sure about that, are you? The guys with the guns aren't going to get confused and hit a hospital by mistake?"

"I'll be far behind the lines."

He nodded, but didn't say anything. He turned back to the garden.

"If I don't go," she added, "who will? Why shouldn't I go?"

He faced her again, putting his hands on her shoulders. "I could think of a few reasons, starting with me," he said softly. "But I won't because I *know* why you're going."

She wondered at the inflection, but didn't have the chance to ask. Penny called from the doorway.

"Okay, you love birds. Time for dinner."

As Lissa and Josef entered the house, Penny looped her arm through Lissa's, stealing her from Josef's side. In the weeks since she had started sharing her family's roof with Josef, Penny had developed what looked like a cautious tolerance of him. And her smile was nearly back, even at church where her fear of being judged harshly hadn't materialized. "Only three weeks from today, Liss, we're off to New York, and then France. I told Caleb I want him to be a regular flag-waving cheering squad. He said we'd have to wait 'til we get to New York for that, if we get one at all, being 'just girls,' after all."

"That's right," called Caleb from the dining room, already seated at the table. He stood when Lissa and Penny entered. "Don't forget who you're going over to support, Sis—the soldiers. They're the stars of that show."

"Now there's a thought," Penny said. "Perhaps if we stop sending soldiers the war will end. Can't have a show without the stars, after all."

"But you can't stop the show until the last act comes out the way we want it," Caleb shot back. "Isn't that right, Josef?"

"I'm probably not the right one to ask about this war," Josef said, "but it seems to me any war would be better off short."

"Yeah, sure. It would be nice to go over and get a taste of what it's like, though. You know, if this really is the last war, like they say. What do you think, Josef? Wouldn't it be nice to be cheered by a crowd of pretty French girls?"

"I like the cheering French girl part," Josef said with a wink, "but maybe not the rest of it. Don't know much about war, but I doubt it's as glorious as the draft board calls it."

Lissa couldn't agree more, from what she'd read in the newspapers. Nonetheless it was good to see Caleb's interest in Josef. Conversation filled the room, most of it generated by Caleb telling Josef about his university experiences and New York. From Caleb flowed a deluge of questions. Josef's lack of answers didn't appear to dissuade him.

Dinner eventually passed, and as Ulu cleared away the dishes, Penny, Caleb, Josef, and Lissa went out to the porch. It was great company though Lissa wished she and Josef could find some time alone. She knew the next few weeks would fly by, between Cassie's wedding plans and the preparations Lissa needed to make before leaving for overseas. She wasn't willing to share all of the remaining time with Josef's family.

Josef obviously had the same idea. After a while, he stood, holding out his hand to Lissa.

"We're going for a ride," he announced when there was a lull in the conversation.

"Where to?" Caleb asked.

Penny put a hand on his arm when he looked about to rise. "It doesn't matter, little brother. We're not invited."

He appeared momentarily confused, but when he looked between Lissa and Josef, obviously noticing for the first time that they were holding hands, he settled back in his seat. "Oh. Okay, I get it. Hey, Liss, Penny always did want you for a sister. Now I guess the pressure's off of me to bring you into the family."

Lissa laughed. "Yes, Caleb, you can rest easy now. You don't have to marry me, cooties and all."

He hooted. "I found out girls don't have cooties when I went to college. At least not some girls."

Josef put an arm around Lissa's shoulders. "I'm pretty sure this one doesn't."

Lissa pushed him playfully away, but let him reclaim her hand and lead her toward one of the Tanner Buicks.

"Let's go to the lake," he suggested.

She noticed a small vial on the driver's seat, which Josef picked up before sitting behind the wheel. He handed it to her. "Ulu's insect repellent," he said.

"I see you planned ahead."

He nodded, looking unabashed and pleased with himself.

They drove down the smooth Tanner lane, cutting off to a trail not much better defined than a deer's pathway to water. It was bumpier along the rutted offshoot, not unlike a typical county road. The sun was almost completely gone, leaving a rosy glow on the western horizon. Still, in the dim light, Lissa could make out the wildflowers edging the birch and pinewood, spreading a welcome mat before them. The scent of wild pink roses and white azaleas met them as they stepped out of the vehicle. Hyacinths looked like a rolling blanket around the edge of the lake.

When they were sitting side by side on the dock, Josef uncapped the small glass bottle. Reaching for Lissa's arm, he sprinkled a few drops of the rosemary and wormwood oil mixture on her skin, then gently smoothed it on like a caress, first up, then down, still holding her hand in one of his. He didn't speak as he touched her. He studied her arm, as if the motion took every bit of his concentration.

Then he turned his attention to her other forearm.

"Larisa," he whispered, setting aside the oil and at last looking at her face. His eyes focused upon her, as always with rapt attention. It was as if, by his scrutiny, he might read each thought and emotion, each memory or hope. He enveloped her, absorbed her into him, and their spirits connected. It brought them closer than any physical intimacy, which they had agreed to limit. This was unity on a level Lissa had never felt before, an openness and the willing vulnerability of complete trust.

"There's something on your mind," she whispered. She knew there was. Otherwise he would be kissing her right now.

He gave her a quick smile and then took both her hands in his and nodded. "It's been on my mind a few days. I wanted to be sure before I brought it up, sure of what I'm supposed to do."

By his serious tone, Lissa knew that whatever he had to tell her had nothing to do with them. Except that perhaps everything they thought or did now had something to do with each other. But this was something having to do with Josef alone.

A tingle of apprehension began at the base of her spine.

"I asked Hank if he knew my draft number."

Lissa's throat tightened, her breathing stopped.

"He doesn't." Momentarily the grip on her hands increased. Then he let her go, leaning back and looking at the lake. "He's keeping something from me. I know it. If I could just remember." He let his tone drift off, but the force behind the words was clear. He looked at her. "From what he's told me of the man who raised me, I'm not sure I was encouraged to register. The man who is my legal father is in jail for helping somebody who was working for the Germans. Why would he let his son register to be drafted into an army that was going to fight against everything he must believe in?"

He sighed heavily, his gaze returning to the water. "What kind of man was I, Larisa Rose? A coward? Did I let that man do my thinking for me?"

Lissa reached for one of his hands again, holding it in her own, feeling his strength, his resilient energy. "I am no expert on memory loss, Josef, but I do know we're born with our basic temperament. The fact that you've forgotten a large part of your life doesn't mean you've become someone else. I've come to know a lot about who you are. You work hard. You help anyone who needs it. You even play hard on the ball diamond or the tennis court. And when you're done with the day's physical challenges, you exercise your mind and fill it with things you find worthwhile, like the Bible, history, and news. So I know you're not only intelligent but hard working and anything but lazy.

"And I know you're loyal," she went on, because she considered herself the best student of who Josef Warner was, perhaps a better one than Josef himself. "I saw that on the Sunday morning when we were standing outside the church. Those two petty gossips said what they did about Hank, and you turned the corner and put on your most charming smile. You thanked them for sharing their prayer concerns, telling them you were grateful they understood how hard it must be for Hank to withstand the stares. Hank's mistake caused the gossip. It's a consequence of his sin that you, unfortunately, have to pay, too. Yet you defended him with kindness, the way the Bible tells us. Your loyalty is fierce, I think, once it's stirred."

She smiled, wondering suddenly if she was saying too much.

He didn't say anything, just stroked the top of her hands with his thumb.

"I think of what's happened to you, how you woke after your accident not knowing anyone, not even yourself. It took courage to come here with Hank. I can't imagine how much courage it must take to face a world of strangers without a single memory, and yet somehow find a way to smile and trust people. I never realized I took comfort in my own history, the good and the bad. It gives me a familiar place from which to look at anything new or uncomfortable.

"And, one more thing about you, Josef: Even if it was a long time ago that your faith was born and it wasn't nurtured through the years, and even if your life wasn't firmly in the palm of the Lord before you came here, I know it is now."

He nodded slowly. "I can't take any credit for the faith God gave me, but I'm glad He gave it. I don't think I could make sense of anything without it." He leaned toward Lissa. "You know why He's placed you here, Larisa. You have the skills of a nurse, combined with the courage and patriotism this country needs right now. He's shaped you to be who He wants you to be, to serve Him and the country in which He's placed you."

She didn't reply. Yes, she believed that, but right now her apprehension was growing again about what Josef intended to do. "Now, tell me what's really on your mind. You're not just thinking about who you might have been."

He took a deep breath. "I'm twenty-six years old. The draft age goes up to thirty, at least for those of us who are unmarried and fit. I'm even a good shot, judging by my pheasant hunt with Hank the other day. I can't ignore the call."

"Call?"

"Nothing heavenly. I'm talking about Uncle Sam's call. But I can't separate God from what I feel, either. I'm alive now, Larisa. He put me here in a time of war. I'm of the age to go, mature enough to help all those twenty-one-year-olds who are raring to get behind a big gun. The ones Caleb talked about at dinner. I'm without obligation or responsibility, but old enough to bring some sense of responsibility. You said it yourself: How can I *not* go?"

Lissa pulled away her hand, feeling a shudder and unwilling for him to feel it, too. Yes, he had no obligation to her, she had to agree. The emotions tying them together weren't an obligation or even the promise of one. It was still just a hope. She entwined her fingers firmly with each other. Something inside whispered her own duty. Every generation of her family had sent off someone they loved to war. Could she be different? Could she fail her family heritage?

Oh, God, how easy it would be to beg him not to enlist. Oh, God, I want You to keep him here. Keep him safe. Keep him with me.

For the first time she realized how hard it was for her parents to support her decision to go.

But she didn't speak any of those thoughts. Her brow furrowed as she swallowed back that recurring knot in her throat. No, she wouldn't totally abandon her heritage, yet she couldn't let him go so easily, either.

She chose her words carefully, pushing back the uncertainty. "Volunteering to answer our country's call is what we're all supposed to do. It's . . . patriotism." She looked down at her hands, clasped so tightly together, wondering if she would be able to find the words to express her thoughts without completely departing from her own values. She gave him an ambivalent smile. "Oh, Josef, I don't know how to say it. You said it earlier, the idea of war is more appealing than what the reality must be. When I read the news of the last two years, I think it must be horrible. And yet what's down in black and white can't really capture the awfulness, can it, even with photographs?"

She touched his hands again, able at last to look him in the face. "I shouldn't say what I really feel. All of my emotions are selfish and motivated by something that has nothing to do with God. It's fear. I am afraid, Josef. Everything in me wants to argue with what you're saying. But if I do that, where is my faith?"

He covered her hands with his. "I'm afraid, too, Larisa. But I've concluded the same thing you did when you joined the Red Cross—I can't come up with a good reason not to go. I could use you as an excuse, I suppose. I want to be with you, and I have to be alive to do that." He sucked in then released a quick breath. "I'm no expert on how to know the will of God or why He sometimes makes it such a struggle to find out what His will is. We may struggle plenty to figure what it is He wants us to do. But it's easy to know what He ultimately wants; He wants us. As best I can see things, this decision fits with what I know of His will. So I've got to go. Do you see that?"

She didn't want to nod. She wanted to shake her head, pull away, and run screaming all the way home. Having him ship over to France was entirely different than going herself. He was practically volunteering to be one of her patients, or one of the men in battlefield graves. How could she let him do that?

But it wasn't her place. God's will sometimes was simple. To Josef, this decision sounded simple, and she wouldn't—couldn't—stand in the way.

He put a gentle finger to her chin and raised her face to his, giving her a lopsided grin. "Maybe I do have some of that 'war fever.' Maybe I want to be a hero. We don't get many opportunities for that. Is it so wrong?"

She managed a chuckle. "I don't see anything wrong with it as long as you're not a dead hero."

"I'll do my best."

"Have you told Hank yet?" she asked after a moment.

"No. Tomorrow."

She cast a shy glance at him. "I'm not leaving for three weeks yet. Won't you stay until then?"

Gently, he traced the outline of one side of her face. "Yes. I'll come to New York with you and volunteer there."

CHAPTER *Ten*

THE NEXT three weeks soared by as fast as one of those new aeroplanes Lissa sometimes saw flying overhead. Time was gone with nothing but a cloud of memories left behind.

Other than the Culpeper horse fair in July, Cassie's wedding was the highlight of the summer. Everyone else knew Cassie was the most beautiful woman present because she was the bride, but Josef whispered his personal opinion to Lissa: It was a shame that she outshone the bride. The remark was silly, but it made Lissa feel admired and secure and took away the lingering self doubt she'd felt since her high school love had rejected her. She even found the boldness to wear lipstick on those lips she'd always wished she could hide. Because she smiled so often lately, she thought perhaps her lips were just big enough to fit the little bit of heaven she was feeling.

News quickly spread about Josef's enlistment. His love of hard work had brought acceptance in a town that valued the six days of labor nearly as highly as they did the Sabbath rest. Most were as proud of him as they were of all the young men who were off to do their duty. Lissa's parents were also proud, but concerned, too, which endeared them to Lissa. They were concerned for her sake, and for the sake of this new loved one who was going into danger.

Hank's reaction caused the most curiosity. He was as patriotic as could be. The whole town believed that if he were young enough, he would have enlisted, even if the war was against his old country.

But when Josef announced his plans, Hank never broke from his stoic demeanor. He expressed neither anger nor support. It was impossible to guess what he felt. Perhaps Mrs. Tanner knew, for the two seemed closer than ever, as if the thoughts of one belonged to the other. But neither Josef nor Lissa had a clue as to how his father felt, even when he finally did make an odd acknowledgment of it.

"You must be baptized," Mr. Tanner announced at dinner one evening. Josef and Lissa had exchanged glances. Was it fear that had kept Hank so quiet in the past couple of weeks, fear that Josef would be killed in action, and must be baptized before dying? But Hank revealed a more pragmatic reason. Josef would need proof of his identity. He didn't have a birth certificate, and a baptismal record would suffice, even a recent one, as long as it was witnessed and signed.

Then Hank went back to his silence, not even to answer Josef's inquiries about whether he might just go to Washington to retrieve his birth certificate. Hank refused to give any information as to how Josef might find such a record.

So Josef was baptized on the Sunday after Cassie's wedding. The Tanners and Parkers joined in a celebration, inviting a host of friends from town. Since Josef would leave with Lissa and Penny in two days to enlist in New York, it also served as a send-off party for all three of them.

Although the entire town approved of the reason for their trip to New York, the prospect of Josef traveling alone with Lissa and Penny posed a problem until Aunt Bobbie volunteered to serve as chaperone. The train ride to New York lasted the morning, with many stops along the way, but Lissa laughed as if on a holiday ride. She had to laugh, or she would cry. If she'd been the only one going overseas, good-byes would have been hard enough. But knowing Josef would soon follow, as a soldier going to fight, was a thought she couldn't ponder. She'd learned something from her mother, after all. She could avoid, deny, and push away thoughts too painful to handle.

Josef took his bag to an inexpensive rooming hotel Hank recommended, since Josef would have to wait some days for his orders to be processed. Lissa and the others settled into their hotel room then met Josef for dinner at a restaurant Penny suggested. The establishment was more extravagant than Lissa was accustomed to, with its 1890s gilt and glow. Josef seemed perfectly at home, choosing wine and ordering food from the French menu as if he were a man of sophistication. The image didn't quite go with his working man's Norfolk suit, belted at the waist. Its box pleats accentuated his square, masculine chest. He still managed to fit the role of the wealthy city dweller as well as he had the farm hand in blue denim or casual tweed.

What is he, really? How can someone fit so well in such varied surroundings?

She could no longer imagine life without Josef. How easy it was to forget that only weeks had passed since they'd met. She hadn't given much thought to Mr. Tanner's initial reluctance over their friendship, especially since he seemed to accept it, much as her own parents had. Obviously there was something in Josef's past that Mr. Tanner thought was better left alone. Lissa hadn't forgotten the words she'd overheard, but she began to question whether she'd heard aright. Surely the Tanners had not really spoken of a lynch mob. Mr. Tanner might have feared that Josef would be punished because of his association with the man who had raised him, the man now in jail for treason or sedition or some such thing. Mr. Tanner seemed to want Josef to forget him. But like Josef, she had a strong impression that Mr. Tanner wasn't telling everything he knew.

"This is so much fun, I wish we really were here on holiday," Aunt Bobbie said as the waiter cleared away her plate.

"My mother and I love New York," Penny said, finishing her tea. "She did invite you to come along on one of our shopping sprees—was that two years ago, now?— but you declined."

Aunt Bobbie laughed. "Yes, well, I'm a widow on a budget, my dear. A Tanner shopping spree is a bit beyond my means if it's to be done properly."

"Just charge everything to Mama's room. That's what I do. She wouldn't care, and she'd never be able to tell your expenses from hers. She just signs any receipt that comes her way. Father doesn't mind, especially since Mama spends her own money from her daddy and his great big bank."

"Oh, my, I shall remember that, Penny," Aunt Bobbie teased.

Lissa was barely aware of the silly banter around her. Josef was looking at her, as if memorizing what it felt like to be in her presence.

"Aunt Bobbie," Josef said quietly, "I know you're a loyal chaperone, but would you trust me to walk Lissa alone back to your hotel?"

She reached across the small dinner table and patted his cheek as if he were a precious child. "I trust you, dear boy. You two haven't really been a part of the conversation since the appetizer anyway." She glanced at Penny. "Shall we be truly decadent and stay for dessert?"

"Of course. I don't think the Red Cross will be offering anything sweet apart from doughnuts, and those go only so far after noon. I intend to enjoy every epicurean delight tonight."

Josef took Lissa's hand, and they started off.

"We won't be long, you know," Aunt Bobbie called after them with a twinkle in her eye and a conspiratorial wink at Penny. "Liss, I must report back to your father that I've done my job."

Lissa leaned down and kissed her aunt, then let Josef lead her away.

The hotel was two blocks from the restaurant, but Josef steered her in the opposite direction down the busy street toward Central Park.

"I know Hank said I lived in Washington all my life, but this city has a familiar feel."

Lissa looked up at the tall buildings snuggled so close together. She loved visiting such a limitless place, but she preferred the more restrained architecture of Washington. "Maybe you were here to sell—what was it— glass? Or coal?"

"Bottles from one factory and coking coal from another. Coke is harder than regular coal. Less sulfur so a lot less smoke when it's used in industrial furnaces. At least I remember that much. Yes, you're probably right. I suppose New York is a good marketplace."

Once inside the cover of the park, he took her into his arms. The sun was setting and the shadows surrounding them were fueled by the early golden glow of electric streetlights just coming on. But even with the sporadic spill of the lights at the street, they stood in the shadows of twilight.

"I've been wanting to kiss you all day," he whispered, then did just that.

Lissa put her arms around him, something she'd never have done in public back home. There was something freeing about being in a city, far from anyone who knew them.

"I've been wanting you to kiss me all day."

He kissed her again and raised the tip of his finger to trace her lips. "You've been smiling all day, Larisa."

"What else could I do? Inside I want to cry because I'm leaving, but I'm with you now. I'll smile until I'm not with you any more."

He kissed her again. "Thank you," he said.

"For what?"

"For telling me you want to cry." He held her tight and she couldn't see his face any more as he pressed her cheek to his jacket. "It's what I want to do, but I can't admit it, can I?"

"Heroes can't shed a tear? Is that it?"

"Something like that."

Already Lissa was feeling her pledge slip away to smile until she wasn't with him any more. "Oh, Josef . . ."

He raised his finger to her lips again. "No, Larisa," he said, "don't give in. If you do, I might. And I want you to think I'm stronger than that, even if it's a lie."

She pulled away because that was the only way to find strength. After tonight she wouldn't see him again—for how long? Forever? Lissa refused to believe that. She would see him again.

"Let's walk a bit then," she said, and he fell into a slow step beside her.

The air was cool after a hot summer day. A breeze rustled the trees now and then, and they heard voices of others who were enjoying the evening air. Lissa didn't know what to say. Every thought in her mind led back to this being their last evening together. She wished they were simply enjoying being together, enjoying their love and life. But she wasn't that good at fooling herself when the end of the evening was so close.

He bent down and picked up a twig, snapping it in two and tossing it aside.

"Sometimes I think this would all be easier if I had the memory of a long line of patriotic ancestors who were breathing their support from the grave, like you do," he said, stooping to pick up another twig. "I'd send you off tomorrow without a doubt that it's the right thing to do. I'd go to the recruiting office and let them send me over, knowing I was carrying on as those before me would expect."

She gave him a wry grin, stopping close to him. "You think I don't have any doubts because of my family history?"

He nodded. "Yes, as a matter of fact, that is what I think."

She walked around him, and he fell in step again beside her. "It's not that way at all."

"But you're always so certain of what you should do in the tradition of every Parker from the Mayflower down."

She glowered at his exaggeration.

"Okay, from the Revolution down," he amended. "But having the tradition does seem to help. Americans *owe* families like yours for the freedom we enjoy, the fact that we have an elected president and not some king or a kaiser who needs military power to back up his laws."

"No one owes us a thing. I imagine those who've gone off to war did it for their own families as much as for the country."

"But how many families are like yours, Larisa? Look around this city." He waved a hand in a sweep, as if to take in everything beyond the trees surrounding them. "You're a minority here, Larisa Rose. Most of the people around here are first-generation Americans. And yet they're going off to war for America, too. I'm just trying to figure out which should be easier."

"Maybe the ones who chose to come here have a stronger conviction about fighting. They chose to be Americans. They weren't just born into it."

"People like Hank." He nodded. "Yes, I see that. I just wish I could remember some of my old convictions. I'd have a history to keep me going when I won't have you around to remind me. I suppose I must have had some feeling for the United States. Otherwise I'd probably be sitting in jail next to that man Otto who raised me. I just wish I could remember. Part of me thinks whatever I hold, I hold firmly."

Lissa shivered, the words sounded so oddly familiar. Then it came to her. "I remember reading the newspaper accounts back in the early days of the war, when the kaiser was quoted so often. He talked about conquered lands, Belgium, maybe, and said, 'What we hold, we hold firm.'"

"I guess I have at least one thing in common with the old kaiser besides German parents. Stubbornness."

They walked a bit farther, and Lissa was glad that conversation had ended. They hadn't talked about the war all day, for which she'd been grateful.

It was different now that he would be part of it. She'd been a regular Betsy Ross, but now . . .

He took her hand as they reached the nearest set of lights leading back to the hubbub of the city. "We should go to your room. Aunt Bobbie will be counting the minutes."

She nodded reluctantly.

Soldiers and sailors were among those enjoying an evening walk, another reminder of what Lissa wanted to forget. The hotel wasn't far, though, and she was glad to step into the quiet lobby. Lissa tapped on the door to the room, but there was no answer. Apparently the others hadn't returned. She fished in her small handbag for the key, and a bold thought occurred to her: She would ask him in.

Her hand trembled and the simple task of unlocking the door was suddenly more than she could handle.

Then his hand was over hers, steadying her. If Josef guessed the reason for her sudden quiver, he didn't give it away. She watched him open the door, and the faint smell of beeswax mingled with the scent of the fresh flowers Mr. and Mrs. Tanner had sent to brighten their room as a farewell bouquet. Lissa would have reached for a lamp but stood frozen to the spot, as the trembling his hand had stilled reignited, spreading quickly to the rest of her. She was alone with a man in a hotel room, so far from home.

Before a single coherent thought took shape, she was in Josef's arms, and he pulled her closer, even as she did the same. Her handbag and key were in the way of holding him, so they fell to the floor. She didn't shut the door, and Josef obviously had no thought for it, either. They stood holding each other as if it really was the last time they'd see one another.

When his lips came down to meet hers, her passion met his. Every sensible thought, every caution, every bell that restrained them when they were back home sharing a kiss was drowned in a flood magnified by their surroundings. At that moment, nothing mattered except what was between them.

Josef lifted her from the floor entirely into his arms, and she felt the door at her back being gently pushed closed, even as his lips never left hers. He settled her back to her feet, but her head swirled, and she barely felt the carpet beneath her shoes. She pulled at his jacket as he slipped her sweater from her shoulders. The jacket and sweater fell to the floor, but she couldn't see where they landed with the door closed and the room dark. Her cotton dress felt like a winter coat in the heat of the room. His kiss deepened, and yearning engulfed her from head to toe.

And then, as quickly as his kiss began, it ended. Josef didn't step away, and she felt his unsteady breathing in her ear. Taking his hands from her waist, he put them on each side of her, palms down, on the cool, flat surface of the door behind her. Then he leaned his forehead against it, the rest of him still merged against her.

"I'm sorry," he whispered, "you deserve better than this."

She stood motionless. He was so close she knew any movement on her part would press them closer, and for a fleeting moment temptation flared again. One movement, even slight, and maybe he would be unable to control the passion he fought. But as overwhelming as her own feelings were at that moment, she shared Josef's struggle. They must follow what the Lord would have them do, whether they were home and surrounded by their own familiar morals or in a far away city where strangers might not judge. The Lord hadn't been left at home.

"We're coming back, you know," he whispered. "You'll go to France and I'll be there soon, and we'll both do our duties. Then we'll come back. And we'll be glad we waited. We'll have a wedding as big as your sister's, and then a wedding night, one where we won't have any memories haunting us about what happened tonight."

Carefully, barely even breathing, Lissa turned her face to his. He still had his forehead on the cool wood of the door, and he suddenly looked exhausted. She might have laughed she was so giddy, except that she didn't want to move. At that moment he'd never been more handsome or more dear.

He tilted his head to meet her gaze. Her eyes had adjusted to the dim moonlight filtering in from the open drapes at the window, and he had a look of glowing triumph.

"I love you, Larisa Rose Parker," he announced, "and I hope you'll agree to become my wife."

Her arms were already around him, and he could not have been much closer. Yet she squeezed and he felt closer still.

"Yes, Josef Warner," she said with equal formality, "I would be honored to be your wife."

Just then they heard Penny's laugh, and they separated as quickly as they'd come together. Josef found the electrical switch and turned on a light, while Lissa scooped up their abandoned jackets before Aunt Bobbie opened the door.

CHAPTER *Eleven*

USS TRANSPORTER 135, SEPTEMBER 1, 1917

Dear Josef,

I am sitting on the deck of what was once a huge merchant ship, now converted to a camouflaged support transport. My training is complete and New York is fading behind me, the endless Atlantic lies ahead. It's hard to imagine I shall soon be in France, after having waited so long for this goal to materialize. I wish it were harder to imagine you facing this same ocean, but I'm afraid it's all I've thought of since stepping aboard. Part of me still wishes that vision would never come true. Forgive me.

Penny is here, and we've made great friends already. We're all equally excited and afraid, I think, because we really don't know how we will react to real soldiers with real wounds.

I just have to trust that God will give us strength when our own fails.

Please know that I think of you each hour of each day. I received your letter this morning before we shoved off. I'm sorry you've had to wait so long to get into training camp. What an unexpected mess, to have too many recruits and not enough camps or equipment. But I'm sure the time will pass quickly once it all unfolds for you. At least you will be able to see your family again before it all begins.

Soon you'll be looking at what I see. The ocean is a pretty sight but I'm reminded this is no romantic undertaking that I'm about to face. I know that I'm totally "green" when it comes to war. In training we've learned how to treat men injured by all the ways man uses to fight his enemies. I fear all of that for you. I'm really thankful that the Army's training camp has taken so long to open for you. My prayer is it'll all be over before you—or any other Americans, but especially you—cross this ocean.

Love,

Liss

VIRGINIA, SEPTEMBER 9, 1917

My dearest Larisa Rose,

I don't know how this letter will find you, so far away, but I'll trust the army knows how to deliver it someday, somehow. I wish I could deliver it personally.

My orders have come through at last, and I leave tomorrow for training camp. I feel like a kid waiting for the first day of school (one who wants to go!), but I remind myself that I'm all grown up, and this is real. Sometimes it's hard not to get roused with all the rest who seem to think we are off on an adventure that happens to include war games. I still have that childish hope of coming home a hero to impress you.

The news of this letter is that Caleb is coming along. He turns twenty next month and decided not to wait for the draft. Hank got the melancholies again when he heard, a little like when I joined. I think down deep he's proud of Caleb. For all Hank's patriotism, I know he can't be happy that we're going to be fighting against people from where he was born.

But I promised to keep an eye on my little brother, and so I will, even if he claims he doesn't need it.

I had another dream that I think is a memory. I was in a schoolroom. I must have liked school. Maybe that's why I'm looking forward to boot camp.

This letter is my last as a civilian, and my next will have to pass more strict censorship and rules. So, even though I'm sure I'll write many times before I get there, who knows what I'll be able to say. So I'll say it now—see you in France. Tomorrow starts my first step toward you, my love.

> *Love,*
> *Josef*

FRANCE, SEPTEMBER 22, 1917

Dear Josef,

We landed yesterday. I know I'm not supposed to say where. Other than a brief storm, and one harrowing false alarm about a U-boat attack, the ride over couldn't have been less eventful. The false alarm was exciting, I must admit. A terrible siren woke us all, and we scrambled to our safe spots with our life jackets, all loud and chaotic. It turned out they'd spotted nothing but a school of whales spouting under the light of the full moon, not a U-boat periscope at all. But at four a.m. we couldn't find the humor in it, with our hearts still racing and having been crouched in mortal fear for half an hour.

I don't have to look far to see that France is someplace foreign and far from home. The villages are quaint and old. From afar I saw a cathedral, which was impressive. The towns we pass along the way all have a more modest church and a pub. I guess the battle between our spiritual and carnal natures has been fought since time immemorial.

It's impossible to be here and not think of history. I remember how Louis XIV sent his ships to war with England. I could almost imagine ships of old dodging cannonballs and the ghosts of sailors like Dugay Trouin escaping from English prisons to return to beloved Brittany, and fight on the seas again.

I wonder what it was like to see the docks filled with booty from English merchantmen, fragrant vanilla, and cocoa beans. There's nothing like that here now. I wished I could go out and investigate some wreckage we saw floating along the shore. But we aren't here as tourists. And even though the sights have been exciting, I long for home and you.

I suppose I should look forward to the days ahead, with work enough to keep my mind from wandering to my homesickness and loneliness.

Love,

Liss

FORT DIX, SEPTEMBER 25, 1917

Dear Larisa Rose,

I long to hear from you, but I know it'll be nothing short of a miracle to get letters between wherever you are and here.

Let me tell you how six of my seven days a week have passed since I got here, though the term "passed" doesn't quite do justice to describing what goes on at boot camp. First call at reveille is five thirty. We have fifteen minutes of sitting up exercises, then five minutes to straighten our cot, wash, and fall in for mess at six. We wash our mess kits, then roll call (and sick call for anyone who couldn't make it up). Then we fall in for drills all morning—field work, hiking with full packs, obstacle courses, bayonet drill. Eleven forty-five brings lunch, and afternoon drills start at twelve fifty-five and last until four. From four to five we have school, training the mind so to speak, although they don't seem to want us to think for ourselves, just do as told. Mess is at five. Evenings are for study and French lessons until we drop to our cots in an exhausted heap.

Some of the men who are harder to fit are still in civilian clothes. We have shortages of uniforms, boots, and blankets. We just got a shipment of guns, so we're equipped with what's important. They haven't let us loose on the rifle range, but artillery training is set to start next week.

Some of the men are complaining. It's strange, but I'm actually enjoying every minute of it. I think they could work us harder and probably will. Almost everybody else, especially Caleb, thinks they ought to show a little mercy.

Not sure what any of this means in terms of my past, except that I must be used to a life of discipline.

I pray my letters reach you without too much omitted by the censors (but I know you guys who read the letters help keep us safe).

Love,
Josef

FRANCE, SEPTEMBER 25, 1917

Dear Josef,

We were all under the dim-witted impression that they would ease us into this war, but within the first week, Penny and I and the others have been working ten hours a day, six days a week. We're seeing the toll of the fighting on the men who've been here a while. So far we see mostly soldiers wounded a while back, who can now be transported to this hospital, some distance from the fighting. We can't hear the shellfire, but our patients still do. It's so awful to see them shake and stare, their bodies consumed with battle fatigue and shock. I wouldn't call it fear, it's something beyond that. I don't know how any of them will recover.

Meanwhile we're all developing a form of fatigue of our own. I find it impossible to write more than these few lines.

Good-night, my love.

Liss

FORT DIX, OCTOBER 3, 1917

Dear Larisa Rose,

Did I say I thought they would get tougher on us? Well, we're considered tough enough now to withstand twenty-mile hikes over unpaved roads with full packs. I'd complain like the rest of them except I know I'm getting stronger every day. Somehow that makes it worth it.

When we're at marching drill they say these silly tunes— chants, almost—to keep our heads, and therefore our feet, in time. It got into my head that Psalm 100 could be chanted in such a way to fit this pattern. While they're saying their meaningless jingle, I'm praising the Lord with every step. But—surprise—they don't like it when somebody doesn't participate, even though my feet were in perfect time. So they made me lead the banter. I started out okay, but before I knew it I was chanting "Know ye that the Lord is God!" Half the guys echoed, "Know ye that the Lord is God." The other half were so surprised they stopped altogether, and the rest fell over the ones who'd lost step. The sarge had me out of there quick. Ever since, I'm in my own drill, the "holy roller drill." Anybody's free to join me, but so far I'm alone. Even Caleb hasn't been willing, but I think he will one day, once he gets to the truth that the Lord's opinion is more important than the other guys.

They sent me to the Chaplain, I guess to "get all that religious talk out." He's a good guy, that chaplain. We prayed together and suspect that God is already at work on the others.

I'm missing you. At night, when my mind is at last free to go where it wants, it rushes to your side. Hope you are receiving my letters.

Love,
Josef

P.S. I know now that I either had chicken pox as a child or am naturally immune. They brought in a guy from one of the tents because he had chicken pox. Instead of quarantining the poor soul, they made sure he passed his rash on to the rest of us in the barrack so we'd all get it over with. Better to get it here than over there, I guess. Anyway, he was assigned to the bunk next to me. I'm still well three weeks later. Quite a few others weren't so lucky, and they're still itching. Before we ship out, we'll get our vaccinations against typhoid and paratyphoid A & B. They're making us safe, Larisa Rose, so we can all come home again.

FRANCE, NOVEMBER 15, 1917

Dear Josef,

I received your first letter! I can hardly describe the joy of holding in my hands something you've held in yours. But it was bittersweet, because it made me more aware of how desperately I miss you.

I'm sure the letter you sent is old news by now. They do tell us a quicker mail route has been established.

What a surprise to hear that Caleb has come along. Well, it's not too much of a surprise that he's joined. I had a suspicion that he might, especially after you decided to. But I am surprised that they assigned you to the same camp. Do look out for him. He seems so young sometimes.

I'm reluctant to talk about my work here, and I'm sure the censors won't let me say too much. I want to spare you and Caleb what these young men have faced. Perhaps it's best if I do tell you some of it. I hope you've been warned already.

Josef, it's so awful. I've been moved to another hospital. It's closer to the fighting but still miles away. Everything I saw before this was bad enough. I've seen men whose lives have been hollowed because of the cruelty and violence inflicted upon them by men in the opposing trenches. It's inhuman, but some of them, at least for the time being, have forgotten what it's even like to live a humane life. Some have been on the battlefield two years, with few breaks from the battle fire.

I didn't see much death at the other hospital, not physical death anyway. Here we see it every day. I told myself I'd be ready for this. War inevitably brings death. But my first day at this hospital I was at the side of three young men as they died. None were older than twenty-five. I felt helpless and inadequate. I couldn't imagine why the doctor seemed so unmoved. I finally realized that a doctor would go mad if every death affected him. He's a good doctor, and he does everything he can, which often isn't much.

The injured receive their first treatment at a field hospital. We get the worst cases from there. So many of them don't make it. My job sometimes is not to be a nurse so much as a companion for a moment to a dying man, to keep him from being alone as he leaves this world for the next.

I long to see you, Josef, only I couldn't bear it, not here. I'm sorry I'm so weak that I have to share all of this with you. Perhaps I shouldn't even send this letter.

Love,
Larisa

FORT DIX, NOVEMBER 20, 1917

Dear Larisa Rose,

Training camp ended, although we've been told we will get more training once we get to France, once they find a way to get more of us over there.

I had another memory, this time while I was awake. I remembered playing a game in a forest somewhere, a child's war game where we were using an ancient method of attacking the enemy with just a few soldiers at the enemy's weakest point.

I think I was reminded by a lesson in training school yesterday. We're supposed to be learning something called infiltration. They said a Frenchman came up with the idea and wrote it in a pamphlet, and the pamphlet got into the hands of a German, and they started using the technique. But I know it's neither German nor French.

It's ancient Greek. I used to play it all the time with a childhood buddy. I even remember his name—Karl Bonner—as well as his face. After I get back from France, I'm going to look him up.

Meanwhile I'm feeling like that school boy again, because
I know I'll be leaving for France soon. Closer to you. It's a
long shot that we'll be able to work out seeing each other,
but somehow I find it comforting that we won't have the "big
pond" between us.

Love,
Josef

FRANCE, NOVEMBER 21, 1917

Dear Josef,

We've been assigned to live in a hotel near the hospital. This
morning as I left my room it struck me how normal this small city
appears early in the morning. Of course, I've never been to Europe
before, so I don't really know what "normal" is. But just after the
sun rises, before the soldiers on leave come out, before the supply
trucks rumble through the streets, if the ambulances aren't racing in
from the fields, before I realize there are no young men to be found
anywhere except those in uniform and when there's a lull in the
distant rumble of the big guns, I can almost imagine how lovely it
must have been to live here before this terrible war.

I'm told this is where Louis XVI met Marie Antoinette and
where Napoleon later met her. Not far from here is the Hotel de
Ville, the spot where Joan of Arc was abandoned by her troops and
taken prisoner.

The little town is surrounded by huge oak and beech trees.
A woman comes out to sweep the brick walkway at her door, a
scarf shielding her head from the fall breeze. A shopkeeper in a
stark white shirt and a brown, sturdy apron comes out to wash his
windows. The many flower boxes are empty. No one has the heart
to grow anything but vegetables these days. But I imagine what it
would look like—a fairy tale town.

Then I reach the hospital and the cries of suffering men bring
me back to the war. I think I would like to visit here someday when

France is itself again. I pray that day will come soon. The people here deserve that much, don't they?

Love,
Your Larisa Rose

USS MAGNOLIA, DECEMBER 3, 1917

Dear Larisa Rose,

Somehow, the mail system has actually worked. I was beginning to lose confidence since it's taken so long to hear from you. I'm not losing confidence in you or us, but in the delivery system!

Yet here it is, right in my lap, your first letter from France. You sound tired and yet strong, my love. You said at the outset of this adventure that God would provide the strength when your own fails, and I know you will continue to depend on and trust that truth. Don't forget He's put you there, and those battle-shocked men will be comforted just by seeing a face as pretty as yours. But don't let them admire you too long, my love, or they'll have to deal with a broken heart on top of their shell shock, once they find out you've been claimed.

I'm writing this aboard ship, heading as fast as allowed to your shore. I'll post this once we land. Maybe you'll get it before it's too many weeks old. We left yesterday, not long after I received your letter dated September 25. I don't know how subsequent letters will find me, but don't let that stop you from writing. They assure us that mail is vital to morale, and they consider it a high priority. So I won't give up, even though the delivery task seems monumental. Our letters are censored by our second lieutenant, but I don't care if the whole world knows I'm nothing but a schoolboy with a crush on you.

Caleb and I had a heart-to-heart yesterday. We've been a little distant ever since the issue of the "holy roller drills." Anyway, the small drilling group of one (me) finally grew by a couple of people. Sarge disbanded us. Evidently it was okay only as long as I didn't have anyone marching with me. I think Caleb wanted to join us, but there was too much pressure, especially from Dack. He's the Sarge. Caleb really looks up to that guy. I think he's a good sergeant and not a bad guy, but he doesn't seem to think much of me.

Anyway, things are better between me and Caleb. That's good since we've been assigned to the same section. That means we'll be spending as much time as ever together.

Lights out. Can't see to write any more, but my thoughts are with you as always.

In case you've forgotten, I love you.

Love,
Josef

FRANCE, DECEMBER 23, 1917

Dear Josef,

It's gotten so cold. With the holidays approaching, I'm homesick again. I have visions of sitting near a Christmas tree with you, sharing a cup of hot cocoa, looking forward to the family festivities with you at my side. Sometimes those thoughts are the only relief I have in a day otherwise filled with things I'd rather not write about.

Lt. Rochelle, the ranking Red Cross nurse at this hospital, has tried to make the holidays bearable for "the children" as she calls our patients. We decorated a tree with whatever we could find, like ribbons and candles borrowed from our rooms. The lieutenant even bought little gifts like bon-bons and chewing gum. I was able to provide some hard candy Mama sent. The patients had a little glimpse back into what life used to be before all this madness began. Even the head surgeon was impressed by our efforts.

Mama's packets have been so helpful. She sends cotton and oilcloth and flannel bandages, things we always seem to need. She also sent warm clothing, which has been of great help to me. I was even able to share a few things with some of the villagers. We were only allowed to bring one suitcase so most of us had to send home *for more. I had this silly wish that they might pack you up and send you to me, to keep me warm. But the photograph my mother took of us together has helped. She said she would have another copy made to send to you. I hope you've received it by now.*

She also said she would send you other provisions. She's quite an all-around mother, worrying if we're eating enough. Her goods and hard candy have made me very popular with both patients and the village children. For purely selfish reasons, I'll ask her to send some paper to you along with one of those new self-inking pens. That way, a shortage of supplies won't keep you from writing to me. There's a YMCA canteen not far from where I am. They usually have a ready supply of such things for me.

I've begun learning to knit so that I might fashion a pair of socks for you. I have so little time, I'm afraid I may not finish until spring. Then what good will they be?

Most of us are working twelve-hour days, every day, even the Sabbath. We take comfort in the memory that our Lord healed on the Sabbath, too.

Right now it's colder than I imagined possible, and rumors among the soldiers say that supplies have been slow to arrive. There is a shortage of blankets and long underwear. The short summer drawers have finally arrived, now that it's the end of autumn.

We get to some very personal conversations around here sometimes, it's just the way things are. If it wasn't so tragic, we'd probably have a good laugh over it. Unfortunately everybody's too cold to laugh much.

In your letter, you mentioned having another memory. I'm glad for you, Josef. I hope one day soon it will all come back to you. I know we'll only be stronger for having you whole again.

I love you, though, with or without those memories.

> *Love,*
> *Larisa Rose*

CHAPTER *Twelve*

"From Caleb!"

Lissa smiled as Penny approached at a brisk pace, waving a letter as if it were a white flag. Lissa held up one from Josef she had just received at that morning's mail call.

Penny caught sight of Lissa's letter. "Oh, then you know they're here. They've been here for weeks." Out of breath and with a lopsided smile, she added, "I don't know whether to be excited or sorry."

"Sorry. Definitely sorry, Penny," responded Lissa with a glance back at the ward she'd just left.

Penny walked beside Lissa. "You're right. I am sorry." Then her eyes brightened. "But, just think, Liss, we might actually get to see them. Caleb said he's applying for leave first chance. I'll bet Josef will, too."

Lissa nodded. His letter had said as much. Things had settled down a bit at the front, with the most recent big offensive over, so there was hope that Penny and Lissa might be able to get a day of leave, too.

"Okay, what's with the silent treatment? How come you're not jumping up and down at the prospect?"

Lissa smiled at last. "I am. It's just, well . . ."

"What?"

"It's you, Pen. What'll they do when they find out your brothers have shipped over?"

"Brothers?" Then she shook her head as if pulling in clear thinking. "Oh, sorry. It's still hard for me to think of Josef as my brother, too. Well, so he is. What of it? Why should that affect me, other than making me excited about seeing them?"

Lissa stopped and faced Penny. "We're not supposed to have come over if we have family here."

"Oh, that. I don't see a problem. Besides, that goes for you, too, when they talk about loved ones, boyfriends, and such. They weren't here when we volunteered; we didn't know they'd be coming when we first signed on. I can't imagine them sending us home when they can barely spare us for a full day's leave."

Lissa nodded, accepting Penny's logic. They started walking again toward dinner in Hut 7. The hastily built wooden buildings varied little among the camps set up behind the lines. They were aptly called huts rather than buildings. Most looked as if they might blow over in a good wind. But both girls worked, ate, and often slept in such a place and had seen them weather a few storms in the four months they'd been in France. The huts were hot in summer and cold in winter, but none had lost its roof yet.

"What does your letter say?" Penny asked as they stood in line for vegetable stew and bread pudding. Food in France for the soldiers and medical personnel was plain but plentiful, compared to what Lissa had heard about refugee camps where people waited in long lines for bread and soup. But that was better than the food available in German-occupied northern France. It was said that people were dying of starvation there.

Lissa took her tray and headed toward a bench at one of the open tables and said a short blessing before answering. "Josef's spirits always seem high, but there seems to be trouble, when I read between the lines."

"Like what?"

"Maybe I'm reading too much into it."

Penny didn't even reach for her fork. "Tell me."

"A while back at camp, the drill sergeant had him doing drills by himself."

"Is that all?"

Lissa cocked her head. "Does that sound normal?"

When Penny averted her eyes from Lissa's stare and focused her vision on the bland stew, Liss set aside her fork, too.

"What do you know, Pen? Has Caleb said something?"

"I don't think—"

"Look," Lissa interrupted, "today's letter came from where they're training here in France. Josef makes a light reference to the sergeant of his platoon telling him to clear the road of debris so the wagons could get through. Josef makes it sound like it was nothing, but it sounds dangerous. He's standing up for his faith and I think he may be getting bashed for it. They're sticking him with the worst jobs."

"They probably don't want the men thinking too much about anything except getting the job done."

"Yes, but when that job may mean death, that seems a good time to be thinking about God."

"I agree with you, Liss, it's just . . . maybe there's another reason they target Josef."

"I don't think it's ever right to single somebody out. I've seen what it does to children. Why should adults be any different? Besides, what could Josef possibly have done to deserve being treated with anything but respect? Don't those officers respect the Lord?"

"I'm sure if any of them have been on the battlefield they thank the Lord every time a bullet misses them. Don't worry, Liss. Whatever Josef is facing now, if it's only because of his faith, it's temporary."

"I don't know what else they'd dislike him for."

Penny rolled her eyes. "Goodness, Liss, he's the quintessential teacher's pet. Except in the army, even the teacher doesn't like him. There must be a reason for that."

"Teacher's pet? Why should you say such a thing?"

Penny took a bite of her stew, and Lissa looked down at Caleb's letter on the table. "Caleb did say something, didn't he?"

Penny raised her fork again, then set it down. "All right, but don't be angry with me for telling you, or with Caleb, because he told me not to say anything."

Lissa put her fork down, too.

"The thing is, it sounds like Josef has been acting like a machine. He's always the best at the drills. He does everything he's asked and more. He's mastered everything so quickly that men think he must have been through all that training before. He's making everyone else look bad, like shirkers or incompetent."

Lissa pursed her lips together. "Then it's jealousy, pure and simple. What any one of them wouldn't give to be like Josef. He's disciplined, strong, energetic, and intelligent."

"Yes, yes, I know all about the man who does no wrong. And don't forget that he's handsome. Now wrap all that up in a 'holier-than-thou' attitude."

"You don't know that! He's never had that attitude around me or anyone in your family."

Penny reached across and placed her hand on Lissa's. "Let's not argue, Liss," she whispered. "There's no reason to. I know you care for him."

"But you don't."

Penny withdrew her hand and looked at her stew. "I've never said a negative word about him, well not since that first day. Why do you think I don't care for him?"

"For one thing, you forgot he was your brother a moment ago. Have you written to him even once?"

She shrugged. "I write to Caleb and send my greetings through him. Besides, you send him enough letters to keep him reading day and night. He doesn't need more from me."

"I think he'd welcome a word from you."

"Why? He doesn't even know me, and I don't know him. What would I write about?"

"Some of the same things I write. Your work, how life is here, how you're handling it all."

"I write all that to Caleb and my folks. I don't need to write it three times. Anyway, Liss, let's not talk about it any more. All this stuff with Josef will clear up once they're on the battlefield and they're all crying out to God."

"Now there's a cheery thought."

———

Cheers cut the air in the bull ring training ground—the same air through which at night, they could hear the big guns booming from the east and north. A smaller war was being waged in front of them. Two-dozen men stood in a circle three deep, giving the pair in the middle plenty of room. Moments ago the men had been practicing carefully choreographed bayonet thrusts, but the minute Josef's partner had stepped out of the training regime for a try at hand-to-hand fighting—the kind that wasn't choreographed—Josef threw down his gun and took a swipe back. Somebody yelled "Fight!" and a crowd formed before the next punch was thrown.

Josef knew he was an idiot to have returned that punch. He knew he'd been set up. Birchall Burton was nearly twice his size and weight, and he'd had it in for Josef since the day they'd met aboard ship. Josef was sure Sergeant Dack had paired them for bayonet practice with the hope that this fight would erupt.

Josef was quicker, but his punches couldn't match Birchall's power. He thought he'd had it when the second, then the third punch landed square on his cheek, just below his eye. But after a shake he was back at it, surprised at his own strength. Josef knew his fists were hardly more than a bug bite to Birchall. Anybody with brains would back off, and maybe the Lord would've turned the other cheek. Josef wasn't fighting to hurt the guy anyway. But he knew how much some of the men disliked him, how they wanted to be doing what Birchall was doing. The time had come to let them know he'd noticed.

"Break it up! Break it up!"

Vaguely aware of men suddenly standing at attention, Josef took his eyes off Birchall—who landed one more punch. The last thing Josef saw from the corner of his eye was that huge, bare fist.

———

If someone said memory loss caused by one blow to the head might be cured by another, Josef now knew it didn't work that way for him. But at least he retained what memory he'd had before the fight.

He hadn't expected a fight to change anything, and now he felt like a fool. Shame filled him. He'd given in to anger, let his pride get the best of him. But the Lord had taken pity on him anyway and sent an officer to step in so Josef wouldn't get killed before he saw his first German.

"Hey, Warner."

Josef turned and saw Andy White, who had been assigned to the camp dispensary since he'd broken a couple bones in his foot on one of the many obstacle courses they had to master.

"Heard you went up against Big Birchall. What are you—a block-head?"

"Guess so," he responded weakly.

Nurse Edna must have heard, because in a moment she stood at the foot of Josef's bed with her familiar glare. Nurse Edna was with the Red Cross, but she wasn't most men's idea of a ministering angel. She was old enough to be a mother to most soldiers but without a trace of maternal benevolence. Her gray-streaked hair was pulled back so flat the shape of her round head looked small on her otherwise bulky body. No one minded keeping the rules about not talking to the Red Cross nurses when it came to Nurse Edna.

"Private Warner, they dragged you in here, but you've had all the attention you're going to get. I stitched up the cut above your eye while you were out cold. Soon as you think you can stand without falling over, get your carcass off that bed to make room for somebody who merits care in a war zone."

"Yes, sir," he mumbled, momentarily confused by the authoritarian tone. "Er, yes, ma'am."

He stood, though still woozy. All he needed was a good meal and he'd be right again. Mess call for lunch had probably already sounded.

Just outside the dispensary hut, an MP stood in Josef's path.

"Private Warner, you will follow me."

With a glance toward the dining hut, Josef reluctantly did as ordered. The food wasn't good, but it was filling. It stuck to the bottom of the stomach for a while. Didn't the MP hear Josef's stomach growl? If he did, it wouldn't make any difference as he led him to the hut of Second Lieutenant Armand Brooks.

Lt. Brooks was younger than Josef, but everybody knew the lieutenant thought himself lucky to have been born when he was. If his military family had taught him anything, it was that war offered the best opportunity to prove himself. Since he knew their secrets because his duties included censoring every letter that came in or went out of camp, he didn't seem to mind sharing thoughts of his own.

The MP announced Private Warner's arrival. If he hadn't, Josef's growling stomach would have revealed his presence eventually. Lt. Brooks dismissed the escort and waited until the door was closed before giving Josef the once over. Josef stood at attention, at the same time taking in the surroundings. A battered wooden desk took up most of the room, with letters, rubber stamps, scissors, and black ink strewn about on top. Another desk was at Josef's right, and behind that on the wall hung a map of Europe. Pins were stuck here and there on France. That desk also was a clutter of smaller maps and paper lists.

"Private Warner," mused the lieutenant thoughtfully as he took a seat but left Josef at attention. "Your name has come up more than once from a couple of the NCOs. Not all the reports have been favorable, I'm sorry to say. I've pressed for the reason why you manage to get on the wrong side of people when you seem to be a good trainee. The only reason I can get is that they're afraid you're going to come up with conscientious objections once you get closer to the front."

Josef looked straight ahead, hoping permission would soon be given for him to defend himself.

"Now why would an enlisted man do such a thing? You volunteered, Warner. What happened? Did the town back home shame you into it?"

"No, sir." Josef replied instantly, eyes forward.

"Evidently you show all the signs of being an objector: praying, Bible talk, worry about ethics. Somebody swears around you, Warner, and they suddenly rethink their words."

The lieutenant pushed back his chair with a scrape, tipping it to rock beneath him. Josef knew he was being scrutinized, as if the officer was trying to divine some truth by merely looking at him.

"Now, I have no problem with any of that if you do your job, private."

He paused, and Josef stole a quick glance to see if the officer showed signs of being finished.

Finally Lt. Brooks stood and came around his desk and into the line of Josef's vision, so close Josef could smell the man's chewing gum.

Looking Josef straight in the eye, he said, "Half the guys out there—no, more than that—don't know why they're fighting. Americans are just getting into this. We've had two years to study what's going on over here, and you know what? Nobody seems able to explain it. You talk to any French poilu. He'll tell you they don't know what started all this or why it's gone on so long or why half their family has had to die. And they're the ones with the most to lose: their own soil. So our soldiers have some cause to be a little confused."

He looked Josef in the eye. "What about you, Warner? Why are you here?"

"May I speak freely, sir?" he asked, still stiff, his tone as formal as his rigid body.

"At ease, Warner. And yes, speak freely."

Josef loosened his knees and swung his arms behind him to clasp his hands at his back. He looked at the lieutenant.

"My answer can't be separated from the faith that got me into trouble to begin with."

The lieutenant propped himself on the edge of his desk. "The Army doesn't discourage faith, Warner, it just doesn't like extremists, unless the extremism is in devotion to duty. But go on."

"I believe God places each of us by design, sir. I was born an able-bodied American. My country is at war. I should not have to ask why they want me to fight if I'm loyal to where God put me."

"You'll just blindly obey, like the fifteen-year-old German boys we've captured at the front? Didn't God give you a brain to think with?"

"I wouldn't know about the German boys, sir. And yes, God did give me a brain, and He expects me to use it. I believe I have. He laid the foundation in my time and place of birth and the God-given ability to fight. God doesn't love us any better than He loves those German boys, sir. I'm pretty sure He's not too happy with either side these days. I don't think this war was His idea. But if my country needs me to do my part, I'll do it. I think democracy is the best way to run a country, sir."

"You're willing to give your life for democracy, then?"

"I guess I'd have to think twice about it if I thought this life was all there is, sir, but I know there's more. So I am willing to give that much."

"Democracy. That's the whole of it for you, then?"

"Yes, sir."

The lieutenant stroked his chin. "Some tell me they thought what the Germans did to Belgium was a crime. Some signed up because a U-boat sank the Lusitania. I've even had one fellow tell me he was doing it for his mother. Most mothers want to keep their boys home. Not this one. She wanted a hero, even a dead one. But I don't hear about democracy very often."

The lieutenant stood. He was somewhat taller than Josef, but suddenly he looked more youthful, with his soft beard and narrow jaw line. He returned to the other side of his desk, not taking a seat.

"Do you know what the common complaint is against you, Warner? When I get the people who don't like you pinned down, it seems you try too hard, so they say." The lieutenant leaned forward, hands on the desk, knuckles down. "I'm assigning you as corporal to Sergeant Dack. You convince him you're true blue and that you're not going to bail when the time comes to sink into those front line trenches, and you'll get his job as soon as he's done with it."

Josef stared. Sergeant Dack? His punches might not be the physical sort Birchall threw, but they were every bit as real. Yet, even with Josef's reluctance to work closely with the sergeant, he couldn't deny that he was pleased. Someone had finally put confidence in him.

"Yes, sir," Josef said, standing again at attention. This was a promotion others would have been immediately grateful for, so he added, "Thank you, sir!"

"That's all, Warner. You're dismissed."

Josef turned and headed to the door. Before leaving, he stood beside the threshold at attention again. "If I may inquire about the leaves, sir?"

Everyone knew the lieutenant was the real power behind the lieutenant colonel, whose signature was required for leaves. Papers without Lt. Brooks's approval could get lost on his desk for weeks.

"All local leaves will be approved for this weekend, private. You'll have your stripes before you get to Paris."

"Thank you, sir."

This weekend. Three more days, and he'd see Larisa.

Josef left the office, making a swift path to the mess tent. He hoped he wasn't too late.

Various soldiers, no doubt sated from the heavy food, lingered outside. Josef ignored them, intent on the door.

"Hold it, Warner."

He would have ignored the call if hadn't come from Sergeant Dack. Josef stopped, without turning around.

Dack came up behind Josef. He was shorter, built like a pit bull. With his nearly shaved head and thick neck, he almost looked like one, too.

"Awhile back I put in for a corporal before we get to the front. Who should stop me not a minute ago but Lt. Brooks. He tells me I got my corporal. Then he tells me who it is. So you and I's gonna be workin' together. Just one thing. You keep your holyfalutin' ways to yourself, or I'll make sure you're the easiest target out there for them Jerries. Got that?"

Josef nodded, never looking at the other man. He finally reached the door of the mess hut and to his relief the crew hadn't yet given things over to KP.

CHAPTER *Thirteen*

"How LONG does it take for one train to go down one track?"

Penny had no answer, but Lissa needed to ask someone, just to vent her frustration. She glanced again at the watch from her pocket. The timepiece was not only hopelessly out of style but it was also a man's—her father's. Almost everyone even remotely involved in the war used wristwatches, which were far more practical. She would have to get one, even if the watch in her pocket did offer the comfort of connection to home. But at the moment, the pocket watch was her enemy.

They'd received a letter that Josef and Caleb would arrive today, Friday, for three days of leave. Train schedules being what they were, emphasis was on moving active troops and not soldiers on leave, and the soldiers were hours past their planned arrival time. It might take most of another day to get back to their unit.

But that wasn't the worst of it. Lissa didn't have three days' leave. She had travel orders, which would put her on an outbound train this very night.

She'd only learned that morning that she was to be transferred to the Red Cross Infant Welfare Unit at Evian-les-Bains. It would be a relief to work with children again instead of the devastating wounds of soldiers she saw each day.

But the timing was all wrong. She had to leave for Lake Geneva at seven o'clock. Three hours from now.

Penny looked every bit as fretful as Lissa felt. Seeing her distress mirrored so clearly brought tears to Lissa's eyes. It was all too obvious: Penny didn't think their reunion would happen, either. This hoped for day was just another fatality of this horrid war.

Lissa turned away, swallowing a lump that nearly outsized her throat, closing her eyes to the rush of hot tears. She'd already tried to get her orders changed, to delay her departure one more day, but she'd been refused. The Red Cross, too, was at the mercy of the military trains.

And then she heard it. The clank of iron, the spout of steam, the squeal of brakes pulling back on the wheels to slow the engine around the misty bend.

Lissa grabbed Penny's hand. This was the second train since noon, and they'd met that first train eagerly, only to be let down. Lissa didn't know what she'd do if Josef wasn't on this one.

A huge black engine came into sight, pulling colorless boxcars behind, each marked with the same bold instructions as to how much they could hold: forty men or six horses. Within minutes those boxcars banged open, and men, horses, supplies and the inevitable wounded soon filled the damp outdoor station. Lissa's gaze moved frantically through the horde.

"Josef! Josef!"

She didn't see him. He might not be here, but she called anyway, willing him to appear. If he didn't see her immediately or she couldn't spot him, the sound of her voice would lead him to her.

Penny squeezed her hand, maybe to remind her to keep her head, no matter what happened. Lissa squeezed Penny's hand back, a swell of hope filling her. There were so many men; surely there had been room for just one more?

"Larisa!"

She heard his voice and saw him at the same time, shouldering his way through the crowd of uniformed men. Unbounded joy bubbled up to eliminate every frustrated worry. Then she was in his arms, off the ground, twirled around, his lips pressed to hers.

"Josef, Josef," she laughed and cried his name though the sound was muffled by his mouth, which never left hers.

He held her so tight she could barely breathe, but she wouldn't dream of asking him to loosen his hold.

"What do you say we run away, forget this whole war business, and take our honeymoon right now?"

She laughed. "Sounds wonderful."

Penny cleared her throat but Lissa never took her eyes from Josef's.

"Not too many sights to see around here these days," Penny interrupted, "so you might want to postpone those plans."

"Penny!" Without letting go of Lissa, Josef opened one arm and scooped his sister inside the embrace. "Caleb's right behind me. It's a family reunion."

Though Lissa looked, she didn't see Caleb anywhere nearby. Finally she spotted him, still near the edge of the track, evidently trying with less exuberance to make his way through the chaos.

Penny shouted his name.

He was beside them before long, but Josef didn't break his embrace with Lissa. He just let Penny squirm free.

"Let's get away from here," Josef shouted above the din.

Lissa and the others followed the suggestion. The rain that had been falling intermittently began again. Penny and Lissa had planned to head for a little café two blocks from the station, and Lissa hurriedly led the way. The café was crowded with soldiers on leave: British, American, French, and a few Belgians, but they managed to find a place to sit following Josef's leadership. Soon the four of them were seated and drinking hot coffee around a worn, unadorned table.

"We've been on that train all day," Caleb complained.

Penny laughed. "What do you think this is, Russia? France isn't that big, you know. Why did it take so long?"

"One delay after another. It's a mess," Josef said. "We didn't know until we got here how bad things were. We haven't even seen much outside of a training camp."

Lissa and Penny exchanged glances. They'd had their surprises when they were thrown into duty so many months ago.

Josef must have caught the look. He reached over and grabbed Lissa's hand. "We don't know how bad it's been for you, but we can guess after seeing all the wounded men, day after day."

"Naw," Caleb said in an exaggerated, wry tone, "we don't know about a lot of things, except the mutinies in the French army, the shortages in the English army, and the retreat of the Russian army. Oh, and Germany is basically winning the whole thing."

"Are the Russians really making a separate peace?" Penny asked. "We've heard the rumors."

"Before we left the states it was in all the papers how the Bolsheviks have taken over and are telling the soldiers to come home. They're supposed to shoot their own officers if they try to stop them." Josef stroked her hand with his thumb. "That means the Germans will be free from having to fight on two fronts."

"And they'll be sending everybody this way," Lissa said. Anger and fear mixed with her happiness at having Josef beside her, but she pushed those other feelings away. The sadness, the worry, and the prayer to give those worries to the Lord would all come later. Not much later. She'd have to leave too soon.

"Do you have any clue where they might send your company?" Penny asked.

"That's a whole other mess," Josef said. "The only thing we hear is that Pershing wants us under American command, but the Brits and the Frogs—you know that's what everybody calls the French—want to absorb us into their ranks. I guess I see their point. They've been at this for three years. Why should we come in and think we can do better?"

"I don't want to fight under anybody but an American," Caleb said.

"A couple of privates don't have a vote, so we'll just do as told."

"Well, one private, anyway," Caleb said, looking at Josef.

"What does that mean?" Lissa asked.

Josef squeezed her hand. "I made corporal. Doesn't mean much yet, I don't even have my stripes. But it's in the works."

"Oh, Josef." She was dismayed by her own tone, which showed her disappointment.

"Isn't this where you're supposed to be proud of me?"

She put on a smile. "Yes it is. I should say congratulations are in order."

"Well, well," said Penny, looking at Josef. "Not even out of training camp and already rising in the ranks."

"You know what they say. Extraordinary times make for extraordinary opportunity. It's just a temporary position, while the war lasts. Once this thing's over and we're back home, I'll go back to being a plain old private for the duration of my two-year stint."

"Think it'll be over in two years?" Caleb asked.

"Now that we're in it, are you kidding? We'll beat 'em any day now."

Everybody laughed, even Lissa, who was having a hard time adjusting to Josef rising in rank, even to corporal. She had watched too many officers die. With the responsibility came greater risk. There seemed to be only one end to greater risk.

"I thought maybe you were getting special treatment of a different kind," Lissa said. "When did you find out you were being considered as corporal?"

"Just a few days ago."

Caleb leaned forward. "Can I say something about that special treatment you mentioned, Liss? Josef has been nothing but a rock. I wish I had half his guts, but I talk better than I act. I'm ashamed of it, but I haven't even stood up for my faith like Josef has. You can be proud of him. I am."

Josef put a hand on Caleb's shoulder. "Thanks, Caleb, that means a lot to me."

"Well, now is as good a time as any to bring up the bad news, Liss," said Penny.

Lissa frowned. She didn't want to spoil a second of their time together, but Penny was right. They had a little over a couple of hours left, when Josef was expecting an entire day.

"What bad news?"

"I'm being transferred."

Josef grabbed Lissa's hand. "Where? Not closer... not to a *field* hospital."

She quickly shook her head. "No, no. Actually, I'm going to one of the children's hospitals. It seems they've waded through all the paperwork of those of us who've been here a while. They decided they could use my experience with kids. Between the villages who've been without a doctor since

'14 and all the refugees and orphans, the children are in a crisis. Nobody back home ever hears about it."

"I'm sure the kids are kept well behind the lines. You'll be safe. Where's the bad news in that?"

She pressed her hand into his. "I leave tonight. At seven o'clock, to be exact."

"What? Can they do that, just ship you off when you have leave?"

"They already have."

Josef looked so forlorn she wanted to put her arms around him. Then he grabbed both her hands in his. "God must have something else planned for us instead of spending the next twenty-four hours together. Maybe it's best."

She couldn't believe his words. "Best?"

"*Safer* might be a better word—for our own good."

She knew then what he meant. They had been vulnerable in New York, and it would be worse here, so much farther from home with so much danger in every direction. He was right. But her heart registered only disappointment. He didn't let go of her hands, and even though Penny and Caleb still shared the table, it was as if they were alone. Lissa didn't take her eyes from Josef's.

"We should be grateful the Lord is getting you away from all this."

She nodded. The cries, the smells, the blood, the amputations, disease, disfigurements, death. Sometimes she thought she would rather die herself than watch one more man breathe his last.

"Are you sorry you came?" Josef asked softly.

In spite of it all, the truth was easy. "No. I've never felt so . . . useful. I just hope we won't be sorry that *you* came."

CHAPTER *Fourteen*

SOMEWHERE ON THE SOMNE RIVER, MARCH 19, 1918

"PRESS ON!"

"Over there!"

Shouts and cries rang in French and English, muffled between blasts. Men fell around Josef like turkeys at a shoot. The earth rumbled then burst open in smoky geysers of dirt. Light bursts sent shrapnel cascading onto the exposed troops.

Josef jumped into a shell hole and looked for targets. From here he had a better view of the ground between him and the Germans, who were coming his way. Limbless trees, stripped bare even of bark, rose like ghostly fingers that beckoned to the living things that were about to lose their lives. Mud and blood and something putrid stung at his nostrils. At least the Germans hadn't used poison gas yet during this battle.

Then he placed the odor: burning flesh. He saw flame throwers farther down the line.

"There!"

Suddenly a man landed beside him. Josef didn't look to see who it was, just that the other soldier's gun was pointed the same direction as his, at a machine gun nest on the far side of the German trench.

Josef shot at one shape and then another, and both went down in quick succession. He was about to aim at a third when the helmeted head went down. He glanced over for the first time and saw Sergeant Dack next to him, taking aim again.

"Got to get closer," Josef called.

Dack made his way out of the shell hole beside Josef, and the two of them scurried belly down to another hole, this one filled with mud from last night's sleety rain. It was little different from the comforts of the trench they'd left behind.

Between them they cleared another nest.

In a lull, Josef sank down, and Dack did the same. "I been followin' you, mister. You've done good," Dack said.

Another blast blotted out whatever else he might have said, and both men swiveled back, guns pointed.

"Stick with me, Joe," Dack called. "There's another nest about twenty feet that way."

Josef scrambled to his heels to follow when something else caught his eye—a still figure not far away, face down in the mud. Something was familiar about the color of the hair a helmet had once covered.

"Hey, Sarge; it's Brooks."

Without waiting for a reply Josef held his gun in one hand and bellied his way toward the fallen officer. He couldn't see any blood, but Brooks was so covered in muck that even if he'd been bathed in red, Josef couldn't tell. He looked for a sign of breath, but in the shell wind and ruckus he couldn't feel a thing.

Dack was not with Josef any more, he was in the next shell hole, covering Josef. Whether Brooks was breathing or not, Josef knew what he had to do.

There was no easy way to get the officer to safety. Josef couldn't stand up. He flipped his gun over his shoulder, grabbed the prostrate man by the arm and leg, and heaved him onto his back. He crawled, dragging the lieutenant from the cover of one shell hole to another. Bullets whizzed by, the ground beneath him thumped like an underground heartbeat while men nearby were pitched up then tumbled to the ground at the sound of exploding shellfire.

Fifty feet turned to forty, then thirty, twenty. Ten. He heard the whine of more bullets, but Josef kept going to the last foot.

"Medic! Brooks is hit. Medic!" He heard the cry, desperate like a boy's, and it was coming from his own mouth. In a moment someone was there. Charlie, the medic. Charlie. From Anaheim where the sun always shines.

Just as Charlie bent over Brooks, Josef leaped back over the top. Dack was waiting for him, and they had another nest to clear.

SOMEWHERE IN FRANCE, MARCH 22, 1918

Dearest Larisa Rose,

> *We had what everybody's calling our "baptism of fire" for the past two days. It beat the boredom of sitting in wet trenches, but I can't say I want to go over the top again any time soon. Caleb and I are both okay. Not a scratch. We have four days off before we go back for another four, but the guns never stop even if we do.*

> *Some of the Brits said we might get lucky enough to get a "bon blighty" next time, a wound that's enough to get us out of the trenches but one that won't change our future, if you know what I mean. So here we are, not exactly seasoned, but not blissfully green any more, either. We have to go back, though. Part of me is downright dizzy to be alive. Another part of me never wants to go back.*

> *Can't say more, it would just get censored anyway. The nice thing is that Sarge is starting to trust me. He's a good guy.*

> *The Lord is with us, and He always will be. He's going to see us home, Larisa. I'm sure of that. If you could see how many bullets we dodged, you'd believe it, too.*

> *Anyway, now that we've proven ourselves, so to speak, they'll probably be using us more.*

> *Love,*
>
> *Josef*

A seven-year-old girl lay dying on a narrow cot. Her dark hair took up far more space on the pillow than her tiny face. She couldn't cough any more. The disease had sucked the strength from her lungs. Only spots of blood colored that bed, since her pale skin blended starkly with the white of the pillow.

Lissa saw it too many times. Some of the children came to the chateau hospital without any symptoms, on orders of their caregivers or as part of a routine transport check. "Go and get your lungs looked at," the children were told. "The radiograph will tell if you need rest or not."

And so they would come, and a nurse at the chateau took a picture of their lungs, saw the lesions, and had an idea of what would come: fever, fatigue, night sweats, chest pain, coughing up blood, and then death.

They lost dozens a day to tuberculosis, until the chateau looked more like a charnel house than a once-upon-a-time scene of elaborate parties. Within its gilt walls, children came to die. If it weren't for the nurses, they would have died alone.

EVIAN-LES-BAINS, APRIL 5, 1918

Dear Josef,

Why, oh, why, did I think this assignment would be easier? It's so much worse. I cannot even describe the pain I see daily. Mostly it's tuberculosis, but we see tetanus and more and more influenza, the same we've been seeing from the trenches.

But these are just little ones, Josef, who trusted their parents' generation for something so simple as a chance to grow up.

I've never longed for home so badly, and yet I couldn't let the children down by leaving. What right has anyone to a content, happy life when there is so much suffering?

Throngs of refugees are leaving Paris because the Germans are getting closer. Their big guns extend their dreadful touch farther every day. Many of those fleeing have come to us. We take what patients we can, but we have no room for more. I don't know what happens to those we send away. Perhaps I don't want to know.

I suppose I should find it incredible that someone lies in hiding out there, concealed in the bushes, with only one thing on his mind: to kill me. Death is such a permanent, personal attack. Is it the only solution to ending this?

Is war ever right, Josef? Is this one?

Love,

Larisa Rose

"You all done pretty good out there these past weeks." Dack spoke to six men nearby, but Josef felt the sergeant's eyes on him. They huddled in a dugout of earth shored up with wood planks like the rest of the ugly trench work marring France. Even as Dack spoke, sand and dirt showered them now and then after the pound of cannon sounded above. "You're some shot out there, Joe."

He waited for Dack's usual punch line that would negate the compliment, but one didn't come. Such digs had grown sparse.

They sat on wooden benches, six of them in the hovel. "You're all good—even our young'n Caleb over there." Dack paused, rubbing a hand over his chubby, lined face.

"Look here, fellas. I ain't gonna lie to you. This here's a suicide mission, plain and simple. Just thought I'd tell ya so you wouldn't think otherwise. They's callin' us to make enough ruckus to bring the guns pointin' our way. Then some more experienced Brit yahoos down the way can come chargin' across and do the routing.

"It ain't even like we's gonna get the glory for this. But let me tell you, them guys ain't gonna get across without us cannon fodder neither. So it's a go. I chose the lot of you 'cause I'd like a chance at makin' it back. Only way that'll happen is with steady boys who can lay down good fire. You guys are the best around.

"One more thing. I didn't know 'til the other day that two of you is brothers. I don't like sendin' brothers out, in fact there might be a regulation against it. If there ain't there probably should be. It's up to you guys, but I'd shore like both of you coverin' my back side."

Neither Josef nor Caleb said anything, just nodded. Josef looked at the other dirty faces. Caleb, Birchall, Dack, and three other guys he'd known a few months. To the percentage of his life he remembered, it might as well have been forever.

Caleb sat beside Josef, and from the look on his face, Josef wondered if he felt more excitement than fear. The boy was uncharacteristically quiet, but the light was in his eye. He'd been complaining about being under British command, and here was their chance. The Yanks get to go out and divert fire.

"We're gonna need luck on our side in about five minutes," Dack said, cocking his head to the doorway, "right after we go out there." His gaze went to Josef's. "You got anything you want to say?"

Josef couldn't hold back a smile, and it made a dent in the fear stuck to the pit of his belly. "Luck, Sarge? If I thought some mindless thing like luck was going to decide my future, I wouldn't go."

From Dack's satisfied nod, Josef knew that was the kind of remark he'd been expected to make. Nothing like a battlefield to welcome any reference to God, even an indirect one.

"Okay then, Joe. You say a prayer and we'll be on our way."

. . . Or a direct one.

Not even Birchall scowled. Josef prayed what he'd prayed every time he woke up in these trenches, a sacred rhythm of praise followed by a request for protection and guidance for every step.

When he ended the prayer, he looked at Dack.

"We can do this, Sarge."

"Then let's go."

Less than a half hour later Josef's words haunted him.

It should take longer than twenty-four minutes to change somebody's life.

Thoughts were sporadic. Who could think, with the pounding, pounding noise blasting into his brain. Even without shrapnel embedded in it, the body gets to the point that nothing seems to function, not the brain or the heart or even the kidneys.

Two hundred yards from the relative safety of the crumbling dugout, Josef crouched and fired, hobbled forward, crouched and fired again. A blizzard of cannon and machine fire sounded behind them as promised. It was the promised cover for them to cross no man's land.

He saw Beckmann's body thrown like a toy and split in two. It wasn't like he was a human with a mother waiting for him, two sisters who baked enough cookies for him to share with his platoon, and a father who prayed for his safe return.

Murdock was next. He was tossed into the air like on the wind of an invisible giant's breath, and he came back down to earth whimpering, writhing, and legless. Josef was behind him and paused, despite the screaming order from Dack to keep going. Before Josef took two steps, Murdock was still.

"Joe."

It was Caleb's voice, right at his elbow as they charged for the next cover. "I . . . gotta tell you something." He stopped yelling, or maybe it was just the shell exploding nearby that robbed his voice of sound.

Josef didn't want to hear what Caleb had to say, not with so much fear on his brother's face. "Tell me when we get back, Caleb."

His eyes widened, the whites bigger than their blue centers. "No, we're not gonna make it."

Josef stopped so abruptly Caleb rammed into his back, and the two flopped sideways into the pit of a shell hole. Josef let his gun slip from his hand and grabbed the strap of Caleb's kit strapped across his chest. That kit held everything they would need to get through a few days if they became separated from their company: a couple of hundred rounds of ammo, two grenades, a rifle grenade, canteen, packet of gum, two iron rations, and two slabs of chocolate. He intended them to eat that chocolate when this was over.

"We're gonna make it, Caleb! Now get behind me and shoot at anything that gets in our way."

He didn't give Caleb a chance to argue. He jumped out of the shell hole. Moments after Caleb leaped out a ball hit the spot they'd vacated. Josef pounced on Caleb, but they were under the arc of the blast and shrapnel sailed harmlessly beyond them. The concussion was another thing. Josef's ears rang and he could hear nothing else.

But he tramped forward anyway, pulling Caleb behind until he took up the leapfrog over mounds of earth and fallen trees through the mortar fire and blasts. Before long the fire sailed farther away; Josef couldn't hear a thing, but the rumbling beneath him wasn't so strong. They came to the German barbed wires and cut through. By now it was darker than when they'd set out. It was a strange darkness. Not so much black as an eerie gray-white wall of fog. Josef felt both deaf and blind now.

He knew then the fire would cease before long. Who could see friend or foe in this? But they had to press on, and Josef prayed for something other than the sound of ringing in his ears. The tone was maddening, closing in on him like bells stuck inside his ears. He shook his head again and again, but it did no good.

Josef scanned the area in front of him but could see no farther than a few feet. Dack, Birchall, Corcoran—nowhere to be seen.

He prayed he was headed in the same direction they went, even as the earth soon ceased trembling from the blasts. No sense wasting fire power if the target couldn't be seen. He wished again that he could hear. The heavy artillery might be gone, but that didn't mean gunfire was lessening. He prayed it was.

Making sure Caleb was still behind him, Josef stopped every few feet. His little brother must be deaf too, since every now and then he reached out to touch a boot or limb instead of trying to speak.

They snaked their way forward. The ringing in Josef's ears was finally easing. He could hear the rustling beneath his chest and limbs again, but little else. The gunfire had ceased altogether.

But the fog was still heavy. He saw nothing, but the land had changed, sloping upward beneath his crawl. Upward, through the fog. He wished he had the guts to stand and get his bearings. He knew they were behind enemy lines, but he didn't know where or how to get back.

"Caleb, can you hear me?" he whispered.

Though he'd heard his own question, he heard nothing from Caleb. Josef could see almost nothing through the haze, but he felt Caleb's presence nearby. He felt until he found his brother, then groped for his face and turned his chin toward him.

"Caleb. Can you hear me?"

Caleb opened his mouth, but no words came out. Instead, horror widened his eyes as he looked over Josef's shoulder.

"Ach, *mein freund*, we can all hear you."

CHAPTER *Fifteen*

VIRGINIA, JUNE 3, 1918

"MIND IF I come in?"

Hank eyed the unwelcome face of the young federal agent before opening the door wider. He was thankful his years as an investigator had taught him to keep his thoughts and sudden fears a secret. There was no way this young whippersnapper was going to figure out he was the last person Hank wanted around.

"I brought you this, from the trial."

It was a file Hank had handed over when he'd been subpoenaed for Otto's trial, months ago, containing all of the notes he'd taken along the way following Josef's whereabouts. There were observations and records of expenses and payments. It looked authentic enough, Hank had made sure of that. But some things had been removed, and it contained only a skeleton of what he knew. That was something else the young agent wouldn't find out.

"Thought you might like to know the old man's health has taken a turn for the worse in the past few weeks. He's in the sick ward at the prison. They're pretty sure he won't live out the sentence."

Any glib response fled from Hank's brain. Even the grave news the agent brought about Otto faded from importance. Just behind the agent was a picture, the only picture Hank had of Josef. It was Addie Parker's photograph of Josef and Lissa together, smiling on the front porch of this very house.

Hank snapped his gaze away.

"Yes, well, thank you for the file and for the information, but as I made clear during the trial, Otto von Woerner is not a personal friend." He steered the agent back toward the door with a light hand to the man's shoulder. "I'm sorry to hear he's sick, but I have no plan to visit him."

The agent laughed. "Didn't think you would, considering he almost got you into a mess of trouble."

Hank wanted to dispute that, but more than that he wanted the agent to leave.

He put a hand on the doorknob. "Thank you for the file, Mr. Donahue. You could have sent it in the mail, but thank you for delivering it."

The agent appeared in no hurry to leave. He glanced over his shoulder and Hank had to squelch an urge to propel the man out the door.

"You here all by yourself today, Mr. Tanner? Last time I was here I think you said your son was home. He here today?"

"No, Mr. Donahue. He's in France."

"France, eh? Fightin' the Jerries?"

"Yes, that's right."

He almost had him out the door, it was swung wide in anticipation of the exit.

"Hank?"

Both men turned to the sound of Jaylene's voice.

"I'll be right there," said Hank, hoping that was the extent of the interruption.

"I didn't know you had company," said his wife pleasantly.

"Just a delivery," Hank said.

But to his profound dismay Agent Donahue turned to Hank's wife, a cordial smile on his young face.

"Ah, you must be Mrs. Tanner." He turned and took two steps farther inside the home and extended his hand. "I'm Special Agent Donahue, from the Bureau of Investigation."

"Oh? And a delivery brings you all the way from Washington, Mr. Donahue?"

"The case is closed, and I'm behind in cleaning out the files. Since your husband helped in the conviction, I thought bringing back his property was the least I could do."

"A shame you made the trip all the way out here, Mr. Donahue," she went on, so friendly. Hank wished he could whisk her from the room without the action bringing attention. "My husband is often in the city. It would have been easier for you to bring it to him there."

"Oh, it's no trouble, ma'am. No trouble at all."

While Donahue spoke, Hank stepped behind him, placing his body between the agent and the framed picture on the hall table. He caught his wife's eye at the same time. She'd read enough of his silent language to sense something was wrong.

"Your husband says you have a son at the front," Donahue said, still amicable. "Must be hard on you, ma'am."

"We trust the Lord to keep him safe. Both of them."

Hank's jaw dropped and he stared at her so hard she obeyed his wordless will. She looked at him, and he saw a little of her color drain away.

"Both, ma'am?"

When she looked back at the agent she smiled, albeit rather tremulously. "Our daughter is there as well, with the Red Cross."

"Ah," he said. "My, you certainly represent the best of our country, then, don't you? Pitching in to get the job done?"

"Well," said Hank, clearing his throat to attract attention back toward the door, "thank you again, Agent Donahue, for the file."

The young man took another step closer, but Hank still wasn't breathing. He wouldn't take another breath until this man was out the door.

And in a moment, he was. With a tip of his hat as he replaced it on his head, the agent finally stepped outside. Hank closed the door, fighting the urge to slam and lock it.

"Hank, what was all that about?"

Hank didn't answer, just raised a finger to his lips. He wanted to be sure the agent was gone before they spoke.

He didn't risk going to the window, afraid he might be spotted. But he didn't hear the sound of a motor yet.

Then he heard something else, the sound of another knock at the door.

"Get rid of the picture," Hank whispered, and Jaylene jumped to do his bidding.

Hank opened the door again, but this time rather than letting the agent back inside, Hank stepped out onto the porch. It was early June, but the air outside was unusually warm, hotter than inside. Jaylene opened the house every morning to let in any breeze, closing it again once the sun was high and the air still.

"Just one more question I forgot, Mr. Tanner."

Hank folded his arms in front of his chest.

"I stopped in town before I came here," he said, his tone still friendly. "You do have lots of friends, Mr. Tanner. Oh, yes. I spoke to a Mr. Lindstrom at the market. He knows you, that's for sure. He told me how proud folks are that you have a daughter and two boys over there."

Jaylene appeared at the door, obviously having hidden the picture. Hank had a sinking feeling it didn't matter, after all.

"Beg your pardon, ma'am," said Donahue, tipping his hat toward Jaylene, "but I heard something in town I need to verify. Your husband has two sons?"

Hank answered, because he knew he had no choice. "That's right."

"Odd thing is, one goes by the name of Josef Warner?" He turned to Hank again. "That's W-A-R-N-E-R, I'm told. Not W-O-E-R-N-E-R."

"Yes, that's right."

"Now, I don't mean to bring up personal matters, sir," he said. "But since the whole town knows about the son with the different last name, I was wondering if you might tell me where he is right now?"

"France."

"In France," he repeated, letting out a slow breath. "Fighting—with the Americans?"

"That's right."

Then he fished something from his breast pocket. "This is a picture I'd like to have you look at, Mr. Tanner. Take your time, and tell me if you recognize this man."

Hank knew who'd be portrayed before glancing down. A sense of calm grew over him that he could finally drop the charade, even as the rest of him knew that something awful was going to happen. But he had another thought that also brought calm: "I am sovereign, Hank. I am."

"It isn't a clear picture."

"Hmm," said Donahue, looking at the picture as well now, but still holding it before Hank's face. It was indeed Josef, taken in front of a munitions plant when he was probably a college student. He was protesting arms sales to other countries eager to build up their arsenals. It occurred to Hank that if anyone had listened to the protesters and stopped selling bigger armaments, the whole war might never have begun.

"I showed this picture to Mr. Lindstrom. He thought it looked just like your son. Funny how their names are almost the same, too, isn't it? Josef von Woerner—Josef Warner? Pronounced the same, spelled different, after you drop the fancy *von*, of course."

Hank noticed another car coming up the drive, another black lizzie. Federal reinforcements?

"Why don't you get to the point, Mr. Donahue."

Agent Donahue tucked the picture back into his pocket.

"You're under arrest, Mr. Tanner, for aiding and abetting a criminal. The same crime that got good old Otto two years and one hefty fine."

Hank wanted to comfort Jaylene, who'd gasped at the first few words Mr. Donahue uttered. But Hank didn't move. Instead, he watched the car pull to a stop just beneath his porch, and wondered why he hadn't recognized Frank McPhearson's tin lizzie. Not reinforcements at all.

"Got a telegram for you, Hank," he said in his slow drawl, obviously oblivious to the drama being played on the porch. Perhaps Hank's face was calm, he'd willed it so and hoped, for Jaylene's sake, that he'd succeeded. But Jaylene was crying. Didn't Frank see that?

"Gee, I'm sorry, Jaylene," said Frank as he neared and looked at Jaylene's distraught face. "How'd you know? Did Martha call ahead? I told her this was official business, and she don't have the right to warn people. They get to read the telegram first, that's the rule."

Confused, Hank accepted the telegram as Jaylene stepped outside.

Regret to inform you, your son, Caleb Tanner, is missing, believed killed in action. Details to follow from State Department.

There was no other information. He might have pulled it close to his chest so Jaylene couldn't read the words, but it was too late. Hank let the paper fly just in time to catch his wife before she fell in a faint toward the hard wood of the porch.

Lissa did what she did every morning, splashed her face with water, dressed—since today she wasn't already wearing the clothes she'd collapsed in the night before—then left her room for the wards. She had been moved to yet another children's hospital, this one in Lyon. It had once been a German consulate, an elaborately ornate mansion boasting a central heating system that hadn't worked when they'd first moved in. They'd finally learned a zealous caretaker had cemented all the chimneys shut when the Germans evacuated so the place would be useless to the Allies. The worst of it was that the loyal caretaker had been French.

Now the suite in which the German emperor once slept was an operating room, the library a recovery room, the mistress' boudoir a nurse's dressing station, and the parlors and dining room wards lined with narrow cots.

On her way to the wards, Lissa always stopped at the front hall. It was a huge, inviting area, with beveled, wood paneled walls and arched doorways, mullioned windows and curved handrails along either side of a wide oak staircase. It was the only place in the mansion not crowded with beds, supplies, or equipment since it was reserved for sudden influxes of sick or wounded when time was needed to sort them out and find them places.

But Lissa didn't go there for the freedom of space or the beauty of the entryway. She went to the table strewn with lists—lists of missing, lists of wounded, or lists of dead. It was part of her daily ritual, an integral part of her most fervent prayer time.

She always started with the killed in action list. Better to get that one over with first, with its never ending additions. She might have felt something when she read the new names except that she'd long since grown desensitized. She couldn't help it. If she'd imagined herself a year ago looking at such lists with indifference, even with only strangers' names recorded, she'd have been shocked at her own callousness.

She thanked God another day that Josef's name was not there.

She heard a ruckus outside and peered through the multi-paned window. Another group of children was arriving, probably evacuated from an orphanage or another hospital, making room for more soldiers. She should go out and assist.

Quickly she scanned the other two American lists and breathed easier when she found no familiar names. She started to turn away when another sheet, half tucked beneath the ones she'd scanned, caught her eye. "Missing Believed Dead," a British list. As the sounds outside pulled at her, she allowed herself just a glance at the bottom of the alphabetized roster.

Caleb Tanner.

Josef Warner.

Lissa stared. Her feet, which had been about to take her outside, locked solidly into place, fixing her to the spot. Her breathing stopped then resumed in short, shallow, rapid increments, her heartbeat seemed to halt and race at a wild rate all at once. She stared at those names, unbelieving, confused, then looked at the heading again: "British: Missing Believed Dead."

Missing Believed Dead. She read it over and over until the words blurred.

A mistake—it had to be. Josef and Caleb weren't British. Why would their names be on a British list?

Even as she tried to convince herself that it must be a mistake, she knew that many American soldiers still fought under English and French commands. It was the bane of every American commander, that they were not allowed to field their own independent army.

"Donner un coup de main, n'est-ce pas?"

Lissa heard the nun behind her. Sister Mary Michel was one of the oldest nuns at the hospital, yet she moved among the quickest. She was already at the door. It registered in Lissa's mind that she must lend a hand as the sister had asked, yet she could not move. She couldn't even move her gaze from the page.

"Lissa? Est-ce que tout va trés bien?"

The sister turned from the door and took a few, slower steps closer. Sister Mary Michel was not tall, reaching just above five feet, and from Lissa's peripheral gaze she saw the nun's face at just about the height of the page in her hand, the page that shook as if in a storm.

Gently, the sister pried the paper from Lissa's fingers. "Lissa, something is wrong, yes?"

Lissa shook her head. "No, it's a mistake. Just a mistake." She pointed to the names. "You see? There are my friends' names, but on a British list. They aren't British." She turned back and clutched one of the other pages. "These are the American lists, and their names aren't on any of those pages. So, it's a mistake, you see?"

Sister Mary Michel's strong, wrinkled hands covered Lissa's. The nun pressed tight, even as such contact crimped the page in Lissa's grip. She took the sheet from Lissa and laid it back among the others, still holding one of Lissa's hands.

"Come with me." She led Lissa away from the hall.

They went to what had been a small office, now a supply room. It was dismally void of supplies needed for a hospital of over one hundred beds, so there was plenty of room in the center for the two of them to stand.

"Lissa, I say to you as to others in *détresse* ... distress. You pray now, then you work. *Le travail sera bon pour vous, garder votre ésprit occupé. N'est-ce pas, Lissa?* Work will ease your mind. It is the only way."

But Lissa still shook her head. "No, Sister Mary Michel. I'm all right. It's all a mistake."

The sister stared at her with ancient eyes of compassion, eyes that understood grief.

"We need you, Lissa. The children, yes?"

Lissa stood still, unable to wrest her gaze from the older woman's. For a moment she felt the sister's strength and calm, her singleness of purpose. Sister Mary Michel wouldn't let anything stand in the way of what needed to be done.

Lissa, too, knew what needed to be done. She saw the children every day, more of them all the time. They weren't just short on supplies, they were short on nurses as well. Too many demands of the war to spare the numbers needed. Lissa couldn't shirk her duties just because her life went upside down.

She wanted to run very fast, very far—all the way home. She wanted to find Josef there, the way it used to be. And Caleb. She wanted to see Josef's smile, have him hold her in his arms. How she wished to be home. She wanted to feel her mother's arms around her and hear her say everything was all right, that she didn't need to feel this pain and grief threatening to overcome her. Everything was all right because Josef and Caleb were all right. They were home, waiting for her.

Instead, she stared into the beseeching eyes of Sister Mary Michel. The children needed her.

"I go now," said the sister, heading to the door. Before opening it, she said, "It is your choice how you meet grief. We all have our own way."

Lissa watched her go. With the Sister's steady gaze went Lissa's precarious calm. A swell of panic followed a wave of fear. Then came a surge of chaos. So fierce came each emotion that they grasped her body like some war germ that attacked invisibly but rendered her helpless.

The children. The children need me. God, oh, God, how can I help anyone? How can I think clearly enough to be of any good to anyone?

Work would give strength, according to the nun.

But how? How do I move from one moment to the next, without breaking?

Lissa heard the words almost audibly: "Work and you will find the strength. I am with you." Rather than finding comfort, something else burst deep within. She fell against the door of the little room, collapsing to the floor with her head cradled in her arms.

No, I can't feel You. I can't see You. How can You be here? How can You be here, if You let Josef die? Why did You bring him to me, only to take him away? I can't trust You!

"Be still and know that I am God."

How can I be still? How can I do nothing? I have to look for him, I have to know what's happened. I'll go to every military power until I find someone to help me find him.

"Trust in the Lord your God, and lean not on your own understanding."

Tears ran hot down her cheeks, and she let them flow without trying to curb them. God would catch them, she'd been taught as a child. He put them in a bottle. She felt as if she'd done nothing but cry since she came to France—cry for the soldiers, cry for the children, and now cry for Caleb and Josef. How full must her bottle become?

CHAPTER *Sixteen*

Mary Downing added another bundle of personal belongings to a growing stack in the sidecar that had been modified to fit her Henderson motorcycle. Each satchel represented some aspect of a soldier's life: a bundle of letters, identification tags, eyeglasses, personal New Testaments from the Pocket Testament League. All things no longer needed by the missing, presumed dead, soldier lost to no man's land.

She drove down the rutted roads that were, thankfully, dry today. On many days in the spring and fall, the roads were nearly impassable to all but cycles like hers that could skirt the road altogether. So Mary drove fast, pretending to herself she was an ambulance driver. She could have volunteered for that duty, but going from hospital to hospital to gather information about missing soldiers was as close as she wanted to get to all that blood, not to mention her duties as a searcher kept her well behind the lines. Ambulance drivers sometimes penetrated far into danger zones. Mary was ashamed to admit that she just didn't have the guts to go there. Not yet anyway. Perhaps she hadn't mustered enough anger against the Germans yet.

Today's destination was another hospital. She would finally give up that one bundle, the one she'd considered some kind of companion. She'd even found herself talking to it a couple times, or to the letter inside the bundle.

She was really talking to a man no longer alive, the author of that letter. It wasn't a long letter, but it was memorable. Ever since she'd read it a month ago she couldn't quite let it go. That was why she had mixed feelings about finally delivering it today. But a month to a waiting loved one was probably a lifetime. Lyon was farther south than she normally ran, and there were lots of other bundles in her sidecar that needed tending. So it wasn't only her reluctance to part with this particular bag that made her slow to deliver it.

She glanced down at the sack again. It still showed dirt from the trenches, despite the surprisingly clean contents. "Today, Josef. Your letter will reach her today at last."

Pulling to a stop before what had once been a German consulate, she suddenly felt sorry it had taken her so long.

"I'm looking for Nurse Larisa Rose Parker," said Mary to the first person she met. Mary spoke French, but the nurse didn't seem to understand, except perhaps for the name. Mary tried English.

"Oh, sure, Lissa's inside. Try upstairs in the infant ward."

Mary entered the consulate-turned-hospital, noticing the buzz of activity, more so than in most hospitals she visited. The supply boxes stacked by the door, what few there were, seemed to indicate an evacuation. Mary felt her jaw harden. Another civilian hospital being made available for soldiers? Would it never end? Where were all these children supposed to go?

But she said nothing of her thoughts, asking the first nurse she saw to point out her target.

Larisa Rose was every bit as striking as Mary expected. Large, almond shaped, golden brown eyes sparkled at the baby in her arms. The accompanying smile that dominated the entire lower half of her face was infectious. She was tall and perhaps a bit thin, but everybody in all of Europe was thinner these days. The top of her head was covered by the traditional white cap, but from what Mary could see, Larisa Rose's hair matched the color of her eyes.

Yes, I can see why you loved her, Josef. She can still smile.

So many in France had forgotten how—including Mary herself.

"Larisa Rose Parker?"

Startled seemed too mild a word to describe the look on the other woman's face. She jerked her head up, and her face wore a look of fear.

"That's my name," she said. "How did you know?"

"May we talk a moment?"

She had gone pale, and Mary felt sorry for the baby who was suddenly no longer the object of attention as she was laid back in the crib.

Without a word, the woman called Larisa Rose led the way to a balcony off the room that must have once been a lavish bed suite. She closed the tall glass doors behind them, and they stood outside in the warm June air.

Mary held up her sack. It felt like hers rather than Josef's, so long had she been carrying it. Suddenly it looked small, inadequate to represent the man.

"My name is Mary Downing. I'm with the Searchers Unit of the Red Cross. I brought this to you."

"For me? What is it?"

She must have an idea already. She's going more pale.

"It's a few personal belongings of Josef Warner. Normally we'd send them to family, but there was a letter with your name and unit on it, so I was given permission to show the lot of it to you the next time I came this way. It's not much, just some socks and a small Bible, some paper and a clean uniform—and the letter."

"Letter?"

Mary heard the tremor in Larisa's voice and nodded. Because the woman looked incapable of movement, Mary withdrew it from the sack and held it out. Still, Larisa looked as though she couldn't move.

"Would you like me to read it to you?"

"No. I'll read it."

Mary doubted the woman could, with her eyes suddenly tearing. But Larisa Rose wiped at her eyes and turned away, unfolding the thin sheet. It was the kind of paper mothers sent with care packages.

Mary knew what it said. She remembered the words but didn't want to read them again. She envied the kind of love these two shared, but she wasn't going to stoop to blatant vicarious living.

April 2, 1918

Dearest Larisa Rose,

> *I think I know a little more about why some of the patients*
> *you saw at your first assignment ended up as they did, the ones*

you called shell-shocked. Bullets fall on us constantly, like a never-ending sport. All one has to do is stand above the trench for a sniper to end your life.

My only link to sanity is when I think of you. I'm convinced God brought you into my life to keep me alive. Surely if a German hasn't gotten me by now through some rash or unwise move of my own, I'd have been driven insane by the lonely helplessness all around me. I'd flee to no man's land for release. But instead, through God's grace, I flee to you.

I just got word that Lt. Brooks died today. I tried to save him, did I tell you?

Love,
Josef

Though Larisa had turned away, Mary could see her shoulders shake as she read. Who wouldn't cry? He'd obviously loved her, and Mary could see that the feeling was mutual. Pity and sorrow filled her, along with a burst of real anger at this awful war. Maybe she'd end up an ambulance driver after all.

Then Larisa squared her shoulders and sucked in a deep breath of air. When she turned back to Mary, her eyes were streaked with red, but she had a look that had nothing to do with grief. It was a sort of desperation. Mary guessed that the letter had sent her beyond grief.

"Where did you say you were from?"

"The Searchers Unit."

"What's your job, exactly?"

Mary was fascinated that the sadness seemed to have passed, pushed out by what she'd thought was desperation. Now she saw that it was hope.

"Mostly we look for information for the families of those who are missing in action."

"Do you know anything more about Josef Warner's whereabouts, then? Do you have information for me?"

Apprehension grew in Mary. "I can't tell you the details of his last mission. They never tell me that. I do know that seven men went on a mission, and they believe none survived. One body was found close to their return spot, but the rest had been headed over the German line. Their bodies couldn't be recovered."

"Not if they were taken prisoner," Lissa said quietly. Mary heard absolute conviction in the woman's voice. So, that's what she thought.

"It's possible," Mary said slowly, comfortingly, though she didn't believe it herself. It was what Larisa wanted to hear. Germans didn't take a lot of prisoners, especially when the highest ranking soldier in the unit was a sergeant who could yield little information if interrogated.

More to the point, if they were prisoners, the Red Cross would have been given a record of it from the Germans running the prison camp.

"Larisa, I want you to know the truth. The Germans give us cards through channels with the names of those captured. We should know if he's a POW. He would have been listed as taken. On the lists I've seen, there are no names of prisoners matching the names of those from that mission."

The golden brown-flecked eyes looked at Mary steadily, and she saw that same look still there, only now edged with a determination so strong it was as if by pure will this woman would get others to believe as she did.

"Until I see Josef's body, or until somebody tells me they've seen it, lifeless, with his spirit gone from this earth, and can tell me where he's buried, I won't believe it. He's not dead. I would know if he was."

Then she fished in a pocket of the red dress beneath her white apron, no longer desperate but now rather giddy. "Do you know, your being here, your position, it's just possible God has a new assignment for you. To look for him."

Mary stood still. Grief sometimes did strange things to people.

"I can't very well if he's a prisoner of war, now can I?"

"Well, of course that's just one scenario. Here's another. Josef was wounded, someone on this side of the line picked him up and brought him to a hospital somewhere." She spoke with a laugh, light and happy, the likes of which Mary hadn't heard in a very long time, at least not when delivering pouches of deceased soldiers.

"Then we'd know it," Mary said softly.

"Not if his dog tags were lost. Not if he's hit his head again."

"Again?"

By this time Larisa Rose had found what she'd looked for.

"Here, this is Josef Warner. Blond hair, very light. His eyes are blue. Handsome, everyone thinks so. You'll notice that first. His teeth are white and even. He has just a hint of a dimple. Do you see it there?"

Mary took the photograph from Larisa's eager hold and studied it from a more comfortable distance. Mary wanted a good look at Josef's face.

"He is handsome, isn't he?"

Larisa nodded. "He's twenty-seven years old now. The picture was taken just last summer, so he hasn't changed much, unless he's grown a beard because he hasn't been able to shave. He wouldn't be able to if he's wounded. We nurses don't have the time to shave anybody."

Mary watched Larisa closely. She really believed what she was saying. Every word. Mary knew she shouldn't encourage this denying of the truth. Larisa was fabricating a web of possibilities to avoid facing what had actually happened. How could Mary encourage the nurse to hold on to such a fantasy? It would only hurt her more when she was forced to acknowledge Josef's death.

Nonetheless, Mary was a searcher. That was her job. She didn't have the skill of the nurses or the guts of the ambulance drivers, but she had an acute ability to remember faces and names. She could offer to do her job, at least.

"Does he have any birth marks? Any identifying features—beside his handsome face, of course?"

Larisa thumped her forehead. "He has a scar right here. Other than that, I don't know. We're only engaged, not married. I did see his chest once. Smooth, taut, and muscular. Is that enough?"

"The scar on the forehead helps. His hair must be hiding it in your photograph. Seeing that picture helps, too."

"You'll remember and notify me when you spot him?"

"*If* I spot him, Miss Parker."

Mary nodded. She could tell the other woman was eager to talk. Talking sometimes helped. Maybe it would help her sort through the grief to the truth. She had to leave soon to deliver more bundles to the port for shipment back home, but she could take a few more minutes. "How long were you engaged?"

"We met early summer a year ago, and he asked me to marry him before I left with the Red Cross last fall. So eight months. There's one reason in particular I'm sure he's just missing, Miss Downing, and not really dead as the British think. There is something not even his commanding officers know: Josef lost his memory. He was in an accident just before I met him, and his entire life was blanked out. He only remembers bits and pieces. So it's very likely, if he was wounded, he might be experiencing more memory problems. If he's lost his dog tags, how could anyone identify him if he can't identify himself? He may be lying in one of any number of hospitals, here or in Germany, unable to tell them who he is. They can't list him as wounded or a prisoner. That's part of why I'm so hopeful. It's a perfectly feasible scenario. The more I've considered it, the more likely it seems."

Mary nodded. Well, this was a new one, at least. And as unimaginable as it sounded, Mary found herself wanting to believe it, too.

It was a lot better than looking for a grave.

———————

Josef climbed onto the back of the wagon, collapsing on the hard bench seat. There wasn't room to sprawl out. Men already filled both bench seats, and several sat in between on the floorboards. They stank, just like he did.

Josef and the others were taken from the prison camp every morning, searched, poked, prodded. Then they were transported to various places. They cleaned out abandoned or damaged houses to billet soldiers or worked in fields to harvest turnips or cleaned out railroad cars or moved heavy ties for repairs along the tracks. Once Josef was taken to a munitions factory to fill casings for aerial bombs and artillery. Handling the explosives turned his skin yellow, but he was so covered with dirt that it didn't seem to matter. His skin hadn't been the color he'd been born with since he'd jumped into his first trench more than five months ago.

He liked fieldwork best; he could swallow some turnips nearly whole, dirt and all. If he was caught he'd be knocked down or hit in the head, but that didn't hurt as much as the hole in his belly.

At the end of a fourteen-hour day, he was taken back to the camp, searched, poked, and prodded again until the Germans were convinced he wasn't trying to smuggle anything in. He was given gruel to eat, some sort of soup or mush depending on its thickness, which varied day to day. It was worse than tasteless, but he ate it anyway, like everybody else. Josef had no idea what was in it.; certainly no meat, but there was an occasional green. If it had any nutritional value it was purely accidental.

He and the others were confined from eight in the evening until six the next morning in a deserted factory with brick walls and a cement floor. At six AM, the cycle started again. They were fed another foul meal, searched, and transported. At seven in the evening they were hauled back from the work site, which sometimes took as long as an hour. They ate their second meal of the day and returned to their barracks and its cold or heat, its filth, hunger, and darkness. He wasn't sure those first fresh breaths of air in the morning were worth it when he had to return to the old stenches at night.

Josef moved over when the wagon stopped again, to make room for Caleb and Dack. They never spoke outside the barracks. Guards listened, so even uttering mundane words felt like a violation.

On the way back to camp the driver took a different route, as he often did, probably to prevent the prisoners from seeing military activity. Maybe a battalion was being gathered at a train station for transport or there was movement of heavy artillery.

Not that having such knowledge would make a difference. At their camp, they could do nothing with covert information. They'd heard rumors about camps that were lax, even downright comfortable compared to what they endured.

The Germans were ultimately snobs, Josef decided. They bestowed different treatment according to a determination of status. Camps housing commissioned officers and downed aviators were comparatively cushy places where prisoners were treated with a measure of respect. Those with low rank and non-commissioned officers didn't command much honor.

This camp was unregistered. Rumor had it that their residence here was only temporary. Germans used slave laborers until they were too sick or overworked to be much good. Then they were taken to another camp to be registered, fed, and clothed under the watchful eye of international law. There even Red Cross packages could come from home. How long they might be forced to stay in the present hell was anybody's guess.

When they entered a village, Josef was glad they were in a wagon instead of on foot. In the weeks he'd been a prisoner, he'd come to hate passing through the villages. Civilians were unpredictable. Once, he'd been passed a potato that he'd shared with Caleb before they reached camp. On other trips they'd been spat upon, tripped, or ridiculed. They were hated more often than they were pitied.

There was another reason he disliked villages. He hated seeing the faces of common Germans. He hated seeing up close what this war and those in power had done to every person not wearing a uniform. The soldiers were fed. Perhaps not well, but enough that they remained strong enough to wield a weapon. Civilian faces, from the oldest to the youngest, were gaunt, pale, and sick. He'd seen a woman carry a baby so malnourished that he was sure the child was dead until he saw the enlarged dark eyes blink.

Shame over his German heritage engulfed him. He was glad his parents had left this land where the army was valued above all else.

He closed his eyes when the wagon plodded through a village square so he wouldn't have to see those faces again. When the cobblestone faded back to dirt, he opened his eyes. They passed a field unplowed and unused. Abandoned fields were everywhere with so few workers. He saw green hills on both sides, and wildflowers grew freely in between, expressing the glory of a creative God. Josef looked away, too tired to appreciate it beyond the simple acknowledgment of the Master's hand. *Yes, I do praise You, Lord. It must be You keeping me alive. It sure isn't the Germans or myself, any more.*

Then he unwillingly looked back at that field, unable to look away. Flowers. He remembered the flowers at Hank's place. Jaylene had been proud of her lilies. Another yard, another garden came to mind. It had been a city garden, more elegant. There were lilies there, too. And daisies, tall hollyhocks, and glads.

His mother's garden.

His gaze scanned the countryside. She was here somewhere, buried in Germany. Suddenly her face came to him as if it had only been yesterday that he saw his mother's loving smile.

For a moment Josef wasn't in that wagon. He was home, where he'd always lived before Hank had fished him out of that river.

Vivid memories filled his mind. He could see each room of the house, far more elaborate than he'd expected to remember. There was a library of wall-to-wall books, and plants everywhere, all reaching for the light that filtered through tall windows. Plush furniture, an ornate dining room that boasted too much food at every meal.

And Otto. He remembered the man who believed he was Josef's father, a successful businessman who worked all of the time. He'd once only owned the coking factory that stunk so bad everyone in the family hated it. Later, he worked in the glass factory, making all those bottles. Yes, Otto von Woerner had worked in both factories, even though he owned them. Josef had worked in both of them as well, at least for a while.

Otto, the distant father—for whom work was more important than family. But that thought was somewhat unfair. He was sometimes kind, when he was around.

Josef tried to remember more. A few memories came, like riding a bicycle and rowing a boat when he was a boy. He recalled going to someone's house. A neighbor's? No, the house was too plain to belong in the same neighborhood as the one in which he had lived.

Then the wagon reached the prison camp, and the new memories ended.

Body searches were just an inconvenience now, no longer humiliating. After that, Josef ate with the other prisoners in silence, then trudged to the barracks. Once inside, conversations bubbled up here and there, like a pot of water finally at a boil. Josef took his spot on the floor. Prisoners had been given hay and a few blankets to cover the cement, but Josef wasn't sure it mattered. It was just one more layer for the bugs to infest.

The camp was filled with a limited variety of men. Most were French, so there was a language barrier. There were even a couple of Russians, left behind when their army retreated. Their government had signed a separate peace, but these men and some others were forgotten; lost in the system. They stayed to themselves. The Germans seemed to hate the Russians most. Dack was the only one with a rank as high as sergeant, but the others paid him no attention.

Josef lay on his blanket, putting one arm under his head and the other over his eyes. He heard someone approach, either Dack or Caleb or maybe both. He didn't look up. He wanted to think. He wanted to remember.

"Been giving any more thought to our little project?" Dack asked in a low voice.

Josef pulled his arm to his side, looking up at the sergeant. It was the only interesting topic of conversation—escape.

"Still want to, after what happened yesterday?"

Two Russian soldiers had run off during work detail. Both had been shot in the back.

"We won't be so stupid," said Dack.

Caleb took a seat between the two of them, folding his legs underneath.

"Think we'll get back to that factory assignment next week, like we've been hearing?" Caleb asked.

Josef shrugged. That assignment had been promised and postponed four times already. Not that they liked the work. Stuffing bombs and bullets to be used on their old trench mates wasn't the kind of work they welcomed. But they did like the diversions there. There was a real break at midday, with water and crackers. It was there that Josef had devised a plan for their escape.

"How much powder do you think you'll need for that bomb, Joe? Enough if the three of us line our shoes with it?"

For some reason he couldn't imagine, Josef remembered all about how to make a small pipe bomb. The memory was clear and detailed. And though he'd worked in that munitions factory only four days, he knew that even a minor explosive, placed just so, would destroy the whole building. It would touch off a chain reaction with the plant's own powder stock. They could blow up the place.

In the chaos, forewarned prisoners could make their break. Some would be instantly caught or killed, but at least a few would make it to freedom, if they survived the blast.

He had liked the idea from the start. Something about destroying ammunition appealed to him. If he could slow down the supply, he might help speed the end of the war. It wasn't that big of a plant, so the difference he might make would probably not be much. But it was a step.

Caleb and Dack liked the idea, too. They just had to figure out a way to get the prisoners out of the building before they blew it up.

"Getting fire to set it off will be the hard part. Probably not too many smokers on that job—not that we could borrow a light anyway."

"The soldiers have plenty of cigarettes," Caleb said, and Josef knew it was true. "We could try to swipe a match."

"It's a risk," Josef said.

The other two pondered the possibilities, stretching out on straw near where Josef lay. But when the conversation ended, so did Josef's attention. His mind went back to his new memories until, not much later, he fell asleep.

Flowers filled his mind again. The garden. With the clear vision of his sleeping mind, he saw the colors, smelled the scents. Then he saw *her*, wearing a white dress. Her hair was light like his own, burnished gold in the sun, swept up in a loose knot. A breeze moved the wavy tendrils. She offered a daisy to Josef, and he was a child again, happy to be by her side.

"God's flowers," she'd told him, "and you're God's child, Josef. Don't ever forget that."

Something dripped from the flower. Petals? No, blood. First it stained her dress, then it poured into the trenches and fell on the gaunt faces of all those German civilians he never wanted to see again.

Pounding. Shellfire. The wind and whistle of bullets and grenades. The ground opened. Suddenly he stood amid the smoke of the guns, at a gravesite where his mother's name was chiseled on the headstone. A shell passed overhead. It didn't touch him, but the grave beneath his feet burst open, and there she was, the top of her coffin blown away. She lay there peacefully in the white gown, her hands folded stiffly around a red lily. Her skin was pasty white, the kind of white that comes with death.

"Hey, wake up."

The words didn't belong here. He didn't want to take his eyes from his mother. He wanted to see her, even if she was dead. But then he felt the hand on his shoulder and he couldn't shake it away.

He opened his eyes and wiped a dirty hand over his face. It was damp with perspiration.

"You sick?" asked Caleb in a hushed, worried voice.

Josef let out a deep breath, and rubbed his face again, this time with both hands. The only source of light or air in the building was open vents spaced sporadically near the roof. One vertical ray of light shone on Caleb's concerned face, and for a moment Josef didn't know who he was.

Then he knew. He remembered.

He remembered the old and the new. He remembered everything.

Josef shook his head. No, he wasn't sick. Not any more.

"Nightmare? You were making so much noise, I thought you might bring the guards."

Josef realized he was trembling. So many memories flooded his mind he wasn't able to sort reality from dream.

"Did I say anything?"

"You called for your mother."

Josef sat up. He wanted to get out of the horizontal position that had opened his mind to the images. They were too real. He held his forehead with the palms of his hands, staring into the darkness of the floor.

Parts of the dream were still in front of him.

"Yes, I dreamed her grave was being shelled. Her body was there, on the ground, in the open. She was dead, but not decayed, even after all these years. She looked like she was sleeping."

"I thought you didn't remember her," Caleb whispered.

Josef looked at his young half-brother. Every memory of his life bombarded him—confusing, frightful, bitter—and he wasn't sure what to say. Some of what he remembered he knew he couldn't share.

"I remember her," he said, low, and left it at that. "Go back to sleep, Caleb."

Caleb didn't take much persuasion. He rolled onto his side and was breathing heavily a few moments later.

Josef was afraid to lie down again. The dreams might come back and stoke the fire of his fear. But there was no escape. His loyalty to Germany, his blind love for this fatherland. He remembered his love for Otto, too, and his old wish to please him. He wanted to please his father enough so that he might stop working and spend time with Josef. He remembered the longing that Otto nurtured in him to come to Germany.

He remembered missing his mother.

He remembered Liesel Bonner, the woman who'd betrayed him. She'd chosen America over him. And he'd chosen Germany over her. Josef looked around. He didn't need light to see his surroundings, both inside and out. He looked through narrowed eyes. This? This is what he'd been taught to revere? Germany didn't look much different from America, with its hills and valleys, its lakes and towns. America might be bigger and more spread out, but it wasn't so very different. What had he expected? A land of milk and honey? Streets paved in gold? Heaven?

Germany's history still beckoned him, with it richness and culture. The music, the literature, the strength. The Josef he'd been since he'd awakened in Hank's flat never knew why this war was being fought. The Josef he was before thought he knew: German culture was worthy of a new and bigger empire.

The new Josef tried to meld old with new, but came up with nothing except confusion.

He remembered how Hank must have found him. Josef lifted a hand to his forehead, long since healed. He'd been shot by that federal agent Liesel brought—shot as a traitor to the very government he now served.

Josef was a criminal. A traitor. His pulse raced, his breathing went unsteady. *He* was the criminal that Otto went to jail for helping.

He swallowed hard. Liesel had betrayed him. Pain sliced through his middle. How could she have done that? She'd known him her whole life. They'd planned to be *married*.

Yet, he knew she hadn't been raised the way he had. He knew even then that she would disapprove of his actions. So would Liesel's father—and Karl, Josef's best friend, despite his apparent repugnance of war. Karl had never hated the war because he loved Germany, the way all the German newspapers taught Josef to believe. Karl hated the war because he hated *war*.

Josef pressed his hands on his head, wishing some of the thoughts were lies. But with biting clarity he knew exactly what was true and what was a dream. Josef was wanted by the United States government.

Even as his brain tried to deny the truth, the memories couldn't blot out the two most important discoveries he'd ever made, memories with an impact on his past, present, and future. His love for God and his love for Larisa Rose Parker. He was engaged to be married to one of the most patriotic women in America. The daughter of one of the oldest, most patriotic families in America. A Daughter of the American Revolution.

Nausea rose from his gut, but there wasn't anything in his stomach to empty.

CHAPTER *Seventeen*

"ARE YOU sure you won't come with me?"

Lissa shook her head despite Penny's plea. "I signed on for a year, Pen. I still have two months left."

"Doesn't take long to feel like we've been here a year," Penny said. "But with all that's happened, I'm sure they'd understand."

Lissa reached across the canteen table and squeezed both of Penny's hands. "I know they would, just as they understand why you're going. But you know why I'm staying, Penny."

Penny frowned. "Oh, Liss," she whispered.

But Lissa shook her head again. "No, Pen. Don't tell me I'm foolish to believe he's still alive." She gripped her friend's hands again, leaning forward and smiling. "I *know* he's alive, Pen. I know it! I plan to be here when he's found, even if it means extending my stay to the end of the war."

Lissa watched a progression of emotions cross her dear friend's face: sadness, impatience, even a touch of anger.

"Liss, don't you think I want it to be true, that I want Caleb to be alive, too? But it's been three months."

Lissa refused to speak or to listen. They'd argued about it for the last time. Her face must have revealed her resolve, because Penny gave up.

No one believed what Lissa believed; she knew that. She wasn't sure when she'd started believing Josef was alive. Maybe she'd just never accepted his death. But thinking he was out there somewhere was the only thing getting her through each day.

"I'll miss you, Penny. Part of me wishes I could go home, too. But it's not only Josef, you know. You'd be staying if your family didn't need you so much since the news came back about Caleb being missing. There's so much work here."

Penny nodded. "Yes, much as I hate every stinking moment, I've never felt so needed. I'm glad I don't seem to have much of a choice. Mama's letter sounded just frantic enough that I don't feel a tinge of guilt at leaving so much behind me. Who knows? Maybe I'll be back."

"No, Pen, don't come back. Let someone else take your place. Maybe it'll be over soon."

Rumor had it the Germans were finally backing down, but there had been similar scuttlebutt ever since the Americans had joined the Allies. Not a single rumor had proven true. All Lissa had seen since they arrived was German military might, in all its ugly force, while Allied troops couldn't seem to cooperate with one another.

Lissa and Penny stood. Penny had pleaded for enough leave to get down to Lyon before traveling west to the port of St. Nazaire to meet her passage home. They'd spent a few hours catching up, but it was already time for Penny to go.

Lissa drew Penny close. "My friend," she whispered, holding back tears. Lissa already felt more alone than ever, knowing Penny wouldn't be a train ride away. Sorrow, envy, and relief filled her. Penny, at least, would be free of all this. But never, never, did Lissa doubt she was making the right decision to stick it out. Lissa held her friend at arm's length. "Be safe, trust in the Lord—and *write* to me, Pen. I'll miss you."

"Do you know what I'm going to do when I get back home?" Caleb asked.

Josef looked at him. He tried not to view Caleb differently than he had the day before, tried not to feel differently. He didn't think he was succeeding. Josef wasn't sure what to feel, but he knew one thing: If Caleb knew the truth, it would undoubtedly change the way *he* felt about Josef.

"What?"

"I'm going to take a bath," Caleb said as he picked a cootie out of his shirt. "I'm going to take a bath every day. I'm going to take a bath twice a day if I want to. I'm never, never going to get dirty again."

Josef grimaced. "That'll be easy on a farm. You'll stink like horses again, probably the first day you get back."

Caleb laughed. "Yeah, well, horses smell better'n me these days."

"That's for sure."

"Yeah, and they smell better than you, too."

Josef saw the smile on Caleb's whiskered face. Incredible, he thought, how he'd had a brother and a sister all these years and never knew.

That thought brought the Bonner family to mind, the family he'd "adopted" into after his mother had died. The Bonners had embraced him, so much that he'd felt more at home with them than he had with his father. What were the Bonners thinking now? They must know, as everyone must know, that he'd worked to stop American involvement in the war. Were they disappointed in him? Ashamed that they'd taken him into their fold? Did they regret caring for him?

He tried to defend himself against his own accusing thoughts, but everything he had once believed was colored differently now. Before, he'd only seen the German side, the side he'd been raised on, the side of the German schools and newspapers, German clubs, and German associates with whom his father mingled.

Josef had thought Hans Bonner a fool for his Americanized ways.

But Hans had always claimed he wanted to live where his vote counted. From what Josef had seen of German citizens, he wondered if those German patriots would choose to vote for the military regime that commanded their country now. How could they, and then come home to look into the starving faces of their wives and children?

Josef didn't think Hans a fool any more.

Before the sun was high off the horizon, Josef and the other prisoners were working on the rail line, offloading cars, but myriad thoughts so filled his mind that he forgot his pain. He remembered his driving passion to do whatever he thought necessary to aid the German cause. He'd been so convinced, so sure he'd been doing the right thing. Had he been wrong?

He was sure the American government would see it that way. He'd known what he was doing was illegal, but he'd hated the use of American weapons to kill German citizens so much that he didn't care about staying within the boundaries of the law.

Had he really loved Germany more than the U.S., where he'd been born and raised? One country was the only land he knew; the other an idealist's dream. If the only true citizenship that counted was that of heaven, what would God have had him do?

Josef looked around, wiping sweat from his brow with his forearm. From the open rail yard he could see the countryside, hilly and green, trees parting here and there. What made Germany right and the Allies wrong in this war? He'd been so sure that Germany was the righteous state. He no longer knew why.

He bent back to work, shoveling coal out of a rail car, very much like the coal he'd once sold for Otto. Why had he thought he ever knew any answers? God was probably disgusted with both sides. Josef might have thought the Allies right when he joined the American army last year, but wasn't he just following a blind sort of loyalty then, too? He assumed he should do his duty for the cause of democracy, or was it simply that he'd been raised in America? The Allies weren't right, he knew that as well. He had seen what the Allied blockade had done to the German population. The German military regime might be distributing the sparse food supply unfairly, but the fact that there was too little to go around was a direct result of the blockade.

Visions of Liesel came to mind, but he pushed them away. His initial feeling was anger over her betrayal. Maybe she had never loved him the way she should love the man she was going to marry. How could she if she'd been willing to send him to prison? They never should have been engaged at all, given the fact he'd kept so much from her, and when she did learn his secrets, she disapproved. But the fact remained, if she hadn't loved him, then the least she could have felt was loyalty. They'd grown up together. He'd eaten at the Bonner table at least as often as he'd eaten at his own. They were part of each other's lives. How could she give him away?

Then thoughts he most didn't want to face detonated in his brain: What would Larisa have done had she been in Liesel's situation? He knew. Larisa Rose Parker was part of a family that had fought for America since its independence. He knew exactly what she would have done if she'd found out about Josef's covert activities—the same thing Liesel had done.

Only maybe she'd have done it sooner.

His heart went cold at the thought.

CHAPTER *Eighteen*

"SISTER! SISTER Mary Michel!"

The old nun acknowledged Lissa's call with a turn of her head but kept walking.

"There's a military physician downstairs. He wants me to leave the children's ward."

"Do as he says."

Lissa had expected that answer, but the decision broke her heart. Ambulance after ambulance had arrived, full of American wounded. There were no beds available except those just vacated by the nurses and nuns from their night's sleep. Barely cooled, the cots were filled with soldiers before an hour was up. Now they wanted the children moved, two to a bed.

Lissa cringed at the sight of familiar wounds and the festering faces of those who'd been gassed. The masks had been effective until the Germans started using mustard. That gas burned any exposed skin, blinded the eyes, and if it got into the respiratory tract and lungs, it meant death. She offered what little she could as she cut away their clothing, pulled mud-caked, bug-infested cloth from yellowed, puss-covered skin, whispering comfort into their blistered ears. "You're safe now, soldier."

Among those who weren't fatally exposed, often the blindness wasn't permanent. Those who could walk came in pathetic rows, following the soldier in front of them by a hand on the shoulder. They snaked along, led by a medic or an unwounded fellow soldier. Those probably would survive, but received care last.

And Lissa was too busy to acknowledge her own odd fatigue.

Josef sat in a circle with the three men of his unit, Dack, Caleb, and Birchall. The four of them were the only Americans.

"Okay," said Dack. "Listen up."

Josef knew he wasn't the only one giving Dack rapt attention. Caleb looked the most excited, which was no surprise. He was young and still thought himself immortal, especially after surviving the mission that killed the others with whom they'd set out. Birchall seemed the most discerning, despite what Josef had once thought of him. He was about the same age as Josef. What Josef had mistaken for a backwoods mentality was really more the wisdom of a farmer. His livelihood depended on hard work and trusting God, even though Birchall didn't acknowledge that it was God he trusted for every crop. They'd given each other a wide berth after exchanging fisticuffs, but they trusted each other now. Birchall had even asked about Jesus once, not long after their capture.

"We have to be ready when the conditions are right," Dack said. "That village we're cleaning out is in a low valley. That means fog, if there really is a God." He aimed a glance Josef's way, as if any reference to God was somehow connected to him. "And that's when we break for it."

"The only thing is," Josef said, "the day can't start out in a fog. The Jerries will never take us out on a morning when they can't see past the end of their own nose."

"They ain't the only problem," Dack added. "Which direction do we head once we're out of the valley? The Frogs think we're south of Stuttgart. My geography ain't so good, so what we have in store for us might be more a challenge than just sticking it out here. What do you say, then?"

Caleb looked at Josef. He knew his brother's hero worship was fully restored, but Josef expected to lose that respect again once Caleb knew the truth about Josef's past.

But the notion of escape made Josef's pulse race with anxiety and anticipation. He wanted to get Caleb out of this hellhole before it sapped that invincible light right out of his eyes. Josef hadn't known much about German geography when they'd first been taken prisoner. Now he remembered all the maps he'd pored over as a child, the villages his father talked about, the cities, the rivers, and the hills. If they were near Stuttgart, he knew which way to go.

"This is what we do. We look at the sky every morning." He kept his voice low so it wouldn't go beyond their huddle. "The sun rises in the east. We get our bearings and look south, find some landmark we can aim for inside the village to point us in the right direction when the fog is thick. Then we head for the river we pass every day. That's where we'll meet. The river flows north, to the North Sea, so we want to go against the flow, south to the Swiss frontier."

"Okay, then," said Dack, "we pray for a fog, a thick, heavy, blinding fog. A fog got us into this mess, I guess we can hope for one to get us out—before we get carted off to someplace else."

Josef did pray, and in between supplications for safety he prayed for a clearer head. He'd once been naïve to think that if all his memories returned he'd feel more complete, more secure, stronger and better equipped to offer Larisa a confident, stable future. He had nothing to offer her now except her freedom to find someone else. She needed someone who fit the profile of the man she thought he was.

Thoughts like those made the prospect of escape less appealing. He was willing to give his life for his brother's freedom, but as for himself, it didn't matter any more.

That was why his own plan didn't frighten him, the one he would execute entirely alone. But he needed that fog first.

———

"Oh, Mama, I've missed you!"

Penny hugged her mother close. She was home.

"Where's Daddy?"

"Right here."

Her father's tall frame filled the archway leading to the parlor, and Penny slipped from her mother's arms to rush into his.

"Daddy!"

"Why didn't you telephone?" her mother asked through her tears. "We would have met you at the station."

Penny brushed away her own tears, staring at her mother as if she'd never seen her before. She knew neither she nor her mother was a great beauty, but even at near fifty her mother was called *pert*. Penny used to be annoyed when someone called her pert, too. "Pertie Penny" used to grate on her, but at the moment the word only connected her better to her mother. "There wasn't time. Our ship docked in New York and I could barely catch the train. I didn't want to ring from the town station. It would have taken twice as long for you to come and fetch me as for me to come along on my own. Oh, it's good to be home." She drew both her parents near at the same time. "Where's Ulu?"

"She's gone to town to help with the care packages for the children Lissa wrote about. Caps and nightgowns and such. I was just headed there myself, but I'm glad I was delayed."

Penny hugged her mother again, then looked between her parents, searching their faces. "How are you both, I mean, with Caleb . . . missing?"

Her parents exchanged frowns. "We're holding up," her father said.

Her mother looked to one of the photographs on the table behind them. Caleb in his uniform took center spot. "We miss him terribly. But there's still hope, you know. They aren't saying that he's definitely . . . gone."

"Now you sound like Lissa," Penny said. "She's convinced they're still alive, somewhere, somehow. But Mama, I don't want you hoping for something that's not very likely. As disorganized as some of it is over there, they have a pretty good system for keeping tabs on the men. POWs are supposed to be reported, dog tags and all. And the British, they think . . ."

Her mother nodded. "We know, Penny. We know what they think about our boys."

"Our boys?" Penny repeated.

Hank spoke up. "Caleb and Josef."

Penny's gaze never left her mother's face. "I guessed that, but it's just a little surprising to hear you refer to Josef that way, Mama."

"Well, he's your father's son, isn't he? And since he came here, he's become part of our lives. He wrote to us often, you know, before he disappeared. He's very dear to both of us."

Penny nodded then looked around the familiar room to see things she'd only dreamed of for more than ten months. Nothing had changed, not the afternoon light chasing away every shadow or the furniture and the scent of lemon wax Ulu used to polish it.

"I might as well wait until Ulu gets back before I go into tales of what's happened to me for the past ten months. How about you telling me what's been going on around here?"

Her parents exchanged a look but no words.

"Oh, come on, you must have something to tell." She looked at her father. "Without me and Caleb around, you and Mama have probably been living it up, making all kinds of trips to the city." She turned to her mother. "What about it, Mama? Have you spent time in New York, shopping? Or better yet, become a partner in Daddy's investigation office?"

Her mother gave an awkward, tight smile and averted her gaze. "He's given up his office in the city, actually."

Surely she hadn't heard right. Her father had been an inquiry agent ever since he came to this country. He might not have earned his living from it since they'd opened Saddlebrook, but it had always been a source of interest, even for Mama. Or so Penny'd thought.

"Why?"

Her father took her hand and led her to the sofa. It felt a lot like the day her father had led her to the sofa to tell her that Josef was her brother.

"Let's sit down, Penny."

Penny stood still, sudden stiffness setting in. "What's happened?"

Her mother came up behind her and slipped a gentle arm about her shoulders. It didn't help. In fact, Penny grew colder, more rigid.

No one took a seat, rather they stood in the comparatively cramped space between the flowered sofa and the two conversation chairs just opposite.

"I gave up my license, Penny," her father said. "And, since you'll hear about it when you get to town, you might as well know it wasn't my idea."

Penny was confused. "Whose was it, then?" Who could make her father give up his license? Certainly Mama wouldn't.

"Now, Penny, I don't want you to get upset," her mother said, and the warning had the opposite effect. Penny's heart raced.

"They don't allow persons convicted of breaking the law to hold a license," her father said.

"Persons convicted of breaking the law? What are you talking about?"

Her father sank to the couch and rubbed his hands down his thighs to his knees, where he patted them once, then looked up at her as if to invite her to sit opposite him on one of the chairs. When she didn't move, he spoke anyway.

"I was arrested a couple of months ago, Penny. Around the time we received the news about Caleb."

"Arrested! What for?"

"It's a long story. But, it's better you hear all the facts from us. Sit down, Penny. This'll take some time."

CHAPTER *Nineteen*

"You're next, Birchall," said Josef.

Even as he spoke with calm assurance, Josef's heartbeat pummeled his chest. When he'd fought at the front his pulse kept steady pace with the booming shells. Not since working for the Germans had his blood pumped this hard.

Today had been a long time coming. Even Birchall had become desperate enough to pray for this fog, because they all worried they'd finish cleaning out the bombed village in the valley before a fog settled in. And here it was.

Birchall shook his head. "Nope, your turn, Joe."

Josef swung around. This was no time to argue. They stood in the middle of what had once been a living room, except half the roof had caved in. German guards had just been through, routinely checking progress. The village was so badly damaged they weren't rebuilding. They just wanted to salvage what they could, from timber for fuel to the smallest spoon to be melted down and used in a bullet casing in the munitions plant up the road. The munitions plant stood undamaged while the village lost nearly every home.

Time was not a luxury Josef and Birchall could afford. Caleb had left, and Josef prayed Dack was already gone from whichever building he'd been assigned. They should be headed for the river where it was assumed they'd meet up, sooner or later.

"It's all planned, Birchall. You're next."

Birchall didn't move, just leveled a stare at Josef that he hadn't seen since boot camp days.

"Look, it's your little brother out there. Nobody wants to see him out of this place more'n you. You go on and watch over him. Now git."

They'd discussed how the one left behind took the greatest risk. Making enough noise to sound like a team would be difficult, but having more than one run at a time seemed too dangerous, even with fog. Too noisy in all the wrong places. And so Josef had volunteered to go last.

"See that beam over there?" Birchall said, pointing to the heavy oblong object. "After you leave, I'm gonna lift it and push it out that window. Nobody outside will think one man could do that alone, and we'll buy a few minutes before they check around again. So go on, the plan's done and I'm not changin' it. Standin' here arguin' about it won't make no difference."

Josef could see from Birchall's face that he wouldn't budge. "Okay, throw the blasted beam, then follow right behind. Got it?"

Birchall nodded, and Josef took off out the back, along the route they'd planned, under the cover of a thick cloud. But he didn't head for the river.

The village looked odd in the murky air. Shadows offered blurry outlines. Distance was hard to judge. Sounds, too, were different, muffled, as he scooted low and kept silent. Voices echoed off the remains of buildings— German voices. Josef understood every word. Someone was being teased about the size of his boots. Evidently he had small feet.

It was late in the afternoon, as far as Josef could tell. He wouldn't have long to wait.

Josef removed his shirt and shoved it under a bush. That was for the benefit of the dogs, if they were brought in to search once their absence was noted. He left it in the direction heading away from the river.

Drizzle dampened his skin. Once he reached the higher ground at the edge of the low-lying village the fog thinned but did not entirely clear. He thanked God for that. He'd need all the help he could get.

He found his target and slipped into a ditch. Today's rain added to the water already there from days of rain. He shivered, but again he was thankful. The water added to his cover. The cold magnified the disparity of adrenaline blazing through his veins. His target was there, smoke rising from its chimney, the roof solid. Aerial bombs had damaged a building nearby and pock marked the road. But the arsenal was intact and in operation. So he waited.

Every shout from a distance pushed his pulse faster. When a child called for his mother nearby, Josef nearly jumped from his hiding place. A while later he thought he heard a distant ruckus, and his head pounded with his heartbeat. Had their disappearance been discovered? Was the search party headed this way? It was what he feared most: They would sound the alarm and secure the building before he got there. But even when a pair of soldiers sprinted along the road, they bypassed the building altogether. Josef raised a prayer of thanksgiving. Surely the Lord is with me. The words of a psalm sang in his heart.

Rain started in earnest, pelting him cold and stinging in the fall weather. Wind whipped at him, but he relished it. Nobody was out in this weather except the sentries.

He watched the building empty and the night watchmen come on duty. No one came his way. There was no need since the small village behind him had been destroyed. Instead the workers, who were either refugees or prisoners from other camps, were taken away in wagons, heading in the opposite direction. They'd been told the workers were too few for a nightshift. He hoped it was still true.

Josef watched the sentries. From his memory of the four days he'd been assigned to work in that building, he devised his plan of access. There was a door at the back, most likely locked and guarded. But that was the door he planned to try first. It was well out of sight from anyone either still in the building or in front of it. No windows faced that side; it was brick from top to bottom.

Josef slipped from his hiding place just as the sun peaked out from parting clouds, only to sink rapidly beyond the not-so-distant western front. Thick trees and underbrush served him well, allowing him close access to the back of the building.

From behind the bushes but near enough to see the features of the German sentry, Josef quietly pulled off his shoes, his pants, even his bug-infested underwear. Stark naked, he walked from the wood, doing his best to ignite the fire of insanity in his eyes.

"I am Field Marshall Paul von Hindenburg." He spoke fluent German, just as his mother taught him so long ago. "I have come from the western front. Stand at attention, soldier."

The soldier stared. He couldn't have been more than sixteen. If he had any experience firing his Mauser, he couldn't have done much damage. He'd have to get over the astonishment on his face first.

"I have come to inspect your weapon. We kill the All-Lies! We kill the All-Lies! Let me see the weapon, soldier."

Josef swiftly approached and, rather than reaching for the weapon, Josef pulled at the alarm whistle that hung about the boy's neck, breaking the thread and throwing it to the ground.

"This is for cowards, boy! Do you want to be a man? Now let me see that weapon."

The boy pulled back, the gun beyond Josef's reach.

"Do you want to go to the front, soldier? Or do you want to be in the boy's league all your life? Let me see the weapon!"

The sentry finally made a decision and lunged for the whistle. Josef kicked it away and swiped at the rifle at the same time, twisting it from the young soldier's grip.

He held the gun to the boy's face, knowing exactly what he should do. Shoot.

"Do not get up, boy," he continued in his flawless German, "or your Mama will receive a notice of your death before the sun sets on another day. And we don't want that, do we?"

"What . . . is it that you want?"

"I want you to open the door."

"I don't have the key."

"Oh? Then I have no alternative, have I?"

But still Josef couldn't bring himself to shoot. At a faceless enemy he could aim a weapon, but at a boy? Nonetheless, he turned the butt of the rifle on him and slammed it down hard. The child had at least a chance of survival, if he woke.

Josef dragged the boy to the bushes, stripped him of his uniform and boots, and put them on. The boy was skinny but lanky, so while the length was all right, Josef couldn't button the waist, even trim as he was. And the boots pinched his toes so badly he couldn't walk, so he pulled the standard pocketknife from the boy's pants and savagely cut the sole away from the leather upper, thanking God it left enough room without his toes sticking out altogether.

He started back toward the plant, but an itch on his bearded face stopped him. Such unkempt growth would be an immediate signal he was no sentry. Rushing now, knowing he hadn't much time, he opened the knife again, bending down at a nearby puddle and splashing his face to soften the wiry hair. Then he scraped the blade along, removing the worst of it. No time for more than that.

He ran back to the boy's post.

He tried the door. It was indeed locked, and it held fast despite the rust. Josef knew he didn't have much time. He had to be bold.

"Time to switch." Josef swung around, seeing another guard approaching at a confident stride. This soldier was every bit as youthful as the one Josef had already knocked out. Where were all the real soldiers?

This one, however, recovered his shock rather quickly at not seeing a familiar face in a familiar uniform. He drew his gun on Josef.

"Where is Jurgen?"

"I sent him to retrieve you. There has been trouble in the village, and you should walk together," Josef said, cheerful but firm, hoping his age would be enough to see the boy past his confusion and suspicion. He tilted his head in the opposite direction from where this boy had come. "He went that way."

The boy passed Josef, heading around the building.

Josef acted quickly. He pounded the lock with the sturdy butt of the rifle until it broke. Soft with rust, it didn't take long, and Josef was inside within moments.

He closed the door behind him then went to the spot he'd chosen. He knew there were no grenades stored here, which would have made his job so much simpler. He would have to devise his own explosive. Josef knew exactly what to do, mixing a powder from one keg and a chemical from another and rolling them inside a length of cotton stored nearby that was used in the manufacture of the explosives. He placed it at the base of a barrel with the word Brennbar boldly stamped on the top and sides—"Flammable." Josef recognized the chemical. Then he rushed back to the door. It was not a large building, and he stopped at the threshold. Without a match he would have to mix the chemicals to start a fire that, he hoped, would lead to an explosion.

His own shadow filled the doorframe. He took aim. All he had to do was hit the side of that barrel. Enough of the liquid chemical would pour out, and once it touched his makeshift bomb, that would be it. Flame would shoot in all directions, igniting the rest of the powders and chemicals in the arsenal.

"What is this?"

Josef felt the tip of a rifle poking him in the back.

"What are you doing?"

"An intruder is inside!" Josef shouted.

The boy raised his gun away from Josef, looking over Josef's shoulder. It was enough of a diversion. Josef turned on the boy in an instant and smashed the rifle into the youthful face. The young guard stumbled back but did not fall.

Yet it was enough for Josef to have the advantage. He righted his own rifle and aimed it at the boy.

"Set aside your gun, young man," ordered Josef.

The boy stood stubbornly immobile.

Josef had little patience and less time. He grabbed the end of the gun, pulling then thrusting it into the gut of its holder. The boy stumbled again, this time to his knees. Josef now held two guns, one of which he threw into the building behind him.

"Run for help, boy. You'll need it to put out the fire."

The boy scrambled to his feet and ran before Josef could tell him twice.

Josef turned back to the building and pulled the trigger.

Then he ran. The river was just beyond the trees.

Behind him one explosion set off another and, as fast as Josef could be in those boots, he felt the heat chase at his heels.

"Can we stop, just for a minute?"

Sergeant Dack slowed but did not stop. Both men looked over their shoulders, but Caleb saw what Dack did—nothing except hills and trees, and the rushing water behind them.

"Maybe Josef and Birchall aren't far behind."

"Yeah, well, we can't wait for 'em," Dack said. "You want a bullet in the back? They won't take time to hang us. They'll just shoot. Come on, keep up."

Caleb didn't want to keep up. He wanted to turn back to see for himself what had happened to the others. But he didn't dare.

"How far is it to the border, do you suppose?"

"Of that, my boy, I got no idea."

Caleb looked over his shoulder. He wished Josef were here. They'd have some hope then.

Josef veered off the river when he heard the shout of soldiers ahead, pursuing Caleb and Dack. He went east, seeing that the water wound around from the direction of the mountains. He'd allow plenty of space for the search party, fairly confident that they wouldn't turn around and look his way, especially with the borrowed clothing and shoes to avoid the dogs catching the scent of a prisoner. He kept running.

He wasn't so tired as he was hungry. He passed an abandoned farm and spotted an apple tree, swiping as many as his pockets could hold, eating one on the run.

Then he headed back to the cover of trees. It was there he heard them, closer than ever: at least three German soldiers. And then, out of a bush, a young soldier suddenly appeared in sight.

"I've got this flank!" Josef shouted, and between his German uniform, gun, and good diction, the soldier didn't even hesitate to go back in the direction from which he'd come. Josef silently thanked his mother and Otto for always speaking German at home. Josef swerved farther off, leaving the search party that now headed away from the river.

He prayed Caleb and the others were wise enough to keep up their speed. With the Lord's help, he could catch them before the sun rose, if he wasn't caught first.

Josef wasn't sure when he got the idea, but once it was formed, he couldn't shake it. He didn't want to give in to the thought, it meant they would not take the shortest course to the Swiss frontier. His idea would delay their exit to safety.

But he couldn't get it out of his mind. He prayed as hard as he ran. *Help me clear this notion, Lord.* But it wouldn't vanish; it wouldn't even ease. The harder he prayed, the more vivid came the desire to follow what seemed a foolhardy plan.

He would see her grave.

He knew where it was. He knew the little town was north of the last village he'd passed—the opposite direction from the frontier and freedom. Ever since he was a little boy he'd wanted to see where those men had taken her. Now he was so close. So close, yet to see it now might mean his life.

He had to find Caleb and the others first. Make sure they were safe and on their way.

The river was ahead, and he knew he'd made good time. The shouts of the soldiers had faded. Clearly they did not have Josef's trail. He raised yet another prayer of thanksgiving.

It was dark, and he knew his appearance, at least from a distance, would alarm his old trench mates. He also knew they weren't armed, and so aside from hoping they wouldn't sound a loud protest, he hoped he could waylay them and either join their flight or at least wish them well, while he went off on his own final, reckless mission.

Would he be so bold, he wondered, if he thought Larisa would be waiting for him? But how could she? She'd want her freedom from a traitor as soon as she knew who he really was.

But he didn't let himself dwell on thoughts of her. It took too much energy.

Then he saw movement. He slowed, not wanting to attract attention to himself until he knew who was up ahead. In the dark he could not see whether their clothing was tattered Allied uniforms or crisp German ones. No buckles glinted from the moon, which was a hopeful sign, but caution stilled any noise he might make.

There were two figures, not the three he looked for, and they were not giving away their heritage through language. He thought one silhouette looked like Caleb, but he needed to get closer to be sure.

They splashed through the shallow edge of the cold water. Josef was above the banks, darting from tree to tree and never far from the water's edge. If the two figures below were his fellow soldiers, the Germans were no more than ten minutes behind them. No time to spare.

Then one stumbled and the other cursed. That was Dack all right.

"Hey, up here. It's me!"

"Josef?"

"Shh! Follow me."

The other two did as Josef said.

"Boy, am I glad to see you!" Caleb said, catching up to Josef, already on the move again. "Where's Birchall?"

"I was just going to ask you. He was the last to leave, but he should have caught up to you before now."

"We haven't seen him."

"Shouldn't we be heading the other way?" Dack said after a minute.

"We're going to Lilie See–Lily Lake." It was all so clear now, even that he should take them. "It's a detour. They know we're headed to the border. If we go the other way it'll throw them off."

"But if we make it to the border first, it won't matter."

"The Germans are only a few minutes behind us," Josef said, keeping the pace quick even as they talked. His voice was all confidence now. It made perfect sense. It was the Lord directing his path, not his own silly wishes. Suddenly his wishes and the Lord's will were the same. "If we keep going that way we can't make it to the border without them catching us. Follow me, Dack."

Dack stopped altogether, and Josef looked back, barely slowing.

"It's up to you, Sarge," said Josef. "Maybe we can make it, but we have a better chance of hiding out and going for it from a different direction."

Caleb never wavered, and in a moment Dack caught up to them.

Josef looked at the stars for his directions. Lily Lake couldn't be more than a few hours' run. They could make it before the sun rose. There they could take cover and rest before making their final bid for the border.

Dack fell in step with Josef. They ran, fueled by pure desperation.

Josef led the way. When they'd first been captured, their own sturdy boots had been commandeered, exchanged for old, ill-fitting, and worn shoes. Caleb and Dack alternately stumbled or winced, having stepped on something other than the spongy lowland ground. Josef wasn't sure how much longer they could keep up to him in his stolen German boots.

A sudden yelp halted him. He looked and saw Dack on the ground.

"Grab the other side, Caleb," Josef said, pausing only long enough to pull Dack along.

Caleb was clearly waning. His breathing sounded heavy, and he wasn't much help getting Dack to his feet. Moaning and out of breath, Dack cursed, but the three made progress. Josef's hope grew, particularly when the shadow of a church spire loomed below in the distance. Lily Lake. That spire was his goal. Somewhere nearby would be the cemetery. Josef felt a renewed burst of strength and all but carried Dack along the route.

Birchall Burke knew it was over. He'd slipped out shortly after Josef, making it to the river without incident. But he never caught up to the others, and when he slipped on a rock and twisted his ankle he knew he never would.

That's when he decided to leave the river and create a trail away from the others. Better one not make it than all four.

And so he left his scent for the dogs in the distance and they followed his direction, due south to the border, the route they were expected to take, the route the others would have taken, but not so soon, as agreed. When he fell a second time he dragged himself forward, knowing his feet wouldn't carry him any farther.

It wasn't long before the howls and stomp of heavy boots caught up to him.

"Wait here," Josef whispered.

He helped Dack to the ground. Once settled, the sergeant sucked in a quick breath and then fell back, sprawled out. Josef took a quick glance at the wounded leg. Dack had fallen hard on rough ground, splitting open his knee. It was bleeding, swollen twice the size of the other.

Josef turned to Caleb. "Stay with Dack. Rest here." He handed him one of the two apples left in his pocket, tossing the other to Dack. "I'll be back. Just don't move."

Josef left the cover of thick underbrush, feeling bold enough in his German uniform to complete the plan that had sprung up during his flight. He'd have to get close to find her. The weather had cleared, and the moon was bright in the late night sky, giving him all the light he needed to read the inscriptions on the headstones.

That light might also give his presence away.

Before he reached the church, he thought to check something first. All of his calculations had been correct so far, about the river and its flow. They'd seen hills begin to graduate to mountains, matching what he knew of the location of this village, which was north of the Swiss frontier. But every guess had been based on a starting point of Stuttgart, the biggest city they'd passed when first captured. They were relying on the guess of the Frenchmen they'd been imprisoned with. Were they right? They'd all been blindfolded in the back of that truck. Who really knew?

Josef went to the front of the church in search of the Saint's name for whom it was built. If he found the right name, he'd know they were exactly where he hoped. If not, he wouldn't get to visit his mother's grave, and the Swiss border might not be where he believed it to be, either.

It took a few minutes to find the cornerstone. And there was the name of the patron, Saint Wolfgang. Gratitude saturated Josef, sending him to his knees in a wordless prayer of thanksgiving. They'd make it now.

Then he headed back to the cemetery.

He made a quick assessment. The grave would have been added almost twenty years ago. Not a new grave, but it wouldn't be found among the oldest either. He decided to start in the middle of the small yard and circle out.

As he went from site to site he noticed the yard was scrupulous. He'd seen farmyards on his marches through France and Germany that weren't tended so meticulously. Who had time to keep up a gravesite?

He had no answer, but he was silently grateful for the flowers, trimmed grass, and straight headstones. Not a weed grew through the rocks that were placed here and there. It was, he had to admit, a fine place to leave one's remains.

A chilling thought struck him. If he went back to America, he might face a sentence that could put him into a grave of his own. That conjured a picture of Otto and a big black motorcar taking Josef's own oblong box to the dock to be buried alongside her.

Maybe that's why the Lord had wanted him to come and visit her, to see where he would be himself, at least the physical remains of himself. He knew where his spirit would be.

And then he saw it. He'd bypassed that one at first, thinking someone of importance must have been given a place of prominence. It was set higher than the other graves, with a small iron fence surrounding it that somehow hadn't been ripped up by the army and reformed into weaponry. The largest tree in the yard was overhead, giving shade in the summer, its massive trunk offering a break from winter winds. Hardy autumn flowers lined the knee-high fencing, with what was in sunlight, no doubt, a crescendo of color winding upward at the back of the headstone. The moon's light wasn't enough to reveal the tints of each flower. Nonetheless it cast its glow upon the yard, an island of beauty amid a country that was pock marked and dying.

Josef stepped over the fence, careful not to crush any growth. She would have liked it here, so like her own gardens. It was as if someone who loved her took care of the yard.

He touched the stone, and his hand trembled. Stark clarity of memory hit him: her face, her smile, her love, the disappointment she would feel if she knew the mess he'd made of his life.

"I'm sorry," he whispered.

Then he remembered her words. He'd been young, but they came back as if twenty days had passed instead of twenty years.

"Your faith. Someday, Josef, you will claim it as your own," she'd said when he sat at her bedside, not long before she died. "I know you're young and you want to believe what I believe, because it's brought me peace and happiness. But someday my little boy will be a man fully grown. Your faith must be your own, not an inheritance from me. You'll remember, Josef, and claim it, and you'll know that I smile with the Lord when you accept His precious gift."

"I do claim it," he whispered now, and brushed her name with his fingertips. Not her faith, nor Hank's, nor even Larisa's. It was his own. How else could he have survived, except through the grace of God?

"Who's there?"

Josef heard the gruff words but didn't move. He still had the gun over his shoulder, he still had the confidence that came with the uniform in this land full of German soldiers. He could pass a soldier or be caught a spy. Did it really matter what happened to him now?

At last he looked up. The man before him was solidly built but stooped, as if he'd spent his life slouched or bent. Middle age had not set well with him. His skin sagged around the mouth and along the jaw. Perhaps a beard would have covered such a flaw, except that if it were gray like the hair along his temples, it would only exchange one sign of age for another.

It was, however, the look on his face that was so curious. He stared at Josef as if he'd seen the face from one of the gravesites around them.

"What are you doing there?" he asked, and his voice was throaty, as if he were even older than he appeared.

"My name is Josef von Woerner," said Josef in his easy German tongue. "This is my mother." He swept an open palm over the site at his side, as if presenting her in living flesh.

The man's eyes changed from suspicious scrutiny to momentary astonishment. He took a step closer, never taking that intruding gaze from Josef's face.

"Yes," he said, stopping when only the low fence stood between them. "Yes."

"Yes?"

"Yes?"

"You are like her."

"You knew her?"

His gaze left Josef's face for the first time since he'd looked up. He looked at her headstone as if he saw another face there. "Yes, I knew her." The gaze returned for another searching look. "Everyone knew your mother, before she went to America. We all know the von Mannheim family here."

Josef said nothing. He knew so much about Germany and its history, but so little of his family. Otto hadn't told him much about that—his own or of his wife's.

"So, you came back to fight for the fatherland, eh?"

The man seemed neither impressed nor disgusted by the observation, so Josef said nothing.

"I came to visit her grave," he said. "I wanted to see where she was." He started to turn away but stopped after he stepped outside the iron border. "Do you take care of things here?"

The man nodded.

"She would have liked this."

The man nodded again. "Like all von Mannheim's. It's the flowers."

Josef started to walk away.

"Why did you come back?"

Josef stopped again, but had no idea how to answer. He'd been a spy in America, and now it seemed he could be caught a spy in Germany.

The man stepped closer. He was shorter than Josef, but perhaps only because he couldn't stand up straight. He had a look of open disapproval.

"You weren't born here. Why come back to fight?"

Josef averted his gaze. He had to be careful, but he knew the correct answer. The answer most Germans would want to hear. "My parents are citizens of Germany. That makes me a citizen as well. The fatherland."

The man snorted and turned away, facing the church. "The fatherland is not what it used to be before the Kaiser crushed it in his palm." Then he looked at Josef again. "You are a fool. I'm glad your mother is dead and cannot see you."

Josef looked around. What kind of words were these, spoken so easily, which would be thought treasonous to Germany?

"Many men have died for the fatherland," Josef said softly, "for the Kaiser. You turn your back on it so easily—on them?"

He faced Josef again and shook his head. "No, not on them. But on the Kaiser?" He spat on the ground. "This is what I think of the Kaiser."

Josef looked around again, expecting at any moment a squad to come and arrest the man and Josef with him. Was this some sort of trap? Did he suspect Josef of being an Allied soldier?

Whatever the truth, Josef thought it would be safer to go back into hiding. He suddenly felt as though he'd been too bold.

He started to walk away.

"You might as well follow me," the older man said quietly. "I'll give you food and take you to the border."

Josef turned around, blood surging again, veins swelling to allow greater flow. He scanned the horizon, but there was no one around.

"Three men escaped from Camp Sixty-Eight yesterday. Search parties have passed through, two waves of them. You are not fighting with the Germans, are you, Josef, but with the Allies?"

Part of him wanted to run, to get away from whatever knowledge this man had. But he was too tired, and he'd run too many times before. Besides, it made no difference. He had no home now, not in America or in Germany.

He offered neither a defense nor an admission.

"Come with me," the man said.

Josef could have run, resisted, or even overpowered the older German. But he followed.

The man led him to a cottage not far from the church. No one else was on the narrow dirt street at this pre-dawn hour. He opened the door to a low-ceilinged, one-room home, with a door as solid as the man himself. The contents were clean and uncluttered, the furniture simple and sturdy. He went to a cupboard and pulled out a loaf of brown bread, cutting a hefty slice for Josef.

"Take this. It doesn't offer much by way of taste, but it's probably better than what you've had lately."

That much was true. It could have been the flakiest French pastry ever made, it was so far superior to the gruel he'd been eating. The man pulled forward a cane-backed chair for Josef and sat on the bench at the other side of the table.

"Where are the other two?"

Josef said nothing. It was one thing to take a risk for himself, especially when it came with bread, but it was another altogether to betray the whereabouts of his fellow soldiers.

The man accepted Josef's silence. He leaned on the table and folded his hands before him. "We are seventeen kilometers from the Swiss border. The hills are the shortest route, but it is snowing already across the Swiss border in the Alps. The pass is guarded twenty-four hours a day. You have no choice but to take the high route."

Josef swallowed what was in his mouth. "Why are you doing this?"

The man smiled. "You mean to ask why you should trust me?"

"Something like that, yes."

"Because I have seen enough of this war. Because I now care for the gravesites of half the men in this village. Because I'm hungry and poor. Because one of those graves is my son's. It is a fool's war. I'm sick of all the death that the Kaiser brought to us. He's not Bismarck."

Josef took another bite, wondering why the man hated the Kaiser, and asked him.

"Let us say only that my loyalty is to the von Mannheim family first. I am a von Mannheim. Your mother was my sister."

CHAPTER *Twenty*

THE SUN glowed beyond the eastern horizon as Josef found his way back to Dack and Caleb.

"What took you so long?"

"Where'd you get that bag? What's in it?"

Josef withdrew half the bread that his uncle Gustaf had wrapped and placed in the leather pouch. From beneath that he pulled a pair of shoes that would be too large for Dack but far better than what he wore. He had another pair for Caleb.

"Where'd you get this stuff?" asked the sergeant.

"Somebody gave them to me, along with some very good advice. Soon as you've put on those shoes, we'll get out of here. The searchers are due back in this area any time now."

The shoes were well worn but sturdy as boots.

"How's the knee, Sarge?" asked Josef.

"Fine," he said, rubbing off a crease of dust on the new footwear, as if he'd just purchased them at a store. Josef knew better than to believe him about the knee. It was still swollen. They'd been warned about punctures and tetanus back in the trenches.

Josef searched the bag again, though it was nearly empty now. "Here. Pour some of that on it." It wasn't exactly medicine, but it would have to do.

Sergeant Dack sniffed the amber colored liquid and his eyes lit up. "Are you kiddin'? I'm drinkin' this!"

Then he had a swig and offered it to Caleb.

"It's for your leg, Sarge, if you want to keep it."

Disappointment crossed Caleb's face. Josef took the bottle back, sliding Dack's plain dark cotton pant leg up to reveal the wound.

"Want me to do it, or do you want to do it yourself?"

"You can have the honors," Dack said, looking away. But with a quick glance back, he added, "Just don't use it all."

Josef applied the burning, cleansing liquor sparingly but thoroughly. Dack winced, and his muscles tensed from head to foot. When Josef righted the bottle, looking to assure himself that he hadn't missed any part, Dack snatched it from his hand. "That'll do," he said, and swallowed the remains that swirled at the bottom of the small, clear bottle.

He tossed the empty glass over his shoulder, looking at the same time at Caleb, who was busy finishing the rest of the bread.

"Any more of that?"

Josef pulled the other half from a cloth. "We'll have to get going," he warned. "We have a long day ahead of us. Grab the old shoes, Caleb. We'll pitch them down one of these hills. Maybe those dogs will pick up the scent. That'll distract them awhile."

Josef and Caleb pulled Dack to his feet, and they were on their way. Josef knew exactly where they were going.

"See that hill over there? We're going over it. On the other side is a lake. A big lake." He didn't mention that unless Gustaf met them there with a boat they wouldn't be able to cross. It was too wide to swim.

Once they reached the other side, the high country would be a lot harder to cross than the low-lying hills around them now. But he wouldn't tell them about that yet.

If the others looked horrified, Josef didn't want to see it. He didn't want to see their faces at all. If they didn't think they could cover the ground, most of it wide open with nothing more than a dip or roll to hide in, he didn't want to know. And, if they thought they could make it, he didn't want to know that, either. Both options seemed foolhardy. They must flee not only patrols but a civilian population warned to be looking for them. Josef forged ahead, hoping the other two would follow.

Dack had little choice, despite his protest.

"There's bound to be a pass," he suggested before long.

"Yes, a well guarded one," Josef said. "It's this way or we go back to the German camp, Sarge. Take your pick."

No one uttered any more qualms after that.

They stayed off the road and kept any bushes or tree knolls in view for possible cover. They saw a few farms, but no people. If anyone still inhabited the homesteads they kept to themselves.

"We saw an explosion after we got away," Caleb said after a while. His voice was near breathless from their pace and from alternately helping Dack. "We thought it was an Allied bomber, come to save our skins. But we didn't hear any planes, just bombs exploding. Know anything about that?"

"It was the munitions plant. There was an accident."

Caleb's eyes widened. "You mean you . . . ?"

Josef said nothing, but even Dack looked at him sideways, impressed.

"Find anything out about Birchall?" Dack asked.

"Reports say three prisoners were on the run. Birchall must have been caught."

That quieted all three for a long time. When anyone spoke again it was only to complain about the terrain or Dack muttering a curse.

At the sound of motorcars or wagons passing in the distance, Josef hit the tall grass and pulled Dack down. Caleb quickly followed until the air was quiet again. Later, when there were no trees to provide cover, they crawled at the slightest noise. Dack pulled himself along without assistance. They traveled through mud and weeds, a creek and over rocks.

Josef led them far off the road. They needed a wide sweep if they were to make it undetected. Uncle Gustaf had told him there were soldiers looking for them, but not many around here. There were few left this far from the front anyway. The men left behind were as old and stooped as him or too young to leave their mamas.

The air grew cooler the farther they traveled up the hill, and they stopped talking. With each step Josef grew more hopeful. Dack tried to hobble on his own, a sturdy stick aiding him.

"It isn't far now," Josef said, something in his gut telling him it was true. It had to be; they'd come farther than he expected already.

"I was thinkin' that same thought two hours ago," Dack complained.

"It's true now," Josef said. He believed it, and he'd make them believe it, too.

Then they heard the soldiers again, and the baying of dogs. He knew then his forced hope had been precarious at best.

He looked back. Three Germans with two dogs straining on long leashes. Only a furlong away.

Josef rushed to Dack's side. Making a run was their only choice. If Josef's guess was right, the lake wasn't much farther. Maybe they'd be able to see it over the next crest. Caleb joined him on Dack's other side.

"Let me go, guys—go on your own. You'll never make it with me."

But Josef clung all the harder, looking at Caleb.

"Get over the hill, Caleb. Run. Look for a man in a boat."

Confusion clouded Caleb's face, wasting essential moments.

"Run!" Josef commanded, and his bark was nearly as vicious as the ones behind them.

Caleb took off faster than Josef would have believed possible. His little brother might make it. That was all that mattered.

Josef felt Dack's weight. He saw new blood on the sergeant's pants, felt each burst of pain in the other's labored breathing. But Dack ran, miraculously keeping up the pace Josef set.

A shot whistled by, followed quickly by a closer growl. Josef pulled the last of the food from his pocket, throwing it down. The dog was probably starving like the rest of Germany. He might stop the chase for the crust of bread. Snarls were soon heard from behind as the dogs both went for the bread.

The soldiers weren't so easily deterred. Another shot went off, and Josef felt something graze his clothing. But he felt no pain. It must have missed. He ran harder, pulling Dack along.

The summit of the hill was only paces away. Josef gasped for air, but his lungs couldn't fill. Dack tripped, pulling Josef downward, but Josef heaved him up and the two were righted again. At the crest he saw what he was desperate to see: the lake, crystal blue and wide. Just opposite lie Switzerland and the Alps.

"We can make it!"

Caleb had disappeared into trees at the base that edged the lake. Caleb would make it. They might all make it.

Then Josef felt the sting. Barely more than the prick of a bee at first, until blood spread over his uniform, warm and oozing from the shoulder that held most of Dack's weight. Josef's arm went limp, and Dack went down.

"Go!" Dack gasped. "Get out of here."

But Josef didn't listen. Instead, he pushed Dack with all his weight down the long, steep incline. He rolled and slid faster than either of them could have navigated the slope on foot. Josef followed, only moments behind. He landed nearby, not far from the trees that offered blessed cover. Hauling himself up, he pulled on Dack, and with his good arm he hoisted the other along.

"The lake is there, and if we make that—we're free!"

The sergeant heaved himself forward. Josef didn't know where either of them found the strength, except that with each step he praised the Lord.

One dog had resumed its chase and stumbled down the hill. Josef had no more food to throw him off. But the dog did not bite when he reached them, only lunged as if trained to trip the prey and not bring damage. Josef jumped and swung Dack along, pulling him over the dog yet too weak to succeed. Dack's feet landed on the dog's back and just as Josef yanked the sergeant off the animal, it rolled out of the way with a yelp. The animal lurched away, resuming its persistent barking from a safer distance. Bullets thumped into the trunks of nearby trees, but Josef saw the edge of the water and new energy burst to his limbs. Dack must have seen it, too. It was just as Gustaf had described. Lake Constance. Josef knew the name from old maps. This was the northwestern finger that jutted from Switzerland into Germany. All they had to do was get to that boat and row like they'd never rowed before.

The trees ended and the shoreline loomed close. Josef panicked. No sign of Caleb or Gustaf. Then from up the way he heard a shout. Caleb waved his arms like a flagger in front of Gustaf and his boat, rowing toward them, keeping close to shore.

Another surge of strength came from Dack. He was almost pulling Josef for a moment. They splashed into the icy water, scrambling to Caleb's outstretched arms.

Then the shooting behind them stopped. It simply stopped. Even the dog, now panting beside the soldiers, sat quietly and watched as the boat took Josef and the others away.

CHAPTER *Twenty-One*

L*ISSA* *SAT* on the edge of her cot, letting the curtain separating her from the next bed fall back into place. She was so tired she didn't think she could take off her shoes, let alone her jacket, apron, cap, or dress.

"Hey, Liss, can I come in?"

"Sure," she said without moving. Only her eyes looked up.

Minnie Osborn laughed. She was a relatively new arrival and barely over twenty-one, but with the energy of a teenager. "You look done in, friend."

"I am." She raised her feet from the floor, careful to keep her dirty shoes off the edge of her cot. She didn't need to sleep with the mud, too. Without being asked, Minnie unlaced Lissa's shoes. "I just wanted to see if we could switch shifts tomorrow. You have the morning off and I have the afternoon. But just looking at you, I can tell you need the morning to sleep."

Lissa nodded, turning over on her side after kicking off her loosened shoes. "Sorry, Min. Maybe next week."

"Okay, sure. Oh, I'll just leave this for you to read tomorrow, then. I picked it up with my letter by mistake."

Lissa didn't open her eyes. "What is it?"

"A letter from the States. Return marked P. Tanner."

"Thanks," she murmured, but didn't have the strength to open it. Tomorrow was soon enough to read Penny's letter.

———————

Josef savored each sip of hot chocolate, comfortable for the first time in what seemed a lifetime. He looked at Caleb and Dack, who were asleep in bunks. The house was more like a cabin, like a place Josef had pictured in the wild West back home. There was a single room with open wooden beams holding up the ceiling, plain whitewashed walls, massive fireplace on the far end. A round table sat on top of a multi-colored rug over a polished wood floor, and a cupboard with Dutch china sat off to one side. The only light came from the snapping fire in the fireplace.

Adelbert Bálint stoked the fire, then pulled a chair from beside the table to face the light and warmth.

"Fever's gone, I see." Adelbert spoke without looking Josef's way.

"Yes." Josef wondered how the old man could tell without laying a hand on him. But Josef had learned that when the Lord touches something, amazing things could happen. Having Adelbert Bálint find them wandering the snowy Swiss Alps was one of those amazing things.

Maybe it wasn't so amazing to Adelbert, the retired Swiss physician who said he spent his days looking for those just like Josef and his two companions. His hunting cottage was filled with blankets, food, and such luxuries as the chocolate Josef now sipped. A small hut Adelbert had once used to skin his catches was now a delousing shed where men washed off the filth of war while their clothes were baked and brushed free of vermin. At least that was what he did when the clothes were worth saving. Theirs weren't.

Dack's leg had been cleaned and sewn shut, with no sign of the dreaded tetanus. Caleb once more had escaped without a scratch, to Josef's relief and chagrin. It would reinforce his brother's sense of indestructibility. Josef's shoulder, grazed by a German bullet, was healing nicely.

They might have wandered the Swiss wilderness for days had Adelbert not been on one of his hunting trips. Before the war he hunted game. Now he hunted escaped refugees, deserters, or former prisoners like them. He'd picked up their trail and found them only hours after Uncle Gustaf had sent them off with blankets and a meager sack of food. Adelbert had helped more than a hundred such escapees since that first fall of the war, back in '14. Gustaf von Mannheim knew of men like Adelbert and sent them off in his direction. Then Uncle Gustaf had gotten back in his boat and returned to Germany.

"Tomorrow, then," Adelbert said, looking at the sway of the fire rather than Josef, "someone will come to take you to the village."

Adelbert spoke of the wagon or sleigh, depending on the weather, that came by every couple of weeks to drop off supplies and pick up whatever strays Adelbert took in. Adelbert didn't keep any pack animals himself, so he'd made the arrangement with the baker down in the village, who was as sympathetic as Adelbert to the plight of anyone escaping Germany or Austria-Hungary.

Josef stared at the fire as well, wondering what direction he would go from here. Knowing his identity, he couldn't rejoin the American Expeditionary Force. He was bound to be found out sooner or later. He'd be dishonorably discharged and likely face charges of treason. But what other option did he have? He could claim his old name and demand sanctuary with the former German Ambassador to the U.S., Count Johann von Bernstorff. Bernstorff most likely would not know Josef's face or even his name, but Josef was fairly confident he remembered the covert activities he'd suggested. He would be granted an audience; might even be offered a commission in the German army. That's what he'd once hoped if he ever made it to the fatherland—the place Otto had always told Josef was home.

The lights of the fire jumped and bobbed, and Josef stared at the gold flecked sparks. What he saw instead of the fire were the golden eyes of Larisa Rose. Home. The word was as warm as the heat from the fire, and somehow he couldn't separate the feeling of home from the memory of Larisa's face.

His jaw hardened. She wouldn't give him a chance, once she found out about his past. She wasn't some casual American who cared little about this war. Though he tried to steel his heart to her rejection, the ache of emptiness gnawed him. If he went to her, confessed everything, begged her to forgive him, maybe . . .

What then? She'd forget about his past deeds against the country she loved and go on the run with him? They would hide out for the rest of her life so the authorities wouldn't find him? Now that was just the sort of secure future he wanted to offer the woman he loved.

Josef leaned against the headboard. He closed his eyes and held steady the warm cup in his hands.

Lord, tell me what to do.

He knew what he wanted to do; that feeling was no different after praying for guidance. He wanted to go home. He wanted to go back to the United States.

He remembered the way it was before the day he woke with Hank hovering over him—when he thought Otto was his father and he sold glass and coking coal, and met with German infiltrators on some of his "business" trips. Josef had been convinced that Germany had all the answers. The fatherland held the path to a brighter future for all. He'd said as much to Liesel that day she confronted him. He'd been so sure his furtive work was noble, not the dishonest, dishonorable mischief Liesel seemed to think.

She'd been the wiser. She'd told him to go and fight openly for the Germans, not sneak around and use innocent Americans to further Germany's goals. So now he had come to Germany, but it wasn't home as he'd been told from his earliest recollection. Hadn't Otto always said they were Germans, not Americans? But what else had Josef known, except that country? He'd been born there, he was a citizen. Germany wasn't what he'd expected. It certainly wasn't home. Not like America.

Josef moaned as he contemplated his dilemma.

"You have something on your mind other than the war, I think," said Adelbert in his heavily accented English.

Josef opened his eyes and spoke in German, "I've heard about shell shock. Maybe that's all this is."

Adelbert laughed. "I've seen shell shock and you don't have it, young man. And you could have told me you spoke German earlier, instead of making an old man work so hard."

Josef let out a long, slow breath. What did he have to lose? He glanced over at the other two narrow beds. They were probably still sleeping, but even if they weren't, what was he going to do, hide his past forever? They'd know something was up if he didn't get on that train for France tomorrow.

"I have a decision to make, without a good choice."

Firelight shadowed Adelbert's face. He had an angular look, a sharp nose and chin, high forehead, and stark white hair. It was not a handsomely aged face by any standard, but a distinguished one. Perhaps it was the look in his eyes of wisdom that came with a long life.

"We all come to those places, sooner or later."

Josef nodded. "I suppose. But this decision—it isn't just whether to get married or be faithful to a wife or cheat my neighbor. Those decisions for me would be easy. God gave me a conscience, and now I have a desire to do what is right." He leaned his head back again and stared ahead, seeing only the door in the center of the opposite wall. By the time he left tomorrow, he'd have to know where he was headed. "I have to decide how I'm going to spend the rest of my life—a man dishonored but of free conscience who sits behind bars, or a coward on the run."

"It sounds as though you have made your decision."

"I know the right thing to do, the honorable thing. But I don't know if I have the strength to carry it through."

He heard Dack stir from the other side of the room.

"Just thought I'd let you know I'm listening in, Joe. Not that it matters, I can't understand a word. Why didn't you tell us you spoke German?"

He sat up, swinging both good and bad leg over the side.

"I didn't remember how until we were in the prison camp."

Caleb sat up as well, without a hint of drowsiness. "I couldn't make out much either, but do you remember your past now?"

Josef pulled himself to the edge of his own bunk and placed his feet on the floor without getting up. He stared intently at Caleb, knowing that what he had to say would have an impact on him, too. "Yes, Caleb. I remember everything."

"Since when?"

"Since the night you woke me from that dream, when I was dreaming about my mother."

Caleb nodded. "Why didn't you say something?"

"It's complicated," he began, but even as he tried to offer that evasive answer, he knew Caleb deserved more. "I remember things that could get me—and your father—into a lot of trouble."

"My father? Why?"

"He helped me avoid being arrested and going to prison."

Dack and Caleb exchanged glances. Adelbert, whose smattering of English obviously included that word, looked at Josef just as curiously.

"What did you do?" Caleb asked. "And how did my father help you?"

"You might as well know, your father—our father—lied to both of us about my name." At Caleb's look of shocked disbelief, Josef shook his head and held up a hand before Caleb could voice a protest. "He only wanted to protect me—both of us, I guess, but mostly me. I guess he was trying to make up for lost time. He wanted a chance for a part in my life."

Josef caught Dack's confused stare. "I'm illegitimate," he explained. "Caleb is my half brother, as you know from our different last names. Only my name is Josef von W-o-e-r-n-e-r, not Josef Warner. Our father was hired by the man I thought was my father to get me out of trouble."

"What kind of trouble were you in?" Dack asked.

"I was working for a German network in America, before—and for a while after—we got into the war."

Dack whistled. "You mean you were a spy?"

"A saboteur, actually," Josef said. "I set up rallies to make people think pacifism was the wisest course, not to fight. I told them to avoid the draft. I infiltrated munitions plants to start strikes. I helped plant firebombs on private ships loaded with ammunition that were being sold to the Allies."

Dread grew on Caleb's face, as clear as any look of admiration he'd ever shot Josef's way. "And my father helped you. Was he working for the Germans, too?"

"No, no! When he found out I was in trouble, he took the chance to help me. That's all. But it's enough to get him into trouble for aiding and abetting. He sheltered me. If I'd gotten my memory back sooner, he might have done whatever he could to get me out of the States."

"Well, you're out now," Dack said. "Let me get this straight: you didn't remember all that spy stuff you did? You forgot?"

"I forgot every memory of my life. When I joined the army I didn't have a clue who I was."

"You passed the physicals?"

Josef shrugged. "They took my height and weight and checked my heart. They didn't ask about anything in my head."

Dack rubbed his hands over his face, as if embarrassed by the entire United States Army. "How many nuts do you think they take in a day?" He looked at Josef with a sheepish smile. "Hey, I owe you my life, buddy. Here I thought you were some kind of squeaky-clean missionary, and I find out you're a man with a past. I'm just tryin' to figure it out, that's all. So, what are you, American or German?"

Josef looked from Dack to Caleb, who seemed just as interested in how Josef answered that question. But Josef wasn't ready to say. There was no easy answer.

"I'm sorry, Caleb."

Caleb plastered his eyes on Josef. "Sorry? Sorry you're a traitor? Or sorry you had to tell me?"

"Both, I guess."

"So what are you going to do? Go back to Germany? Guess you're some kind of hero there."

Josef said nothing.

Dack spoke in his place. "It's a cinch he can't go back to the States, ain't it? But I don't know what kind of traitor he can be, the way he saved our skins and blew up a German ammo factory. You want to see him go back to America, to jail?"

"Maybe that's . . ."

Though Caleb cut himself short, Josef didn't need to see the guilty look on Caleb's face to guess what he'd been about to say.

"Yeah, you're right," Josef said.

Caleb looked away.

There was silence for a while, then Adelbert quietly asked for translations of a few things he hadn't caught, and Josef explained it all in his fluent German. Josef was aware of Caleb watching him, as if he didn't know who he was. He looked like a kid who'd lost his best friend. Maybe he was.

"So that's it. Born in America; raised a German."

"I was born in Germany," Adelbert said quietly. "Many in these hills were born across the border."

Josef eyed him curiously. "It's a good thing your country has been able to stay neutral, then. Easier for you, I mean."

The older man stood and went to the plain wooden mantle upon which sat a pipe. He took a reed from a cup beside the fire, lit it in the flames, and applied the end to the tobacco. The pungent smoke permeated the room.

"Is it easy to define patriotism?" he asked without looking at Josef. "Switzerland is many peoples, German, French, Italian. We have long struggled to define what it is to be Swiss. But this *war* . . ." He said the word after a pause, as if it were harder to say than all others, ". . . has helped us to do so. It has united neighbors, who no longer are *Italian* Swiss or *French* Swiss. Patriotism is a decision, Josef. It often comes without any feeling of jubilation. Does a mother feel joy to watch her son go off to war? No, there is no joy in that duty. Patriotism is a duty, perhaps not an emotion at all. It is a duty greater than leftover attachments to the place we left behind."

Josef thought of America, "the melting pot," and how many people had made the decision Adelbert described. He thought of how similar he was to this old man, who had been born in Germany.

"How do you do your duty to Switzerland, Adelbert? You've helped us, but it goes against Germany."

"I prefer to think I'm not working against anyone but rather for . . . all people. I am a physician, a Swiss physician. I help humans, not POWs."

"Nothing political about it, then," Josef concluded. "Really, for me there wasn't either. I never did what I did to go against the United States. I was only against the ammunition being used to kill Germans." Then he asked, with all the innocence of a child, "Do you think Germany is wrong in this war?"

Adelbert puffed again on his pipe and took his seat. Josef heard Caleb and Dack talking quietly, probably wondering what they discussed in German. But he desperately wanted to hear what the old man had to say.

"If I were to listen to my cousins across the border, they would remind me it was the Russians who attacked us first. They would say France would have attacked if Germany hadn't. The French have always wanted Alsace Lorraine returned. They want a bit of revenge that Germany took it in the first place. Italy has wanted to push her frontier up into Austria. Do you know Germany was not a united people until several years ago? As an empire, Germany was left behind with its own quarrels while other countries went about claiming colonies all over the globe.

"So I understand why they did what they did. They alone are not to blame. Many European businesses were enjoying the profits from that ammunition you blew up. I think it is not so much a matter of right and wrong any more. The question is which side is the greater fool for having let it last so long with so little purpose on either part."

Josef leaned back, finishing his now tepid chocolate. Adelbert's words were of little comfort. There was no right and wrong to this war, which made it all the more difficult to choose sides. Adelbert had chosen loyalty to his adopted country, but if Switzerland had chosen to war against Germany, would he be so patriotic then?

Adelbert rose from his seat and played the host, cutting bread and hard cheese, distributing it to his guests. A pall covered the room, making the prospect of their rescue gloomy rather than the triumph it had been the evening before. Josef could feel it, smell it as he smelled the smoke of Adelbert's pipe.

Josef didn't know what to say, how to break through. He guessed the trail of Caleb's thoughts, how he must wonder where Josef's loyalties lay. Was he somebody else, now that he had his memories? He was no longer Josef Warner, American soldier, but Josef von Woerner, German spy?

Caleb was the first to break the silence. "You blew up one of their plants." He said it like it nagged him, like a gnat flying around his ears.

Josef didn't deny it.

Caleb stood up. "You can't go back . . . to Germany, I mean. People saw you. It might get out. And I'm not sure you even want to."

Josef continued to sit without a word. He offered neither confirmation nor denial.

"Whose side are you on now? Ours or theirs?"

Finally Josef stood as well. They were about the same height, and the room wasn't large. For a moment it looked like a face-off, except that Josef felt nothing but compassion for the confusion on the younger man's face. He wanted to call him brother or refer to their blood tie. Certainly they'd become that in the past few months. Sharing the trenches could easily take the place of a lifetime of sharing the same roof. But he couldn't speak of that.

"I don't know if this'll make sense, Caleb. I don't feel like I'm on either side when it comes to the war. I'm on God's side."

"Oh, here it comes. The conscientious objector finally steps out." Dack said. But he didn't sound disgusted the way he used to. He sounded amused. He stood too, and placed himself between them. He was shorter than either of them and glanced up from one to the other. "Look, Caleb, whatever this here brother of yours has been up to, the faith business was no act." He looked at Josef, adding, "Not that I doubted it, the way we razzed you, and you just took it all those months."

He turned back to Caleb. "What I'm sayin' is, to me it don't seem to matter which side he's on. He saved our skins, didn't he? Got us outta that camp? It wasn't like they was followin' the rules of war back there, was they? They coulda' killed us and gotten away with it when they was done usin' us as slave labor. Now, I fer one wouldn't want to join a side that did that to prisoners, even lowly ones like us. But that's up to Joe, see, Caleb? You remember who got you out when you look at him like he just betrayed you and the whole United States of America. Got it?"

Dack winked Josef's way. "See? Not a single curse word in any of that."

Caleb didn't seem to appreciate Dack's humor. He scowled. "He's not your brother. You don't have to go back and have the whole country look at you and say, 'There he goes, the brother of the traitor.'"

Sergeant Dack looked about to say something, but Josef shook his head. "Just like it felt when the whole town was whispering, 'There he goes, the brother of the bastard?'"

Caleb took a step back, turning to the fireplace. "I suppose, somethin' like that." He looked back over his shoulder. "Only I didn't care about the bastard stuff. That only bothered the women. This is different."

Dack slapped Caleb on the shoulder, none too gently. "What'ya think, boy, this is about your social status? Shoot, kid, Joe's got to start over from scratch, and you're worried about what people'll think of you?" Dack turned from Caleb as if disgusted, then faced Josef again. "What ya gonna do, Joe?"

The blunt question was the one Josef couldn't stop asking himself. He ran a hand through his hair, turned back to his bunk and sat down, holding his forehead in his palms and staring at the floor. "I don't know."

"Looks to me like you got no choice. You can't go back home, at least not until the war's over. Maybe then people won't be of a mind to hang somebody they can blame for all the boys gettin' shot over here. Heck, Caleb's prob-

ably right. I'm not sure you can go back to Germany and claim that fancy-schmancy von-whatever name, neither. You blew up one of their munitions plants. Maybe going back there's not what you want, anyway. Maybe you can go and join the Bolsheviks. They told all them Russkies to go home and stop fightin', didn't they? Maybe you can be the rock solid pacifist I always thought you were. I don't know.

"You get what some people who mess up don't, though. You can start over and pick a new life. Listen, me and Caleb'll go back and swear Joe Warner got shot a hero—an American hero—gettin' us outta that camp. They ever connect the Josef von-whatever to Joe Warner, they got no case against a dead man. So you're free to live your life as you choose, without anybody on your trail. Got it?"

Josef watched Dack's earnest face, fully convinced he would do what he said. He would lie to protect him. He glanced over at Caleb. He wasn't sure it would be so easy for him.

But Caleb didn't let Josef look at his face for long. He turned his back.

Josef stood again. "Just start over." But saying the words was far easier than entertaining the concept.

Even as Dack's plan made the most sense, the ache that had begun the moment his memories returned loomed greater at the prospect.

Start over without Larisa?

"Just one problem with the plan, Dack," said Josef, but he was thinking aloud rather than speaking clearly enough for anyone in the room to easily hear him. "Just one problem."

When he didn't expand, Dack looked from Josef to Caleb and back again, obviously waiting for some explanation.

Caleb nodded. "Larisa Rose Parker."

Josef didn't deny the truth.

CHAPTER *Twenty-Two*

LISSA WOKE with the immediate feeling of having overslept. She sat up quickly, then remembered she wasn't due back at the wards until noon. Fishing in the pocket of the dress she'd never taken off, she found her father's timepiece. Eleven o'clock. She'd slept twelve hours.

She had just enough time to wash and change into the clean clothes in her cubbyhole. On her way out, she stepped on the letter Minnie had dropped off the night before, scooped it up, and tucked it into her pocket.

The wards were so full, the army had built a temporary wood hut in the yard for the nurses. She dreaded to think of the coming winter. If it were anything like the last one, the hut wouldn't be warm enough. She sighed as she entered the back entrance to the consulate. Maybe the war would be over before another winter set in. Rumors were rampant again, about how the Germans were in retreat all along the four hundred and fifty mile front. Maybe this time the rumors would prove true. How long could they hold out, now that more American soldiers poured in every day? An endless supply of fresh blood to soak into the fields of France.

Lissa planned to read Penny's letter over lunch at the canteen. But Sister Mary Michel arrived at the same time, and the two of them shared the meal and discussed patients instead.

The day went as all others had. She eased what suffering she could, rationing out what few supplies were on hand. The day had one bit of a reprieve: no shipments of new patients. That was just as well since they had no free beds.

Lissa still had not been able to return to the children's ward, which was now entirely upstairs. But she didn't miss the suffering there, either.

Her day ended two hours later than she'd been scheduled. After she ate and returned to her bunk, she was nearly as tired as she'd been the night before. With a yawn, she rubbed her eyes, wondering if she had the energy to stay awake long enough to read Penny's letter. Lissa reclined on her bed and pulled the now crumpled envelope from her pocket.

It was dated only a few weeks ago, the first one she'd received since her friend had returned home. It would be good to get her perspective on things back home. From the weight, Lissa guessed it was several pages long.

But as she withdrew the stationary, newspaper clippings dropped into her lap. Lissa read the letter first.

> *My dearest friend,*
>
> What I have to say will not be easy for you to hear. I have wrestled with my conscience, whether or not to be the bearer of ill tidings, but I cannot help feeling honesty is what you need most, more than the protection of ignorance.

Confused by such a dour opening, Lissa skimmed down and noticed Josef's name written several times. Her heart thudded hard against her chest. Anxiety rose.

> Josef Warner, the son my father so gallantly brought home to help start a new life, is not the innocent illegitimate child we all believed him to be. He's a traitor, Liss, and what's more, he's wanted by federal authorities.
>
> My father—Josef's father, too, I have to remind myself— risked his own peaceful life to save Josef. I'm sure he was spurred by guilt because of the way Josef was born. But my father paid a price. He was arrested while I was away. It seems a very dedicated federal agent spotted Josef. He came back and snooped around and

found out that Josef Warner is none other than Josef von Woerner,
a notorious saboteur who worked for a network of German spies.

He's guilty of all kinds of crimes, Liss! He blew up ships! I'm
sending you some clips from an old D.C. newspaper I was able to
dig up at Cooper's. You know he never throws anything away. Our
papers barely covered the story, but the D.C. story included a sketch
of Josef. The reports say Josef died in the river, but we all know good
ol' Daddy fished him out and saved his life.

As incredible as it sounds, your dear, precious Josef isn't worth
the deep denial you have sunk into since his disappearance and
probable death. He was a criminal. If he were still alive, they'd
arrest him on the spot.

Father says the French police have been notified by our
government to keep an eye out for him, just in case he did somehow
miraculously survive as you so desperately want to believe.

I'm so sorry, dear Lissa, but you must know the truth. I want
you to be rid of his memory, so you can get on with your life. Finish
your tour of duty over there if you must and come home and find
someone else to love. You deserve to be happy.

And if you want to know my opinion, I think Josef
remembered everything all along. It was all pretty convenient,
wasn't it, to have my father protect him? What greater purpose had
he than to get home to his precious Germany? I tell you, Liss, if
Josef really is alive as you so passionately hope, I'll bet he took that
mission to penetrate German lines so he could get back to the other
side to his German cronies. Only problem is, he took Caleb with
him. I'll never forgive him for that.

Father has had to give up his investigation license because of
his involvement with Josef. He had to sell out a quarter of his stock
to pay the fines. Imagine, my father suspected of sedition for helping
Josef! You can bet the town's had some fun with all of this, except
their gutter gossip is subdued because they think Josef's dead. And
they feel sorry because of Caleb. But I know they talk. I've seen it
on every face when I go to town.

*Come home, Liss. Your tour of duty is almost up. I know
you've had a notion to stay in hopes of Josef being alive, but even if
he is, it's useless now. Come home. The air is fresh here.*

Love,

Penny

Lissa read the letter, confused. It was ridiculous, all of it. Josef, a spy? It was too silly to imagine.

Then she saw the clippings, the minor headlines on the death of a suspected spy. Perhaps some of the article was written as propaganda, just to feed the public's ready fears that the German enemy was at the doorstep. But soon the words she'd overheard in the Tanner study came back to her, about saving Josef from a lynch mob.

Oh, Josef, Josef, could it be true? Could any of it be true? Could you have worked against your own government?

It was inconceivable. It would be like betraying one's own family, the very foundation upon which life was lived, the freedom, the protection, the order of a country run by its own people. Who could ever betray it?

Lissa studied the letter and clippings again. They were from a familiar Washington paper, *The Star.* The caption below a sketch of a smiling Josef read: "Suspected spy lost in the Potomac." Below that the article began:

> Josef von Woerner, whose parents immigrated here from Germany, is presumed drowned in the Potomac River after fleeing federal officials. Von Woerner has been connected to covert action with the sole purpose of slowing American involvement in the European war, from sedition to arson, planned and funded by a German network right here on American soil.

She skipped down a paragraph, numbness giving way to an erratic heartbeat.

> His whereabouts were tipped off by another German-American, Liesel Bonner, reported to be his fiancée. Bonner is not thought to have had any involvement in or knowledge of von Woerner's illegal activities. She is

hailed a patriot by the Federal agent who headed the case, claiming her help was instrumental in ending the criminal's nefarious career.

Lissa saw the papers in her hands tremble. A criminal. A nefarious criminal. With a fiancée. It couldn't be true. He wouldn't have kept all that to himself. But he didn't. He couldn't remember. In spite of what Penny so eagerly suspected, Josef wouldn't have been able to hide the truth. Not if he truly loved another woman.

Could he?

The moisture of warm tears on her cheeks was her first indication that she was crying. But she brushed the wetness angrily away. It wasn't true! All of it was a lie! Josef loved her. He hadn't fooled them just to bide his time until he could get to Germany. He'd joined the American army. He came to fight against the Germans.

And he'd loved her!

"Oh, Josef," she cried, and fell to her pillow, a mass of pain and confusion.

———

Josef watched Adelbert standing at the open threshold. The fresh mountain air was warmer today than yesterday. "The wagon is coming up the hill," the older man said over his shoulder. Rather than going outside he took a step back, leaving the door open. "It will take another ten minutes for them to reach us. Looks like there are two riders today."

He went to the table, wrapping the leftover cheese that he'd served with breakfast, taking the soiled cups to the wash basin. But he didn't go outside to the pump for water; he turned instead to Josef.

"I do not know which direction you'll head when you leave here, Josef, but if it is to France, I have a word of caution."

Josef gave his full attention.

"There are few Swiss guards at this section of our border because we no longer fear invasion from the Germans. The only Germans near this border are on rest leave. But there are many Swiss troops at the northwestern border, where France and Germany meet Switzerland. Three divisions, so they say, and three in reserve. According to the Hague agreement back in 1907, we, as a neutral, are allowed only the passage of sick and wounded. We cannot let cross any robust soldiers ready to return to the fight. You will not be allowed to rejoin your troops, if that is your aim, unless you work it out with your officials first."

Josef nodded, then translated for the others.

"What!" Dack exclaimed. "We're prisoners here now, in Switzerland?"

"We have to go to the American consulate in Zurich, that's all," Josef assured him. But he wasn't nearly as sure as his tone of voice indicated.

The sound of bells on a horse and the clatter of a wooden wagon reached them through the open doorway. Josef followed Adelbert outside, the others close behind. Two men hopped out of the wagon, and one headed up the hill toward Adelbert's cottage while the other stayed behind to unload sacks.

"Trouble arrives already, Josef," said Adelbert quietly, and Josef came up behind him. "That fellow with my baker friend is a newspaper reporter. He shows up from time to time to write stories of my escapees." Adelbert turned and looked Josef eye to eye. "Decide right now what your story will be. They will stand by you." He glanced toward Caleb and Dack.

Adelbert held Josef with a firm grip to his forearm. "Think first, young man. Think what the Lord would have you do."

"*Guten-tag*, Adelbert."

The reporter was short in stature, stocky and with splotchy skin, but he was smiling and already looking past Adelbert with obvious curiosity. "I see I was lucky to have come today. Three of you. Welcome to Switzerland."

"Only one of them speaks German, Helmut. They're with the AEF. You might as well speak English."

"Ah, Americans! That's goot . . . goot. I have not reported to American papers yet. New market." He held up the camera hanging from around his neck. "I take pictures, very goot? You will be famous!"

Josef felt the others' eyes on him, and in a moment the reporter was staring at him, too, perhaps following the lead of Adelbert.

"Where are you from? What is your story?"

Dack spoke up, drawing attention to himself. "We escaped from a Jerry prison camp, and let me tell you, it wasn't one of them cozy places for officers, neither. We were slave labor on a starvation diet at a camp where they didn't even register us."

The reporter whisked out a pencil and notepad and started scribbling away. "Do you know the location? The camp number?"

"Sixty-Eight, that's all we know. We were about a day and a half run from the border, though. Got close to a big lake, and once we were in the boat the Boche chasin' us just turned around and stared, like there was some kind of invisible wall protectin' us all of a sudden."

The reporter nodded and spoke even as he frantically wrote. "Yes, yes, one Frenchman tell me when he cross to Switzerland the Germans are chasing. When he reach border, they wave, as though glad he made it. Just like comrades. That's how it is now. It used to be different, back in da beginning, you know. They don't care any more, the ones who patrol the border." Then he looked up at Dack. "You tell me names, and spell them please, so I get them right. You first."

Dack told him.

He turned to Caleb.

Finally he looked at Josef. Everyone stared, and it made Josef pause. "My name is Josef von Woerner."

"Von Woerner? Ah, dis is goot! An American-German fights the land of his fathers! Tell me, did your family approve of you coming over to fight your cousins?"

"Look," said Dack, stepping closer to the reporter, "he ain't got no cousins over here. Caleb here's second generation German-American, too. There's lots of 'em in the American Army, all fightin' the Kaiser."

"Well, then, what about you?" the reporter asked Caleb. "Did your family approve?"

Caleb nodded. "Wholeheartedly. They're patriotic Americans."

"The American patriots send over their sons. Yes, yes, that is goot." He made more notes. "How did you escape from the camp? I see you limp, Mr. Dack."

"That's Sergeant Dack," he corrected, though there was no way for the reporter to have guessed since they all wore the Austrian country clothing Adelbert had supplied.

"How did you manage to get over da border with an injury?"

"I had help from this guy here who wouldn't give up on me, even when I shoulda been a goner." The reporter glanced up from Dack to Josef, then back to Dack when Josef said nothing.

"Is this a modest hero, then? Why don't you tell me, Sergeant?"

"Oh, I got plenty to tell. It started with a fog. . . ."

Dack didn't even watch the reporter taking the notes. Instead, he looked at Josef as if he had a plan.

". . . And you want to know somethin', mister? Them bombers missed one of their targets, but Josef von Woerner here, he made up for it."

The reporter looked up, obviously intrigued.

"Let me tell you about an American hero," said Dack, "and I'm lookin' at him."

———————

"I suppose I should say thanks," Josef said, when they were comfortably settled in the passenger car of a train headed west. In the village, they'd been given more food and shoes that fit, all charged to the benevolent Adelbert, who had an account for those delivered from his care. They were given directions to the nearest American authorities, where they could have identity papers drawn up. The Army and their families would be notified of their whereabouts.

Josef looked at Dack. "I think you went a little overboard when you said I was the best soldier at the front. I think the Brits and Frogs might think they know of somebody out there better than me over the past four years."

Caleb laughed, and it surprised Josef. He seemed lighthearted for the first time since Josef had confessed his past. "Sarge, that reporter probably expected Josef to walk on water back to France, after all you said about him."

But Dack wasn't smiling. He looked from Caleb back to Josef, who sat opposite him and Caleb on the passenger seats. "When you admitted your real name, you made the choice to go back and face the music, Joe. You're gonna need all the help you can get. Better hope that reporter has lots of readers all the way across the big pond so it'll do some good."

Josef nodded, suddenly as grim as Dack. He looked out the window at the snowcapped Alps, pine trees, and a lake in the distance. When he'd admitted his name that morning, he knew what he was doing. It was the first step home—to a jail cell. Home, and Larisa. And yet, the strongest reason of all was that it was what God wanted him to do.

The stop at Zurich came soon and the three disembarked as if they were natives. They even looked the part, with their traditional Swiss knee pants and halters. But once they left the station, they were lost. Josef asked directions and the three of them set off.

When they stood before the gated, official looking brick building, Josef paused.

"This is where I leave," he said softly.

Caleb turned on him quickly, Dack more slowly. "What do you mean?" asked Caleb.

"I'll catch up to you, but there's something I have to do first."

"What?"

"I have to go to France."

"That's where we'll all end up," Caleb insisted.

"If I go in that building," Josef said slowly, "I'll be tied up with Army brass until they get our whole stories. Who knows how long that'll take? They may already be looking for me if they think Joe Warner survived the mission. If I turn myself in now, I won't see Larisa again, at least not as a free man." He stepped closer to Caleb. "Do you understand, Caleb? I'm not running away. I'm going to do the right thing because that's what the Lord would have me do, and I follow Him. But first I have to talk to her."

Caleb said nothing.

"Wait a minute," Dack said, cautiously. "Maybe we all oughta wait before we go in, then. How else are we gonna keep our stories straight, and tell them exactly what happened?"

But Josef shook his head. "You can't wait, Dack. Regulations say if we're liberated . . ."

"Yeah, yeah, we go through immediate debriefing. But I don't see where we've got any vital information, except about the plant you blew up. Heck, they probably think it was already bombed, since our planes tried. Maybe they don't even know they missed. It's not like they got those fancy aeroplanes flyin' into German territory every day. Who knows? What I do know is that the safest thing is for us to stick together. We go to France, see this gal, then report to HQ together and tell them our stories."

But Josef was shaking his head. "I don't know. I'm not sure you should be sticking so close to me. If they know Josef von Woerner is alive, they're looking for me. Being involved with me would only . . ."

"Only nothin'. Where'd you say she was?"

"Lyon. That's south of here."

As Josef spoke he noticed the curiosity on Caleb's face and it struck him like a blow. "What are you staring at, little brother? Afraid I'm making this up?"

Caleb lowered his gaze and when he looked at Josef again his eyes were damp, full of confusion and regret. "I don't know. It's like I don't even know you."

"Hey," Dack said, pulling Caleb's arm and leading him down the street, away from the building that flew an American flag. Josef followed. "Are you dense, kid? The guy gave his real name to that reporter. You think he's gonna take off now?"

Caleb shook his head, bowing his head again. "No. It's just . . . I think we should stick together, that's all."

"Yeah," Dack said, "that's what we're doing, too."

"We don't have any money, Sarge," Josef reminded him, "or papers. It might be as hard to get into France without IDs as it was to get out of Germany."

Dack shrugged and started walking.

"Where are you going?" Josef demanded.

"Back to the train station. Then on to France."

"How?"

Dack grinned. "Didn't I tell you I spent a summer hobo-in'? We just jump a train headed in the right direction. We figure out what to do at the border along the way. Come on."

Josef exchanged a glance with Caleb, who was watching him closely. Against all caution, Josef shrugged much the way Dack had a moment ago, then followed.

Caleb suddenly laughed as the three headed off together. "Woo-hoo! I always wanted to be a hobo!"

CHAPTER *Twenty-Three*

Lissa gripped the corner of the table as she poured water into the basin. She ignored the aches and pains, the cough, the growing weakness infiltrating her body. Day after day exhaustion was finally catching up to her.

Her emotions were raw enough to ignite pain in every nerve. She longed for numbness and sought solace in work, which was as urgent and endless as ever. Yet between each task, her mind stubbornly conjured images of Josef blowing up ships, kissing a woman named Liesel, and laughing in a German beer garden over the victories of his countrymen against the United States. With each image her heart tore a little more. It ached, and the ache permeated her being.

He's alive, and he loves me. He couldn't have been lying about that. Why would he?

Yet the images persisted. Even if he had no memory, *someone* had done those awful things. The government must believe him guilty. That he fled authorities in Washington seemed to support the story. But couldn't he be a victim of the times? Many crimes were being committed against German-Americans. The victims simply had the unfortunate circumstance of having parents born in Germany or having a German name. They were hated and ostracized, blamed for what the Central Powers did to the boys. Maybe Josef was nothing more than a victim of hatred and propaganda. Someone else did those things he'd been accused of.

Lissa dropped a bedpan, and it fell to the floor in a clatter. It was empty, so she had no mess to clean, yet she couldn't still her trembling hands. She felt weak, too weak to carry out the simplest duty.

There were wounded to tend, along with an alarming influx of sick, soldier and civilian alike. She would continue her duty, no matter how her head spun. Clutching the bedpan, she headed to her patient. But before she reached the next bedside, the bedpan once again hit the floor as Lissa collapsed alongside of it.

Josef plopped to the floorboards of the train car at Dack's side. Caleb was nearby. Of the three of them, he was the only one not sucking in his next breath.

"You had me worried that time, Sarge," Josef said. "Your leg is worse than it was yesterday."

"Aw, it's nothin'. I had a broken bone in my ankle once and hopped a train in Springfield. Nothin' to it."

"We're home free now," Caleb said, settling back and propping his head under folded arms. "All we have to do now is enjoy the ride."

Josef wanted to believe him and tried to relax. Their journey toward the French border couldn't have taken longer had they decided to walk. Trains in neutral countries were evidently as backlogged and overscheduled as they were in the warring countries. The first train they'd hopped sat eight or ten hours in one place. When it finally moved, it only went half as far as they'd expected. This train was headed in the right direction, though, so they hoped it might be their last. They didn't want to waste another day. But Josef's effort to enjoy the ride, as Caleb had invited, didn't linger. The train screeched to a halt shortly after they left the train yard, and any trace of the calm Josef had tried to gather quickly vanished.

Dack leaned to peer out the open door. "Hey, this ain't no scheduled stop. No station. We better skedaddle. Oops, no time for that. Somebody's coming. Get back!"

The three scrambled to opposite sides of the empty car. There was nothing to hide in but darkness.

Josef heard voices, men speaking French that he couldn't understand, except for a word or two he'd picked up in boot camp classes. He couldn't hear a thing from the others, not even breathing.

Boxcar doors clanged open and shut over shouts and commands. Josef wished he could peek but didn't dare. The voices neared.

Suddenly a man in a Swiss uniform hopped into the boxcar, flashing a bright lantern in a slow rotation. Josef stood before it reached Caleb's corner, drawing the beam to himself. He held up his hands. "I'm unarmed," he said in English. "I'm an American." He tried to lead the armed soldier to the edge of the boxcar, to exit before the others were spotted, but the man didn't budge.

He held the light in one hand, a gun in the other, and called for help. Other soldiers jumped in, and Josef raised his hands atop his head the way the Germans had made him do, not all that long ago. But even as he tried to hold their attention by walking to the edge of the boxcar, the first soldier rotated his light, landing on Caleb, then on Dack.

They were escorted to an officer who spoke rapid French. At least the soldier aiming his rifle their way pulled it to his side.

Josef stepped forward. "*Sprechen sie Deutsch?*"

The officer nodded.

"We are American soldiers trying to get back to our unit," Josef explained in German.

"There are certain channels lost soldiers must follow. Stowing aboard a Swiss train is not one of them. You must come with us."

He would have turned, except that another soldier whispered something in the officer's ear, causing him to take another look at Josef. The officer remained while the other ran back to a passenger car. He returned with a newspaper.

The officer opened the paper and studied it a moment, then looked at Josef again. "What is your name?"

"Corporal Josef von Woerner."

Suddenly the brown haired, brown eyed young man burst into a wide smile. He looked from Josef to Dack and Caleb. "And which one of you is the Sergeant?"

Dack tentatively raised his hand, like a kid in a schoolroom with an answer he wasn't quite sure was correct.

The officer stepped closer and patted Josef's back. "Come. Come." He led the way toward the passenger car. "Let us welcome you, Mr. von Woerner, and your brave friends. Never let it be said the Swiss pass up an opportunity to share a toast with a genuine hero who saved the lives of his compatriots."

Josef learned their story had been in that morning's paper, complete with his picture. Though the reporter seemed to have included all the details Dack had supplied, the Swiss soldiers wanted to hear it all again, from the conditions at the illegal prison camp to the hasty race across the border. The three were fed amid apologies that it was simple food and not plentiful. Shortages touched every country, even the neutral ones.

After some time, the Swiss officer had a discussion in French with his soldiers. Josef could catch none of it, with the voices kept low anyway. At last the officer spoke again, in German.

"We regret we are unable to take you into France," he said. "It is against the international rules of the Hague Convention. However, there is a Red Cross unit not far from our last stop inside Switzerland. They have a Visitors and Searchers team, and they are more concerned about people than they are the rules that we, as a noncombatant army, are bound by. We believe they can get you across the border."

Josef's heart jumped. A Red Cross unit. This was more than he'd expected. They could do more than just get him back into France. They could get him to Larisa.

CHAPTER *Twenty~Four*

"Josef von Woerner," said the judge from the tallest courtroom bench Lissa had ever seen, "you are sentenced to death by hanging for treason. You are the vilest of traitors, one who tasted the freedom of our nation and was foolish enough to spit it out. Death by hanging. Death, death, death."

Lissa cried out, but no sound came. She tried to raise her hands, but they were leaden, too heavy to lift. The next image was no less horrid, of Josef alive and well, married to a woman he called Liesel. The woman smiled and presented him with a baby. A small child with a strangely large head who wore the mustache and spiked helmet of Kaiser Wilhelm.

She saw dying soldiers and Sister Mary Michel and Penny, all of them covered in the putrid stench and blood of death. Death was everywhere. The only escape was through an open, bottomless grave. She fell into its smothering blackness.

In a rare moment of coherency, she saw Sister Mary Michel with a wet cloth, wiping something from her face. Lissa couldn't speak, though she heard the Sister say something about influenza and that she wasn't going to lose another nurse.

Lissa was confused. Lose her? How would she get lost? She couldn't go anywhere, she couldn't get out of bed. Sister Mary Michel worried too much.

Besides, the sun was lovely as it sparkled in the sky. Cool, fresh air caressed her cheeks, and for a time Lissa had no cares, no sadness, no regrets. She knew her Savior was there with her. The sun shone here, just like in America. Maybe she was home.

Then she saw someone else. Was this a heavenly vision? She heard his voice, felt his touch, and knew he was real. "Larisa," he whispered, "I'm right here, and I won't leave you. You've got to get well. Will you do that for me? I love you, Larisa Rose. I love you."

"Josef?" She closed her eyes. Maybe he was here to take her to heaven. But no, then he wouldn't tell her to get well, would he? That was for the living. But she didn't want to live without him. How could she know what to do? She tried to open her eyes again, but they wouldn't obey. She was so tired, and when she opened her eyes the cough came back. Sleep was her only escape.

Josef caressed her forehead with a cool, damp rag. She was deathly white, almost ashen. They'd arrived at the hospital an hour before, with an enthusiastic Searchers Unit escort named Mary Downing. Their unit so rarely received good news they'd been more than eager to help reunite Josef with his loved one.

Josef had refused to cave in to the emotion that roiled through him when they'd arrived at the chaotic hospital. He'd forced his way through the crowd of sick outside the doors. The line was a weak, confused, unsteady mass. They were sick, all of them, waiting for treatment—and turned away. No more beds. No more room. No one available to do more than take temperatures.

Anyone with a low fever or still capable of standing was turned away immediately, the rest were given a cot outside if one was available, or else a blanket was spread on the ground. The people outside waited for the sick in a bed to die and be moved away so another could take their place.

Josef's horror and fear multiplied inside the hospital itself, threatening to overthrow his resolute control. These were the conditions in which Lissa worked? He'd waylaid the first nurse he could find, who told him Lissa Parker wasn't working any more. She was a patient herself. But the nurse didn't know where she'd been taken. He ignored the upheaval threatening inside of him, ignored the uneasiness and pity on Dack and Caleb's faces. He went from bed to bed, seeing soldiers and civilians. He forced himself to look at each face, from the wounded to the pale to those with an oddly blue tint. Those were the ones who barely moved. And he prayed as he never had before.

Caleb and Dack said nothing. Once Josef thought he saw fear on Dack's face, fear of death. How had so many gotten so sick? Was it a germ from the war? Was it catching? He told Dack and Caleb to go. They didn't reply but kept up the search with him.

They went outside, through a door that led to a yard in the back. It might have been an appealing place once, with a yew garden now grown wild and flowers that fought the weeds for ground. Interspersed in the untended jungle were rows of cots. There he spotted her at last, in a cot off to the edge of the yard, near a hut that had been hastily and recently built, judging from the freshness of the clapboard. He fell to his knees beside her, crying her name and whispering that he needed her to get well and that he loved her.

He wasn't sure she knew he was there, not until she said his name. He felt his first hint of hope, and tears tumbled down his cheeks.

The sight of Caleb and Dack watching helplessly dragged him to his feet. He felt no shame for his breakdown. At that moment, all he felt was rage. He left her side to stop the only nurse he saw, one heading to another cot down the row. He grabbed her arm. "I demand to know who's in charge here."

She raised wide, alarmed eyes to him and shook her head, uttering something in French he couldn't understand.

"Doctor," he said slowly, repeating himself again. She pointed to the building, trying to pull back the arm he gripped. Josef let her go. "Stay with Larisa," he said to Caleb, then went to the tall building. He covered his nose when he entered. He hadn't noticed the stench before and wondered how he could have missed it. The smell of blood combined with countless other foul odors. He stopped three nurses before he found one who could speak English.

"Most of the doctors are in the surgery upstairs," she said, "but Sister Mary Michel is down here somewhere. She heads up the nurses and makes most of the decisions about patients. There." She pointed to a small nun scurrying from bed to bed on the opposite side of the room. By the time Josef caught up to her, she was headed outside.

The fall air was still warm, for which he was silently grateful. Still, he meant to see that Lissa was given better care. He picked up his pace to catch up with the little nun.

He caught her by the elbow, and when he closed his hand around her arm, she looked up at him with annoyance rather than the fearful surprise the other nurse had exhibited.

"I am here to help Larisa Rose Parker," he said, taking his hand away. Then he cocked his head in the general direction of her cot. "But she's out here, totally ignored by you and your staff."

She started walking again, heading to the first row of cots, and spoke over her shoulder. "She is where I put her, *monsieur*."

"She is one of your nurses, isn't she? This is the thanks she gets for working here, letting her die in the outdoor air?"

The little nun stopped and faced him, with a raised brow and such a formidable, level gaze he might have backed down. He stood his ground.

"You know nothing of what happens here, *monsieur*, and I suggest you find out before you judge."

"What I see is that she is ignored and left outside."

"You see nothing. She has the influenza. A hundred have died of it in the last week. They die faster inside where the beds are close, and the air is full of stench. She coughs, *monsieur*. She gasps for air. Do you want her to gasp the foul air of death or the air God has given? I have moved influenza patients outside to give them a chance, not to kill them, I assure you!"

She started to turn away, but Josef boldly grabbed her arm again. He wiped the threat from his face, helpless and desperate. "Tell me . . . tell me if she will die."

The nun lifted a hand. "I cannot say. She is no better after two days. She will either get better in a few days more, or the lung fever will come on her. Most do not survive this. Some do."

"What can I do?"

"Give her water when she can take it. Make her comfortable. Pray."

She turned away again, heading once more to her other patients, but added, "When you leave her side, wash your hands. Those who tend others often are the first to die."

———————

Josef held her hand as tightly as he dared, but she was limp and offered no response. He tried to get her to take water, but it dribbled down the side of her face, onto the damp pillow. She never opened her eyes.

Dack and Caleb stayed by his side until the little nun demanded that they make themselves useful. Not even Dack could ignore her command. Josef wasn't sure what she had them doing, but he had the grim idea that it involved moving bodies.

With Larisa's hand in his, pressed to his lips, Josef never ceased praying. He'd tried to stop hoping for their life together, convinced she wouldn't want him once she knew of his past. But the thought of losing her to death was one he couldn't comprehend. She must live.

It started to rain and he pulled a tarp over her cot, stretching it from the edge of the hut to the sturdy trunks of nearby arborvitae. The canopy was large enough to shelter several beds, and he rushed to help others cover the rest.

He found Sister Mary Michel after that. She still scurried from patient to patient.

"Will you look at her?" he asked.

He didn't care if he sounded pathetic. Having her look at Larisa was all that mattered. She followed.

The little nun somberly pressed a palm to Larisa's forehead, then felt for her pulse.

"She has stirred today?"

Josef shook his head.

"She has taken liquid?"

He shook his head again.

The gentle rain tapped on the tarp like an ancient rhythm dance. Josef watched the nun's face, and his heart felt like an anvil inside.

"I tell you, *monsieur*, that I do not know if she will live. But it is in God's hands."

"Sister! Sister Mary Michel!"

The frantic call drew both to look. Another nurse, a few cots away, looked up from the patient at her side. Surprisingly, Caleb was there, too.

"Th-this one was dead, Sister," she stammered in English. "No pulse. No breath. He was dead, but he moved, just as this man was going to take his body away."

The sister came to the nurse's side. Judging by her English, she was an American. Sister Mary Michel nodded and placed a hand on the nurse's arm, which was all it took to calm her.

The sister leaned close to the patient, feeling for a pulse, listening for breath. She raised a perplexed glance to the nurse. "You are certain he moved?"

"Yes, Sister, I left him with his hands folded across his chest before stiffness sets in, to show that he was dead. I do it in case I can't have the body moved right away to free the bed. I get distracted with all the—"

"And his hands, Nurse? He moved them to his side?"

She nodded.

Sister Mary Michel looked at Caleb. "You did not change his appearance when you came to move him?"

Caleb shook his head. "I never touched him."

The old nun looked between the two of them, as if hesitating. Then she bent over the patient and vigorously rubbed his arms, his legs, his chest. She pressed her mouth to his, blowing, counting, holding his nose closed while she blew into his mouth.

Josef watched, fascinated by her dedication. She'd said herself it was contagious. She'd told him to wash his hands. Yet here she was, sharing breath with a man dying of this germ.

How long she worked he did not know, breathing life into him, massaging his blood flow. At intervals she checked for pulse. He couldn't guess whether she found one, but she kept working.

When she stopped at last, she looked breathless herself, worn out.

"Give him water when he can take it," she said, then walked away.

The wide-eyed nurse exchanged glances with Caleb and then Josef. Tentatively, almost fearfully, she picked up the man's wrist, and her eyes widened more.

"He's alive!"

Josef turned and ran to catch up with the nun.

"Teach me," he said. "Show me how you revived him."

"I will not, *monsieur*," she said. "It would be death to anyone else."

"But not to you?"

She shook her head. "Last spring I was sick with something like this, only mild. Barely a day, and it was gone. It has left me stronger than others, I've known that for two months now, since the first time I gave the breath to one on the deathbed."

She started to turn again, as if that had been explanation enough.

Josef stopped her again, with a gentle touch to her arm. "I would do that for her. If I can't find you. If she were to need this. I need to know, Sister. I don't care about the risk."

The nun looked him over as if determining whether to believe him. "Your dedication to her is admirable, *monsieur*. But first you should look in her pocket." Then she left, calling over her shoulder that if he read the letter and still wanted, she would teach him.

Josef returned to Larisa's side, aware that Caleb hovered nearby. What had the nun meant by a letter? Gently, he fished beneath the blanket and found a thick, folded envelope in Larisa's pocket. He pulled it out, despite a silent warning in his head.

"Is that a letter from Pen?" Caleb asked eagerly. He must have recognized the handwriting or saw the address.

Josef nodded. He read it through. Each word was the truth, except Penny's accusations. Pain or anger at his sister might be justified, but he felt neither. He looked at Larisa, desperate to tell her, desperate for her to hear the whole truth from him. He hadn't wanted her to learn it this way.

Without a word, Josef handed the letter to Caleb.

———

Josef slept on the ground next to her cot. He didn't know where Dack and Caleb slept. Throughout the night he checked her, as Sister Mary Michel had shown him, searching for a pulse, ready to give her his breath if she needed it, the way the nun had reluctantly instructed. Larisa's weak but steady pulse was still there, and he thanked God.

Caleb came to find him just after the sun rose.

"How is she?"

"The same."

"I was thinking about everything, Josef," he said, low. "If she dies . . ."

Josef shook his head, turning his back on Caleb to look at Larisa.

He felt Caleb's hand on his shoulder. "You've got to leave, Josef," he whispered. "There were MPs here last night."

"What were they doing?"

"Just checking, I guess. But they must know."

"I don't care."

"They'll arrest you. It was in Penny's letter. They know what you look like."

Josef said nothing.

"I'll stay with her, Josef," he said. "If she comes round—when she comes round—I'll tell her where to find you."

Josef looked up at last, but it wasn't the idea Caleb presented that intrigued him. "I thought you wanted me to do what's right, Caleb. Isn't going back to the States to face the charges the right thing to do? You know, prove I'm an American and all?"

Caleb shrugged. "I don't know what's right any more. I know you love her. I know you want to do what's right. I think you deserve a chance to be with her, that's all."

"Take her with me on the run? Even if she was willing, I couldn't." He shook his head. "It's too late, Caleb. If they saw that Swiss paper, they know I'm alive."

"That's why you've got to leave now."

He did not respond, only sat beside Larisa, immovable.

"They could hang you, you know," Caleb whispered.

He knew.

———

Larisa's pallor grew more ashen, and the coughs went sparse from lack of strength. He gave her water, and it still spilled down her cheeks. He massaged her hands and arms the way Sister Mary Michel had shown. Twice that morning he was able to bring the sister to Larisa's side, but she said there was nothing to do except wait.

He didn't want to eat but forced himself to keep his body strong, prayed to keep his spirit strong. He told her that he loved her to keep his hope strong. Surely if she knew how much he loved her, she would somehow forgive him for his past.

But each time he watched Dack or Caleb or some other able-bodied helper carry away a body, his strength ebbed.

The sun set again and he'd barely left her side. He slept on the ground another night, rousing to check her heartbeat, listen to her breathing. One or two of the patients nearby seemed to be getting stronger. They called for water from time to time, and Josef gave it to them. Even as he watched them improve, he alternately felt renewed hope and desolate loss. Larisa's condition wasn't changing at all.

And when he ran out of hope Josef checked on the man a few cots down. The man was weak but still alive. That helped.

The sun shone again and Josef pulled back the tarp. The light touched her face, but her skin looked whiter. Sister Mary Michel insisted he let the sun reach her, calling it the sun cure. But even as the rays warmed his own skin, they seemed powerless on Larisa.

By midmorning one of the patients nearby was sitting up. He asked for more water and was given a bit of broth. Josef helped him. Before he'd even finished, another patient stirred, then another, and Josef brought them water. For the first time the insidious nature of this influenza occurred to him. These were not the very young or the very old. These were the strongest, those in their prime. Those felled by the sickness were like Larisa and like him.

He tended to the others longer than he had before and was anxious to get back to Larisa's side. There was always one more need, one more call he couldn't ignore. He watched Larisa though, still asleep, still so weak. But when was the last time he'd seen her move, he wondered? He went to her, ignoring other calls.

He put a hand to her skin. It was damp and clammy. Was that a good sign or bad? Surely if it was blazing hot, as it had been before, that would have been worse. Then he picked up her wrist.

His own breathing stopped when he felt nothing. He moved his inexperienced fingertips, searching for the life sign but found none.

"Sister!" he called, to no one in particular. He wanted Sister Mary Michel but he didn't dare take time to search. He massaged Larisa the way the nun had shown him, striving for control, striving for steadiness even though his thoughts and fears threatened to overwhelm him and make his efforts useless.

A nurse passed by and Josef called to her, beseeching her to find Sister Mary Michel. And then he tried his own effort at the life breath, pressing his mouth to Larisa's and breathing the way the nun had shown him. He was so frantic, his own breathing was unstable. He knelt beside her, closing his eyes, willing himself calmness, offering the briefest of helpless prayers. And he began again.

From the corner of his eye he saw someone approach. He hoped it was Sister Mary Michel, but he wasn't going to stop until she told him. He tasted salt and realized it was his own tears. Maybe he should let the nun take over. But he couldn't stop. He did what she had done, massaged and breathed, massaged and breathed. He never took his eyes from Larisa.

"Is that—normal?—what he's doing to her?"

"He's trying to save her life, sir. I think we should not disturb him."

"Look, I've never seen anything like that before. Is this a game or what? I'm not leaving here without him. If it's a delay, it won't do any good."

Josef heard the words but they made no sense. He kept working.

Then he felt a hand on his shoulder and looked from Larisa for the first time. It was Sister Mary Michel.

"Let me help," she said, and he fell back for the first time. His gaze went inevitably to the man three cots down on whom Sister Mary Michel had performed this technique. He was still asleep. Josef suddenly wanted to check on him again, to be sure he was still alive.

He stood, but didn't make it farther than the foot of Larisa's cot.

"You're under arrest, Josef von Woerner. You'll have to come with us."

Josef looked at the two American MPs, confused and dumbfounded. Surely they were joking. He couldn't leave now.

"Look," Josef said wearily, "I'm sure you've got a job to do, and I'm not going to resist, but you can see—"

"You'll have to come now," said one.

Josef ignored him. He stepped around and went toward the other cot, but the MP, along with the other at his side, grabbed Josef's arms.

Josef struggled, but their grip was firm. "If you could just *wait*."

But they didn't listen. They strong-armed him toward the yard's gate.

Once on the other side of that gate, Josef saw Caleb at the front of the hospital amid what looked like the same crowd of sick from the other day.

"Caleb!"

He looked up, already frowning, but his jaw dropped open at the sight of Josef. The clipboard in his hand fell to the ground and he rushed to catch up. The MPs didn't slow.

"Go to Larisa, Caleb!"

"But—I should come with you. Help you."

Josef was already shaking his head. "Stay with her, Caleb. Then find me and tell me if she's all right. Go, Caleb, go now!"

Caleb turned and ran.

CHAPTER *Twenty-Five*

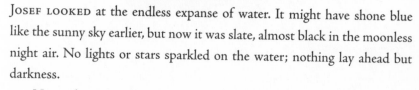

JOSEF LOOKED at the endless expanse of water. It might have shone blue like the sunny sky earlier, but now it was slate, almost black in the moonless night air. No lights or stars sparkled on the water; nothing lay ahead but darkness.

He was bound at the wrist, allowed an hour on deck under armed guard. He'd left France after a week in a military prison. Now he was on a troop ship of sick and wounded, all headed back to the States for recuperation. All of those on board would go home a hero. All but Josef.

He didn't care what lay ahead any more. While Josef had been held all those days, he'd prayed constantly for Larisa and asked for news of her condition. None came and no visit from Dack or Caleb. When he'd asked his guards repeatedly for information about her, he'd been ignored.

Surely Dack or Caleb would have been able to get word to him somehow if she was all right. But would they have tried if the news were bad? He leaned forward, rubbing both his hands in his hair, bound as they were. Visions haunted him of Larisa being carried from her cot and added to the others in that overcrowded cemetery.

No one had spoken to him since he'd come aboard. They'd given him a small cabin which was locked night and day. He was fed but allowed few other comforts. His daily hour on deck was the most generous allowance, though today they'd forgotten until after dark. He felt the chill of advancing autumn, but he didn't care if he ever saw the sun again. It hadn't cured Larisa.

He tried to pray, but words no longer formed. He tried to remember verses from the Bible that offered hope, about things working together for good, and trial leading to greater character. There were verses about a God of comfort and trusting Him even when everything around seemed hopeless. That God was faithful and true, forever unchanging and loving and good. He was a God Who had suffered, too. He offered a place in heaven where there were no tears. That was where Josef wanted to go and where Larisa probably was.

There were others on deck, soldiers and sailors. Josef walked in silence with his thoughts.

"Two more today, Doc," said one of the voices from the rail.

Josef stopped.

"I don't know, Jim. I don't know how many of us will finish this one."

Josef looked their way. Their tone of voice matched his own mood, except they sounded more tired than he felt. He could tell one was an Army doctor and the other a colonel by their uniforms.

"Sam—you know, the crazy attendant—thinks it's a judgment from God," the doctor said. "God's ending it all his way instead of letting us do it to ourselves in a war."

The colonel shrugged without a laugh. "Maybe he's not so crazy."

"I'm not even sure they'll let us disembark in New York. Rumor has it a ship from Norway pulled into the harbor and was told to turn around. It was full of the sick. A voyage like that would be a living hell."

"But we're not from Norway, are we?"

"Half of New York is closed down."

"Well, once we're home I suppose we'll all go hide, same as everybody else," said the colonel, turning around and facing Josef's direction, leaning on the railing with his elbows behind him.

Josef moved slowly, pointing with both hands the way he wanted his guard to allow him to go.

"Pardon me, sir. I know how to help."

The one, already facing him, looked astonished, either at Josef's presence or at the pronouncement. The doctor turned around curiously.

"Help with what?"

"To take care of the sick," Josef said. "I came from a hospital. I helped with the influenza there."

The men exchanged wary glances. "You're the traitor, aren't you?" asked the colonel. "The one going back for trial?"

Josef nodded, no sense denying it.

"Why would you want to help?"

"Because I'm going back to be hanged," he said flatly. "I don't care if I get sick. I guess if somebody other than God is going to end my life I'd rather go out helping somebody instead of some judge ordering my death."

Another glance passed between the two of them, obviously skeptical.

"Look, what could I do if you took off these shackles?" Josef asked. "Take over the ship? Jump? Consider my options. I'm willing to work."

The doctor stepped closer, looking over Josef from head to foot in one quick assessment. Then he spoke to his companion over his shoulder. "We have the influenza patients separated. Nobody wants to work in there. It would free up another set of hands."

"I don't know. He's a prisoner. Regulations at sea. We'll have to consult the Captain."

Josef watched, but the man with the gun spoke before anyone else could. "Begging your pardon, sir. His time on deck is up. I need to take the prisoner below."

Lissa opened her eyes, breathing the fresh air and, for the first time in nearly a week, not coughing the air from her lungs.

Minnie Osborn handed her a glass of water. "You look much better today, Liss."

Lissa nodded. "I feel much better, well enough to stop using the bedpan."

She tried to rise but Minnie put a cautioning hand to her shoulder.

"Better wait until Sister Mary Michel gives the okay for you to get up."

"I don't want to bother her with this. I want to use the bathroom, wash my hair, take a bath. Well, I can take a sponge bath. I'll have to go into the hut for that. Will you help?"

Minnie nodded. "I'm just glad you want to do all that, Liss, and that you think you can."

"Of course I can."

But her head spun when she tried to stand and Minnie brought soap and water to the cot and washed Lissa's face and hair. She assisted her with the bedpan again, under the privacy of blankets, and helped her into a fresh nightgown.

"You mustn't push yourself too fast, Liss. After all, it's a miracle that you're here at all. If your fella hadn't been here . . ."

She stopped abruptly, and Lissa eyed her curiously. "What fella?"

"Did I say fella? I meant Sister Mary Michel. She saved your life."

Lissa shook her head. "No, you said fella, Minnie. What did you mean?"

"I—think I'd better get Sister Mary Michel."

Before Lissa could ask another question, Minnie fled.

Lissa's thoughts rushed to her dream. It had been so real, she wanted to believe that Josef had been at her side, kissing her and telling her he loved her. She hadn't told anyone about it, but from the moment she woke, she thought only of getting in touch with Mary Downing to see if the Searcher Unit had news of Josef.

Had Josef's visit really been a dream? Lissa looked around. Of course it was. If he'd been here, he would be here now.

Maybe he was here. Lissa pulled the cover away. She had to know. She couldn't wait a moment longer.

"Ah, you are much better today, yes?" Sister Mary Michel appeared at her side, but rather than helping Lissa to rise, she gently pushed her back and replaced the cover snugly up to her chin.

"Yes, I am much better today, I think. But I have a question you must answer, Sister."

"Oh? Yes, we shall talk. But first you will eat. Minnie is bringing you some broth."

"I must know something first. Is Josef—my Josef—here?"

The Sister pursed her lips together, creating more wrinkles around her mouth. "I must tell you that I read the letter in the pocket of the uniform you wore the day you collapsed."

"Oh, that nonsense. It was all Penny. She's so . . ."

"Your Josef. He was here."

What she said did not match the look on the Sister's glum face. These were wondrous words.

"It—it wasn't a dream? I thought . . . I knew I felt him at my side."

"Yes, he was quite devoted."

"Oh, Sister." Lissa squeezed the nun's hand. "He's alive!"

She hardly looked pleased, despite the tears of joy filling Lissa's eyes. "Listen to me, Lissa. He was arrested. This is why he is not here at your side this moment. He and his two companions, all three of them were taken by police from your army."

Lissa heard, but her happiness was undimmed. "They'll want to clear up this nonsense about his past. Tell me, was one of his companions Caleb Tanner? Oh, everything is going to be all right. It's a misunderstanding. Josef has been a victim of propaganda."

Sister Mary Michel offered no comfort, no assurance. "I spoke to this Caleb, after Josef was arrested and before he also was taken away. You must listen to me, Lissa. Josef von Woerner told his friends that he did the things they say. He came here to tell you about this. If he was a spy, this is a serious matter, even in your wild and free America."

Lissa looked away, shaking her head. "No, Sister, Josef is none of what you say. He's an American, true blue."

"He is a charmer, that I will say. And the feelings he has for you seem real. He might have gotten away if he had not stayed by your side. Even so, you must face reality. If he were in France and found guilty of treason, he would be shot."

Lissa sucked in her faltering breath. "He mustn't be guilty, Sister. How can you even think it?"

"I would not, except his friend said such words came from Josef himself."

"Bed six, von Woerner," said the doctor, who did nightly bed checks in the wards. "Winding cloth and overboard."

Josef nodded, despite his exhaustion from another day's activities. He fetched water, brought food, cleaned bedpans, washed floors of blood-traced spittle that spewed from the mouths of the sick, and heaved bodies overboard.

He'd expected the news on bed six. When the doctor wasn't around, there was only a nurse or two. They were so overworked with wounded in the other sick bay that they barely made it to this ward. Josef checked patients himself, felt for a pulse, asked if they were able to take liquid, added blankets to the chilled, wiped brows of those whose fevers came and went, and kept company with those who tolerated him. Josef never left the ward. He slept on a blanket in the corner. The ward was locked anyway, to keep the influenza patients who were still strong enough from wandering and spreading their germs to the rest of the patients. The locked door probably had been the deciding factor in allowing Josef out of his own locked cabin.

Josef wound the white cloth tightly around the corpse, tying it off at top and bottom. From the corner of his eye he saw the doctor at bed ten. Josef knew that patient was weakening, but he'd checked himself only an hour ago and there was still a pulse.

"This one next, Josef," said the doctor as he turned from one bed and headed to another.

Maybe it was exhaustion, maybe it was hopelessness, or maybe he was sick of death. Josef snapped inside—an immediate and instantaneous crack, like a physical blow to his head. He left bed six for ten, his pace deceptively calm, smooth. Josef bent over the patient, his ear to the soldier's nose, fingertips to pulse. He heard nothing, he felt nothing.

And so he massaged vigorously. He put his fingertips to the man's nose and pinched, then opened the man's mouth and blew. Counted. Blew again. Massaged again. Breathed again. He saw the doctor's shadow at the foot of the cot; he might even have spoken. Josef didn't hear.

Another shadow joined that one. Josef ignored that, too. He worked. He worked until a third shadow came, and this one loomed close. Josef felt a hand on his shoulder, pulling him away.

"He's dead, man. Who do you think you are, God?"

Josef struggled, but Sam the assistant was already pulling him away. Between Sam and the doctor, they jostled Josef to the aisle.

"Check him," Josef insisted. "I saw a nun do this and save a man. I saw it. Check him."

The doctor did so, but shook his head afterward. "He's gone."

Josef made a move toward the cot again but Sam pulled him back.

The doctor came to Josef's side, putting a hand on his shoulder. "You're overworked, Josef," he said from behind his face mask. "Go to a real bed tonight. Get some sleep."

"Should I take him out of the ward, sir?" asked Sam.

The doctor was already on his way out of the ward. "Let him do as he pleases."

Josef stared at the patient in bed ten. Had he done something wrong? His training was limited, but if he hadn't helped this man . . . maybe he hadn't helped Larisa, either.

CHAPTER *Twenty-Six*

LISSA STOOD on the dock, the single bag she'd been allowed to take gripped in one hand. New York.

And yet it seemed like someplace else. There was the usual bustling as passengers disembarked the huge transport ship, but otherwise the dock was strangely quiet. It had never looked so big. People weren't milling about or standing in conversation, loitering here and there. Instead, those who were here seemed to go about their business quickly and with as little interaction as possible.

She left the dock to catch a trolley, but it was blocks before she came upon one that was available. The ones she saw were full—and sometimes not with people, but with boxes. To her horror one was full of coffins.

The only street vendor she saw was selling gauze masks, singing a chant: "Obey the laws and wear the gauze, protect your jaws from septic paws." Many, though not all, of the people she saw wore them. Lissa didn't bother. Gauze masks hadn't helped stop the influenza from spreading when she worked with the sick in France, so why should she trust one now?

No one spoke to her.

Lissa went to the station for a train heading south. Soldiers still crowded the railways and had first priority for tickets, despite persistent reports that an armistice was to be signed within days.

She got on a passenger train designated to carry civilians and claimed an empty seat and the newspaper that had been left on it. The Washington *Evening Star* headlines proclaimed German retreats, Allied plans for retribution, and the names of heroes who were coming home.

In between war accounts were notices of prominent civilians who had died of influenza. She found no report of the impact influenza had on the soldiers.

Nor was there mention of espionage arrests.

When the train passed through Washington, the streets looked as deserted as in New York City. She read in the newspaper that churches, schools, and theaters were closed. Even the Capital was closed. She saw Red Cross trucks, so familiar in France, probably transporting the sick or dead. Lissa closed her eyes. How had the world become so small that an ocean as big as the Atlantic couldn't stop the spread of something like this? Did God send this plague because He was tired of this war, like everyone on earth? Or was it some kind of new germ that had been let loose by all the carnage? Some speculated it a weapon gone awry. Others said it was spread by German spies.

Spies. Josef, the German spy. No matter how she tried, she couldn't match the face of a cold-blooded saboteur to the easy-going, happy face of the Josef she loved. She wondered where they had taken him. She'd heard nothing more than what Sister Mary Michel had told her. There was no information at the Army base near the hospital in France. They didn't seem to be trying to keep something from her. Rather, it appeared they couldn't tell her what they didn't know.

She'd gone to the Searchers Unit and asked Mary Downing if she could learn something, but she'd come up empty-handed as well. The AEF, she'd learned, was hush-hush about its prisoners, especially American prisoners.

Lissa searched every page of the newspaper twice, but there was nary a word about a spy having been arrested.

Not one letter had reached her from home since before she'd been sick with the influenza. The Red Cross sent word to her parents that she was en route home and she'd hoped someone might come to meet her. But with the world so out of kilter, she wasn't surprised no one had been there. Moving mail must be a low priority when there were bodies to move instead.

Mainly she longed to know what had happened to Josef. She couldn't take Penny's advice to simply forget him. He was part of her. He'd permeated her life, and she had no hope or dream that did not have him in it.

Yet she wondered about her own wisdom. She prayed, hoping God would give her a sign or change her emotions. She loved the Josef she'd known, the Josef without a past. This new Josef, who evidently had his memory, was a traitor, wasn't he? Despite everything, neither the newspaper articles nor the admission by Josef reported by Sister Mary Michel convinced Lissa. She had to know the truth.

Her love for the United States wasn't like the love she felt for Josef. It wasn't passionate or romantic or external. It was like a love felt for oneself, something that couldn't be separated from who she was. A homeland was the foundation of everyday life, the background for every dream. How could the Josef she knew betray that?

Even if everything was true, she didn't want to judge him. She wanted to understand. Was he a different person now that he remembered what he had done—and why? She'd never believed Penny's accusation that Josef had faked amnesia. Lissa was convinced Josef hadn't remembered any of his former life. Once he did remember, why didn't he stay in Germany? How had the government found him? Since he'd told Caleb the truth before being arrested, he must have regained his memory before that. When *had* he remembered?

And had he remembered his other love—Liesel, the woman to whom he'd been engaged? The woman who was to have been his wife?

The realization that Josef had been engaged to someone else before her no longer jabbed Lissa the way it once had, nor was she numb about all that had happened. Waves of pain had gradually been replaced by prayer. She read in the Bible of God's promises and love each time misery rushed in. God knew both Lissa and Josef and even the woman named Liesel. He knew what was best for each of them. Lissa must trust that He would heal them all.

Lissa had no doubt Josef needed healing. Was he confused about his loyalties? Was his love for Germany so strong now that all other loyalties faded into insignificance? Was he confused about her, or had his feelings for her become insignificant, too?

Lissa prayed through all of these questions and in spite of her pain. She took hope in her confidence that his faith was genuine. Surely Josef must want God's will as much as she did.

Only a few passengers got off at Culpeper for lunch at the Waverly. Lissa almost couldn't bear to look at that grand old, three-story hotel. She remembered the happy evening when she and Josef had dined there. When he kissed her good-night, she had decided that nothing would make her happier than to spend the rest of her life with him.

Lissa looked for Mr. McPhearson at the telegraph office, but he wasn't there. He must be making a delivery. She shivered as she walked up the hill from the station on Davis Street, though the November air wasn't even cool. The chill came from seeing all the shops closed, doors shut, and windows covered. It was like a storm loomed, one that didn't show signs of moving on any time soon. People were still getting sick, and she well knew how this sickness ravaged the body.

She turned at the sound of a motor and saw Pastor Eldridge rounding the corner from tree-lined Main Street. She waved at him. Pastor Eldridge was a ruddy-faced Englishman, quick with a smile and always ready to help, a true shepherd of his people. But when he caught sight of Lissa, his smile was slower in coming than usual.

"Hello, Pastor. Could you give me a ride?"

"Welcome home, Lissa." He had a tired glint to his eye as he reached to open the door to his motorcar. "Hop in. I've just finished my rounds with your father."

"Rounds?"

The pastor drove down Davis Street, not looking at her. "Some of us go around to the houses outside of town—like you used to when you were nursing here. We call to see if they need anything." His mouth tightened to a grim line. "Lots of folks can't get out on their own."

"Oh, Pastor, it's like a judgment! Between this and the war, will there be any of us left?"

She was sure his smile meant to offer reassurance, but his eyes didn't convince her. "It's not a judgment. But maybe, just maybe, without this the war over there would never end."

"I'm glad my father is all right," she said. "What about my mother and Cassie and everybody?"

"Your mother is home," he said. "She is fine, or was this morning when last I saw her. Your sister is there, with your mother."

"With my parents? Why isn't she home with William?"

"William is dead."

"Oh." It was more a sigh than a word. Sympathy and sadness filling her.

"Lissa." The Pastor said her name slowly, and something in the warning tone made her look up. "Cassie is sick."

A moment passed before Lissa took in the statement. "Cassie has the influenza?" She asked the question calmly, though her insides retaliated against everything such words meant.

He nodded.

Lissa grasped the dash. "Hurry, Pastor Eldridge. Please hurry."

———

Not even Josef had held Lissa so tightly. Her mother and father swept her into an embrace that seemed to contain as much desperation as affection, and it nearly took her breath away. She was still tired from her own battle with the influenza, but being held in her parents' arms eased the lingering discomfort.

"I want to see her," Lissa said.

Her mother shook her head. "No, Liss. I don't want you anywhere near her."

"But I can help. All I've done these last few months is treat people with influenza."

Even her father shook his head. "The fewer people who have contact, the better. She's in her old room. Mama is tending her."

"Daddy, I've had the influenza. I survived. I can take care of her."

Her mother put both hands over Lissa's and looked at her with somber eyes. "I won't have it, Liss. Just because you've had it doesn't make you immune. Some in town had it and then relapsed."

Her father put his arm around her shoulder. "Let your mother and me tend to Cassie. It doesn't seem to go after folks our age. Right now we want to hear what's happened to you, Lissy Rose. We wrote, but we haven't had a letter from you for almost two months now."

"I was too sick to write, but I'm okay now."

Her father kissed the top of her head. "Thank the Lord for that. Did Pastor tell you about William?"

She nodded.

"And I suppose you know about Josef," her mother said with a mix of caution and sympathy.

"I haven't seen any papers. Well, I did see an *Evening Star* on the train but there was nothing about him. The Army wouldn't tell me anything. I don't even know exactly what the charges are or if he'll be tried in a military or a civilian court. So I don't know much."

Both her parents looked away, as if unwilling to look her in the eye.

"What do you know? Where is he?"

Her mother looked to her father, who answered. "He's being held in New York. The courts have all closed, there are no public gatherings of any kind."

"He's in New York? Where? With prisoners of war?"

His father shook his head somberly. "Tombs Prison."

"That's a civilian jail. That means a civilian court?"

Her father nodded. Lissa turned away, not trusting her wobbly legs to hold her much longer. She sank to the nearby couch and put her face in her hands. "I don't know if that's good news or bad. Is the public any different from the men he served with? They've lost sons and husbands and brothers."

Tears fell to her palms, but when she felt their warmth she brushed them away. Her parents had enough to deal with upstairs without Lissa adding to their burdens.

Her mother took a seat beside her and put an arm around her shoulders. "We love him, too," she whispered.

Lissa looked up, but in that single moment she saw her parents exchange a glance that tinged her gratitude for her mother's words. They were as confused as she. How could they love a traitor?

Lissa stood, shaking off the emotions that threatened to sink her. "We'll just have to wait and see what comes of it all."

Her mother stood, too. "Don't you want to see him? Don't you want to ask him to his face how he could have done those things?"

Lissa turned her back to both of them. "I don't know what I want." She regretted her tone but glanced over her shoulder anyway. "You taught me well, Mother—avoid dealing with the hard things. That's all I'm trying to do."

Lissa couldn't tell whether she offended her mother or not. She didn't demand a discussion or tell Lissa she was wrong. Instead, she let a long moment of silence pass, then whispered something about checking on Cassie and left the room.

Lissa looked at her father, who still stood in place. He never interfered.

"What about Aunt Bobbie?" Lissa asked.

Her father frowned, and it made his face look older than he'd ever looked before.

"She's been gone for a few days."

"Gone? Where?"

Now it was his turn to land in a nearby chair. "I don't know."

"How could you let her go off somewhere alone, the way things are now? If she gets sick, who will take care of her? How will we know?"

He raised his palms in a helpless gesture. "She announced she was going to visit friends but wouldn't say who or why. I couldn't stop her."

"How long has she been gone?"

"A week now."

"But why wouldn't she tell you where she was going?"

He shrugged.

Lissa turned away again, toward the window. Everything outside looked the same, just like home, but nothing seemed the way it used to be. "When did William die?"

"Going on two weeks now, I think. Made his coffin myself, from some of that old wood we had out in the shed. They ran out of coffins in town. Let's see . . . to tell the truth, I can't remember just how long ago."

Lissa was struck again by how his face was more lined than when she'd left for France just a year ago. He looked so tired.

"Father," she said slowly, "what do you think? About Josef, I mean?"

He cast her a steady gaze. "I was surprised, like everybody else, and maybe a little angry at Hank. He was the only one who knew the truth all along. Then, after it sunk in, I knew I'd have done the same thing in Hank's place. He wanted to save his boy's life, and he did. How can I blame him for that?"

"But what about Josef, Father?" She pressed her eyes shut against tears too ready to fall. "He saved my life, you know. He came to the hospital when I was ill, and stayed by my side when everyone else was too busy. That's where they arrested him. How can someone so good be guilty of so much?"

Her father shook his head, as if an answer was impossible. "Hank said the man who raised Josef was a staunch German. He reared Josef as a German citizen, not an American. Hank told me the Germans recruited Josef, secretly of course, when Europe seemed to be heading toward war. Perhaps Josef felt he had no choice but to do the things he did, because of the way he was raised. I can't say. I can't judge him or his motives."

Lissa looked away. Maybe her father wouldn't judge, but others would. Penny had.

She absently took in the sight outside the window again, but didn't really see the familiar bushes and trees and the expanse of lawn.

He was in New York.

"I fired him."

"You what?" Josef stared incredulously at the woman he still called Aunt Bobbie, although she was Larisa's aunt and not likely to become a relative of his.

"He was a pompous idiot. An incompetent, pompous idiot at that. The man I've hired is named Morgan. Anthony Morgan. He's a bit young, but he has everything we need: a belief in justice and dedication to hard work."

Josef leaned back in the chair, letting his breath out between tight lips. "A regular paladin."

"Yes, yes, that's it—a champion."

Josef leaned forward again. Only a scarred wooden table separated them, but the armed guard standing at the door of the unadorned, painted brick visiting room of Tombs Prison was enough to remind him not to make contact. Josef let his palms rest on the rough wood, his wrists shackled. "Look, Aunt Bobbie, I don't have any money. What I did have has been tied up in the government investigation. I don't want you spending your money on some over-eager lawyer who is feeding you hope about how things can turn out if you hire him. I'm guilty. Justice will be served. Now get in touch with that court-appointed lawyer again and tell him he's back on the case."

Aunt Bobbie shook her head, eyes closed resolutely. "I'll do no such thing. I'm only doing what your father would do if he were here. Mr. Morgan is coming this afternoon, and I expect you to cooperate with him. You listen to me, Josef, and one day you'll thank me. When you're bouncing your grandchildren on your lap with Liss at your side, you'll thank me."

Josef looked away when Aunt Bobbie spoke Larisa's name. He'd been in a cell for two weeks now, after a nightmarish sea voyage. He'd figured he would save the Parkers and his family a lot of grief by picking up the influenza. But it hadn't worked. Dozens below deck died while he was healthy as ever, evidently immune.

He'd been convinced Lissa was dead, since no one had gotten word to him otherwise before he'd left France. He'd been taken from the ship at the Port of New York to the Federal Building in Park Row and finally to the Tombs to await trial. Here he learned about Larisa through Aunt Bobbie. A letter had arrived at the Parker home from Caleb, the first definite indication that he was alive.

They'd learned of Josef's arrest, and Caleb's, too, who would face a disciplinary hearing for disobeying regulations after their self-designed flight from prison camp. He said he was relieved to hear from a nun at the hospital that Larisa had survived her sickness with influenza and was homeward bound. He'd tried to get word to Josef, but the Army hadn't let him. Caleb's letter had reached home before Lissa had.

The day Aunt Bobbie read Caleb's letter, she had made up her mind to leave Culpeper for New York to see what was happening with Josef. It had taken days to find someone who would give her permission to visit the recently arrived prisoner. She'd finally broken through the governmental barriers and came to Josef with tales of how Hank had sailed to Europe after he'd gotten word of both his sons' arrests, hoping to help, or at least offer support. They'd received only a telegram from him saying that he'd arrived safely, but the Army wasn't being cooperative. He mentioned no names, perhaps fearing the censors would prohibit the message altogether.

Jaylene had sent word to Hank when she read in the newspaper that the spy Josef von Woerner was in federal custody in New York, but they hadn't yet received any response.

Aunt Bobbie had shared all she knew of this whirlwind of activity. She told him Larisa would be home any day now, and would soon be coming to be at Josef's side.

Josef was anything but convinced about that. Sitting in a cell had given him plenty of time to think. He didn't need to read the newspaper accounts of his arrest and impending trial to know he was a hated man. Why would Larisa want to be associated with him? Aunt Bobbie wouldn't have risked coming to see him except for Larisa. In her own impulsive, romantic, naïve way, she was doing what she thought Larisa would if she were here. That spoke of her deep devotion to her niece, but it was all a waste of time and money.

If Larisa was back in the States, she certainly wasn't stopping in New York to see him. He didn't expect that she would.

"I've given your new lawyer, Mr. Morgan, the name of the family Caleb references in his letter to Lissa, parents of a lieutenant you tried to save."

"What?"

She ignored the protest. Aunt Bobbie was nothing if not resourceful. "Mr. Morgan thought it an excellent idea. We're going to need character references. He is contacting them today."

"I tried to save him, Aunt Bobbie, but I failed. Lt. Brooks is dead. You think his parents should be bothered with my problems? I want you to tell that lawyer not to pester them. They're dealing with their own grief and don't need to be tangled up in my mess."

"Oh posh, boy, they may want to help. And why shouldn't they? According to Caleb, you risked your life to get that young man out of harm's way. Even if he did eventually die, you did all you could. They should be as grateful to you as to the doctors who tried to save him. Does it make the Army doctor any less a hero because he couldn't save him?"

Josef shook his head. What good would Aunt Bobbie's efforts do? Most likely it would only do harm. She was so ready to believe he had a chance. "This is crazy, Aunt Bobbie."

"Caleb said you saved him and your Sergeant, too, so I'm sure both of them are trying to get back here. Maybe your father can speed that along. Now, is there anyone else you've been saving that I don't know about, or someone who knew you . . . before?"

Josef noticed Aunt Bobbie's sudden discomfort. "You can hardly speak of it. You mean from my past as a spy. A criminal. A traitor. You can't even look at me when you mention it. I don't know why you're willing to do all this. If you're doing it because you think Larisa and I might still have a future, you can forget it."

Aunt Bobbie pursed her lips and looked at Josef so closely he felt a prickle of discomfort.

"Are you telling me that since you've recovered your memories, you no longer love my niece?"

Josef held steady that piercing gaze. He leaned forward again, placing his cuffed hands down, this time open-palmed and, because of the cuffs, only inches apart. "Larisa is a part of me, and I'll never stop loving her. But that doesn't mean we can, or should, marry."

"Don't be ridiculous. I know she loves you."

Josef shook his head. "Aunt Bobbie, I know you mean well, and I am grateful. But I've been able to do a lot of thinking about this from the moment I was able to remember everything."

"Yes, yes, I know all of that, how you could've stayed in Germany, or fled in the opposite direction once you escaped that prison camp. I'll venture that it was your love for Liss that made you come back when you knew you'd be found out. Once she knows that, if she doesn't already, she'll fly to your side."

"It was my love for Larisa. But I also want to make it right because it's what God wants." He wished he could find words that explained all the thoughts he'd kept to himself. "God worked a miracle when He moved Hank to save my life. He directed me to a more worthy object of devotion. He directed me to Himself. Otherwise I might not have understood that the things I did before were wrong. Before, I believed what I did was worthy of doing whether right or wrong. But after reading in the Bible what true devotion is, I knew I had to come back. To call myself a Christian, I have to face my crimes."

Aunt Bobbie nodded and reached over as if to pat Josef's hand, but caught herself mid-air with a quick glance to the watchful guard nearby. No touching. "Of course you wanted to do the right thing. If I didn't believe that, I wouldn't be here."

"But do you know what that means? I gave up my future with Larisa. To be worthy of her love I did the right thing. God wouldn't have it any other way. But I won't ask her to marry me. The government will make sure I can't anyway. If by some miracle I'm not sentenced to hang, I'll be in prison the rest of my life. I'll be a memory to her, but at least I'll be a memory of somebody who did the right thing."

To his chagrin he saw Aunt Bobbie's eyes fill with tears. That's all he needed, a hysterical woman to comfort when he couldn't even offer a shoulder to cry on.

Reaching for a handkerchief from her pocket, Aunt Bobbie sniffed. "Oh, Josef, I knew you were the one for her the moment I met you." She wiped her eyes and nose, then looked at Josef earnestly again. "You've just reinforced my resolve to have you represented by the best, Josef. And Mr. Morgan is the best . . . well, the best willing to take on this sort of case, of course. I can hardly wait for him to get here!"

Josef shook his head again. She hadn't heard a word he'd said.

CHAPTER *Twenty-Seven*

"How DO, Jaylene," said Frank Parker, when she answered the door. He took off his hat. Frank hadn't seen Jaylene Tanner in a couple of weeks, since Hank had left for Europe. With church services prohibited and most of the stores closed in town, little opportunity remained to mingle with the neighbors.

"Hello, Frank. How's Cassie doing?"

"Better today, I think," Frank said. "Thank you for asking."

"Is her fever down, then?"

"Comes and goes," he said. "Lissa says she's not out of the woods yet."

Jaylene stood so stiff it was as if she'd forgotten the carefree days when she and Addie would visit over a cup of coffee, and he and Hank would join them when chores were done. The four of them played cards together every Friday night, between planting and harvest seasons. Some of their neighbors would have been scandalized that they would indulge in the sin of card playing, but they didn't see anything in the Bible about it. Their daughters would go off to their own activities, best of friends since they first learned to walk. Now here she and Frank stood like a couple of strangers, though they'd known one another for more than twenty years.

"Came by to give you this," Frank said, pulling the telegram out of his pocket. "Went on my rounds with McPhearson and told him I'd save him the trip and swing by."

She opened the door wide enough to accept the envelope and tore it open. Frank didn't mention that McPhearson had violated every rule of his office by sharing with him the contents of the message. In France, Hank had gotten a telegram from Frank's own sister Bobbie, telling him to get Caleb and the sergeant out of jail as quick as he could and come home. Josef was in a New York jail, and he needed them.

Hank's telegram was to let Jaylene know he'd be home before month's end—with Caleb and a man named Dack.

Jaylene raised moist eyes to Frank. "They're coming home. Both of them, Hank and Caleb."

Just then Penny tripped up the porch steps, out of breath.

"Oh, Mr. Parker! I saw your car and hoped Lissa was here."

"Home and gone again," Frank said. "Came home yesterday and took the train to New York this morning."

"Oh?"

The girl looked less surprised than Frank would've expected. Maybe she had guessed what Lissa would do when she got home.

"I suppose you know Josef's there," Frank said to Jaylene, as if that was explanation enough.

"Yes, we heard," Jaylene said. "I went to see him. He looks fit, despite everything. A bit thin, though."

Frank watched out of the corner of his eye as Penny walked past and disappeared into the house without a word. She had an abashed look on her face, sort of like when he'd caught her and Lissa breaking a rule.

"You know, Frank," whispered Jaylene, "all the headlines are full of the Armistice these days. Peace at last. But once that feels like old news and Josef's trial starts, it's bound to get . . . uncomfortable. Hank and I will understand if you—and all your family—want to steer clear of us. Josef said I should tell you that, and I agree."

"As for me and Addie, we'll be at your side, same as always. Can't speak for Liss, but given that she rushed off to New York, my guess is she'll be there, too. Obviously my sister already is. You know she never told us where she was goin.'"

He saw Jaylene's forehead pucker and tears come, so he looked away, wishing Addie were here. This woman was in need of a hug, and Frank couldn't give her one, even if they were neighbors.

———————

Lissa stood outside the tall, turreted Tombs Prison, knowing inside one of those fortified, steel cells sat Josef. He was alone but surrounded by all of New York, awaiting a trial to judge his illegal activities. Awaiting a judge and jury to decide what punishment his crimes deserved.

A north wind whipped at her skirt. It wasn't cold, even for November, but it was colder than France had been, and she shivered. She couldn't stand on the steps leading to the doors that were centered between those columns forever. She must go in or go home.

All the way from Culpeper, she'd wrestled with her thoughts. Part of her wanted to rush up those three stairs, past the half-iron and half-cement-block fence, and demand to see him. She wanted to touch him and tell him how much she loved him. But another part held back, emotions she couldn't sort out that left her immobile. She hated indecision in others, and no less in herself. Yet here she was, two parts of her mind and heart warring, neither side winning. She wished she could sign her own armistice, the way the Allied Command and Central Powers had. The war was over as of the eleventh hour of the eleventh day of this eleventh month—peace.

That's all she longed for within herself, too. She'd prayed but wondered if wanting to see Josef again really was a leading from above. Or was it her own selfish desire to be with him again, no matter what he'd done or how he felt about her any more?

She wished she knew how he felt since he'd become whole again. Had he been able to merge his old self with the new? Or was he only the old Josef, and the one she knew and loved was a temporary aberration who no longer existed? The old Josef loved Germany above all else, and a woman named Liesel.

Lissa forced her stiff limbs to comply. She wasn't going to turn around now.

Inside, after going through the offices of a receptionist, superintendent, and warden, well beyond the barred windows, she came to a guard station where she stated her business once again. The man had a wrinkled uniform, which was only the first indication of his unkempt person. The smell emanating from him was the second.

"Josef von Woerner," he repeated. He didn't look at any roster or list, yet he seemed to recognize the name.

Lissa nodded, feeling a blush when he looked her over.

"Well, that traitor don't lack for female companionship. I guess his women don't mind he went up against Uncle Sam and the rest of us."

"I beg your pardon?"

The middle-aged man stood shrugging as he pulled a ring of keys from a notch on the wall behind his desk. He wasn't easy to look upon. His skin was marred with spots, his hair wiry and unmanaged. He had a slight paunch and his posture was slumped, and his teeth were black and yellow. From what Lissa could see, he looked more like a warden from the old London Tower than a modern day New York prison.

He didn't seem eager to expand on his comment, though.

"Has Mr. von Woerner had other visitors?"

The man laughed and even from three feet away Lissa got a whiff of his foul breath, which added to his other odors. She raised her hand to cover her nose, feigning an itch.

"Oh, sure," he said at last. "Other than his lawyer, every one's been a woman. One just left a couple hours ago. Thought you was the same one when you first come in, you're about the same height. Her name was Lissa, too, or somethin' like that."

Lissa didn't ask for clarification. Liesel had been to see her love. Suddenly Lissa's feet were too heavy to move. The guard stood at the door, having unlocked it. He looked expectantly in Lissa's direction.

"You comin'? You got to wait in the visitin' room while I send a guard to bring up von Woerner."

Lissa stared at him. She knew he spoke and somewhere the words registered, but she could hardly hear above the pounding in her ears. She turned on her heels and walked briskly from the room, knowing she would faint if she didn't reach the fresh air outside.

My Son,

I write this to you with unsteady hand, but I trust no one here to record my words. I would have to translate to English, and sometimes it is best only to speak in one's own language.

There is much for me to say, much that I should have said long ago. Before I begin my confession, I wish to tell you that I love you and always have. From the day you were born, I loved you as my son, even though I have always known you are not.

Of course you know it now too. I never thought it necessary to tell you. I wanted to keep you as my son. I also wanted a way to take revenge on a man my wife preferred to me, the man who is your father.

I'm told I owe Heinrick for your life. Once again. I learned he saved your life on that awful night when I thought you were killed. I've spent much energy trying to hate him, Josef, but now at the end of my life I find myself thankful to him. He gave you life, and he kept you alive. I knew when I went to him about the trouble you were in that he would do all he could. He did not fail.

Now for my confession. I am to blame for your troubles. I wanted you to keep Germany in your heart as I did. I've spent much of my life here and it is the only home you've ever known, but Germany was always first for me. In raising you, I was not only devoted more to Germany than to you, I was devious. What I must say will be hard for me to write, hard for you to hear. But if I am to go to God with an effort to show my repentance, I must tell you all of it.

I loved you, but I wanted to hate you, Josef, because you were not my own. When I looked at you, I was reminded of what your mother had done. I wanted to raise you so that you would not stay in this country where the man who fathered you lived. I wanted to claim you away from him, claim you for Germany. So I nurtured you on the sweet milk of the fatherland, fed you only its glories and none of its woes. I wanted to believe it all myself, but I knew deep

down I was using that to keep you from the man who could call you his son.

I loved you, resented you, used you. I hoped you would leave America and never come back. I was willing never to see you again if it meant the man who fathered you would never have that chance, either.

For that I am sorry. It is an empty victory. I would not want you to live in Germany where I might never see you again. Such a thought slices through me with pain. This I cannot bear.

You are the product of my twisted thinking. I am a German. I love the fatherland. I hoped Germany would win and gain her place in the sun. I didn't want to see America conquered, I only wanted to see Germany respected and honored as the greatest military power. I believe now that this was a petty and selfish desire. Germany sought greatness through domination and the power of its army, not through the merits of its hard work, science, and culture. Those gifts from our Creator are the measure of the fatherland. Now I think not on Germany at all, but on things your Mother tried to share with me so many years ago. The kaiser is not greater than the kingdom of heaven. This I now believe.

I was wrong in many ways. My delusions of power on this earth bring much pain to your life.

My efforts for grandeur were shown in other ways. They were not simply for my hope in a renowned Germany. I wanted a feast of this world in making my business flourish. I kept you at a distance, too busy pursuing my goals to spend time with you. I did the same to your mother. This is perhaps why she turned for friendship and love to your father. For pushing you away, I am sorry. I realize now I missed much of your childhood. I had your love but was too busy to show you my own.

I have heard there will be a trial for you now. I pray I live long enough to speak on your behalf, to tell that I am to blame. If there is justice in this life, they will listen.

Your loving father,
Otto

The pages trembled in Josef's hands, and his eyes turned hot and moist. But he wasn't alone in the lunchroom where they were given mail with their porridge. Any exhibition of weakness among thieves and pickpockets and far worse brought only the worst result.

He folded the letter and put it in the pocket of his blue denim prison-issue shirt, a shirt like the few dozen men nearby wore. Like the others, he called this place "the pit." If the guards in an unregistered German prison camp were harsh, the guards here had nothing to learn from them.

They were herded back to their cells to make room for the next shift of men for the midday meal. Josef took a seat on the cot that offered small comfort other than familiarity. Since he'd first been delivered to the cell, a trace of self-pity had still sprung up now and then. It was a horrible place, this Tombs Prison. Each inmate was placed in a cell little wider than the spread of his arms, the length could only accommodate the squalid cot on which he sat and slept. The cot itself was revolting, a straw bag suspended on four legs that countless others had used before, judging from its filth, lice, and bed bugs. The steel walls and iron bars were as squalid as the rest of the place. It hadn't taken long for the grime to permeate him.

He could shower with other inmates but found being clean less attractive when he had to step into a shower where grime covered the floor. Back in the days he'd pretended to be a poor factory worker, he'd carefully chosen his own dirt. Even the muck from no man's land was less revolting. He didn't like the bugs, but what was the point of washing them off when there was an endless supply in his mattress to take their place?

He should hate his own arrogance, but he could still thank God that He loved them all, including Josef, when he saw only the ugliness. He had been dirtier than this in that German prison camp. God had delivered him from that.

He pulled out his father's letter once again. Liesel Bonner had brought it to him that morning. No, not Bonner. Her name had become Liesel de Serre. How awkward they'd acted when they first saw one another in the prison visitation room. Josef and Liesel always used to bestow a hug or a kiss upon one another after they hadn't seen each other for a while. That would have been inappropriate, even if it had been allowed. It would be inappropriate even if her name wasn't de Serre.

Days before, Josef had pressed his lawyer about who was named in the case against him. At first he was told only the United States Government. While that was intimidating, Josef wanted to know more details than the name of the attorney general and others in that office who handled the case.

He'd learned that the federal investigator who'd gathered information on him from the start was named David de Serre. And Liesel had married him.

Josef was glad he suspected as much before he saw Liesel, before she spoke her new name. He'd long believed it was best to be prepared. Jealousy had nothing to do with it. When he compared the feelings he remembered having for Liesel to those he now had for Larisa, he knew what he'd felt for Liesel was brotherly affection more than real love. Their relationship had been so comfortable, during a time in his life when he needed comfort and security. Someone he could trust. Her betrayal still stung. If she'd been nothing else, she'd at least been his friend.

Now, he could understand what she'd done. Back when he knew her, when he worked for the Germans, he was so caught up in his blind loyalty, so caught up in trying to impress Otto, that he hadn't seen anything else. He'd never stopped to think what his actions meant.

He hadn't known any of that until he'd met God and Larisa Rose.

"I'm sorry," Liesel had said after that first uneasy moment of silence after they took their seats across from one another in that stark visitor's room.

"Don't be," Josef had said. Then, because he didn't want her to think he was heartbroken, or even resentful, he'd leaned forward and told her the truth. "I'm a better man today because I was caught that night, Liesel."

She'd cried then, tears of happiness he thought, and he was glad she still cared about him, as a sister would. He admitted that he was at peace about being in jail for what he'd done and was ready to face his punishment. Even though he might never be free again, he had the peace of knowing he'd done the right thing. He needed to do what God would have him do. He told her about Larisa. Liesel touched his hand, and the guard gave a stern reminder: "No contact, ma'am." She withdrew and said, "I'm sure you'll have a happy future with her, Josef."

But Josef didn't believe her any more than he'd believed Aunt Bobbie.

When the twenty minutes were up, she handed him Otto's letter, after showing it to the guard. The guard couldn't read a word of it and almost didn't let her pass it across, but decided that even an enemy letter could do no harm now, in this place. Liesel told Josef that her family had been to visit Otto often, and she was sorry to report his health was failing but his love for Josef was strong. Then she'd left.

Now Josef leaned back on the cot, folding an arm beneath his head. He'd been glad to see Liesel. He was comforted by Otto's letter. But it did little to fill the void of the one visitor he hadn't seen yet, perhaps would never see.

CHAPTER *Twenty-Eight*

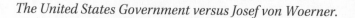

The United States Government versus Josef von Woerner.

Charges: Violation of Federal laws under the counts of: (1) endangering of transport at sea; (2) transporting and storing of explosives within the territory of the United States without a police license; (3) violation of strike laws by inciting illegal strikes; (4) sedition; (5) treason.

LISSA READ the charges as listed in the newspaper. The trial was to begin the following Monday, when the suspect (they still called him that, even though this reporter, at least, seemed convinced of his guilt) would be transported from Tombs Prison in New York to federal custody in Washington, D.C. Because of the nature of the crimes so closely connected to the war, officials were not waiting until Health Office restrictions were lifted and the courts reopened. Rather, in an unprecedented move, they would construct an outdoor court on federal land in Washington. This would prevent endangering court officials, jury, or witnesses by placing them indoors while the plague of influenza still passed from person to person in enclosed places.

271

Days had passed since Lissa had tried to see Josef, followed by nights of insomnia and heartache, indecision and prayer. Each time she tried to give this burden to the Lord, she wrenched it back, sinking deeper into despair. Was he praying, too, she wondered, or did the faith she witnessed in Josef belong only to the Josef who had no memories of his past life—the Josef who no longer existed?

The only bright spot was that Cassie was on her way to recovery. The sisters spent most of Cassie's waking moments together, bonded not only by blood but by grief. Lissa also knew first hand Cassie's fatigue. She wasn't yet over that part of her own battle with the illness. Lissa told herself that was why she had trouble fighting her emotions. She simply didn't have the strength.

She sat on the rocker next to Cassie's bed. She'd pulled the curtain away from the window to afford a view of the fields out back. Beyond those hills lay Saddlebrook, and that reminded her of Josef.

"Lissa."

The voice carried from the base of the stairs and Lissa, with a curious glance between herself and Cassie, rose to answer the call. Before Lissa could answer, she heard, "Never mind. I'm coming up."

Aunt Bobbie. Lissa rushed to the bedroom doorway, greeting her aunt with a hug.

"Oh, it's so good to see you."

Aunt Bobbie returned the hug, then looked at Cassie, who was sitting propped up by a mound of pillows.

"You're on the mend, I see, no doubt because of the good company of your sister and the care your mother has given."

"That's right," said Cassie.

Aunt Bobbie straightened to her full height, which wasn't much taller than Cassie sitting down on her bed.

"So, where have you been, Aunt Bobbie?" Cassie asked. "Father couldn't be quieted when he got your note saying you'd left, but not telling him where you went."

Aunt Bobbie frowned, glancing between Cassie and Lissa. The look gave Lissa an odd feeling that she wasn't sure she wanted to acknowledge.

"I've been in New York," she announced, and looking directly at Lissa added, "where you should be, young lady."

Lissa's odd feeling now blossomed into full blown distress. "Aunt Bobbie, I really don't want to talk about this."

"You don't want to talk about it," Aunt Bobbie repeated. "Very well. If you don't want to talk, then you'll listen. I think it's shameful that you've let that poor boy rot in a jail cell without a word from you—after all he did for you. From what I hear, you might not be alive, and he wouldn't be in jail right now if he hadn't insisted on being by your side when you were ill. And the fact is, you're engaged to marry the man. Don't you think you owe him something?"

Lissa turned away, squeezing her eyes shut against ready tears. "I was engaged to Josef Warner, not Josef von Woerner."

"So that's it? You believe the man you loved doesn't exist, though you haven't bothered to find out."

Lissa turned to Aunt Bobbie, wanting to hope but afraid of the answer. "Does he still exist?"

Aunt Bobbie took both of Lissa's hands in hers. "Of course he does, Liss." Aunt Bobbie laughed, but it didn't match any of the emotions coursing through Lissa. Her aunt sounded positively buoyant.

"If someone had told me ten years ago that I'd be standing here defending a young man in jail as the man my niece should marry, I'd have thought them out of their mind. But here I am, Lissa, doing just that. You made a commitment to him, and you're a Parker. We don't go back on our word."

"Maybe she made a mistake," Cassie interjected. "You wouldn't have her marry a man she doesn't love, would you, Aunt Bobbie? Especially one in jail. I'd say his being in jail is reason enough to change her mind."

"Unless she can stand here and convince us she no longer loves Josef, she'd be a fool to miss a chance at living out that love."

"Well, Liss?" Cassie prompted. "Do you love him or not? You haven't said a word about him since you've been back from New York, but I've also watched you read every article about him, some of them several times. I guess he's on your mind, at least."

Lissa thought she might burst if she didn't speak. "Of course he's on my mind! How could he not be, with all that's happened to him?"

"And this concern is based on what?" Cassie pressed, sitting up a bit straighter on the pillows. "You feel sorry for him? You still love him?"

"I love Josef, but I love the Josef I knew before. Now I don't know what to think. Was his faith even real? And what about his fiancée?"

Aunt Bobbie clucked her tongue. "If that's what you're worried about, that's nonsense. That fiancée was from his past, not the present and certainly not his future. We all have a bit of history by the time we get married, haven't we? I remember a boy at school you fancied, the one who didn't want you to go off to nursing school."

"A school sweetheart is hardly the same, Aunt Bobbie."

"You've long since gotten over any feelings for that boy. What was his name? Oh, posh, who cares? The woman Josef was engaged to is no longer part of his life. He doesn't want her to be, nor does she want to be, as far as I've been able to learn. She married one of the agents responsible for building a case against Josef."

Cassie whistled. "My goodness, she betrayed him."

"I suppose you could look at it that way. Considering what Josef was doing at the time, I'd not blame her. Nonetheless, if jealousy is eating at you, there's really no point in even thinking about her, is there?"

"Was he heartbroken when he learned about this other woman's marriage?"

"Oh, for heaven's sake, Liss, I haven't heard him mention her. You're missing the point entirely. He loves you, not her!"

"I went to see Josef." She turned from the two surprised faces because it was so humiliating to admit the truth. "Evidently this other woman had already been there. The guard told me she'd just left."

"So?" Aunt Bobbie asked.

Lissa turned back again, and this time she was the one surprised. "Don't you see? She rushed to his side in prison. She must have thought him dead. Maybe that's why she married this other man. Now she realizes Josef is still alive, and maybe realizes she made a mistake. Maybe Josef will want her back."

Aunt Bobbie shook her head, her eyes full of impatience. "Lissa, I don't know the story of Josef and this other woman, but unlike you, I've been with him. He thinks you've abandoned him. Josef loves only you, and whatever he once felt for this woman just doesn't compare. That I know. I also know you owe it to him to ask."

Lissa looked to Cassie.

"She has a point, Liss," said Cassie. "You really ought to see him."

Lissa's heart soared and plummeted in that moment. It's what she'd wanted to do all along, it's all she thought about. Seeing his face, his eyes, his smile, close enough to touch, not just the memory of him. She would know in the first moment if he was still the same Josef she'd fallen in love with, the one who loved God—and her.

Or would she? Her heart sank lower with the same doubts she'd had since receiving Penny's letter. Maybe he did still love her. Maybe he would look at her in that old way. Maybe he would smile and her heart would race and flutter, just to be smiled at that way. Maybe that's how he loved that other woman, too. How could she know if she did love this new Josef, the one who'd done the things he had? He had wanted to live in a world dominated by German power. He had worked for an earthly kingdom, not God's.

"I'm afraid," she whispered.

Aunt Bobbie neared, placing her hand on Lissa's forearm. "Of what, dear? He's the same Josef, the same Josef you fell in love with."

Lissa searched Aunt Bobbie's earnest gaze, wanting to believe her. "But how can he be, with everything that he used to stand for, I mean?" She took the hand that so tenderly tried to comfort her. "How can you tell me to go to him, to love him, when he's done things against our country? He was working against us. Of all people, you with your DAR loyalties should tell me to stay away from him."

Aunt Bobbie's face was full of compassion and comfort, without a trace of worry. Obviously she was not threatened in the least by Lissa's words. "If I thought for a moment that he felt no loyalty to America, I'd have left after my first visit without a backward glance. It's so complicated, Liss. I don't understand it all, but what I do know is that he did not act against the United States. He saw himself as trying to save German citizens from the weapons we were supplying to their enemies. And he was raised in a way that promoted blind loyalty to Germany.

"His amnesia and his time here, with all of us, gave him the chance to gain a better perspective. God truly plucked him out of one life and taught him a better way that leads to the Lord Himself. And I believe it leads to you, Liss."

She sighed heavily, resting her hand on Lissa's arm again. "I'll not fault you if you decide differently, but it should be a decision made after talking to him. You must go to him, Lissa. He's convinced you'll have nothing to do with him. He's believed that ever since his memory came back. In spite of all that, he wants to do the right thing. He's ready to sacrifice his life to be worthy of your love, even if you have no future together."

"He . . . said that?"

Aunt Bobbie nodded.

Lissa turned away.

"Lissa, look at me," Cassie said slowly.

Lissa turned to her sister, who was still pale, weak, and tired, but at that moment had a glint of steel in her eye. "Go to him, Liss. You love him, and he loves you. Nothing should come between you except death. I had William such a short time, but I wouldn't trade a moment of it, even now."

Lissa let her tears go. "I'm so ashamed! I should have seen him that day, no matter what. I was such a coward, trying to push it all away."

Aunt Bobbie put her arms around Lissa. "Well, that's from your mother's side of the family, bless her heart, not from us Parkers. But we won't go into all that now. I'm taking the morning train back to New York, and I expect you to be with me. We have a trial to prepare for."

Josef sat on the edge of the straw cot, Bible in hand. He read the words, though he realized he was reading today out of obedience, not devotion. He felt a surge of scorn for himself, something he'd felt often lately. *Obedience.* He was good at that. Was it just an authoritarian vein that ran through him? Was he a utilitarian, who believed obedience simply made the most sense? That kind of thinking had led him to trouble to begin with. Authority figures—his father, then powerful German business associates—had given Josef orders. And he'd obeyed. Obedience for the sake of obedience? Or did he really believe in the fatherland? The fatherland told him he wasn't an

American, he was a *Deutscher Bürger, Sohn von Deutschland*, and his greatest goal should be to protect the *Landwehrleute*. A son of Germany, born to protect the soldiers fighting for the fatherland.

Josef had obeyed this call.

No, obedience isn't the enemy. He remembered Abraham and the prophets and the Lord Jesus. The obedience of Jesus to the will of God had changed the world. Yes, Josef knew so much in his logical mind. He knew it was the object of obedience that mattered. He knew his priorities were finally right. But somehow, in a lice-infested jail cell, it was hard to take much comfort in the fact that he had finally gotten something right.

Inevitably his mind went to Larisa. He knew she was home from Europe, even though every visitor from Culpeper, from Aunt Bobbie to Hank and his wife and Caleb, avoided reference to her. And he knew why. Oh, they were loyal enough to want to see him out of jail, at least out of this jail, but that loyalty didn't include wanting him married to a woman who clearly deserved better.

He did long to see her, just once more. After that, he didn't care what happened.

––––––

Hank sat across the table from Anthony Morgan, who wasn't much older than Josef. Hank's first impression of the young lawyer was just that: he was young; too young and inexperienced to be effective.

But in the short time they'd been working together, Hank had changed his mind about Morgan. He was also smart, hardworking, well educated, and practical. More important, he saw more in Josef than simply the crimes he'd committed. The lawyer seemed to have a firm belief that Josef was a changed man from the days he worked for Germany.

"There will be two stages to the trial," Morgan explained. "The first determines guilt or innocence, the second determines the sentence. We're only contesting sedition and treason. We have a good case to prove he's innocent on both of those counts under the letter of the law. But here's the thing. If we don't want him put away for a good long time, we need to get character witnesses before that judge and jury."

"I'm sure many people from Culpeper will attest to Josef's high moral character," Hank said. "People from Washington, too."

"I don't need his second grade teacher coming in and telling everyone what a good student Josef was. We need recent accounts, testifying to his *patriotic* behavior. Because of the crimes, he was given an automatic dishonorable discharge. We can't let that be all the jury hears about his military record. I have several witnesses lined up, but I'm not sure the judge will allow evidence of Josef's war activities in a civilian court when the crimes were committed earlier."

"Not sure?"

Despite the question, Morgan smiled. "No. But that won't stop me from making a strong argument for it. We both know the judge runs the trial. It's my job to convince him that justice won't be served unless we see who Josef is now, not just how he was when he committed the crimes.

"They're pushing this case through at record speed, and that might work in our favor. We don't have a lot of time to prepare—but neither does the prosecution." Then he frowned anew. "I'm uncertain about one thing, though. I don't know whether to put Josef on the stand. He's too eager to state his guilt, as if he wants to be punished to the fullest extent of the law. That won't look good."

Hank nodded. He'd been with Caleb to see Josef the afternoon before. Between what Caleb had told him and what he'd observed of Josef's demeanor, Morgan was exactly right. Josef wasn't simply prepared for a stiff penalty, he was counting on it.

"But," Morgan continued, "if we could get him to talk about how he feels about America now, and maybe throw in a bit of the faith angle. . . ."

"Faith angle?"

"You know, the conversion. Redemption. Forgiveness."

"This is an angle to you?"

"Depending on how convincing he is."

Hank shook his head. "You have a lot to learn about faith, Mr. Morgan."

Morgan stared at Hank as if he'd lapsed into a foreign language. He raised a small stack of papers in front of him and tapped them into a neat pile before replacing them inside a large envelope.

"All of that may be true, Mr. Tanner. Fortunately I have a good idea how a jury will read things. That's what counts. Here's how it'll go. We need these witnesses in as soon as we can: first, Otto von Woerner, willing to take the blame. He'll be key if he's healthy enough to make it to the courtroom. Then the retired general, Brooks, whose son Josef tried to save. Third, we have the sergeant, what's his name—Sergeant Thaddeus Dack, and fourth we have your other son, Caleb. They'll be helpful in establishing Josef's display of patriotism to America. Fifth, there is a doctor who contacted me, he's eager to defend Josef. The way he worked on that Red Cross ship, Josef is a hero to this doctor. If we can get these witnesses in during the first part of the trial, the second part will be easy.

"You know, Mr. Tanner," the young lawyer added, "all we can hope for is to spare your son a harsh penalty. We have to convince the judge first, and then the jury, that Josef isn't the same man he was before he lost his memory. We need them to hear his actions from this past year. Frankly, without it any hope for a light sentence is impossible."

"A light sentence is all we want." Hank agreed, his voice almost a whisper.

"That's what we want," Morgan said, "but Josef has to want it, too."

CHAPTER *Twenty-Nine*

"PORTER!"

For someone so diminutive, Aunt Bobbie had a commanding voice. It now produced not one but two able-bodied redcaps. She directed them to the bags at the back of the jitney. One porter was sufficient, since most of Aunt Bobbie's luggage was already in New York. She'd only come back to Culpeper for Lissa.

"We'll go directly to Josef," Aunt Bobbie said as they walked toward the huge, brown passenger coach. "After that, we'll go to Mr. Morgan's office. We'll probably find Hank there, and Caleb, too. I believe they were to arrive yesterday."

Lissa nodded, though her thoughts never went beyond Aunt Bobbie's first words. They would see Josef first. She swallowed hard. Apprehension, excitement, and uncertainty collided inside, and she couldn't speak, could barely breathe. She wasn't at all sure she'd be any better when she saw him at last. Possibly she would be worse.

She felt Aunt Bobbie's eyes on her then, and whatever she saw on Lissa's face prompted her to take Lissa's hand and loop it through her arm.

Is she afraid I'll bolt?

"Lissa! Lissa, wait!"

They both turned to see Penny emerge from one of the Tanner Buicks, just behind the jitney.

"I'm so glad I caught up to you."

Aunt Bobbie dropped Lissa's hand and took a small step between the girls as if ready for a confrontation.

"If you've come to stop her, Penny, you might as well be on your way. She's coming with me."

The smile on Penny's face faded and she peered over Aunt Bobbie to look squarely at Lissa.

"I . . . came to see you, Liss. I just came from your house, and your mother told me you were on your way here. I-I didn't want to wait until you came back. Enough time has gone by already."

Penny's face was full of something similar to what Lissa already felt: uncertainty, maybe a little fear, mixed with what looked like guilt.

Lissa stepped around the miniature fortress Aunt Bobbie had made of herself, taking one of Penny's hands. "Oh, Pen, I'm sorry I haven't been by. I've missed you."

Penny pulled Lissa into an embrace. "Me, too."

"Well, this is quite a surprise, Penny," Aunt Bobbie interjected. "I took it from your mother that you want to keep Lissa from having anything to do with Josef. You've expressed quite the opinion of him lately. Do you know where we're off to?"

Her face glistening with tears, Penny stepped back but grabbed Lissa's hands. She sniffled. "I know. You're going to see him." More tears slid down her wet cheeks. "Oh, Liss, I don't know what to think about him, but I do know you're my very best friend. Mother has done nothing but berate me for thinking so ill of Josef. Maybe she's right. Maybe I'm the fool for thinking all those things about him. Except that he's obviously guilty. Oh, I only know that I don't want him to come between me and my family, or me and my best friend. I'm sorry if I've said or done anything I shouldn't. Will you forgive me?"

"As I see it, you were trying to protect me, Pen, in your way," Lissa responded. "I can't blame you for that."

"Does that mean you won't marry him?"

Lissa felt her eyes, already moist, fill to overflowing. "I don't know. I love him, Penny, no matter what he's done. I love the Josef I knew. I'm going to him, and I hope I find out what's to become of us."

"I want to go along."

"Penny Tanner, don't be ridiculous," Aunt Bobbie scoffed. "Is this some kind of ruse to get us to miss this train?"

"It isn't. I'll just tag along, and someone will come to get the car. Mama can send me clothes if I need to stay longer than today. Is it all right, Liss?"

Lissa nodded, eager to have Penny's company again.

"Come along, then. Hurry now," Aunt Bobbie urged.

They found facing seats, and Penny paid the conductor as Aunt Bobbie handed him the tickets for herself and Lissa.

"I want to make one thing clear before anything is said," Aunt Bobbie told Penny. "Lissa is confused enough right now, and I don't want you making it worse. You leave your ill opinions of your brother—yes, your brother—to yourself. Understood?"

Penny nodded, eyes a bit wider than usual as she faced the scolding.

"I'm here for Lissa," Penny whispered, taking Lissa's hand again. "Whatever she wants to do."

Lissa wished she knew what that would be.

Josef lay back on the straw. It was just before noon, but the guards hadn't come by to take them to what they called lunch. After lunch they'd have afternoon work detail: half-hearted scrubbing of floors, toilets, and the shower. The inmates were a maid service without a hint of pride in their work, and it showed.

Josef hadn't showered in three days. His beard had stopped itching, though, for which he was grateful. There was probably enough there now that the little vermin didn't have to pinch so close to the skin.

"Hey, Deutschlander," came the whisper. It came each day, sooner or later. Josef didn't respond.

"You get them Jerry friends of yours to break us outta here yet? Oh, yeah, you and yours lost that big ol' war over there. Lost it but good."

"Are you sure you don't want one of us to come in, at least as far as the guard? They won't allow more than one at a time to see him, but we can wait closer than out here."

Lissa shook her head. "No, Aunt Bobbie. I'm all right. Wait here where the sun shines. There's not much of that inside."

Maybe it was the rays of sun peering through a few puffy white clouds that had started clearing her mind. The Lord had not abandoned her, even if Josef might have. Now she would find out. Pushing away thoughts of him had served no purpose except to make her sick at heart.

Before long, she was inside the visiting room she never reached a few weeks ago. The same stinking guard let her in, but this time she was prepared to hold her breath when passing by him to enter the room. The visitor's chamber was stark, with brick walls painted white. No windows, just bald electric bulbs hanging from the ceiling to light the place. It was an uninviting room in an uninviting place where one would not wish to linger. It was half past two, and one other inmate was there with a visitor, perhaps his mother. They were seated on opposite sides of a table just like the one in front of Lissa. They weren't allowed to touch, she'd been warned about that. A guard on either side of the room made sure rules were obeyed.

Lissa folded her hands and waited. She would let the Lord direct this visit. That's what she should have done the first time she came.

"You've got a visitor, von Woerner."

"My lawyer?" he asked from a scrubbing position on his knees.

Most guards wouldn't have bothered to answer even so simple an inquiry, but this was Newell. "Naw, it's a woman. And, von Woerner? You might want to take a minute and dunk your head in that water. It's cleaner than you are."

"An older woman?"

"It ain't that old one that comes around. I'd say this one is worth cleanin' up for."

Josef bent his head. Larisa? It must be. His first thought was to praise the God he'd been simultaneously trying to blame and ignore. His second thought concerned his abominable appearance. His third, the one that stuck, was to wonder why she had come, after so many days of staying away. If her love was like his, nothing could have kept her away. But if she didn't love him, why come at all?

"Permission to hit the shower first, boss," said Josef, addressing him the way most of the other inmates did.

"Better hurry. Don't want to let this one get away again."

Josef, about to head to the shower only a few feet away, stopped in his tracks. "Again? She's been here before?"

"Not so as I've seen her. But Ackerly said she was here before and ran off."

Josef was tempted to forgo the shower and rush to the visiting room with Newell. Only his appearance would frighten her away if she'd fled once before.

He didn't take much time, and one quick shower didn't get rid of the bugs, but at least he didn't smell as offensive as he had moments ago. Newell even produced a clean shirt, something normally only handed out on Sundays.

Then he followed Newell along the narrow, winding pathway to the room that most prisoners were eager to see.

———

Lissa wished she hadn't given her father's pocket watch back to him once she returned home. How long had she been waiting? The woman visiting the other inmate had already left, and Lissa was alone in the grim room. Weren't they going to allow Josef to visit with her? Or was it Josef's decision to refuse to see her?

She swallowed hard, banishing such gloomy thoughts. She had to know, one way or the other. At last the door opened and her heart bumped into the walls of her chest.

But it wasn't Josef who appeared—or was it? Roughly the same height, but gaunt and dark. His hair that had been so light last summer was now dusky, as if dulled from lack of sun and food. His beard did not match at all. It was closer to the walnut shade of his eyebrows. The cheeks peeking above that beard were sharply defined, with a thin layer of skin hiding his bones.

Around his eyes were circles of faint blue, not like broken veins of a black eye but rather veins swollen from the fatigue of overworked arteries.

But there was the familiar blue of his eyes. It was him, after all.

She stood, and the scrape of the chair on the rough floor echoed in the hollow room. Neither moved, as if that floor had suddenly sprouted tentacles holding them both in place. But what held him so still? An unwillingness to approach her?

Then he stepped closer and she noticed for the first time shackles on his ankles and wrists. She wanted to near him then, to ease the shame of having him move that way. She started to go around the table, but the guards from both sides of the room stepped forward and she knew she had to stay put.

Josef came to the other side of the table, but he did not take the seat. She stared at him, as riveted to those blue eyes as she had been the first time she'd looked into them. She couldn't have broken the gaze then, and she couldn't now.

"Josef," she whispered.

"Will you sit?" he asked.

He was waiting for her to be seated first, still the gentleman, even in this place. Maybe he'd wanted to sit right away, to have the fetters hidden beneath the table. They both took their seats, and she smelled antiseptic. Strong, stinging, but clean.

"You're here," he whispered, still holding her gaze.

She nodded.

"Did you come before? Before today?"

She nodded again.

"But ran away?"

For the first time she let her gaze break from his. "I . . . was foolish."

He shook his head. "You could never be anything except what you are: strong and brave and loyal. Every Parker is."

She tried to smile because he sounded so familiar, even though he looked so different. Everything about him was different, except for his voice and the blue of his eyes.

"I have a lot to tell you, Larisa. I hope you give me the chance."

"I need to know, Josef. I need to know everything."

He leaned forward, putting his cuffed hands on the table. The chains clanked against the rough wood.

"I'll start with this: I am whole now, with a past, as well as a present and a future. Except everything I am is new. I'm not who I was before, and I'm not who I was when I was with you, either. The past is, well, it's there now. Do you believe God has the power to make somebody new? Different from who they were without Him?"

"Yes, I believe that." She held back the tears that shot to her eyes. She didn't want him to know the depth of her relief, because it revealed the depth of her doubt in his faith.

"The first time I read those words in the Bible about being a new creation, I didn't know what they meant. I just took them on faith. I didn't know that God had already done that for me, because I couldn't remember how I was before. Now I see what a miracle it was. I needed to tell you that. And I need to say one other thing."

She waited, knowing that he'd already said enough. No matter if he loved another woman from his past or loved Germany more than he could ever love America, he knew God. That should be enough.

"I need to tell you that I love you, Larisa Rose. I love you more than I can put words to, more than I've ever loved before. I don't know if you can love me the way you did once because of everything I've done, but I'll love you always, no matter what."

"Josef..."

He was already holding up one of his hands to stop her. The other shackled hand automatically followed.

"No, don't speak yet." There was something else in his eyes, something like panic or fear or something else she'd never seen in him before.

"I know who you are, Larisa. I know everything there is to know about you, everything you've shared with me and everything I've been privileged to witness and everything people say about you. All of that is bound up in my love for you."

His hands fell back to the table in a clang. "But you can't say you love me, or you don't love me, any more. You can't say one way or the other, not really. You don't know me the same way I know you. You have to understand why I did those things and how I feel about it all now. You need to know what

I want to do now with whatever time I have left. You can't say you love me or you don't love me until you know it all. So don't say anything about that. Okay?"

She wanted to shrug off all his objections and say she did love him, but his words made sense to her. It went past all emotion to pure logic. Of course she loved him. That love was a permanent part of her. But he was right. She loved the Josef who loved God and America, who'd gone off to fight for their country because he wanted to do the right thing. She loved the Josef she had known, the incomplete Josef.

"Will you let me write it to you? Will you read it with the memory of the love you once had for me? Will you read it for the sake of that part of me you knew?"

"Yes."

He received the word as if it were a kiss. He closed his eyes for a moment and then nodded as he looked at her again. "That's enough, then."

"But Josef, will you tell me, in your own words, right here, and right now, with all your memories intact: Do you believe all the things you did were right?"

He moved his hands closer to hers, careful not to touch her. "I believed I was right at one time. Some of it I still believe. Please, Larisa, let me tell it all to you, not bits and pieces. They won't let me stay long enough right now to do that. The only way I can do it right is in a letter. Don't make any judgments until you know it all. I know I have no right to think you'll still love me or want to spend any time with me. But let me write the letter with at least a little hope that I might be able to salvage some of the love we had."

She stared at him. Even as the love inside her demanded to be revealed, caution rose. Could she believe what he said, what he wanted to write? He must have been adept at lying once if he was a spy.

"I'll wait for your letter, Josef," she whispered.

"Time's up," called the guard behind Josef.

Josef stood, and so did Lissa. But he didn't move away. "I'll give it to Aunt Bobbie to give to you."

She nodded, faintly surprised that he didn't want her to come for it herself. And then he turned toward the guard.

CHAPTER *Thirty*

"WELL? How did it go?"

Lissa felt both sets of eyes on her as she approached Aunt Bobbie and Penny, but she wasn't ready to talk.

"He's going to write a letter to me, Aunt Bobbie. Then he'll give it to you, and you can give it to me."

"Oh?" she said, her brows raising with some confusion. "Well, that's fine. I'll be happy to help."

"That's it?" Penny said, obviously not taking Aunt Bobbie's cue to let Lissa speak in her own time.

Lissa gave her a half smile. "It's all I want to say right now. Where to next, Aunt Bobbie?"

"To find Hank at Mr. Morgan's office." She glanced at Penny. "He'll be surprised to see you, Penny. I'm sure of that."

Aunt Bobbie's prediction understated Hank Tanner's reaction when he greeted his daughter. A number of emotions crossed his face, including surprise and an uneasiness when he introduced Penny to Anthony Morgan. Morgan was young and intriguing, if not downright handsome. His dark hair was long enough to curl like a youth's, adding to the impression that he was not old enough to be the legal representative for anyone.

Lissa, for one, wondered what Aunt Bobbie was thinking to hire a man of so few years' experience in law or life. She wondered why Hank was going along with it.

"The good news is," Mr. Morgan was saying, "I just received word on which judge has been assigned. I know him—he's fair-minded. I think he'll allow all of our witnesses, civilian and military. I knew we could get them in on the sentencing portion, but I want this jury to know the whole Josef sooner than later."

Morgan turned to Lissa. "I want you to be available, of course. As Josef's fiancée, you should plan to be in court every day, to show the jury that he has your full support. I'll give you a list of clothing colors and styles that will make the best impression. We may not need you to testify. Your presence might speak more loudly. We'll see how it goes."

Morgan evidently did not require verbal agreement. He took her full cooperation for granted. She understood why her support for Josef must be obvious by virtue of her presence, but she was a little put off by the lawyer's abrupt attitude and assumptions.

Next he looked at Penny, and Lissa set aside her own affront to watch curiously.

"Caleb will give a major portion of testimony on Josef's actions at home and in their common war experiences. But as his sister, you may be called on as well. I'll make sure a copy of the clothing list is sent to you as well."

Penny opened her mouth to speak, but she must have thought better of it when her father put himself in her line of vision, shifting in his seat near the head of the table. Lissa didn't have to be a Tanner to read that look: Keep dissent within the family. No exceptions.

"Were you going to say something?" Morgan asked Penny, leaning around Hank.

Penny shook her head. "No, nothing."

"All right then," Morgan said, standing. The table before him was strewn with paperwork, folders, and envelopes, loose pages and bound ones. "Hank can go over the details with those of you who've just joined us. I have a court date I can't miss, so I'll be gone for a couple of hours. The government is pushing this case faster than any I've ever seen because of public sentiment.

I'd like it if all of you remain available for me to interview if need be. Sorry to leave so abruptly, but it can't be helped."

When he was gone Penny whispered to Lissa in a tight voice, "Of all the rude, overbearing people. I can't tell if he's too young to have learned any manners, or so spoiled in his ways he doesn't think he needs any."

Hank heard her comment; he looked his daughter's way. "My first impression of the young man was negative, too. But he knows the law, and his goal is the same as ours, to help Josef."

Aunt Bobbie offered Penny the first real smile she'd given her that day. "He comes highly recommended, actually. I might add that there wasn't a lot of choice. Most lawyers would rather leave a treason and sedition case to someone else."

Lissa's heart sank at the reminder of how serious were Josef's crimes.

Caleb neared the door first. "Yeah, well, they've got something to learn, then, because Josef's no traitor."

Then he left.

Hank led the others out of the office, and Lissa was infected with the same anxious melancholy that was evident on everyone else's face.

Aunt Bobbie put an arm about Lissa as they walked outside. "You know, Liss, I don't mean to destroy hope any more than I mean to give you false ones. The facts are there. Josef is in trouble. But we must remember Who's really in control, mustn't we?"

Lissa nodded, but Aunt Bobbie's words only inspired more tears. Lissa refused to let them fall. For the rest of the day, Lissa was in the constant company of her aunt and the Tanner family. Mrs. Tanner had joined them, and they all occupied rooms on the same floor of the New York Hotel, Lissa staying with Aunt Bobbie and Penny.

In the morning they met with Mr. Morgan as a group and, as he hinted yesterday, he wanted to talk to Penny, Caleb, and Lissa individually. Only Penny came away with a frown on her face. Lissa had no idea what transpired between the two, but Morgan certainly now suspected Penny's ambivalence toward her brother. He told Hank that it might be a good idea if she wasn't even in court.

But Lissa found no reason to frown over her own meeting with the aggressive young attorney. She learned, as had Hank and Aunt Bobbie before him, that Anthony Morgan knew his job. He seemed more interested in Lissa today, after having come from a visit with Josef.

"I don't know what you said to him," Morgan told Lissa. "Whatever it was, it worked like magic. Two days ago I was worried about the outcome of this case, Miss Parker. With Josef's new attitude, I'm more confident that it'll have the best possible outcome. Do you know why?"

Lissa shook her head.

"You infused my client with exactly what he needs: hope. Oh, I assured him there was never any real worry that he'd spend the rest of his life behind bars. But until today he gave every indication that it didn't matter how long he spent there. Now he's completely different. He's still willing to accept punishment for crimes committed, but he wants a fair verdict. I can only attribute the difference to you. So thank you, Miss Parker, for allowing me to do my job without my client being the greatest obstacle."

Lissa felt new hope, but Morgan's frown didn't allow the feeling to last long. "Still, I don't want you to expect that any of this will be easy. The prosecution has extended itself all out on this case. I think they've fallen victim to the publicity and timing. They think they can't lose, no matter what they charge Josef with, since everybody is trying to suck the last bit of blood out of Germany and Germans. They're trying Josef for treason and that's where they're making a mistake, Miss Parker. So buck up for a fight, but I don't have any intention of losing."

"Treason is the charge we all expected."

"You and everybody who's read the newspapers. But the laws regarding treason aren't quite so simple as the prosecution wants a jury to believe. You leave that to me and my associate."

Lissa left the meeting with what she hoped was realistic optimism, something she hadn't felt before. For months after first learning he was missing and believed dead, she'd clung to her hope that Josef wasn't dead, as the Army itself presumed. Since learning about his past, she'd alternated between thinking him totally innocent or guilty, perhaps with some plausible explanation.

She needed to know the truth, to know whether she could keep and nourish the love she held for him, even if he was in prison. Her future depended on knowing the truth.

She must wait to read his letter before drawing any conclusions. His own words would reveal if his crimes would matter someday, once the blush of first love had changed to the kind of love rooted in commitment. If they could ever find a future together, would the Parker brand of passionate patriotism rise up in her children? Would those children be able to look to their father with respect and say that Lissa had made the right choice?

Josef's letter would help make her decision.

CHAPTER *Thirty-One*

Dear Larisa Rose,

Seeing you today was like breathing the first air of spring after a lifetime of winter. Words of love brim over, but I hold them for another day, even if such words are all I have to persuade you back to me. But I know that isn't what you need right now, so it wouldn't serve either of us.

I'll try, instead, to bring you into my mind and share every thought, memory, loyalty, and secret. It's only through understanding that either of us will be able to go on, and so I'll try my best to help you see inside my mind, my heart, and the very soul God has given me.

I won't have you thinking I would ever keep something from you, Larisa Rose. And so here are all of my triumphs and failures, as objectively as I can tell them.

There are triumphs, even though I sit rotting in a jail cell. I should say just as quickly that I claim any triumphs in the name of our Lord. He worked a miracle in me, and it's to Him that I shall always give praise and glory.

I was given His Spirit when I was a very young child. The
Lord used my mother to reveal Himself to me. I was secure in the
knowledge that God created me for a reason, and that reason was
different from that of every other person. All creation is a gift, and
we are gifts, too, to Him, to each other, and to ourselves. I don't
have many memories of my early faith. The reason is time now,
instead of my injury. Those memories I do have are of a faith-filled
mother eager for me to know the love of our Creator.

When she died, I was taken to a different church by the
man I thought was my father. I must be careful here, because I
better understand him now and have forgiven him, but I still feel
resentment. One bit of anger is for what he did after Mother's
death. I was plucked from one church, where I was known and
loved because of my mother. I was taken to another where I was
a stranger. Perhaps it wasn't the church's fault. Perhaps it had the
same community and nurturing spirit as the church my mother had
attended—just not toward me. But there I was, a lonely little boy
without a mother to pave the way and a father who was, at best,
distant. By nature, he kept people at a long arm's length. Otto, the
man who raised me, had no knowledge of God except as a habit, an
institution, a rite of society that must be acknowledged. Otto knew
discipline, for himself and for those around him. He was able to
follow the order of the society he chose.

His choice of society led me on a path that ultimately diverted
my attention from Christ and the sort of attachment to country that
most people born in America take for granted. Otto maintained
such devotion to the country of his own birth that he allowed me
none for the country of my birth. So I was raised in the United
States but not as an American. From an early age I was told that
Germany was my true homeland. I went to German schools,
German clubs, a German church, all right here on American soil. I
was nurtured on the idea that Germany was a land blessed by God
in a way others were not.

And I was too immersed in that culture to realize its
arrogance. I was too sheltered, living an ocean apart, to see that

Germany was like other countries. It had beauty but also ugliness. Power and poverty, art and hate, education and ignorance. But I did not know. I learned to serve Germany as a god. I strove to be a son of the fatherland, the best in all I did. Discipline was modeled to me. In that, I excelled.

Yet with each foundational stone laid in me as a stalwart German, I also breathed in the fresh, free air of America, and so American attitudes. How could I separate myself from my surroundings? Every day when I woke, I had the freedom to read both German and American newspapers. I could do it because of the freedom of this country. Had I chosen to order another newspaper, from Russia or the Far East, I could have done that too. I may have been fed the society of Germany, but I was intrinsically part of the freedom of this society and could not, in the end, be separated from that.

I'm sorry my thoughts are jumbled. I want to help you understand some of the motivation behind the deeds that brought me here, to prison. I'll try to give this to you in a sensible order.

Before the war broke out in Europe, I was approached by a wealthy German businessman. He was an associate of Otto's, but I'm sure Otto never knew all of the activities in which he was involved. This man saw potential in my youth, ambition, and eagerness for hard work, combined with my unquestioned loyalty to Germany.

His plan was simple: Represent Germany in the United States well and sympathetically. He wanted to stir the hearts of German Americans to recall their loyalty to the fatherland. I was only too willing. I was certainly well versed on the subject. I began a speaking circuit, holding rallies all along the East Coast. It was easy to find an audience of Germans and others at fairs or in parks on Sunday afternoon.

I stopped speaking when war broke out overseas. It would have been too public. Too many people sympathized with the Allies. Our new goal was to keep America from joining the melee. If I made any speeches, I was disguised. My message wasn't pro-German; it was *anti-war. Keep America out. Remember the advice of American forefathers not to have foreign entanglements. Now U.S. companies were making and selling huge amounts of guns and ammunition, some going to Germany but most to Russia, England, and France. German men, women, and children would be killed with these weapons. So I picketed munitions plants that I knew were selling their products of destruction. I handed out leaflets that urged the cause of pacifism.*

I did not do this just for Germany. I sympathized with the German cause, but I believed the United States should not support or join with either side. I did not want that war to touch this country. Even then I loved the U.S. more than I realized. I'd certainly taken this land and its blessings for granted. I don't think I was exposed to the wonders of America as a land and people until I read the books you showed me in my father's study. Do you remember?

You asked what I now believe. I believe the United States is worthy of loyalty. Whether we should have been in the war or not, America is worthy of loyalty. And its people! So willing to fight for freedom and individual rights—even in another country. This is a land that chose to build itself a government of the people and not hail king or kaiser. They wisely prohibited passing power as an inheritance. Anyone who was smart enough, worked hard, and wanted to serve could aspire to lead. The American forefathers did not tell the people what they could not do. They told the government what it could not do.

My pacifism and feelings for Germany were used to interfere with our entry into the war. I did not believe I was working against America, I worked to save German lives. Never in my mind did I have a malicious intent to harm this country or any person. I tried to ensure that I destroyed only private property and only when no one would be hurt. I am, therefore, guilty of grievous crimes, but those losses were monetary and not irreplaceable.

I am willing to pay for my crimes, and I regret that I was dishonest, destructive, and so dedicated to the wrong god. But part

of me cannot help but believe, even today, that the true God might not think ill of my goal to prevent arms going to the war. I have seen that war at its worst, and I wonder if the better part is to save lives instead of take them.

Many of Hank's books you recommended made an impression. Do you recall Thomas Jefferson's letter to the American minister to Britain way back in 1793? Britain was fighting France, and Mr. Jefferson felt neutrality meant that a country should furnish no aid to one side or the other in a foreign war. That included munitions, as well as corn and other materials a country at war would need. I think the forefathers, in their most moral thought, would have disapproved of the eagerness with which American companies made money from the European strife. You see, Larisa, I do love the United States, but I see its flaws, too. What I have learned, most of all, is to put first allegiance in God. Then patriotism can have a proper perspective.

In the Bible, you'll recall that Jacob is once called a worm. I, too, was a worm but, like Jacob, God took my hand and transformed me into something useful. I am no longer afraid that Germany and its power might not have its way. Not only am I no longer that fragile worm, Larisa. I am no longer a son of the fatherland. I am a son of the Most High. God has worked a miracle in me, and even if it is in the bowels of a prison where He wants me to work, I will.

This is the triumph I spoke of, Larisa: that God should care to save me, a worm and a sinner, from that other life where I served a false god. In Paul's second letter to the Corinthians, you see how God has done this before. It is his way of dealing with people like me. He poured all of our sins into Christ and all of Christ's goodness into us, and here we are, a new creation.

My prayer is that one day you will forgive me for the crimes I committed in my old life and remember the love we shared. I am not the Josef you knew, but the Josef you knew is still in me. When I came to find you in France after I remembered my past, I knew I would be arrested. But I had no alternative if I was to prove myself a child of God, an American, and a man worthy of your love.

I know that you love God above all else and that your love of country is deep and genuine. I know that you are an honest, incorruptible citizen of a nation that is worthy of your patriotism. This is a land blessed by God. The blessing has been proven through those who have an ideal of freedom and equality and generosity of spirit. The blessing was in those who founded this country and those who were with me in the trenches. But this is a nation built by humans, same as any other. I now believe it is the greatest nation that now exists, surely greater than Germany, with its freedom smothered under the Kaiser. America does not deserve blind faith. Loyalty, yes, and perhaps even our lives if we are threatened by an invader like Germany who wants to shove its way beyond its own borders. But true, deepest faith belongs only to our Creator.

I've spoken my heart, Larisa, and I have one last piece of my heart to share. When you visited me at the prison, you were the single window in this place through which I glimpsed Creation as God must want us to see it. Beauty and faithfulness, a gift from a Creator powerful and loving enough to bless us with a world of color and variety we cannot fully comprehend.

I thank Him for you, Larisa, because through you He's given me a taste of His love for all of us. I strive to be more like Him, because He's made you.

I love you.

Josef

CHAPTER *Thirty-Two*

LISSA SAT on a plain, wooden chair, so close between her mother and her father that the cool December breeze barely touched her. Aunt Bobbie sat nearby, along with the whole Tanner family, including Penny.

Lissa studied the makeshift outdoor courtroom, ignoring her feeling of unease. They sat on the edge of a park, where a raised platform of unfinished wood had been placed. Its size was intimidating, even without the judge, who was yet to arrive. To the left was a box with a single chair inside, for those who would testify for and against Josef. To Lissa's right was another raised platform, containing twelve wooden chairs just like the one on which she sat. Around those seats was a gate, blocking entrance except to twelve men who would make up the jury. Directly in front of her was a long, low-hung chain separating the inner court from the outer. Just on the other side were two rectangular tables with empty chairs, awaiting lawyers from the government and lawyers for the defense. One chair would be for the defendant himself. Josef.

She'd read his letter a dozen times, stained it with her tears, prayed over it, thanked God for it. Then she'd followed her initial reaction after reading it the first time and flew to Tombs Prison. She hadn't even told Aunt Bobbie where she was going. All she wanted was to assure him of her love and to tell him that nothing on this earth could keep her from loving him for the rest of their lives.

But upon her arrival at the prison, she'd been told he was already gone, transferred, they said, down to Washington for his trial. She went to Morgan's office to verify this unexpected news. The trial wasn't supposed to start for another week. Surely they hadn't moved him already.

Morgan had gone back to the prison with her, where he was told the same thing. It was some sort of mix up, of that he was sure.

It wasn't until the following day, after Lissa had taken the train to D.C., that the prison system worked out its error. Josef was indeed still at Tombs but was scheduled to be transferred the following day. Lissa thought it best to wait until she could see Josef in Washington when he arrived.

But that plan had failed as well. Because of publicity and the nature of the crimes, Josef was allowed visits only by his legal counsel and immediate family. If she were married to him, they would have let her in. But as it was, she was not allowed access. Rules were rules.

Until today, she'd been angry and disappointed. Now she saw that the rules were to protect Josef. The old words that Hank had spoken so long ago came back to haunt her in the faces of those prohibited by mounted police from approaching the immediate area of the outdoor trial. It looked like the lynch mob Hank had feared so long ago.

All they saw was a traitor. A German who had wanted the Central Powers to win the war. To them he represented the very gun that had taken the lives of so many sons, brothers, fathers, and husbands overseas.

Hank had been the one to arrange access to the trial for Lissa's family. Only a small number of seats had been set up for journalists and fewer for the general public. Cassie had wanted to come, too, but Mama had insisted she was still weak and wouldn't allow her out of the house, even if the weather was uncommonly balmy for so late in the year.

But Mama was there, occasionally taking Lissa's hand or lending a smile. Such hints of encouragement amazed Lissa. Here sat the same woman who'd spent a lifetime avoiding any semblance of conflict. She wasn't at home, hiding from the press, the crowds, and everyone who judged Josef and all those associated with him. She was right at Lissa's side, and Lissa had never felt closer to her.

A family seated behind the Tanners drew Lissa's glance. They were quiet in a dignified way, clearly concerned. Each of them whispered to one another from time to time.

Despite the continuing public phobia of gatherings where the influenza germ might spread, there were swarms of people milling outside the improvised courtroom. Many wore the gauze masks, but evidently they believed the cool outdoor air was safer than cloistered indoor air. Safe enough to take the risk in order to show their animosity toward the man on trial. Lissa hoped the jury was more impartial than the crowd that was blocked off by police. A line of blue-clad officers also formed a living wall from the street. The jury arrived in a specially hired streetcar. Not long after that vehicle pulled away, a closed carriage brought two men in dark business suits. Lissa guessed they were the government prosecutors, confirming that when they took their seats behind the table nearest the gated jury.

At last came Morgan and an older man who sported graying hair and a full belly. He looked so different from his young, lean colleague. Lissa had glimpsed him at the law office, but they had never been introduced, and she wasn't sure of his name.

Lissa longed to see Josef but couldn't spot him. Then her heart quickened as cries around the open air courtroom erupted. She heard shouts of anger and name calling and closed her eyes, wishing she could close her ears to the insults they spewed at Josef.

Then she saw him.

He'd been allowed a suit of clothing to replace his plain prison garb. Though he looked scrupulously clean, beard gone and hair combed neatly, he still looked gaunt.

But his eyes were the same and just then they were searching the audience until they came to rest on her.

Lissa was never so sure that love could be seen and not spoken, felt without touch, than she was at that moment. All she could do was look at him, and everything else, at least for that time she stared into his eyes, disappeared.

Then he had to turn and sit, only to stand a moment later as the judge entered the blockaded area.

The rest of the morning was a blur to Lissa. The prosecution outlined their case first, using evidence gathered by the federal police that included drawings of explosives used, the names of the private ships that were sunk or damaged, a list of the factories targeted for strikes. There were photographs of Josef picketing and speaking at a rally for pacifism. With each piece of evidence, Lissa wanted to shrink into her seat. But she sat tall and straight, chin held high, stoic in her support of the man she loved.

The man she loved was portrayed far differently by the prosecution than the Josef Lissa knew. Where they painted him deceitful she saw him redeemed; they called him a traitor, she saw him as loyal to life.

If only they could know him the way she did.

The day was nearly impossible to endure, but Lissa imagined how much harder it was for Josef. She'd never had insults hurled at her from strangers, never faced the possibility of being locked away in a place as horrible as Tombs. Yet Josef sat there calmly. During a break he managed to turn her way and send her a hopeful smile. She returned that smile with all the love in her heart, even if part of her was finding hope a little harder to muster after so many hours of attacks on Josef's character.

At the end of the day, he was hustled away before any of the family could say a word. Because of the cool weather, the court session was shortened. Lissa watched Josef go. She couldn't fool herself into a very convincing optimistic smile before, so perhaps it was best they couldn't speak now. She didn't want him to know the weight of her worry for him.

She knew worry was wrong. She prayed that God would help her in her unbelief, help her to remember He was in control, just as Aunt Bobbie reminded her time and time again.

Lissa lingered to the last possible moment, hoping she might somehow be able to speak to Josef. Finally Morgan returned to her side and assured her Josef had been taken safely away. They were taking precautions with his transport because of the mobs. Several carriages had been hired, none of them marked to indicate which held the prisoner. Lissa turned from the outdoor court, her heart heavy, her pace slow. She could only see the hatred so many people felt for Josef.

"This way, Lissa," said her father from nearby. She looked up. She hadn't known he stayed behind. Without a word, she followed him away from the dispersing crowd. They hired a jitney to take them to the hotel room they had rented for the duration of the trial, however long that might be. The hotel was extravagant by her father's standards, modest by the Tanners', but they had agreed it would serve the purpose best because of its proximity to the court site.

The two rooms were opposite one another, and the door to the Tanner room was ajar. Lissa's mother called to them as they passed, "Come in, won't you? It was such a madhouse, wasn't it? I wanted to stay with your father and take you back with us, but he insisted I come back here with the Tanners. There are a few people here I think you should meet."

Lissa's only goal was to the door of the suite she shared with her parents. "Oh, Mama, I couldn't possibly meet anyone right now, I'm so exhausted and worried."

Mr. Tanner stepped out to the hall behind Lissa's mother. "Come in, Lissa."

The room was full of people. Aunt Bobbie and Mr. and Mrs. Tanner were with Penny and Caleb and another soldier, a sergeant by rank of his stripes. Near him was the family who had occupied the seats directly behind the Tanners back at the court.

"Come along, dear," her mother said. "There will be time for rest later." Then, keeping Lissa's arm, her mother led Lissa to an older couple. "This is our daughter. Lissa, I'd like you to meet Ilsa and Hans Bonner, and their children, Karl and his wife Katie, Ernst and Helga, and this is Liesel de Serre, and her husband David."

Liesel, the woman who was engaged to Josef.

She was as tall as Lissa, her eyes a lovely pale blue. She was thin like Lissa. But where Lissa was a darker blonde, Liesel was light. Her features were delicate while Lissa's were bold.

She was holding out her hand. "I'm so very pleased to meet you. Perhaps we can steal away for a few minutes later and get acquainted."

"Yes," Lissa heard herself answer, though she didn't want to do any such thing.

And then she felt herself swept up in a hug by the older woman, Ilsa Bonner. "Ah, so you are Josef's fiancée. We were so happy when we learned about you."

The older man at her side stepped forward, pulling his wife a full step back. "Forgive my wife, Miss Parker. She has always thought of Josef as another son, and these last few months have been hard on her."

"Yes, well, no more! We just have to get this silly trial over with, and Mr. Morgan says not to worry. Everything goes well now that his witnesses have been approved. Soon our Josef will be home." She laughed as though she caught herself in an error. "Well, not our home, but yours. We are so happy for you. All we've ever wanted was for our Josef to be happy."

Lissa smiled, but knew it was a weak one. She still longed to be alone, although the Bonner family seemed to genuinely love Josef. She wanted to feel compassion for them, but she was too exhausted. She wanted to read Josef's letter again, to be reminded of his love for her. A love that never would have existed had Josef stayed within the arms of all these loving Bonners.

Her gaze went irretrievably back to Leisel. She wondered how long it had taken after Josef's supposed death for this woman to marry. Her gaze went briefly to David de Serre. Inexplicably, Lissa felt a stab of resentment at him, too, though she knew it was irrational. Her gaze returned to Liesel. The last thing Lissa wanted was to fight another woman for Josef's love. But how could she have gotten over Josef so quickly? If Lissa ever thought she'd lost Josef, it would take a lifetime to get over him.

Mr. Tanner was speaking, and Lissa pulled her attention away from her own jumbled thoughts. "Mr. Morgan said that even though today was tough, tomorrow will be easier for all of us. I've sat in on many cases where it all seems to be going in one direction, and then the scale tips once all the facts are out. Tomorrow will be the day for us to tip that scale."

There was general assent and hopeful comments from every direction, but Lissa still wanted to go out the door. How soon before she could break away unnoticed? Already her father was making dinner arrangements. She was certain she wouldn't last the evening if she had to put on a stoic but hopeful front. All she wanted was to be alone with Josef's letter.

"Mama," she whispered while the others were having their own various conversations, "I don't think I could eat a bite of dinner and all I really want is to take a bath and go to bed. Will you make my apologies?"

Her mother looked about to protest but then saw Lissa's face and nodded. "All right, dear." Then she added with a whisper, "I'm sure everyone in this room thinks this is hard on them, but I know it's hardest on you and Josef. Go on. The door to our room is unlocked."

Lissa gave her mother a brief hug. As many times as she'd thought her mother never understood, today her understanding had been a lifeline. It went a long way in making up for all those other times that meant so much less.

An hour later, comfortable after a bath and dressed in her favorite robe, Lissa sat on the small couch in the center of the sitting room between her room and her parents'. She took out her Bible and retrieved Josef's letter, sure these were the only sources for comfort. She would need such comfort if she were to sleep at all that night and be able to offer a smile to Josef in the morning.

A light tap at the door drew her attention. She'd locked it when she was in the bath; perhaps her mother had forgotten their key.

She stood, opening the door wide.

"Oh! Hello."

Lissa clutched the lapels of her robe, suddenly feeling a mess within its tattered but much loved material. Her hair was wet and dangling. Leisel de Serre stood in the hall, a beautiful woman despite the evidence of her lack of love and loyalty to Josef in her married name.

"I thought you were my mother."

"They're still downstairs dining. I hope you don't mind. I wanted to speak to you."

With one hand on the edge of the door and the other still clutching her robe up to her chin, Lissa had no reply. She didn't want to talk to this woman, even though there was no real reason for such caution or jealousy around her. Josef's letter was proof that he loved her, not this woman. In any case, it was clear that whatever love Liesel Bonner de Serre had held for Josef wasn't the kind that stuck around long.

"I'm sorry," Liesel said softly. "I've made you uncomfortable. I shouldn't have come."

"No, I'm sorry. I'm not myself tonight," Lissa said quickly. Why was she so eager to put this other woman at ease when her presence did the opposite for Lissa herself?

"I've come for a most selfish reason," Liesel said. "I'm not sure what you must think of me, knowing I was engaged to Josef, and now I'm married to someone who helped put him on trial."

"It doesn't matter what I think, though, does it?"

"Please, can we talk, just for a few minutes?"

Lissa felt the pinch of a headache creeping up from the base of her skull. She stepped aside to allow the other woman to enter, then closed the door quietly.

"You're right, of course, I shouldn't care what others think. It's only God, and of course my husband, with whom I should concern myself." She smiled and looked a little embarrassed. "But I saw something in your eyes earlier, something that reminded me of all the guilt I felt for so long over Josef. You brought it right back, as real as can be."

"Guilt?"

"I felt responsible for getting Josef into trouble because I was the one who led the authorities to him the night he was to have been arrested."

Lissa looked down at the floor. She knew all that.

"It was awful," Liesel whispered, and Lissa looked up again. It seemed as if the woman had forgotten Lissa was even there. "But how could I do nothing? No, I couldn't. Even if I did love Josef more as a brother than a fiancé, how could I turn him in? And yet I knew he had to be stopped. He was so misguided, so willing to do anything for the approval of Otto."

Of all the words she'd spoken, a few made the most impact on Lissa. "You loved him like a brother?"

"Yes. That's the main thing I came to tell you, really, so maybe you wouldn't think so low of me for marrying David." She patted her stomach, and Lissa noticed for the first time that it wasn't quite flat. "I've gone on with my life, I'm even expecting my first child. You must know that it wasn't all that long after Josef left Washington that I began a relationship with someone else. It wasn't that I didn't love him. He is very dear to me. But it was never the love a husband and wife feel for one another. We were practically raised together. He was my friend, and everyone always expected we'd marry."

"But he did love you."

"In his way. In priority, I was after Germany, after his work, and after his father, I think. Josef did love Germany and he did love to work. Working for Germany—that was his passion. God and I, we weren't so important."

"He has found his faith now."

"Isn't it wonderful? And he has a true love that, I believe, he'll set before other things. I'm so happy for both of you. My prayer is that we can put this behind us, and you and Josef can start a happy life together. That, really, is what I came to tell you, and to selfishly hope I might have more esteem in your eyes."

"You mean my judgmental eyes, don't you?" Lissa said, but there was no malice in her words. Just a confession of one of her own mistakes.

Liesel turned toward the door, and Lissa followed. She opened the door then held out her hand, which Liesel quickly accepted.

"Thank you, Mrs. de Serre. I didn't want company earlier, but I'm glad you came to remind me that I'm not the only one praying Josef through this."

CHAPTER *Thirty-Three*

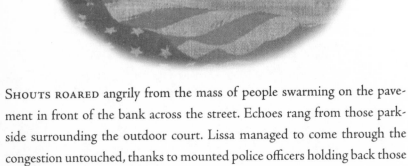

SHOUTS ROARED angrily from the mass of people swarming on the pavement in front of the bank across the street. Echoes rang from those parkside surrounding the outdoor court. Lissa managed to come through the congestion untouched, thanks to mounted police officers holding back those pressing in from all directions on the roped-off area.

The weather was colder, which should have meant fewer spectators. If only that were true. For the comfort of the judge and jurors, barrels had been placed here and there, lit with some sort of fuel to offer a bit of warmth.

Aunt Bobbie was with her, holding her hand as they found their seats behind the table at which Josef would sit. On her other side were her parents, Frank Parker giving his occasional grim smile, offering hope as best he could. Addie seemed the most stalwart of them all.

The defense would now present its case, so the day should be far more palatable for those behind Josef's table. It was time for the other side of the coin. Lissa prayed this side would shine.

Lissa took in the pair of prosecutors seated at one of the tables. Yesterday they had done all they could to paint Josef in the worst possible light. Silently, she'd wished that they could know Josef as she did. Her eyes moved to the jury. If they could only talk to him, see who he really was.

Morgan still did not want Josef to take the witness stand. Initially he feared revealing Josef's desire to be punished. That was no longer the case, but he still didn't want Josef's honest candor to be turned against him on cross-examination.

Lissa would not testify, either. While it might be true that there was no reason to put her on the stand, as Morgan had told her, she still wanted to talk to the jury, to tell them what sort of person Josef was and help them to reach a fair verdict.

Instead she could only sit behind him, give him support with her presence and her smile of encouragement. So she sat and listened, praying the witnesses would be the help Morgan believed they would be.

"Your Honor," Morgan began, then turned to the men in the jury box. "Gentlemen of the jury. Many of the facts presented yesterday we do not dispute, but we very much dispute the characterization of the man behind the facts. To be able to understand whether his actions justify some of the charges brought against Mr. von Woerner, you have to be able to interpret what happened and why.

"To understand that, you need to meet the real Josef von Woerner, not the man presented to you yesterday. That was a caricature of who Josef von Woerner was even in the period when these events occurred. You don't yet know why he did what he did.

"But in this case we are also asking that you put the facts into an unusual perspective. You can't understand the motivations then without knowing the extraordinary facts of the man Josef von Woerner has become. You will see, I'm sure, that the Josef von Woerner capable of doing what he once did is a man of the past. You must see the whole man, past and present, the one who is able to see the world in a truer light. This man chooses to live out his life in America, not Germany, and he will live it out with the integrity to accept your honest judgment.

"My first witness was to have been Otto von Woerner, the man who raised Josef von Woerner and nurtured within him the foundation for compliance when German businessmen, associates of Otto von Woerner's, first approached Josef to speak as an advocate for Germany." He paused, taking a step closer to the jury box. "I received word early this morning that Mr. von Woerner is too ill to be brought here. Since we knew his health is fragile, we arranged for him to make a sworn deposition, answering questions from representatives of the defense and prosecution. I move that we enter this deposition as evidence and that it be published among them as they deliberate."

The chief prosecutor had been involved with the deposition process, so there was no objection.

"So we proceed to some people who can give you a more accurate picture of who Josef von Woerner is."

"My son dictated a letter to a nurse to be sent home from the field hospital," said retired General L. B. Brooks. "He was entirely coherent, as this was before the secondary infection set in which ultimately took his life." He cleared his throat, this dignified, gray-haired gentleman who appeared as though he never lost control.

"In this correspondence," he continued, voice strong again, "my son said he was dragged from no man's land by a soldier he'd recommended previously to be promoted to corporal. He said he'd known from the start that he had made a good decision. He had been more than pleased because this young man had shown himself extraordinarily brave in battle. And then he had saved my son's life."

"And that man was?"

"He knew him as Josef Warner, but he was subsequently revealed to be Josef von Woerner, the defendant."

"And did you bring the true original copy of that letter that can be introduced into evidence?"

The general handed the letter to Morgan. Over objections that the letter described events that occurred after the crimes had been committed, the judge said he would let the jury read the letter and determine its value to their deliberations. Morgan turned to the general.

"Thank you, General Brooks. I have no more questions."

The general turned his steady gaze toward the prosecutor. The government's lead prosecutor was tall and thin, with sparse, unremarkable hair and a prominent nose and Adam's apple. He didn't look as distinguished as the general nor as handsome as Morgan, but he had a presence that commanded respect. His eyes were piercing, as if he could see through any lie. The general did not flinch.

"Your son said in his letter that the man he knew by the alias Josef Warner saved his life. Yet your son died, died for this country."

"That's correct."

"Evidently Josef von Woerner's efforts didn't accomplish much."

"I would say they accomplished a great deal." The general sat stiffly in his seat, but his demeanor softened as he looked at Josef. "I know what the men endured who died on the part of that battlefield known as no man's land. I also know what happened to their bodies as they lay in the field after death. Corporal Warner saved our son from that. And if it weren't for him, my wife and I wouldn't have been able to read and hold in our hands our son's final words. I'm grateful for that."

"Getting back to the facts, did your son describe how he thought von Woerner saved his life?"

"They were part of an advance tactic, routing a German trench. Shellfire from both sides. My son was hit and would have been left for dead during the battle. Corporal Warner saw my son and under fire dragged him from the field to safety."

"And this was during a raging battle that this man dragged your son's body from the field." He paused as if contemplating something, then shot his gaze back to the witness. "Are you quite certain, General, that this man did not so much attempt to save your son but rather use your son's body as a shield to get himself to safety?"

"Objection, Your Honor," said Morgan. "This calls for speculation."

"Sustained."

"No further questions, Your Honor."

Morgan stood again. "Just one more thing, General. Did your son say what Corporal Warner did after he delivered his injured body to the medics behind the line of fire?"

"Returned to the battle."

"No further questions. You may step down."

But General Brooks did not move. He must have heard the instruction, for even Lissa had heard it and she sat much farther away. The general sat still, his chin straight and steady, his mustache barely hiding the quiver of his lips. He looked at no one until a moment later, those dark eyes that seemed to see more than what lesser officers saw, settled on the prosecutor.

"I would like to emphasize something that this court may not appreciate. My son's body was sent home to me from that hospital. If not for Corporal Warner, my son would be in some battlefield grave."

"Objection, Your Honor. Unsolicited."

The general stood even as the judge nodded the prosecutor's way. Between the general's height, which was formidable, and the upraised witness platform, he towered over the prosecutor who had stood to make his objection. The eyes of each juror took in the confrontation.

"If you'd lost a son, sir, to a battleground where flies and rats ate the bodies before the guns fell silent, then you would understand what Josef Warner did for my son and for me. I could give him a decent burial. When you have gone through that, you have the right to say whether Corporal Warner's actions constituted heroism. I'm sorry, Your Honor, but that needed to be said."

He stepped down, without further objection from either the prosecutor or the judge.

"Josef von Woerner approached me on deck and offered his services to help care for the influenza victims," said Dr. Clifton Morris. "I was the only doctor aboard that plague ship. We had some wounded but mostly influenza victims. No one wanted to work with them, but Corporal Warner stayed in that locked ward night and day, giving comfort, and removing corpses. He tried reviving one patient with a risky resuscitation method, breathing his own life's breath into an influenza victim's lungs. The man died, but I couldn't help but admire his determination to save the patient at great risk to himself. I believe he would make a fine doctor, actually."

"What was the attitude of Corporal Warner, Doctor? Did he ever display to you or your staff any indication that would suggest he was anything but an American citizen?"

"Well, we never talked politics, but his main goal was obvious: to save lives and give comfort to the dying. These were all American patients, sir, not Germans. I would say if he was a German soldier, they'd have cause to hang him for giving direct aid to the enemy."

He spoke so flippantly that some laughed, even in the jury box.

Morgan took his seat, obviously pleased.

The prosecutor stood.

"I understand that von Woerner was in chains, quartered in a small, locked stateroom prior to volunteering his services?"

"That's correct. He had been arrested in France."

"By volunteering his services to you, he was given a certain amount of freedom?"

"If you call being locked in an influenza ward freedom. We had to keep it locked for the cognizant patients. They often tried to get out, and we didn't want their disease to spread."

"Be that as it may, this man chose the freedom and diversion of work to the isolation and boredom of a cell in the bowels of a ship. Is that a fair assessment?"

"It's one way to look at it, I suppose."

———

Sergeant Dack gave another lively rendition of Josef's exploits during their captivity and escape. ". . . And that was the second time he coulda' left me behind, but he kept dragging me to that boat, hurt and all. He'd been hit in the shoulder by a Jerry bullet. I wouldn't a blamed him if he'd let me crawl off on my own to be shot. They always shot escapees right off. He just switched arms and hauled me along like a dead weight. I wouldn't be here twern't for Joe Warner. He saved my life."

"It was after you were safely in Switzerland that you learned from Corporal Warner that he was previously known as Josef von Woerner?"

"Yep, he told me the whole story, even what he done when he was workin' against the war. My advice to him was to scram, start over with a new name, and we'd tell anybody who ever put Joe Warner together with Josef von Woerner that he was good and dead, shot by a Jerry bullet for America. Yeah, it's a lie, but he's no traitor, that's for sure. I ain't no traitor neither for givin' him that advice. I'm as American as can be, willin' to give my life for the ol' red, white, and blue. As I see it we should be decoratin' the guy. He mighta' blown up a couple a ships but as I see it he was against the bullets, not America. He blew up a German plant, too. That says somethin', don't it? It was the war he hated, not us or the Germans."

"Objection, Your Honor," said the prosecutor. "The witness is speculating as to what the defendant did or did not feel."

"Sustained. Sergeant, please refrain from presenting counsel's closing argument before he has the chance to do it."

When the prosecutor stood some minutes later, he looked at Dack with a skeptic's eye that could have drilled into his skull. "Tell me, Sergeant Dack, did you actually see the German munitions plant being blown up?"

"No, sir, but I don't know what else coulda made that—"

"And did you actually see the defendant head in the direction of that German plant?"

"Well, no. But—"

"One final question. Sergeant, since you've admitted that you would lie for this man, how do we know that any of your testimony is true?"

"Objection!"

"Sustained."

"That'll be all."

Dack stood, then he sat down again. "I just wanna say I ain't never lied in my life, and I only offered that to Joe, and never actually did it. And today, I'm under oath. I ain't no liar."

Then he stepped down.

"It was like Sergeant Dack said," Caleb testified. "Josef knew the land like a map, and he found food for us to eat on the run. If it hadn't been for him, I'd have had to wait out the war in that camp. And this wasn't like other camps we heard about. We weren't registered. We didn't receive Red Cross care packages. We weren't allowed to write home and we never received a letter, because nobody knew we were still alive. We were slave labor. If that's where a German spy ends up in Germany, well, that's a pretty rotten way for them to treat one of their own."

"Mr. de Serre, you were the lead agent investigating Josef von Woerner's involvement in the crimes for which he is charged, were you not?" Morgan asked.

"That's correct," said David de Serre.

"And through your work on that case, did you become acquainted with the other people in Josef von Woerner's life?"

"Yes, I interviewed most of them, some several times. I got to know Otto, and believe his testimony accurately reflects the control he had over Josef's life. I know the men who convinced Josef to represent the German cause and pacifism and to finally take more radical action against munitions companies. I worked with his fiancée at the time, Liesel Bonner, showing her that he had a life she didn't know about and eventually convincing her that she should help us stop him."

"And did your association with those people end when you thought Josef von Woerner was dead?"

"No, I had developed an admiration and respect for Liesel. And despite her feeling of guilt regarding working against Josef, we became close during that time. Our friendship grew into a deeper love, and she's now my wife."

"So you have about as good a knowledge as does anyone of the type of man Josef von Woerner was during this phase of his life when he caused so much trouble?"

"Yes, I believe so."

"Based on your professional and personal knowledge, what is your objective assessment?"

"Josef von Woerner was passionate about stopping the sale and distribution of munitions. There's no doubt about that. But he never took a life and never showed any proclivity toward personal violence of any kind. He damaged property, tried to persuade people not to join in the fighting, and used his own money to promote antiwar aims. He did meet with men who were agents of Germany, but his motives seemed from the beginning to differ from theirs. There is no evidence he ever acted with the intent to aid Germany in a military action. In fact, his actions, on occasion, robbed the Central Powers as well as the Allies of arms that were being made and shipped to them by private industry. It is my personal belief that his sole motivation was to stop the flow of armaments feeding the escalating destruction on European soil."

"Do you believe your investigation substantiated criminal charges against the defendant?"

"I do."

"What, in your opinion, has your investigation of this man proven against him?"

"Criminal mischief."

"Not treason?"

"Not under the Espionage Act of 1917. He would have had to willfully aid the operation or success of a military or naval operation of our enemies. This act demands the proof of intent to assist enemy combatants. Ultimately, the only intent proved is that Josef von Woerner acted on his personal beliefs, with particular compassion toward the German people."

"Objection. Speculation."

"From your experience as a federal agent who has worked on other suspected cases of espionage, can you draw evidence-based conclusions as to this pattern of behavior?"

"It did not fit the actions of an espionage agent. All we could prove was that he wanted to delay American involvement in a war that we were not, at the time of most of his activity, part of. In the period after the United States declared war on Germany, there is no evidence to support a claim that he acted to aid Germany in a military or naval operation. Therefore, it is my professional opinion that treason was not committed."

When it was the turn of the prosecution to press David de Serre, the lead attorney looked at his notes, at the jury, and then at David.

"Agent de Serre, I find it interesting that a man hired to protect our country's interests is testifying rather strongly on behalf of the very man he was supposed to be working to put away."

"Objection, Your Honor," said Morgan. "It's the defendant on trial here, not the witness."

"Was there a question in that statement, Counsel," asked the judge, "or do you intend to discuss the record of Mr. de Serre?"

"No, Your Honor. I believe Agent de Serre's professional work has been exemplary. His personal life, however, may be clouding his judgment."

Morgan was on his feet again. "Once again, Your Honor, this trial is for Josef von Woerner, unless impropriety on Agent de Serre's part affecting his investigation of the defendant is being alleged."

"Defense counsel has already introduced Agent de Serre's personal stake in this. I am trying to help the jury understand why an agent serving the President I also serve is so quick to jump to the defense of this criminal. Might the jury wonder? Is it because Josef von Woerner is such a 'good guy' that even policemen stand in support of him instead of sitting behind the prosecutor to make sure he gets the maximum punishment he deserves?"

"Proceed."

"Thank you, Your Honor." He paused again, then approached the witness box. "Mr. de Serre, you stated earlier that your wife felt guilty for working against her lover?"

"Your Honor," said Morgan, "that is a prejudicial characterization, and has nothing to do with whether or not my client is guilty of treason."

The judge addressed the prosecutor. "Get to the point, Counsel."

"You have an emotional stake in the outcome of this trial, do you not, Mr. de Serre? Hasn't your wife visited Otto von Woerner in prison and also this defendant at Tombs Prison? Would getting von Woerner off not help end the feelings of guilt you mentioned?"

"Liesel is not troubled by those feelings now."

The prosecutor turned to the jury. "In fact, isn't it true that for months your wife's family believed you were responsible for the death of a man they all loved? Are you the objective professional analyzing the facts, Mr. de Serre, or do you have prejudices that bring you to the witness stand in defense of this man?"

"Objection, Your Honor. Prosecution is filling this witness's mouth with words, presenting the jury with his own interpretation of what he thinks this witness might or might not feel. I request that the entire dialogue be stricken from the record."

"Agent de Serre," said the judge, turning now to face the witness rather than to either of the lawyers, "I believe the prosecution raises a valid point, but both sides seem a bit too eager to speak for you. You do seem unusually supportive of the defense case since you are largely responsible for bringing that case to this court. Why don't you tell us, in your own words, exactly why you are so willing to speak on behalf of the defendant?"

"Your Honor," said David, "my seat may be located behind the defense but I assure you and the court that I am firmly on the side of justice. I am dedicated to this country and to its laws. As I see it—"

"Your Honor," interrupted the prosecutor, "the witness is clearly about to state an opinion. Must we stray so far from the evidence?"

The judge directed his gaze back to the witness box. "Is there any further evidence you wish to state?"

"The prosecutor has referred to my actions when we attempted to arrest Mr. von Woerner and how that night might influence my family relationships. We've all struggled with ambivalent feelings about it, but it has not affected my family relationships or clouded my objectivity. In fact, I believe I'm less biased than a prosecutor who brings charges of treason because public opinion presses for the noose."

"Objection! Public opinion has no place in the courtroom, Your Honor, and has nothing to do with the charges against the defendant."

"I think you've answered the question, Mr. de Serre," said the judge. "You may step down."

Lissa watched as the last witness of the day returned to his seat. The hours had passed in waves: witnesses had started out high and victorious in Josef's favor, but then the prosecutor turned their splash into a ripple. Now all eyes were on the defense team. Closing arguments were scheduled next. In the pause after the last witness had stepped down, various conversations sprang up, and the judge pounded his gavel for attention.

Wind nipped the air of the outdoor courtroom. Lissa glanced around to see if anyone else felt the chill.

The judge spoke. "Because of the hour, and because I wish the jurors to be refreshed for closing arguments, we will adjourn until tomorrow at nine o'clock." As he raised the gavel to end the session, a pop sounded that was nothing like gavel on block. Odd but harmless, it was like a backfiring motorcar.

Lissa's gaze went to the street, expecting to see the black smoke of a sputtering car. She saw nothing.

Another pop.

Without knowing why, Lissa's gaze bolted to Josef. He no longer sat tall in his chair. He clutched at his chest and slumped forward.

Panicked, Lissa sprang to her feet, arms outstretched toward Josef. A moment later, noise erupted everywhere, screams and shouts and another pop. It all sounded strange through the muffling effect of her pounding heart. People ran in all directions while others crouched low. Lissa tried to move forward, but her father held her in place. In the next moment she was yanked to her knees between her parents.

Struggling to free herself from her father's grip, Lissa looked up. To her horror she saw the man she knew only as Morgan's assistant go down, as if some invisible hand pushed him. She knew that it was no hand; it was a bullet. Beyond the chain of the makeshift fence separating her from the inner court, Lissa saw blood stain the back of Josef's light-colored jacket. Gagging on her own breath, she sputtered, "Father, let me go. I must help Josef!" His hand dug into her wrist as she tried to wrench free.

"Lissa, look. He's safe. Look."

Lissa stretched as far as her father's hold would allow, seeing through the scattering crowd a dozen men in blue rapidly surrounding Josef. Lissa couldn't tell whether they protected him or were preventing an opportunity to escape in the chaos. She didn't care as long as they kept him surrounded. They propelled him toward the street where a motorcar waited. She also saw he wasn't walking on his own. An officer helped keep him upright. The defense attorney was carried off on a stretcher.

More shouts, this time from outside the immediate area. A man waved his arms and pointed upward at the building across the street. A squad of police rushed it, silhouettes almost immediately on the roof. Moments later a rifle fell the three floors, landing with a clatter on the pavement. Surrounded by a half dozen armed officers, a hooded man stood with his hands atop his head, a pair of officers behind him with guns held at his back.

The few who remained in the outdoor courtroom appeared as dazed as Lissa felt. She looked where she'd last seen Josef hustled off. He'd been hit. She was sure of that. The panic of immediate danger subsided enough to make room for a new agony of worry: Was he even alive?

CHAPTER *Thirty-Four*

LISSA'S FATHER grabbed her again and urged her with her mother away from the abandoned court. More police officers than Lissa had ever seen assembled outside of a police parade had converged on the area and were dispersing those who lingered.

"I have to find out how badly he's hurt, Father," she cried. "Where is Mr. Morgan?"

"He went that way." He pointed in the direction they'd taken Josef, and Lissa turned to go that way. Her father held on to her.

"There's nothing you can do. Even if you could find him, they won't let you in. Come away from here, Lissa. Come to safety."

She didn't budge. She wanted to move in the opposite direction her father pulled.

"It's what he would want, Lissy Rose, to get you away from here." Hearing her childhood name only reminded her of what Josef called her.

But her father's eyes, so worried and fearful, made her reconsider. She could ignore the danger for herself, but not for her father.

She nodded at last. "All right, Papa. All right."

"We'll go to Morgan's office," Father said, and those words inspired speed in Lissa's stride.

"Yes," she said, "he'll be the first to know Josef's condition and where they've taken him."

There they waited. Father tried to get Lissa to leave for something to eat, or to go back to the hotel to rest. He said Morgan would undoubtedly call her there the moment he returned. Perhaps he was even trying to call her now from the hospital. But Lissa wasn't leaving. She wanted to know the full extent of Josef's condition, and she wanted to be face to face with Morgan when he told her, so she'd make sure he didn't hold anything back.

Near seven o'clock, the door to his office slowly opened. An exhausted-looking attorney stood in the threshold, a hall light behind him, one dim desk light touching little more than the surface of his desk. He approached them, and Lissa stood.

"Josef is fine. So is Mr. Kroller, my assistant, although he was wounded more severely than Josef. But they will both be fine."

"Where did the bullets hit them?" she asked.

"Josef was struck in the upper chest. The bullet had to be surgically removed, and he lost a bit of blood, but the doctor thinks Josef should recover nicely."

Lissa slumped forward, breathing deeply, as if it had been far too long since her last breath.

"And Mr. Kroller?" asked her father.

"The bullet went in and then out, right through his side. Fortunately for him he's got a bit of bulk there, so it missed anything vital."

"Can I see Josef?"

"I don't have too many connections in the prison system, but I'll try, after he's had a night to recover."

Lissa latched on to the slim chance he offered.

Morgan stepped closer to Lissa, grinning. "Hey, this time he wasn't hit in the head. His memory is fine. You know what he told me?"

Lissa waited.

"He said that only God decides when he'll die, not some federal agent or a German bullet or an American sniper. Only God. After all he's been through, I'm beginning to believe him."

Lissa's father came to stand beside them and patted the lawyer's back. "Sounds like the beginnin' of wisdom, Mr. Morgan."

Lissa nodded her agreement, and offered a weary smile.

"Let's go, Lissa," her father said. "You need to eat, and to rest at the hotel after such a day. We all do."

Morgan stepped aside from the threshold to allow them to exit. "Yes, that's right. I plan to press for court to resume tomorrow if it's possible. Josef must be present, so I hope he's strong enough. I want to get this to the jury while our evidence is vivid in their minds. Who knows, Josef being targeted this way might spur some sympathy, especially if he shows how eager he is to move this trial forward, even after being shot."

Lissa touched Morgan's forearm. "The doctors expect him to recover soon enough for the trial to resume tomorrow?"

"When I left Josef, he was insisting that they release him tonight. But in case things are postponed, I wish there was a way to keep up the juror's sympathy. I think many of the witnesses achieved what we hoped, but it would be better to keep the momentum."

"Mr. Morgan!" Lissa dug in her purse. "I know a way you could do that." She pulled out Josef's letter and held it in front of Morgan's puzzled face. "Let Josef speak for himself with this."

The young lawyer opened the letter with obvious curiosity. She hardly cared that it contained so much about her personal life with Josef, his profession of love, and his confessions both private and political. The letter revealed the Josef she loved, the Josef the jury needed to see.

Morgan accepted possession of the letter but didn't offer any assurances.

Over her shoulder, she added, "If the jury only knew Josef the way I do, they would have to love him. Wouldn't they?"

In the dim light, she thought she saw something in his eyes. Determination? Approval? She had no way to tell. Whatever it was, it was the most hopeful thing she'd seen all day.

———————

One morning paper was filled with headlines of the avenging sniper. The shooter was the father of a soldier killed overseas. His statement had been quoted in bold type: "An American bullet for the German, in return for the German bullet that got my boy!"

It seemed his words were more newsworthy than the condition of his victim, at least according to the editor of that particular paper.

Lissa sat on the bench outside a real, indoor courtroom, surrounded by portraits of Thomas Jefferson and George Washington instead of barricades holding off an unruly mob. The familiar faces of American history had probably looked upon proceedings for generations, seeing tellers of truth or lies, those who would give justice or promote inequity, and those interested in grace or only in punishment.

Lissa expected justice, but she hoped it came with a generous measure of grace.

She prayed again as she'd been praying for the last twenty-four hours, with desperation and hope, weakness and strength. For another moment she trusted that God was still in control, until the fear crept up again.

"I understand rules," she said bitterly to Penny and Aunt Bobbie, "but not this. What's the purpose of leaving me out this way? Even Hank . . ."

Aunt Bobbie smiled sympathetically. "I'm sure there's a reason, darling."

Penny, on Lissa's other side, put an arm around her shoulders and smiled reassuringly. Morgan had sent a note to Lissa's hotel room, stating that Josef was able to be in court. The proceedings could continue, but not until the afternoon, giving him more time to recover. She couldn't get permission to see Josef in the hospital. No one but Hank had visited, and he hadn't returned to the hotel at all.

Suddenly she heard a commotion just beyond the double doors to the court building. Lissa exchanged an anxious glance with Aunt Bobbie and stood. The sound of shouting wound its way in through the open doors, echoing on the ceiling and down the hall. The noise sounded different today, and she recognized why almost immediately. The familiar jeering was there, but mixed for the first time with supportive shouts. The supporters were not as loud as the taunts, but she realized that support for Josef had been born. Newspaper reports that quoted some of the defense witnesses must have been read.

Flanked by police, there was Josef, leaning on Hank but walking on his own strength.

"Josef." She stood in his path, one he obviously had no intention of altering.

"Larisa Rose," he answered. The police didn't let him any closer to her, but they paused instead of sweeping her aside. No one moved for a long moment.

"The Lord kept you safe," she said.

He nodded.

She quickly added, "Whatever happens in there, God kept you safe for us."

The explosive flash of a press camera's bulb startled the nervous police. They guided Hank and Josef on down the hall, and she stepped aside. Morgan took her arm.

"Want to walk in with us?" he suggested. The police dropped away by the doors leading to the courtroom. She slipped her hand in Josef's.

"God meant all of this for a purpose, no matter whether we're allowed to live it out," said Josef, looking at her as they walked toward the defense table. "Remember that."

No matter whether we're allowed to live it out?

His words chilled her as she took her seat with the family and looked at Penny.

"It'll be all right, Liss," Penny whispered, as if she could read Lissa's thoughts.

Aunt Bobbie nodded her agreement. "Yes, so let's get this over with, shall we?"

Josef remained standing, still supported by Hank at his chair. Then the judge entered, and Hank helped Josef to sit as the court was called to order.

The prosecution went first. For nearly forty-five minutes, the lead prosecutor recapped his case, summing with the defendant's guilt and his own admission of sabotage, along with his efforts to interfere with America's involvement in the war. Josef was an American citizen, he reminded them, who obviously favored Germany more than the country of his birth.

"That he is guilty is all too clear, gentlemen," the prosecutor concluded confidently. "His actions certainly exacerbated our entry into this war. And this is no German citizen, sent secretly from his homeland to do such dirty work. No, this is an American, born and raised right here on our very soil, so indoctrinated to German ways that America came second to him. His attitude, his actions, and his history all prove one thing: Josef von Woerner is a traitor. He has betrayed the land of his birth and deserves the harshest penalty."

Lissa saw men in the jury box taking notes, and she hoped they would be as engrossed in Morgan's words. She was grateful for one thing: The "harshest penalty" wasn't death, even to this prosecutor. They hadn't raised that possibility from the start.

At last Morgan stood. Piles of paper sat on the table before him, which he motioned toward as he faced the men in the jury box.

"As you go to deliberate this case, each of you will be given a copy of several documents that have been accepted into evidence, which you may use to reach your conclusion. These are offered the same as any witness. I have depositions from a dozen men who knew Josef von Woerner when he was heavily involved in his illegal activities. In the interest of saving time, and with representation from the prosecutor's office, I have collected each testimony in writing. Most of them are easier to read in translation than to hear, since some witnesses speak no English. These are testimonies of Russians and Poles and Italians and other immigrants in this country who worked in the plants Josef tampered with. These twelve live in the Washington area, and each and every one of them is anxious to speak on behalf of Josef von Woerner. These are men from the factories, men Josef worked beside in the hope of stopping production of the arms that were flowing into the battle-fields of Europe.

"One man tells how Josef von Woerner, this supposedly ruthless spy, bought Christmas presents for children of the factory workers. Another man tells how Josef gave him three months pay when strike funds ran out, claiming the money was from another strike fund that supposedly had extra money for those without work. He later learned there was no such fund, and we have a record of this and other financial gifts from Josef's own pocket.

"Another testimony tells of medicine and food Josef delivered, also falsely credited to a charitable—but fictitious—old man. Such gifts came from the defendant. There are more stories, all witnessed, ready for your perusal. Josef von Woerner, or Joe Warner, whichever you choose to call him, was even in his most nefarious days dedicated to the safety and well being of others. He was not some German spy, bent on destroying this country or a single living soul residing here."

Morgan approached the center of the jury box, both hands resting on the polished wood as his gaze seemed to meet each juror one by one. Since the courtroom was now inside, some wore the familiar gauze masks. But Lissa could still see their eyes, each and every one of them.

"I know that it would not be popular for me to stand here and tell you why this war began. Such talk is not welcome these days as we lick our wounds and bury our dead. But if you are to know the man whose life you hold in your hands, you must understand more than just the outcome of the war. You must understand this war from Mr. von Woerner's mind."

Morgan returned to the table upon which sat the papers, and rested his hand on the second stack. "Here is the promised notarized testimony of Otto von Woerner, the man who raised Josef von Woerner. In it is summarized an unequivocal account of the sort of indoctrination Josef was subjected to, growing up in a world that put Germany above all else.

"It cites how Josef was raised in German schools, on German newspapers, German essayists. He was taught Germany's past glories and the country's aspirations for future glory. Tutored in military science, geography, and the history of Germany, Josef was always expected to do his duty and never shirk. Otto regularly corresponded with German associates who had a finger on what the German people felt, since in his heart he'd never left the land of his birth. Through Otto, Josef knew nothing beyond the perspective that he was fed by the propagandists."

Morgan paused, and his glance swept the jury again.

"That is why, as I said, you must understand the origins of the war not just from our point of view, but also from the point of view of Josef, an American by birth but for all practical purposes raised a German. Many Germans still feel that they were lured into the war by their enemies, Russia and France. They were trapped in a war on two fronts with the alternative being annihilation and absorption into the neighboring lands. Some Germans likened it to an iron ring that tightened like a noose while others built their arms.

"Josef von Woerner was sympathetic to all of this talk. How could he not be? The material point was that he never was driven by his support of Germany to the point of raising arms against the United States. He only moved against the weapons Americans sold that would be used to kill."

He returned to the table, placing himself behind another stack of paper.

"I will also provide you with copies of a personal letter. This was not taken in deposition and does not have the weight of evidence, but I have permission from the judge, gained in a closed chambers meeting with prosecution, to share it with you. This is a personal letter, written by the defendant just before the start of these proceedings, to his fiancée, a woman who fiercely supports him. This is a candid account not only of Josef von Woerner's loyalties and efforts, it also shows the perspective with which he looks back on those times since he's had a chance to learn about the country he's also loved. America. Unbiased. An adult now, thinking and choosing for himself what is important.

"I'm sure this letter will be helpful in understanding what kind of man Josef von Woerner is now. As I said in my opening statement, the man you judge must be the whole man, not the half of one he was before."

Morgan turned and glanced Lissa's way, and she smiled with all the calm confidence she could muster since his look had drawn everyone's attention to her. "Miss Parker, Josef's fiancée, said something to me that I found very endearing. She said if you could only know him as she does, you couldn't help but love him." He gave a little laugh, and some in the room smiled. "Of course, that's asking a bit much, considering it is said by a woman who is in love. Yet consider this, gentlemen of the jury. Miss Parker comes from a family with a strong tradition of American patriotism. Each generation of her family has fought for the good of this country. Since she could not be a soldier, she went overseas to give aid and comfort to our troops as a Red Cross nurse. She is a member of the esteemed Daughters of the American Revolution. Maybe she is blinded by love, but is her whole family also blinded, since they have stood solidly with Josef since they learned of his past? It isn't evidence, but I can't help but believe a woman like Miss Parker or her family would be intimately connected with someone they believed to be a traitor. Not to this country, not to their beloved United States."

He stood behind the fourth and last of the pile in the collection of papers.

"Finally, I am providing each of you with a copy of all the pertinent laws of our land that define treason and sedition. You will quickly notice that Josef von Woerner's actions do not meet the criteria of treason. Did Josef von Woerner tamper with property not his own? Yes. But he did not do it to hurt this country, only to save lives. I would remind you that yesterday you saw the defendant and another man become victims of the very kind of ammunition he tried to destroy. As you read the statute defining treason I implore you to understand that the crimes charged here do not fit this statute. Obey our laws and recognize that Josef von Woerner never willfully aided any of our enemies, nor did he assist any enemy against us, or against any branch or member of our American defense. Not one of the ships he tampered with was an American military vessel. Follow the law, gentlemen. You will agree that Josef von Woerner is innocent of any accusations regarding treason.

"He may not be a saint, but he is not a traitor."

CHAPTER *Thirty-Five*

LISSA STARED at the back of Josef's head. Never in her life had prayer so completely engulfed her. No longer did she hear the words around her or feel the floor beneath her. She felt lightheaded without being dizzy, separate from everything physical without losing sight of reality.

Only three hours after they had been cloistered, the jury sent a message they had reached their verdict. She and her family, along with the Tanners and the Bonners, had dashed from the hotel back to the courthouse. Josef was already in the room, and barely looked up when Lissa and the others entered.

He looked as immersed in prayer as Lissa had been for the past three hours. At last the judge called the room to order. He asked the foreman of the jury if they had reached a verdict.

"Yes, Your Honor."

The bailiff ordered the defendant to stand, and Josef did so with the help of Morgan.

Lissa's prayer went on. She closed her eyes.

The foreman, seated on the farthest end, sent a folded piece of paper to the judge through the bailiff, which the judge viewed then handed back. The crowded courtroom was as silent as church before prayer. Lissa didn't know

329

how many were praying just then, but she offered one last plea before the jury foreman opened his mouth.

"Count: Endangering transport at sea. Verdict: Guilty."

She didn't let out her breath. They had expected that.

"Count: Transporting and storing explosives without a license. Verdict: Guilty."

Yes, that, too.

"Count: Violation of strike laws by inciting an illegal strike. Verdict: Guilty."

Lissa felt as though her heart stopped beating. Two counts left. The ones that could bring the stiffest penalties.

"Count: Sedition."

It seemed the entire courtroom stopped breathing in that moment. Even the foreman must have sensed it, for he looked directly at the defendant rather than the paper before him.

"Verdict: Not guilty."

The room spun around Lissa. Dizzying, wild joy bubbled up in her chest.

"Count: Treason."

Lissa caught her breath again. There could only be one conclusion, after the last.

"Verdict: Not guilty."

The room now blurred through Lissa's tears. Her parents swept her up in an embrace that compressed the breath from her. Boisterous cries sounded nearby from the Tanners and the Bonners. Caleb Tanner's voice rang above all others, a boisterous hoot even louder than Sergeant Dack's. Even Penny let out a whoop.

Josef turned around. Lissa squirmed from her parents' hold. Reaching for him, they touched hands before the judge called the room to order again.

"We've all seen and heard the testimony, Mr. von Woerner." The room once again quieted. "I commend the jury for following the letter of the law and not a spirit that sometimes tempts us to follow emotion and not our legal system.

"Your trial will move to the sentencing portion of these proceedings, based on the guilty verdicts presented by the jury. Prosecution and defense may present further evidence at this time if they wish, or they can pass the current evidence to me as the basis for a ruling. Is there further evidence?"

"No, Your Honor," said the government's attorney.

"I have nothing to add, Your Honor," responded Morgan.

"I thought you wouldn't," said the judge, who looked at the paper on his desk, then back at Josef.

"In preparation for this decision, I asked for the collection of pre-sentence reports from the various persons who have had contact with you in custody. I have before me reports from the various prison wardens, guards, and police assigned to you, both behind bars and those assigned to transport you between cells and other prisons or here to the courtroom. Though you have been incarcerated in a U.S. system a relatively brief time, at least in comparison to some of the prisoners these men deal with, I have not a single report indicating you were trouble. You were, as at least one report states, a model prisoner.

"The court will need time to quantify the amount of fines and damages for which you will be liable. Mr. von Woerner, you will no longer be a wealthy man when all is said and done. I am, however, crediting time spent in the prison camp in Germany as well as time served awaiting trial toward the time you will be required to spend in prison."

Lissa's heart soared. Reduced prison time.

"It is my order that, pending completion of the court's financial investigation, Mr. von Woerner, you will be remanded for custody to the federal prison in Atlanta to await sentencing. This is partly for your own protection. Assuming your continued good behavior, I anticipate that you can expect to be held for a fairly short period of time. I hope it will be long enough to let certain factions turn their attention to objects more worthy of their hatred. These proceedings are adjourned."

The gavel hit the block, and the courtroom again burst into noise. Reporters were either gleeful or infuriated, a few spectators voiced outrage, but more noised their support. Lissa barely heard any of that through the joyful thanksgiving she offered.

She saw Josef shake Morgan's hand, then he turned to her, and she stepped forward.

But the bailiff was there, already standing behind Josef. Morgan would meet with the judge in chambers to work through formalities of transfer to Atlanta. A few flash bulbs popped. Then the bailiff escorted Josef away, but Lissa knew it wouldn't be long before Josef would be a free man.

EPILOGUE

SEPTEMBER 15, 1919

JOSEF PUT his arm around his bride's shoulders.

For over nine months, he'd been held at the Federal Prison in Atlanta, an institution so far superior to either Tombs or the German POW camp that it nearly seemed a place to rest and recuperate from his ordeal. As the judge had predicted, the length of time was also enough for Josef to have been forgotten by the news reporters and others who identified him as an object of hatred.

He'd been gone just long enough for Lissa to incorporate the larger Bonner circle into her family and plan their wedding, which had taken place the day before, two weeks after his release.

Now they sat in the back seat of Karl Bonner's new tin lizzie, with Karl at the wheel.

"I'm not sure this driver knows where's he's going," Josef whispered into Lissa's ear and then bent forward to kiss her.

"Does it matter?" Lissa asked with a laugh. "Let's enjoy the ride."

Karl turned at the next corner. "I hate to disappoint both of you, but I know exactly where I'm going, and we'll be there in less than three minutes."

"So soon?" Josef protested.

"This is my neighborhood, Josef. I couldn't get lost if I tried."

Before long, Karl stopped in front of a modest bungalow with a green slate roof, nestled in front of a line of shade trees. The house was relatively new. Even from the street, Josef could see there were no curtains on the windows or flowers in the freshly turned beds around its foundation. He could already see in Larisa's eyes that she thought the house was a definite possibility.

It was certainly nothing like the mansion in which Otto had raised him, but Josef felt no dissatisfaction. He had learned many things about himself in the last couple of years, and one of those things was that a lavish lifestyle offered little appeal.

Maybe the simplicity of trench and prison life had taught him that.

Though he didn't miss the things Otto had provided for him, Josef found that he did miss Otto, who had died a few months after gaining his freedom. He had visited Josef in Atlanta, and the two of them had found a relationship at last, one of honesty and even affection. Josef, the Bonners, and Lissa had all encouraged Otto in his own new faith. Josef often wondered how it would have changed both of their lives if either of them had found such faith earlier.

Otto's businesses had dried up during his scandal and imprisonment. His assets were all sold and were enough, barely, to cover the fines and restitution assigned to Josef at sentencing. As the judge had predicted, Josef was not a wealthy man, but he was free at last. For Josef and for Lissa, that was enough.

Josef now worked for a different owner but at the same glass company Otto once owned. He had feared that he could not find a job, especially not where his name was still somewhat notorious. But once the court documents were opened to the public, they were extensively reported and excerpted. Animosity cooled. Some newspapers delighted in the romantic angle and printed verbatim Josef's letter to Lissa, to Josef and Lissa's chagrin. With stories of war heroes filling the papers, Josef faded from view. That was exactly the way he wanted it.

One surprising outcome was the obsession that Sergeant Dack had come to feel about Josef. He thought it unfair that Josef should have a blemished military record. He reenlisted with the sole purpose of fighting for

Josef's honor—or so it seemed to Josef, for all the efforts Dack extended on his behalf. Dack, in his typical ornery way, thought it would be an interesting battle to convince the U. S. Army to issue medals he believed Josef deserved to a man with a dishonorable discharge. So far, he wasn't succeeding, but Josef appreciated his friend's efforts more than he would have cared for the medals themselves. With a steady income and enough money left to buy a small home, Josef and Lissa were ready to start their new life.

They walked around the vacant house that Karl had found. Josef held Lissa's hand, a rush of thankfulness coursing through him that he could see her smile as a free man that she had accepted as her husband. Lissa was already organizing her plans for this house if they decided to buy it. He found himself eager to carry out her plans, even while Karl was saying that he knew the owners and could assure them that the structure, roof, plumbing, and gravity-fed coal furnace were all sound. Josef barely heard a word.

"Well, Mrs. Warner, would you care to live with me and a child or two in this house?" he asked.

Laughing, she nodded and embraced him. "I believe I would like that, Mr. Warner."

AUTHOR'S NOTE

GERMANY DID maintain slave labor camps like the one in which Josef and his fellow prisoners suffered, but I have found no record of American soldiers interned in them as described in this fictional story. It is well documented that labor camps were used to imprison Belgian refugees.

—Maureen Lang